Dear Liz

Happy Birthday

May '91.

And Happy Writing.

With all our love Genia xxx

Andy xxx

The Slang Thesaurus

The Slang Thesaurus

JONATHON GREEN

ELM TREE BOOKS

London

First published in Great Britain 1986
by Elm Tree Books/Hamish Hamilton Ltd
27 Wrights Lane London W8 5TZ

Copyright © 1986 by Jonathon Green

British Library Cataloguing in Publication Data
Green, Jonathon
    The slang thesaurus.
    1. English language – Slang – Dictionaries
    I. Title
    427′.09   PE3721
    ISBN 0-241-11851-4

Typeset by Computape (Pickering) Ltd, North Yorkshire
Printed and bound in Great Britain by
Richard Clay (The Chaucer Press) Ltd, Bungay, Suffolk

For Lucien and Gabriel

Contents

Introduction

Dr Peter Mark Roget published his *Thesaurus of English Words and Phrases* in 1852 with the intention of classifying and organising the English Language. His topic encompassed the great spread of standard English, and for all that the Thesaurus has become a basic adjunct to anyone seeking a polished style, his initial aim was to reveal through the relationships of words a new and simpler means of communication for everyone.

Since then, the Thesaurus has gone through a number of revisions, the most recent being published in 1982. It remains a vital helper for every type of writer – both professional and general – who seeks the most apt, the most accurate, the most telling and the most elegant expression of their thoughts. In essence, a comprehensive wordlist, arranged as to topic – with all the words that deal with the same idea (and sometimes their opposites and correlatives alongside them) grouped together – the Thesaurus format remains massively popular.

The intention of *The Slang Thesaurus* is the adapting of the thesaurus technique to the slang vocabulary. Unlike a dictionary, which provides a meaning for a given word, the thesaurus provides a variety of words, all of which express a given meaning. As the editor/compiler of a number of dictionaries of alternative language, including *Newspeak: A Dictionary of Jargon* (1982) and *The Dictionary of Contemporary Slang* (1984), I have come to realise that there exists a definite, and often-voiced demand for a book that would provide just such a 'reverse dictionary'. This book attempts to meet that demand.

The range of slang that has been amassed in the *Thesaurus*, with the particular effect of grouping like with like, is intended to offer a variety of appeals to scholars and less professional logophiles, as well as all those many people who simply enjoy browsing through such collections of more or less arcane, exotic and even obscure words and phrases. As the tabulation of the contemporary slang lexicon gradually developed it became interesting to note the way in which certain areas of human life create seemingly disproportionate vocabularies. While all aspects of the language – taking in the prosaic as well as the more dramatic – have been duly included, specific categories do stand out.

'The chief stimuli of slang are sex, money and intoxicating liquor,' opined Dr J. Y. P. Greig in 1938. Bowing to current events one must add drugs to that list. Coupling such pleasures with a good ration of blasphemy, scatology and euphemism, one has a fair cross-section of slang origins. And, given those additions, Dr Greig's sources are still remarkably constant, as the word lists make clear. There remain only a few parts of the body, and a limited number of functions for their employment, but the language such parts and functions create is still evolving without restraint. Although my intention has been to restrict the *Thesaurus* to contemporary usage, many of the words originate in earlier periods. Slang, like more standard usage, develops over the years, responding in kind to the vagaries and developments of the society in which it is created and used. Listing it in this form only underlines such development.

The *Thesaurus* is divided into sections and groups of categories based roughly, although obviously not completely following, on those used for *Roget's Thesaurus*. These are arranged according to the principal or dominant idea that they convey. Within the sections of these categories are words and phrases that are definitely synonymous; they are entered in alphabetical order. In such cases that the words within a given section require a more specific definition other than that offered by the keyword, this will be given. All categories and sections and the vocabulary listed in them will be cross-referenced whenever necessary. As well as the usual abstract categories – 'Volition', 'Emotion' and the like, I have added listings of several specialist vocabularies – 'Crime', 'Prostitution', 'Commercial Sex', 'Drugs', 'Commerce' and 'Gambling'. All of these fall outside the purlieus of the traditional Thesaurus but are repositiories of large amounts of popularly used slang and therefore demand inclusion.

A thesaurus, by definition, is a compilation of facts – in the form of listed, connected words – rather than of etymologies, discursive explanations of the development and origin of a word or of similar philological exposition. For such information one must look to the ordinary slang dictionaries. On the other hand, this comprehensive organisation into specific categories and sections of the enormous body of slang is designed to appeal not merely to wordsmiths but to have, like any of its peers, a practical function. The genesis of *The Slang Thesaurus* was in the requests of those who said to this compiler 'I enjoy the definitions in a slang dictionary, but what I really want is the reverse, something that gives me the slang for the normal word.' Such appeals have been many. It is the aim of *The Slang Thesaurus* to meet them.

The bulk of the material included in the *Thesaurus* has been derived from my own *Dictionary of Contemporary Slang*, much enhanced by subsequent delvings and accretions. To thank each individual for their contributions would be impossible, grateful though I certainly am, but I must thank David Robbins for opening up an area that had hitherto defeated me, notably the patois used by West Indians in England.

Finally I offer my profound thanks to John Nicolson, without whose invaluable efforts, clichéd acknowledgement though this may be, the compilation of the *Thesaurus* would truly never have been possible.

JONATHON GREEN
March 1986

Abbreviations

abbrev.	*abbreviation*
adj.	*adjective*
adv.	*adverb*
aka	*also known as*
Aus.	*Australian*
backsl.	*backslang*
betw.	*between*
Can.	*Canadian*
derog.	*derogatory*
eg	*example*
esp.	*especially*
euph.	*euphemism*
excl.	*exclamation*
facet.	*facetious*
fr.	*from*
milit.	*military*
mod.	*modern*
n.	*noun*
occ.	*occasionally*
phr.	*phrase*
poss.	*possible*
rhy.sl.	*rhyming slang*
S.Afr.	*South African*
Sp.	*Spanish*
spec.	*specifically*
UK	*United Kingdom*
US	*United States*
USMC	*United States Marine Corps*
v.	*verb*
vi	*verb intransitive*
vt	*verb transitive*
Yid.	*Yiddish*
WI	*West Indian*

Abstract Relations

TIME
1. Duration
n. 1. *period of time:* go, space, stretch, trick
2. *long time:* blue moon, born days (all one's), coon's age, month of Sundays
3. *short time:* brace of shakes, jiffy, less than no time, two shakes of a lamb's tail, in a tick, wake-up; spec: mo, sec; short (short service commission)
4. *work time:* hitch (milit.), forty-eight, (milit), gaol break (movies), graveyard shift, lobster shift, swing shift, R&R (milit.)
v. 5. *spend time:* spec. 29 and a wake-up (prison use: period betw. receiving notice of parole and release)
adj. 6. *new, novel:* brand spanking, bran-new, fresh as paint, hot, hot off the press, wen (backsl.)
7. *old:* dillo (backsl.) has-been, over the hill, past it
adv. 8. *during; while:* punch the clock
9. *for a long time:* for donkey's years, for yonks, since God knows when
10. *forever:* for keeps, till the cows come home, till hell freezes over
11. spec. short (near the end of prison term/milit. service)

2. Relative Time
n. 1. manana
2. *crucial time:* nick (of time)
v. 3. *to be late:* stand up
adv. 4. *formerly:* already; spec: space, while back

5. *long ago:* donkey's years, way back, year dot
6. *after:* later! when morning comes (US bl.)
7. *now:* on the dot, this is where we came in (the same time)
8. *soon:* in a brace of shakes
9. *any time:* any old
10. *immediately, shortly:* before you can say Jack Robinson, chop-chop, first crack out of the box, in a jiffy, a jiffy, in a brace of shakes, in less than no time, like a shot, like a shot out of hell, one-two-three, on the knocker, on the nail, PDQ (pretty damn quick), pronto, right off the bat, stat (medical)
11. *suddenly:* bam, bang, bang off, blam, caplunk, kerblam, kersmack, plop, plunk, pop, powee, slap, slap-bang, slap-dab, smack, smack-dab, smacko, socko, wham, whang, zap, zoom, zowie
12. *seldom, occasionally:* once in a blue moon, – a coon's age, a month of Sundays; since God knows when
13. *early:* bright and early; previous
14. *prompt, punctual:* in the nick of time, Johnny on the spot, on deck, on the dot, – nail, – nose, – the spot, pronto, right there
15. *late:* Harry Tate

3. Divisions of Time
n. 1. *day:* good day for it, – for the race; spec. roaster, scorcher, swelterer (a hot day); nice day for ducks (a wet day)
2. *days of the week:* when the crow shits (Aus. payday), Mother's Day (US black), poet's day (piss off early today), TGIF (Thank God It's

Friday); spec. sickie (Aus.: a day's sick-leave)

3. *festival days:* hols, Xmas; spec. buck's night (Aus.: stag night)

4. *week, month:* moon; spec. Hell Week (US college); leo-time (August); play-away (UK society use: weekend in country); beno (menstrual period, there 'be no' fun); wallflower week (menstrual period)

5. *seasons:* dog days, lamb time, silly season

6. *weekend:* dirty weekend

7. *morning:* ack emma, morning after the night before, rooster time, small hours, sparrow fart

8. *afternoon:* arvo (Aus.), pip emma

9. *night:* crash time, flop time, hay time; spec. dog-watch (media: post-midnight broadcasts)

10. *hour:* half (in telling time: half-five, -six, etc); spec. happy hour (cheap drinks period in a bar); mad minute (milit. use: free-fire test period for weapons)

11. *minute:* cock linnet (rhy.sl.)

ORDER
4. Arrangement; Order; State of Affairs

n. 1. *conditions:* how-do-you-do, kettle of fish, lay of the land, lie –, size of it, way the wind blows; spec. lineup, set-up

2. *orderliness, good condition:* apple-pie-order, apples (Aus.), apples and rice (Aus. rhy.sl. = nice), fine as wine (US black) hunky-dory, jake, nice going, squeaky-clean, ticketty-boo, top whack

3. *cleaning, neatening:* doing up, pearl diving (washing dishes in restaur.), policing (milit.), tarting up

v. 4. *to arrange, to clean:* do up, doll up, police up, pretty up, tart up

5. *be consistent:* hang in there, – together, – tight, – tough, hold water, get in line, put one's money where one's mouth is, stand up

adv. 6. hitting on all four (cylinders), up to scratch, – snuff; spec. runner (of a second-hand car)

7. *orderly:* in apple-pie order, kosher

8. *consistent:* according to Hoyle, boilerplate, by the book

5. Disorder

n. 1. Chinese fire drill, dog's dinner, grunge, Horlicks (UK upperclass use), pig's ear, pit, (right) two-and-eight (rhy.sl. = state), scrunge, schmutz, what the cat brought in

v. 2. *to get out of order, get into a mess:* make a dog's dinner (out of), screw up

3. *to disarrange:* arse (ass) up, ball up, foul up, fuck up

4. *to dirty, to soil:* crap on, – over

adv. 5. *messy, out of order:* all to cock, all over the place, – the shop, any how, arsy-versy, cockeyed, everywhichway, fouled up, fubar (fucked up beyond all recognition), gfu (general fuck-up), gmbu (grand military balls-up), gmfu (– fuck-up), grungy, out of whack, raspy (US black), ratty, samfu (self-adjusting military fuck-up), sapfu (surpassing all previous fuck-ups), screwed up, screwy, scruff, sky-west and crooked, sleazy, snafu (situation normal, all fucked up), susfu (situation unchanged, still fucked up), tarfu (things are really fucked up)

6. *infested:* crawling (with)

IMPROVEMENT
6. Improvement

v. 1. *to improve:* be on the mend, – on the up-and-up, get oneself into shape, – together, get one's act together, – arse (ass) in gear, – shit together

2. *recover:* perk up, pull oneself to pieces (facet.), pull oneself together, pull out of it, pull through, snap out of it

3. *repair, mend:* do up, rev, revamp

4. *strengthen:* beef up, jack up, jazz up

7. Impairment

n. 1. *defective object:* dead duck, fuck-up

2. *accident:* balls-up, cobblers, cock-up, howler, mons

3. *wreck, collision:* pile-up, smash-up

4. *ruin, destruction:* blooie, blow-out, blow up, blue ruin, brodie, bust, bust-up, conk-out, fold-up, knock-out, smash-up, washout

v. 5. *deteriorate:* conk (out), die on the vine, pull a fadeout, fade, go blah, peg out, peter –, spec. deteriorate rapidly: do a brodie, go down the chute, – the tubes, hit the skids, take a nose-dive

6. *get out of order, break:* blow (up), bust, conk (out), crack (up), crap out, fold up, get out of whack, go blah, – blooie, – on the blink, – haywire, poop out, screw up

7. *to degenerate, go to ruin:* (to be) all up, (be) washed up, conk out, fold up, go boom, – phfft, – phut, go to the devil, – to the dogs, – the deuce, – to hell, – to pieces, – to pot, – to smash, – to the pack (Aus.)

8. *to spoil, disorder:* balls up, blow, do up (brown), bugger up, foul up, fuck up, gum up (the works), louse up, put the kibosh on, – the skids under, queer up

9. *to hit:* bash, whack

10. *to ruin, destroy:* belt out, christen, clean out, crab, diddle, ding, dish, do, – a job on, – brown, – in, – over, – up (like a kipper),

gimp, knock off, murder, put the kibosh on, – the skids under, sew up, total, trash, wipe out

11. *have a crash:* have a bust-up, – crack-up, pile up, smash-up, total; spec. collide: collect (Aus.), run smack-dab into, tear into

12. *to spoil, upset:* crab, piss on one's parade

13. *broken, out of order:* arsed up, ballsed up, banjaxed, beat up, bollixed, bollocksed (up), buggered up, bust (up), clapped out, cockeyed, fouled up, fucked (up), gone blooie, – haywire, – to fuck, – (all) to shit, on the blink, – the fritz, out of whack, screwy, shot, upgefucked

14. *in poor condition:* all wet, beat up, cheesy, crappy, crummy, low rent, punk, trashy

15. *ruined:* all to hell, – to pieces, – to smash, bought and sold (and done for), done, – up, conked out, finito, fucked, gone phut, – to the devil, – to hell, – the dogs, – to pot, – to smash, (all) shot, washed up

phr. 16. that's torn it

SEQUENCE
8. Sequence; Succession

n. 1. *list:* sked(s), slate

2. *turn:* go, hand, stretch, whack; spec. buying drink: shout; Buggin's turn (next in line for a job)

v. 3. *to follow:* gumshoe, pussyfoot, string along, tag, tail

4. *continue:* go with the flow, hang in (there), keep the ball rolling, stay with it

adv. 5. *in succession:* on the trot

9. Beginning; Commencement

n. 1. first base, first crack (out of the box), git-go, (on the) ground floor, ground zero, jump, jump street, square one, starters

2. *preface:* openers; spec. opening

remarks: er, gosh, hell, I mean, look, you know

v. 3. *to begin:* cut loose, dig in, do it, fire away, get the lead out, – the show on the road, – one's arse in gear, – one's finger out, – on one's bike, go for it, hit it, kick off; spec. jump the gun (to begin prematurely)

4. *at the beginning:* early bird, from the word go, in front, off the top, right from the giddyap, when the balloon goes up

10. End; Termination

n. 1. blowoff, curtains, end of the line, in the death, – the stretch, kiss off, payoff, wrap

2. *stop, cessation:* bust-up, fold, knockoff, quits

3. *conclusive end:* all bets are off, capper, clincher, crunch, end-around, KO, living end

4. *suffixes used in slang words:* -aroo, -eroo, -erino, -ette, -fest, -iferous, -ino, -terino, -inski, -itis, -nik, -o, -ola, -ski

v. 5. *to end:* ace it up (Aus.), bust up, conk (out), fold (up), go over the top, – the limit, take the count

6. *to cease, stop:* call it a day, – quits, drop (it), get one's cards, hand in one's chips, hang it up, knock (it) off, pull the plug (on), put the brakes on, stow it, wind up

7. *to terminate:* break (it) up, call all bets off, clean up (on), floor, fold, knock (it) on the head, polish off, put (it) away, – on ice, – the brakes on, say goodbye (to), wash up, wind up; spec. kill (turn off lights, machinery, etc)

adv. 8. *ended:* all over bar the shouting, all bets are off, all torn up, all up (with), done (for), down the drain, – the pan, – the tubes, in the bag, kiboshed, pegged out, up the spout

excl. 9. can it!, cheese it!, come off it!, cut it out!, drop it!, forget it!, hold on!, hold up!, kill it!, knock it off!, – on the head!, ace it up! (Aus.), lay off!, leave it out!, – off!, – over!, less of it!, stow it!

phr. 10. curtains for you, that's your lot, the deal's off

CHANGE
11. Change

n. 1. *experience:* picnic, set-up; spec. dead man's shoes (US black: an unavoidable unpleasant experience); university of life (learning by experience)

v. 2. *to alter:* go through changes, snap out of (it); spec. go fish (gay use: to act as a woman)

3. *to happen, to turn out:* come down, go down, pan out; spec. peak (to reach the limit of an experience)

12. Substitution

n. 1. *substitute:* dupe, front, ringer, switcheroo

v. 2. *to replace:* ad lib, cover up, double (for), front for, pinch-hit, ring (in)

adj. 3. *fake:* bogue

13. Permanence

v. 1. hang in there, – tight, stay with (it)

RESEMBLANCE
14. Kind; Sort

n. 1. character, lot, number, piece; spec. situation: layout, outfit, scene, set-up

15. Similarity

n. 1. *likeness:* dupe, lookalike, (dead) ringer

2. *duplicate:* ditto, dupe; spec. knockoff (antiques/clothing trade)

3. *imitation:* copycat, takeoff; spec. shamateur (sporting use)

v. 4. *resemble:* not tell t'other from which, stack up (with)

5. *to copy:* make like, me-too
adj. 6. plastic, strictly from

QUANTITY: SIMPLE
16. Quantity; Number
n. 1. *collection:* ballpark figure,
caboodle, grab-bag, whole kit and
caboodle, whole bag of tricks, – ball
of wax, – bang shoot, – boiling lot,
– shebang, – shooting match
2. *zero, nought:* damn all, dick,
diddley-squat, doodley-squat, jack
shit, nisht (Yid.), not a sausage,
squat, sweet FA, – Fanny Adams,
zilch, zip, zot; spec. cricket: blob,
duck, pair of spectacles (two scores
of 0 in the same match)
3. *small denominations:* flach
(backsl. = half), country cousin
(rhy.sl. = 12), oat (backsl. = 2),
roaf (backsl. = 4), net (backsl. =
10), ace, deuce, tray, finif, fiver,
nickel (5 as number or quantity),
neves (backsl. 7), half a dollar, – a
bar, – a sheet, – a yard, – a cock
(£5), half saw, sawbuck, quid,
tenner, cock and hen (rhy.sl. =
ten), cockle and hen, pony
4. *large denominations:* big bucks,
telephone number(s), Nelson (111),
big one, C, century, G, grand, K,
ton, monkey, yard, mill; spec.
gambling: nickel ($500), dime
($1000), big nickel ($5000), big
dime ($10000)
5. *indefinite numbers:* points
(percentages), tall (US black use:
large numbers, often of cash),
jillion, squillion, umpteen,
zillion
v. 6. *count:* dope out, figure out,
guesstimate, reckon, tote (up)
mod. 7. one (as in 'You won't get
dime one out of me!')

17. Degree
n. 1. cut above, notch above
adv. 2. *to a degree:* that (when =
extent: 'I was that pissed!'), the

devil, – deuce, – hell, – on earth
(when preceded by 'what . . .')
3. *at the most:* tops

QUANTITY: GREATNESS
18. Greatness
n. 1. *something large:* blockbuster,
boomer (Aus.), cheese, gorilla,
humdinger, monster
2. *large amount, many:* all sorts, and
then some, bags, barrels, heaps,
loads, oodles, devil of a lot, heck –,
hell –, hulluva, thumping, fat lot,
gobs, lashings, more than you can
shake a stick at, neat sum, tidy –,
pile, pot (of), rafts, scads, tons,
wads
3. *something/body important:* ace,
biggie, big cheese, – deal,
– enchilada, – league, – noise,
– shot, – stuff, – time, – wheel,
– wig, full two bob (Aus.),
something to write home about,
your (yer) actual; spec. important
facts: brass tacks, nitty-gritty
4. *eminence in degree:* (preceded by
'as', 'like', etc) all creation, all
getout, beans, billy-o, blazes, a
house on fire, nobody's business, in
spades
v. 5. *to be important:* beat all, – the
band, cut a lot of ice
6. *to feature:* headline, put in lights,
– on the map, hit the high spots
mod. 7. *large, huge:* bumper,
ginormous, gross, humungous, dirty
great, tearing, thumping (great),
whopping, whacking
8. *great in degree:* almighty, bally,
big-time, blankety, blazing, blessed,
blinking, bloody, blooming, boiling,
clinking, crying, father and mother
of, flaming, heavy, hellacious,
hell-fired, holy, motherfucking,
mollyfogging, motherless,
mother-raping, pepper-kissing,
perishing, rip-snorting, ruddy
(great), serious, some
9. *to a great extent:* and how, and

then some, damn tootin', darn (durn) tootin', as all getout, something awful, – fierce, – terrible, to beat all creation, the worst way, over the fence (Aus.), up the gazoo
10. *very, exceedingly:* all-fired, bang, beastly, blame, blankety, bleeding, blind, blinking, bloody, bust-out, darned, dashed, dead, double, dynamite, ever so, fonky, for sure, goddam, Harry . . . -ers, hell-fired, helluva, pigging, powerful, right, screaming, slamming, spanking, socking, sodding, steaming (great), stiff, stinking, stone, TNT (US black = dynamite), thundering, veddy, way, well, whacking, whopping (great), wonelly
11. *excellent:* raspy

19. Smallness; Insignificance
n. 1. *something small:* (big) hunk of nothing, (long thin) streak of piss, no great shakes, nothing to shout about, – to write home about, not worth a plugged nickel, – a bumper (Aus.), – a hill of beans, small potatoes, small-time
2. *something worthless:* boloney, blah, bushwa, crap, garbage, trash
3. *small amount:* dribs and drabs, bits and bobs, smidgeonette; spec. cough and a spit (theatre: a small role)
v. 4. *not to matter:* cut no ice, (don't) hold no air, no great catch, – great shakes, not amount to a hill of beans, not worth a bumper, not worth a fart in a noisemaker, – in a thunderstorm, – a hill of beans, – a light, – a pisshole in the snow
5. *to lose importance:* to go down the chute, – the tubes, to hit the skids, poop out
adj. 6. *small, insignificant:* airy-fairy, chickenfeed, dinky, footling, half-cocked, – -pint, – -portion, one-horse, milk and water, penny-ante, piddling, pissy-ass, popcorn, sawn-off, teensie-weensie, thin on the ground; spec. -ette (suffix)
7. *cheap:* bargain basement, dime-a-dozen, dime-store, five-and-dime, nickel-and-dime, reach-me-down, two-bit, weak

---

QUANTITY: COMPARATIVE
20. Superiority
n. 1. *act of surpassing:* licking, fading, screwing, shafting, skinning, whitewashing
2. *the best:* A1, capper, cream, daddy, grade A, gravy, monte, payoff, pearler, topper, tops
v. 3. *to beat, surpass:* beat all to hell, – eight ways from Sunday, – out, give a black eye, get the jump on, hammer, have one cold, hype (US black), kick (one's) arse, knock for a loop, knock sideways, – the spots off, – the stuffing out of, lick, run rings round, put away, – one's nose out of joint, put it over (on), steal the show, sweep the board, take the shine off, whitewash
4. *to be best:* beat all, – all get out, cop the lot, take the cake
adv. 5. *superior to:* ahead of the game, a cut above, two jumps ahead
6. *best:* A1, ace, top of the tree, tiptop, up in the paints
phr. 7. *I've won:* read them and weep

21. Inferiority
n. 1. spec. sport: wooden spoon
v. 2. *to be surpassed:* licked, skinned, get on the short end, take a bath, – a back seat, – it on the chin, – one's lumps, – the fall, – the gas, – the knock, (to be) taken to the cleaners
adj. 3. *inferior:* bush, out of the money, – the picture, not in the game, – the picture, – the same league, pipped

QUANTITY:
COMPLETENESS
22. Completeness; Sufficiency
n. 1. *sufficiency:* earful, enuff, full
house, noseful, nuff
2. *superfluity:* bellyful, chokka,
enough and then some, too much of
a good thing, up to one's neck,
skinful, snootful
3. *everything:* ballgame, business,
everything but the kitchen sink, full
monte, full two bob (Aus.), guntz
(Yid.), hook, line and sinker, issue
(Aus.), SRO (standing room only),
whole bag of tricks, – ball of wax,
– bang shoot, – boiling lot, – kit and
caboodle, – shebang, – schmeer
(Yid.), – shooting match, – works
adv. 4. *satiated:* lousy with,
jam-packed, crawling with
5. *excessive:* gross, mondo, over the
top, OTT, far out, too much, out of
sight, outasite, mega-, too-too
6. *complete:* all-fired blinking,
blooming, dead, plumb, regular,
straight-out, straight-up
7. *completely:* abso-bloody-lutely,
bang up, clean (to), clear to hell,
flat, from arsehole to breakfast
time, from soup to nuts, – the
ground up, – the word go, slam,

23. Incompleteness; Insufficiency
n. 1. *share:* cut, divvy, piece (of the
action), slice, split, whack
2. *quantity used in a given portion:*
crack, edition, go, jag, shot, slug,
sniff, throw, toot, toss, whack
3. *nothing:* bugger all, not a lick, – a
smell, – sniff, sod all, sweet fuck all,
sweet FA, zero, zilch, zip all
v. 4. *to lack:* be clean out of, fresh
out of, shy of, light, to be hungry
for, hung for

QUANTITY: VARIATION
24. Increase
v. 1. throw in
phr. 2. all that jazz

25. Decrease
n. 1. dent (in one's wallet),
knockdown, knockoff, letup
2. *riddance:* brush-off, the big E,
– dust, – elbow, – rubout,
– runaround, – slip,
v. 3. *separate, divide:* cut up, cut up
touches, divvy up, go halves,
– fifty-fifty,
4. *eliminate, discard:* axe, blow
(out), boot (out), can, chuck, chunk
(US black), clean house, count out,
cut loose, deep six, ditch, dump, get
shot of, give the air, – the bump,
– the hook, – the brush-off, – the
elbow, – the slip, – the (old)
heave-ho, – the heave, – the knife,
put the skids under, – rollers under,
– the shears to, scarf (US campus),
unload; spec. censorship, editing:
blue-pencil; throw the baby out with
the bathwater (to discard the useful
along with the useless)
adv. 5. *used up:* all out (of), all
shot, done for, fresh out (of),
washed up

26. Equality
1. *inequality:* another story, a
something else (again), a whole new
ballgame, two other guys, a horse of
a different colour
2. *on equal terms:* even-Steven,
fifty-fifty, halvers, quits

QUALITY
27. Goodness
n. 1. *something excellent:* ace(s),
beaut, bee's knees, bells (US black
use), belter, the berries, big time,
bobby dazzler, but good, cat's
pyjamas, – whiskers, corker,
cracker, daisy, dilly, duck soup,
fave rave, the goods, gravy,
humdinger, jim-dandy, kayo (KO),
lily, lulu, McCoy, oldie but goodie,
pea (Aus.), peach, pip, pippin, real
McKay, real McCoy, rip-snorter,
scorch (US black use), Shovel City

(which one really 'digs'), some thing to shout about, – to write home about, topper, trimmer (Aus.),

v. 2. *to be excellent:* beat all, – the band, go over big, – like a million bucks, hit the spot, make it big, take the cake

adj. 3. *excellent first-rate:* A1, all fine and dandy, all wool and a yard wide, AOK, apples (Aus.), – and rice (Aus.), awesome, back of the net, bad, baddest, bagged, bang on, – up, bat, beaut, bitchen, bitchin, bitchin twitchin, blinding, bod, boffo, bonaroo, bonzer, boss, brahma, brill, bully, cas (casual), choice, classic, clearly, cold, completely, cool, copacetic, crackerjack, crazy, d, dandy, dead set (Aus.), def, death, deaf (US black), doog (backsl.) doog eno (backsl.), ducky, dynamite, electric, ex, fab, fantabulous, foxy, gaff, gear, godawaful, good as all getout, great shakes, grouse (Aus.), groovy, handsome, hellacious, high-tone, hot-shit, hotsy-totsy, hunky-dory, irey (Jam.), jolly d., just like mother makes it, – the job, – the ticket, – what the doctor ordered, keen(-o), killer, king, knockout, live, mad (Aus.), magic, major, marvy, massive, mean, mega-, mind-blowing, mondo, nasty, neat, number one, numero uno, on the money, outasite, out of sight, – state, – the box (Aus.), – this world, peachy, peachy-keen, pimp, primo, rad (radical), rich, right up one's alley, righteous, ripper, scrummy, serious, sexy, shit-hot, smashing, socko, solid, spiffy, splendiferous, spot on, superfly, sweet, swell, TB (très brill), that's the ticket, to die, tons, top drawer, top hole, top notch, top shelf, total blowchoice, totally, tough, triff, trippy, tubular, unreal (Aus.), v., vg., vicious, Wee Georgie Wood

(rhy.sl. = good), wicked, wizard, yummy

excl. 4. encore!, far out!, fuckin(g) A!, perfecto!

5. *quite good:* better than a poke in the eye with a blunt stick, – a slap in the belly with a wet fish, close but no cigar, not so dusty

28. Badness

n. 1. *something bad:* asshole, baddie, baloney, bomb, bosh, bum, bushwa, chazerai (Yid. = rubbish), cheapie, cold, cold case, crap, crock (of shit), crumb, dead duck, double-whammy, doodley-shit, dreck, kaker (Yid.), no big deal, nowhere, pain (in the arse), – (in the neck), schlock, small beer, – change, – potatoes, snot, stinker(oo), tinhorn

adj. 2. *poor, mean, second-rate:* bad-ass, basic, bit previous, blamed, blankety, bodger (Aus.), bum, brummy (Aus.), bush league, chump-change, coffeeand, cold, cotton-picking, crappo, crappy, Crow McGee, cruddy, crumbum, crumby, crummy, dashed, dicky, dipshit, ditso, dodgy, dog-ass, g, godawful, gross, gnarly, half-baked, hard-boiled, hole-in-the-wall, iffy, jerkwater, low down, – rent, mean, Mickey Mouse, naff, NG (no good), NBG (no bloody good), no bon, no go, not much chop (Aus.), number ten, on the outer, pisspoor, poxy, punk, rank, ribby, rinky-dink, ropey, schlocky, shag, shitty, stinko, suck-ass, ticky-tacky, tinhorn, two-bit, two-bob (Aus.), unreal, upta (Aus. = up to shit), yucky, zero minus

3. *mediocre:* half-assed, – cocked, Wall Street didn't jump

excl. 4. base!

ATTRIBUTES

29. Weight
n. 1. *something heavy:* gorilla, wodge
adj. 2. gross, nuggety, thumping, whopping

30. Flexibility; Texture; Colour
adj. 1. blue (US black dark-skinned)

31. Temperature
mod. 1. *hot:* hot as a bastard, – a bitch, – buggery, – hell, hotter than hell
2. *cold:* cold as a bastard, – a bitch, – a well-digger's arse, – a brass monkey – witch's tit, cold enough to freeze the hind leg off a donkey

32. Strength
n. 1. get-up-and-go, guts, juice, legs, steam
2. *physical strength:* beef, the doings, elbow grease, jism, meat, muscle, what it takes
3. *directed force:* bang, biff, boot, flash, ginger, guts, jolt, kick, oomph, pep, powie, smackeroo, smacko, snap, sock, sockeroo, swack, wallop, zip
v. 4. *to exert strength:* put beef into, – muscle into, – one's back into, – one's elbow into, strongarm
5. *to be potent:* have a shot in one's locker, – lead in one's pencil
adj. 6. *strong:* ballsy, big ass, built like a brick outhouse, – brick shithouse, bullet-proof, heavy, mean, ruggsy, warry

33. Weakness
v. 1. *to be weak:* can't cut it, – fight one's way out of a paper-bag – get it together, – hack it, – knock the skin off a rice-pudding, – take it, doesn't cut the mustard
2. *to weaken:* bottle out, cave in, chicken out, conk out, crack (up), hit the skids, honk out, lose one's bottle, pull a fadeout, wimp out

3. *make powerless:* bash, bugger up, botch –, do –, do over, do the business on, – up (brown), gum –, put the kibosh on, – out of commission, queer one's pitch, put a spanner in the works, screw up
mod. 4. *weak, flimsy:* weak as catspiss, wet as a dishrag
5. *unsteady:* cockeyed, dotty, groggy, skewiff, wonkey
6. *effeminate:* faggy, he-she, la-de-da, nance, pansy, pantywaist, queer, swish (see also Homosexuals: 404)
adj. 7. *vulnerable:* up for grabs, wide-open
8. *weak:* candy-ass, chickenshit

APPEARANCE

34. Appearance; Looks
n. 1. front, getup, phizog, stackup, turnout
phr. 2. *unhealthy appearance:* looking green about the gills, – like a dog's dinner, you look like I feel

35. Beauty
n. 1. class, dog, spiff
2. *something beautiful:* beaut, cutesie, cutesiepie, dream, dreamboat, corker, daisy, dish, eyeful, hot stuff, looker, nifty, peach, pip, pippin, spanker, stunner, sweetie
3. *ornaments:* fixings
4. *attractive figure:* built, classy chassis, stacked, plenty of what it takes
v. 5. *to look beautiful:* (to be) easy on the eyes, knock dead, – one's eyes out, – out, look a knockout, – fit to kill, – a million bucks, – some, stack up nice
6. *to decorate:* doll up, spiff up, tart up
adj. 7. *beautiful:* beaut, cute, cutesie, dishy, dreamy, dreamboat, fit, foxy, ginchy, hot, keen looking, knockout, neat, no slouch, peach, wow

36. Ugliness

n. 1. *something ugly:* a bag, fit to stop a clock, no oil painting, – prize, something the cat dragged in

adj. 2. *ugly:* bagged out, corroded (US black), grisly, groaty, grody, – to the max, gross, grotty, gucky, hard on the eyes, – to take, hurtin' for certain, icky, manky, pitty, ragged out, ratty, rough, rugy, scrungy, skrungy, scummy, scuzzy, tacky, white bread

phr. 3. *disregarding ugliness for sex:* you don't look at the mantlepiece when you're poking the fire

Space

DIMENSIONS
37. Dimension
adj. 1. *thin:* beanpole, herring-gutted, ribby, skinnymalink, weedy
2. *short:* hammered down, knee high to a grasshopper, – jack rabbit, sawn-off, tee-tee, titchy
3. *fat:* beefy, broad in the beam, built like a brick outhouse, – shithouse, cornfed, double-gutted, fat-assed, pot-bellied, two-dinners
4. *measure of dimension:* wall-to-wall, yea (as in 'yea high', 'yea big')

38. Distance
n. 1. along, chance, piece, ways
2. *long distance:* good way, – piece, long chalk, neat step, tidy –, back of beyond, back of Bourke (Aus.), beyond the rabbit-proof fence (Aus.)
3. *short distance:* close shave, hop and a step, near as dammit, near thing, piece, (in) spitting distance, near squeak
v. 4. *to be near:* be hot, – warm
adv. 5. *far:* back of beyond, cold, to hell and gone, faraways
6. *near, close:* bang up (against), breathing down one's neck, as near as no matter, – dammit, texan rude (backsl. = next door), under one's nose, (by a) nose, up one's daily (rhy.sl. = daily mail = tail = behind), ringside, upside (US black)
7. *measurement:* klick (kilometer), mike-mike (millimeter)

SHAPE
39. Straightness
n. 1. beeline

adv. 2. *straight:* down the alley, in the groove, on the beam

40. Crookedness
adv. 1. *crooked:* all anyhow, assbackwards, cockeyed, crinched, everywhichway, gimped (in), hell west and crooked, screwy, six ways from Sunday, skewiff

---

PLACE
41. Situation; Location
n. 1. posish, sitch
2. *ground:* deck
3. *small place:* manhole (US black)
v. 4. *to put, place:* dock, park, plant, spot
5. *lay down, put down with force:* bing, blop, bop, chuck, flop, kerplunk, lam, nail, peg, plank, plop, plunk, slap (down), smack, sock, swack, whang
6. *to be in a place, to reside:* (drop) anchor, hang out, – up one's hat, park one's carcase, perch, pitch camp, roost
adv. 7. *where:* anywheres, somewheres, any place, some –, on deck, at (as in 'where are you at?')
8. *everywhere:* all over, – the map, – the shop, from hell to breakfast
9. *in the wrong place:* off one's manor, – patch, – turf, on the flip side, on the Jersey side

42. Town; City
n. 1. big city, burg, met, metrop
2. *small town:* jerkwater (town), one-horse town, sticks, tank town, whistle stop
3. *suffix:* -ville

43. Cities: Nicknames
n. 1. Apple (NYC), Bay City (San Francisco, Calif.), Bean Town (Boston, Mass.), Berdoo (San Bernadino, Calif.), Big A (Amarillo, Tx. or Atlanta, Ga.), Big Smoke (Sydney, Aus.), Big T. (Tucson, Ariz.), Cowboy City (Cheyenne, Wyo.), Dago (San Diego, Calif.), Guz (Devonport, UK), Hip City (black use: Cleveland, Ohio), Jew York (derog: NYC), Nueva York (NYC), Nap Town (Indianapolis), P-Town (Philadelphia), Pompey (Portsmouth, UK), Rubber City (Akron, Ohio), Shaky City (Los Angeles), Sin City (Las Vegas, Nev.), the Smoke (London), Tinseltown (Hollywood, Calif.), TJ (Tijuana, Mexico), Windy City (Chicago, Ill.), Yidney (derog: Sidney, Aus.)
2. *imaginary cities:* Shitkicker, Ohio, Woop Woop (Aus.)
3. *areas:* Bible Belt, Borscht Belt, gin and Jaguar belt, scampi belt

44. Cities: Districts
n. 1. Chocolate City (any black ghetto), the Coathanger (Sydney Harbour Bridge, Aus.), the Drain (the London Underground), Dream Street (47th St, NYC, betw. 6th and 7th Avenues), Foggy Bottom (the State Department, Washington, DC), Forty-Deuce (42nd street, NYC), the Bush (Shepherd's Bush, London W12), the Gate (Notting Hill Gate, London W11), the Grove (Ladbroke Grove, London W10, W11), the Junction (Clapham Jnct, London, SW4), Kangaroo Valley (Earls Court, London, SW10), Rods (Harrods of Knightsbridge), Swone One (London SW11), Silicon Glen, Silicon Valley, up West (the West End of London), the Water (the River Thames, London)
2. *spec. college use:* Big Green (Dartmouth), Big Red (Cornell), Bruno (Brown U.), Crimson (Harvard U.), Eli (Yale U.), Farmington (Miss Porter's School), Old Nassau (Princeton U.), St Grotlesex (a fantasy amalgam of US prep schools)
3. *spec. prisons:* the Island (Parkhurst, IOW), the Scrubs (Wormwood Scrubs, London W14), the Ville (Pentonville, London N1)
4. *spec. homosexual use:* Boystown (the gay area of West Hollywood), Queen's Row (Boston, Mass), Swish Alps (Hollywood Hills), Vaseline Heights (gay centre of Portland, Ore.)

45. Countries: Nicknames
n. 1. Bananaland (Queensland, Aus.), Big Ditch (Atlantic Ocean), Blighty (UK), Down Under (Australia), Honkers (Hong Kong), Jamdung (Jamaica), the World (the USA as seen by troops in Vietnam)

46. Region; Locality
n. 1. boonies, boondocks, manor, nabes, neck of the woods, patch, side (W1), stamping ground, turf
2. *unpleasant place:* armpit, bottoms (US black), craphouse, creepsville, dump, lavatory, Motel Hell, muckhole, nowhere city, shitheap, skid row, toilet, wrong side of the tracks
3. spec. blue feature (water area on a map); civvy street, Cloud 9

47. Thoroughfare
n. 1. *road:* blacktop, double nickel, drag, frog and toad (rhy.sl.), M-way; spec. milit. use: redball (enemy road, in Vietnam)
2. *street:* bricks, drag, field of wheat (rhy.sl.)
3. *main street:* Afro set, fast lane, front line, front street, main drag, – stem, set; spec. bread and butter

(rhy.sl. = gutter), Johnny Horner (rhy.sl. = corner)
4. *meeting place:* meat market, – rack; spec. homosexual use: cottage, tearoom

48. Enclosure
n. 1. bullpen, hootch, shovel and broom (rhy.sl. = room); spec. office (any workplace – pilot's cabin, pimp's bar, etc.)
2. *house:* cat and mouse (rhy.sl.), gaff, joint, pad; spec. deri, derry (derelict house), fancy crib, mahogany flat (US black)
3. *sleeping place:* doss, doss house, flop, – house, kip, – house
4. *residence:* crib, dorm, fleabag, padding crib; spec. slaughter house, whip shack (US black: a place for sex); animal house (US campus: the least fashionable fraternity house)
5. *garden:* Dolly Varden (rhy.sl.)
6. *spec. places:* bone yard, silent city (cemetery); cooler (mortuary); caff, greasy spoon, takeaway (cafe); chippy (chip shop); labour (labour exchange); tekram (backsl. = market); farm, funny farm, giggle-house (Aus.), loony bin, – farm, nut house (mental hospital); prison: nick; sport: end (of a football ground); crime: flat joint (gambling), honky-tonk, slaughter (a dump for stolen goods); uni (university); bog, crapper, dike, john, loo, shitter, snakes house (lavatory), grubber (Aus.); spike (vagrants' hostel); trap (club); slide (transvestite club)
7. *homeless:* on the bricks, – stones, – street
8. *unpleasant, dirty place:* pisshole, shithole

MOTION: VELOCITY
49. Speed; Swiftness
n. 1. action, the double, get-up-and-go, go, hot-foot, hustle, lick, pep, quick-time, rabbit fever, zip

2. *going fast:* hot-footing, scoot, scram, skedaddle, spin, whirl; spec. white line fever (driving fast)
3. *something fast:* bat out of hell, blue streak, greased lightning, scorcher, streak of lightning; spec. wham-bam thank-you ma'am (quick intercourse)
v. 4. *to go fast:* ace, ball the jack, barrel (it), belt along, blow ass, broom, do a fair lick, get one's skates on, go full blast, – like a bat out of hell, – a blue streak, – a bomb, – a house on fire, – a shot out of hell, – greased lightning, – like hell, – like nobody's business, – like the clappers, – through like a dose of salts, hightail (it), hit it, – the wind, hoof it, move one's ass, neckbreak (US black), pour it on, rattle one's dags (Aus.), rip (along), scoot off, shoot off, – over, – through (Aus.), skedaddle, snap it up, streak (off), take a powder, take a runout powder, tear ass, – off, turn it on, up and dust, whizz (off), zip, zoom (off)
5. *to hurry:* fall (all) over oneself, get a move on, get one's arse in gear, get the lead out, get weaving, look sharp, make it snappy, move it, – yourself, shake a leg, shift arse, snap it up, step lively
6. *to run:* beat feet, cut dirt, fan one's butt, flap the heels, hightail (it), lay 'em down, pick 'em up
7. *to accelerate:* hop on it, jump to it, let her rip, put the skids under
8. *to make go faster:* put the skids under
adj. 9. *fast:* at a rate of knots, chop-chop, double quick, hot and strong, hot cross bun, (rhy.sl. = on the run), lickety-split, like a bat out of hell, like a dose of salts, like a rat up a drain, like winking, off like a bride's nightie, on the double, on the hop, on the hurry up, on the trot, toot sweet, zippy
excl. 10. where's the fire!

11. *full speed:* all the way, all out, at full bat, wide open
12. *hurry up!:* snap it up, wake it up

50. Slowness
v. 1. *to be slow:* dog it, drag –, go nowhere fast, leadfoot, mosey (along), slowpoke
2. *not hurry:* hold one's horses, hold one's water, keep one's shirt on, take it easy
3. *to slow down:* put on the anchors
adj. 4. *slow:* doggy, drag-arse, lazy-arse

MOTION: DIRECTION
51. Direction
n. 1. U-ie (u-turn)
v. 2. *go straight:* make a beeline (for)
3. *change direction:* flip-flop, hang, hang a Lilly, – a Louie, – a Ralph, – a U-ie
adv. 4. *moving:* back to square one, on the hoof
5. *in all directions:* all over the shop, everywhichway, hell west and crooked, six ways from Sunday
6. *from both directions:* double-doored (Can.)

52. Approach
n. 1. *arrival:* blow in, check-in, drop in
v. 2. *to arrive:* beat (one) to the punch (US Black use = to arrive first), belly up to, blow in, breeze in, drop in, – by, hit, lob in (Aus.), make the scene, roll in, – up, sneaky-pete, tool in; spec. working use: clock in

53. Entrance
v. 1. *to enter:* barge in, blow in, bob up, breeze along, – in, bust in, drop in, – by, duck in, ease in, ooze in, pop in

2. *enter forcibly:* bust in, crash in, gatecrash, muscle in, nose in
excl. 3. emok nye! (backsl. = come in!)

54. Departure
n. 1. blow, bow-out, check-out, the fade, kiss-off, send-off
2. *hasty departure:* bunk, bust (out), hightail, jump, lam, one-two, powder, runout, – powder, scoot, scram, scrambola, scramskie, skedaddle, skip, vamoose
v. 3. *to leave:* amscray, bail (out), beat feet, – it, beetle off, be missing, blow, – out of, boogie-woogie (US black), book (US black), break in, broom, bugger off, bug out, bunk off, buzz off, check out, choof, clear off, cut (out), cut along, – loose, do a bunk, – a powder, – a runner, fade away, flake off, fly the coop, fuck off, get lost, – on one's bike, – the hell out of Dodge, hat up, haul ass, have it away, – on one's dancers, – on one's toes, heel on (US black use), hightail (it), hit the bricks, – the road, – the street, – the trail, – the wind, hive off (Aus.), honk on, hop the wag, iris out, jam (US black), leg it, let's boogie, light out, make it, mug up (US black), nick off, pedal one's dogs, piss off, pop off, pull up stakes, push along, – off, put it in the wind, raise up (US black use), roll out, run out (on), Scapa Flow (rhy.sl. = to go), scarper, scat, scoot (off), scram, shoot off, shoot the coop, shoot through (Aus.), shove off, skedaddle, skip, sky, sky off (US black use), sling one's hook, slope off, sod off, split, take a hike, – a powder, – a runout powder, – it on the lam, – off, – the air, – the wind, tear off, – loose (US black use), toddle off, up and dust (US black use), vamoose, whizz off, zoom (off); spec. move one's belongs at night to avoid rent: shoot

the moon; hand in one's dinner plate (resign from a job)
4. *sneak off:* do a bunk, duck out, ease out, gumshoe, iris out, skip (out), squirrel off, take it on the creep; spec. jump the gun (start off prematurely)
adv. 5. *departing:* ready for the off, off with a bang
excl. 6. *leave!:* be missing!, blow!, break it up!, bugger off! buzz off!, case off! eff off!, fuck off, get lost! – rooted! (Aus.), go pound salt up your arse!, – to hell!, hop it!, kaycuff foe! (backsl.), naff off!, on your bike!, piss off!, push off!, rack off! (Aus.), scram!, shove off!, sod off!, take a hike! vamoose!; spec. lead on, Macduff (exhorting another person to take the initiative)
7. *spec. goodbye:* Abyssinia, catch you later, toodle-pip, TTFN (ta-ta for now)
8. spec. AWOL (milit. absent without leave)

55. Ascent
n. 1. stiff pull
v. 2. *ascend:* shimmy up, skin up, zoom (up)
excl. 3. alley-oop!, upsidaisy!

56. Descent
n. 1. *fall:* bop, brodie, cropper, flop, header, kerplump, nose-dive, plop, plump, purler, spill
v. 2. *to fall:* come a cropper, – a purler, go arse-over-appetite, – arse-over-tit, go kerplunk, hit the deck, take a spill, – a brodie, – a flier
3. *to sit down:* give the dogs a rest, grab a chair, – a flop, park yourself, – your carcase, take it easy, – a log off (your feet), – the weight off your feet
adv. 4. *head-over-heels:* arse-over-appetite, arse-over-tit

57. Irregular Motion
n. 1. bumpity-bump, flitter-flutter, pitapat
v. 2. bobble
3. *to jerk:* yank

MOTION: TRAVEL
58. Travel in General
n. 1. *wanderer:* mumper
v. 2. *to wander:* bat around, (go on the) bum, case (it) around, cat around, knock about, mooch, slap the pavement, swan around, tool around, tromp (around), truck; spec. island-hop: the Grand Tour (campus use); pack (live as a female tramp)
mod. 3. *moving:* on the go, – the trot

59. Walking
n. 1. ball and chalk (rhy.sl.), footslogging, Guy (Fawkes) (rhy.sl.), leg work, yomping; spec. UK royal family: walkabout; US black use: Memphis glide, pimp stride, slidewalk
v. 2. *to walk:* air out, ankle along, bop, diddy-bop, foot it, poke along, ride shanks' pony, walk the dogs

60. Riding
n. 1. *ride:* hitch, spin, whirl; spec. run (Hell's Angels outing)
2. spec. banker (cab-driver's regular route), burn-up (fast riding of a motorcycle), chicken run (teenage virility ritual involving cars), Hollywood swoop (US black use, one vehicle halts the other by passing and then cutting in front of it)
3. *speed of ride:* herbs (Aus.), horses (horsepower)
v. 4. *to drive fast:* ball the jack, belt it, burn rubber, buzz, caravan, deadhead, do a ton, floor, give (it) the gun, – the herbs (Aus.), gun (it), hammer, hit the gas, jam it, lay

rubber, let her go, – her out, peel
out, pill out, put the hammer down,
rev, romp it, sandbag, screw it on,
thrash (Aus.), wind her up
5. *to ride in a car:* spec. ride punk,
ride pussy, ride the bitch's seat (US
black: a woman seated between two
men); ride tough (US black: drive a
smart car)
6. spec. hot-wire (to start a car
without an ignition key), Kojak
(to find a parking place easily), nerf
(to collide with another car), put on
the anchors (brake), run out of road
(to crash, after failing to take a
corner), (have a) shunt (to collide),
soup up (to improve the car's
performance), tailgate (to follow
too closely)
7. *to hitchhike:* bum, go on the
thumb, hitch, push the thumb,
ride one's thumb, thumb it, thumb-
trip
8. *spec. surfing:* to ride the
planks
phr. 9. *what do you drive?:* what are
you pushing (US black)

MOTION: TRANSFERENCE
61. Transference
v. 1. *to transport, haul, carry:* cart,
hump, pack, tote
2. *to pull:* schlep (Yid.), snake,
yank
3. *to reach for:* make a long
arm
4. *to raise:* hike

62. Throwing
n. 1. chuck, shy; spec. cricket use:
dollydrop, skier, steepler
2. *hard throw:* bullet, hot one,
hotshot, hummer, ripper, scorcher,
sizzler, smoker, steamer, streaker,
whizzer, zipper
v. 3. *to throw:* bung, chuck, cut
loose (with), let go (of), rifle (it in),
shy, smoke, uncork

63. Ejection
n. 1. *discharge, dismissal:* the air,
the axe, big E, boot, boot-out,
bounce, brush (off), bump, bum's
rush, chuck, dust, elbow, gate, KB,
kiss-off, knock-back, order of the
boot, Spanish archer ('El Bow'),
walking papers
v. 2. *to dismiss:* blow out, boot
(out), bounce, bump, call it a day,
chuck, ditch, eighty-six (rhy.sl. =
nix), elbow, give the air, – the sack,
the belt, – the brown envelope,
– the (old) heave-ho, – the elbow,
axe etc. (see n. 1), hoof out, put
the skids under, – the screws to,
sack, see the back off, send away
with a flea in one's ear, send
packing, show the door, – the gate,
sling out, turf out; spec. kick
upstairs (move to a senior but less
important job)
3. *to be dismissed:* get the chop,
– the bullet, – the order of the
boot, – the sack, etc. (see n. 1.)
adv. 4. *dismissed:* booted, out on
one's ear, – one's arse

Matter

GEOGRAPHIC CONDITIONS
64. World; Earth
n. 1. *the great outdoors*, Mother Nature

65. Heavens; Space
n. 1. upstairs, up there
2. *the sun:* bath bun, currant bun (rhy.sl.), rays, UVs
v. 3. *to sunbathe:* catch some rays

66. Natural Phenomena; Weather
n. 1. *hot weather:* blazing (down), peas in the pot (rhy.sl. = hot), roaster, scorcher, sizzler, swelterer
2. *cold weather:* brass monkey weather, cold snap, dirty weather, filthy weather, freezer, Naughton and Gold (rhy.sl.), potatoes in the mould (rhy.sl.), taters
3. *wet weather:* bucketing down, pissing down
4. *rain:* Andy Cain (rhy.sl.), pleasure and pain (rhy.sl.); spec. send her down, Hughie (Aus.: an appeal for rain, or good surfing)
5. *fog:* peasouper
6. *winds:* Irish hurricane (dead calm)
v. 7. *to rain:* bucket down, piss down, rain cats and dogs, spit
8. *to be windy:* blow great guns

FLUIDS
67. Liquids
n. 1. *water:* Adam's ale, fisherman's daughter (rhy.sl.)
2. *sea:* big ditch, – lake, briny, Davy Jones' locker, deep, ditch, drink, frog pond, oggin, pond, puddle;
spec. surfing use: Big Kahoona (a perfect wave)
3. *waves:* spec. white horses (white caps on choppy waves)
4. *ice:* rocks
5. *petrol:* gas, juice; spec. hot rod use: nitro
6. *oil:* black gold, crude, lube
7. *thick, sticky liquid:* dope, gism, glop, goo, goop, guck, gunk
8. *glue:* dope, goo

MATERIALS; DEVICES
68. Raw Materials
n. 1. *things in general:* stuff
2. *spec. oil rigs:* mud; iron-, glassworks, etc. grog (refractory material)
3. *gold:* red stuff, yellow stuff
4. *silver:* white stuff
5. *stone, brick:* Irish confetti (when thrown at others)
6. *silk:* squeeze
7. *lead:* bluey

69. Devices; Implements
n. 1. *equipment:* fit-up, gear, kludge, lashup, layout, rig, rig-up, set-up, shebang, works
2. *indefinite objects:* bits and bobs, dingbat, dingus, doings, dojigger, do(o)-dad(s), doodah, do(o)-hickey, gitty-gap, gizmo, gubbins, jig, junk, majigger, motherfucker, oojah, shebang, so-and-so, stuff, thingummibob, thingummijig, thingy, whamdoodle, what-d'you-call-it, whatchamacallit, whatnot, whatsit, whodjamaflop, you know, you know what
3. *new object:* wheeze, wrinkle

4. *tool:* April fool (rhy.sl.), ratfucker, (home-made starting handle)
5. *prizing tool:* jemmy, jimmy
6. *hammer:* Birmingham screwdriver, Irish screwdriver
7. *wrench:* knuckle buster, monkey
8. *household equipment:* asswipe (lavatory paper), B-52, church key (can-opener), band of hope, Cape of Good Hope (rhy.sl. = soap), hottie (hot water bottle), jerry, Ted Frazer (rhy.sl. = cut-throat razor); spec. homosexual use: trick towel (used by male prostitute to clean up after a client)
9. *knife:* axe, blade, charming wife (rhy.sl.), chiv, cutter, flick, nigger-flicker, shiv, slicer
10. *scissors:* snips
11. *shovel:* banjo, Lord Lovel (rhy.sl.)
12. *drill:* kanga
13. *keys:* church key (can opener), twister (house key)
14. *saw:* bear's paw (rhy.sl.)
15. *nails:* monkey's tails (rhy.sl.)
16. *matches:* cuts and scratches (rhy.sl.), strikers
17. *clock:* dickery (dock), hickory dock (rhy.sl.), ticker
18. *stationery, etc.:* blotch, (blotting paper), bungy (eraser), nerd pack (holder for pens)
19. *cleaning:* honey cart, – wagon, pooper-scooper
20. *carriers:* cock sparrow (rhy.sl. = barrow), esky, poly bag (polythene)
21. *covering:* Auntie Ella (rhy.sl. = umbrella), brolly, tarp (tarpaulin)
22. *lights:* finsburies (rhy.sl. f. park = arc), glim, Harry Randall (rhy.sl. = candle)
23. *vehicles:* body and soul lashing (sailing use); George (automatic pilot)
24. *musical instruments:* axe, bull-fiddle (double bass), joanna (rhy.sl. = piano), Strat (Stratocaster electric guitar), taps (drums)
25. *record players, etc.:* boofer box, chatter box, ghetto blaster, Third World briefcase, wog box; nigger box (TV); sides (records)
26. *technology:* bug (surveillance device); spaghetti (a mass of wires), stinger (a light socket extension); number-cruncher (large computer)
27. *contraceptive devices:* flying saucer (diaphragm), French letter, – tickler, frenchie, frenchy, rubber, rubber boot, – johnny, safe, scumbag

---

WEAPONS; EXPLOSIVES
70. Weapon
n. 1. *weapon:* enforcer, heat, persuader, piece, tool
2. *clubs:* life preserver, sap, slug
3. *brass knuckles:* brassies, iron mikes, knuckle dusters, knucks, maulers
4. spec. pimp sticks (a whip made of wire coathangers)
5. *pocket knife:* chiv, toothpick

71. Firearm
n. 1. action piece, bad news, barker, belly gun, Betsy, cannon, chopper, chunk, equalizer, gat, grease-gun, heater, hog-leg, iron, peacemaker, piece, poker, pom-pom, rod, roscoe, Saturday Night Special, speaker, tool, zipgun; spec. thirty-eight (.38), forty-five (.45), Mag (Magnum); pump (pump-action shotgun); sawed off (sawn off shotgun)
2. *machine gun:* Chicago piano, – typewriter, chopper
3. *spec. military use:* arty (artillery), Bouncing Betty (a mine that springs into the air), chopper (helicopter), dick gun (a rubber bullet gun), fast mover (F-4 fighter-bomber), flat top (aircraft carrier), frag (fragmentation grenade), Huey (HU-1 helicopter), Leaping Lena (see Bouncing Betty), MA

(mechanical ambush), slicks
(helicopters), the gun (M-60 light
machine gun), thumper (M-79
grenade launcher), tin can (naval
destroyer), toe popper (M-14
anti-personnel mine), willie peter
(white phosphorus)

72. Ammunition; Explosives
n. 1. ammo, buck (buckshot),
hardware, lead, rockets; spec.
pineapple (bomb or grenade)

73. Explosion; Shot
n. 1. bing, boom, bong, bop, bust,
pam, plink, plunk, pow, whoomp,
whomp
2. *gunfire:* Chicago lightning; spec.
lit up (under fire), incoming (hostile
gunfire)
v. 3. *to shoot:* bust caps, hose down,
lead (down), pop (off), turn on the
heat; spec. dry-snap (to fire a
weapon without ammunition)
4. spec. frag (to assassinate a fellow
soldier with a fragmentation
grenade)

74. Armed
n. 1. drop (being able to draw a
weapon before a rival)
v. 2. *to be armed:* pack iron, – a gat,
rod, etc.
adv. 3. *armed:* heeled, loaded for
bear, packing iron, etc., rodded,
tooled up
phr. 4 spec. rock and roll (milit.:
firing an automatic weapon in a
steady burst)

VEHICLES AND MOTORS
75. Vehicle
n. 1. *car:* auto, boat, buggy, flivver,
heap, iron, jam jar (rhy.sl.),
john-john (WI), motor, ride, short,
wheels
2. *large car:* Al Capone ride (US
black use), big boat, brougham (US
black use), cruisemobile, gangster

doors, – ride, gas-guzzler, limo,
pimpmobile, spivmobile; spec. black
taxi (Aus. official limousine)
3. *old car:* banger, bone-shaker,
clunker, jalopy, junker, rust-bucket
4. *specific cars:* Bird (thunderbird),
cad, caddy (Cadillac), Connie
(Lincoln Continental), deuce 25,
deuce and a quarter (Buick 225),
DV (Cadillac de Ville), geetoh
(GTO), Jag (Jaguar), Jew Canoe
(derog: Cadillac in US, Jaguar in
UK), kitty-cat (US black: Cadillac),
LD (Cadillac Eldorado), Masers
(Maserati), Merc (Mercedes), rado
(Cadillac Eldorado), Roller, Woler
(Rolls-Royce), Vette (Corvette);
black and white (US police car thus
painted); crummy (transport in
logging camps); ringer, tweedler
(UK criminal use: illegitimate cars);
passion wagon (car used for
seductions); dump truck (derog: car
full of lesbians); woodie
(wood-panelled station wagon);
ringer (stolen and disguised
second-hand car)
5. *trucks:* rig, ute (Aus. utility
trucks)
6. *motorcycles:* ass hammer,
chopper, garbage wagon, hog,
machine, one-lunger; spec. wheelie
(trick riding on a motorcycle)
7. *aircraft:* coffee grinder (old,
unstable aircraft)
8. *ships:* halfpenny dip (rhy.sl.),
tub, the tubs (transatlantic
liners)
9. *railways:* Bedpan line (BR line
between Bedford and St Pancras)
10. *bicycle:* do as you like (rhy.sl.)
11. *ambulance:* blood wagon
12. *public transport:* drain, rattler
(London underground trains); swear
and cuss (rhy.sl. = bus)
13. *cabs:* fast black, flounder and
dab (rhy.sl.), spin; spec. bill (a
taxidriver's license)
14. *collision:* pile-up, prang,
rear-ender, shunt

v. 15. *to crash:* prang, shunt, total, write off

76. Automotive Parts
n. 1. *engine:* cams (camshaft), carb (carburettor), crank (crankshaft), headers (manifold)
2. *brakes:* anchors
3. *accelerator:* hammer
4. *seats:* buddyseat (pillion on motorbicycle), shotgun seat (next to driver), pimp post (US black: armrest between front seats)
5. *tyres:* gangster walls (whitewalls)
6. *handlebars:* apehangers (high, extra-long motorcycle handlebars)
7. *interior:* black on black (US black: black car with black interior)
8. *exterior:* rag top (soft top)
v. 9. decoke (to clean spark plugs)
adv. 10. dressed (US black: a car with every conceivable accessory)

77. Motor; Engine
n. 1. boiler, kettle, pot, hog, mule, donkey; spec. four-, six-banger, four-, six-lunger, kicker (outboard motor)
adj. 2. *specially engineered:* hopped up

BUILDINGS AND FURNITURE
78. Building
n. 1. dive, dump, hole, joint, layout, shebang, spot
2. *house, home:* back-a-yard (WI), crib, drum, eemosh (backsl. = house), kip, pad; spec. crash-pad (house where one can sleep temporarily); condo (condominium); pseudy Tudy, stockbroker Tudor (fake 'Elizabethan' architecture)
3. *apartment:* shotgun flat, walkup
4. *lodging house:* doss, – house, kip, – house
5. *hotel:* spec. Hojo (Howard Johnson's)

6. *public house:* battle-cruiser (rhy.sl.), boozer, rubbidy, rub-a-dub (Aus.); spec. drinker (after hours club); public (public bar); balloon (rhy.sl. = saloon bar); nineteenth hole (a golf-club bar)
7. *cafe, club, etc.:* caff, carry-out, takeaway, takeout; spec. clip-joint (club that defrauds its customers); slop chute (USMC bar)
8. *place of entertainment:* bughutch, fleapit (inferior cinemas); cherry hogs (rhy.sl. = dogs = greyhound tracks)

79. Parts of Houses
n. 1. *lavatory:* altar, bog, can, crapper, dunnee, dunnigan, flush, jakes, john, karsy, lav, lavvy, little boy's/girl's room, little office, loo, pisshole, pisshouse, shithouse, shit jacket, shitter, snakes' house, throne, thunder-box; spec. head(s) (naval)
2. *outside lavatory:* one-, two-holer
3. *lavatory paper:* asswipe, bumf, bum fodder, wipe
4. *window:* burnt (cinder) (rhy.sl.)
5. *fire:* Anna Maria (rhy.sl.)
6. *stairs:* apples and pears (rhy.sl.), wooden road to Bedfordshire
7. *floor:* Rory (rhy.sl. = Rory O'Moore)

80. Camp
n. 1. spec. jungle (US hobo camp)

81. Furniture
n. 1. fixings, sticks
2. *bed:* kife, kip, sack, Uncle Ned (rhy.sl.)
3. *pillow:* weeping willow (rhy.sl.)
4. *table:* Cain and Abel (rhy.sl.)
5. *chair:* lion's lair (rhy.sl.), ryache (backsl.)
6. *mirror:* snake in the grass (rhy.sl. = looking glass)
7. *clock:* dickory dock (rhy.sl.)
8. *style:* Jewy Louis (derog: over-ornate

phr. 9. *shut the door:* put the wood in the hole

DRESS
82. Clothes
n. 1. duds, clobber, doodads, drapes, fronts, pieces, rags, rig, schmutter, threads, togs, traps, wrapping; spec. clear cut (US black use: stylish clothes); night clothes (criminal use: dark clothes used for robberies at night)
2. *suit:* piccolo and flute, whistle and flute (rhy.sl.), vine
3. *formal dress:* d.j., monkey suit, soup and fish, tails, tux
4. *best clothes:* best bib and tucker, glad rags, go to meeting clothes, silks (US black)
5. *old clothes:* grubbies, tat
6. *second-hand clothes:* hand-me-downs, reach-me-downs
7. *uniform:* spec. colours, originals (patches, jeans and jacket worn by Hell's Angels); rabbit skin, sheepskin (academic tippets)
8. *civilian clothes:* civvies, dog-robbers (suits worn by off-duty officers)
9. *skirts:* midi, mini, maxi
10. *underwear:* Alan Whickers (rhy.sl. = knickers), BVDs, didies, east and west (rhy.sl. = vest), fleas and ants (rhy.sl. = pants), Harolds (pants), kecks, long johns, passion killers, skivvies, snuggies, UBs (underbodies); spec. falsies; VPL (visible pantie line)
11. *trousers:* bins, council houses (rhy.sl.), daks, kicksies, loon pants (very baggy), petrols (Aus. rhy.sl. petrol bowsers), round the houses (rhy.sl.), strides (Aus.), trou; spec. baggies (shorts worn for surfing)
12. *coat:* benny, boolhipper (US black: leather), crombie, leather piece, nanny goat (rhy.sl.), rod, smother, weasel (and stoat)

(rhy.sl.); spec. bum-freezer (short jacket); pussy (fur coat)
13. *swimming costume:* cossie (Aus.)
14. *pyjamas:* jim-jams, pjs
15. *shoes:* beetle-crushers, boppers, bovver boots, brothel creepers, – stompers, daisy roots (rhy.sl. = boots), dogs, howd'ye dos, reptiles, roach-killers, shit stompers, stomp(ers), waffle-stompers, winkle-pickers; spec. air hose (shoes worn without socks); thousand eyes (US black: heavily perforated leather shoes); wellies (wellingtons)
16. *running shoes:* chucks, daps, quick starts (US black)
17. *hats:* chimney, titfer (rhy.sl. tit for tat); spec. boonie hat (soft military hat for jungle use), skidlid (crash helmet), steel pot (steel helmet)
18. *shirts:* dicky dirt, Uncle Bert (rhy.sl.); spec. fag tag, fruit loop (small loop sewn to back of shirt)
19. *pocket:* bin, Lucy Locket, sky (rocket) (rhy.sl.)
20. *sportswear:* jock, jockstrap (athletic supporter)
21. *tight sweater:* shrink; spec. boob-tube (narrow cylindrical garment, encircling breasts)

83. Accessories
n. 1. *gloves:* turtle (doves), (rhy.sl.); spec. mittens (boxing use)
2. *handkerchief:* bubble duster, snotrag
3. *cane:* whangee
4. *tie:* fourth of July (rhy.sl.), Peckham (rhy.sl. Peckam Rye)
5. *socks:* almond (rocks) (rhy.sl.); spec. pimp socks (US black: socks with thin vertical lines)
6. *spectacles:* cheaters, Lancashire lasses (rhy.sl.), shades (dark glasses)
7. *bag:* diddy-bag
8. *wallet:* dummy, goitre, leather, poggler, poke

9. *watch:* Gordon and Gotch (rhy.sl.)

10. *jewellery:* bobbles, glass, ice, jim, red stuff, rocks, Simple Simon (rhy.sl. = diamond), sparkler(s), tom, tomfoolery (rhy.sl.), tot (WI); spec. patacca (fake, rubbishy jewels)

11. *sanitary towels, etc.:* diaper, do rag, G-string, jam-rag, jelly sandwich (US black), rag, sling shot

12. *contraceptives:* bag, French letter, frog, johnny, rozzer (US black), rubber, rubber johnny

13. *cosmetics:* lippy, slip

14. *braces:* airs and graces (rhy.sl.)

84. Dressing

v. 1. *to dress:* get dolled up, – togged up, pile into

2. *to dress up:* dike down, dog it, doll up, look sharp, put on the dog, spiff (oneself) up, tart (oneself) up, tog (oneself) up

adv. 3. *dressed up:* (in one's) best bib and tucker, buttered (US black), choked down (US black), dap, dressed to the nines, dressed up like a dog's dinner, – like a pox doctor's clerk, dolled up, dyke down, flossed up (of a woman), fonked out heavy (US black), full buf, got up, kitted up, laid out, laid to the bone (US black), piss elegant, pressed (US black), pimped down (US black), pooned (up), ragged down (heavy) (US black), suited (down) (US black), spiffed (up), tabbed (US black), togged to the bricks; spec. drag (dressing in the clothes of the opposite sex)

4. *smart:* clean, clean to the bone, fonky –, mod –, ragged –, silked –, tabbed (US black), neat, nifty

5. *colourful:* jazzy

85. Undress

n. 1. dishabilly

2. *nudity:* the altogether, birthday suit, (stark) bollock naked, (in the) buff, (in the) raw

v. 3. *to undress:* drop the duds, – the gear (Aus.), peel, – down, – off, shuck down, strip (off)

4. *teenage pranks:* drop trou, hambone (Aus.), moon, press ham

5. *to undress someone:* debag, pants

adj. 6. *naked:* bare-ass, peeled, raw, starkers

phr. 7. Charlie's dead (your slip is showing)

8. it's one o'clock at the water-works (your fly is undone)

FOOD

86. Food

n. 1. belly timber, choff, chop, chow, chuck, eats, feed, fixings, fodder, fuel, grease, groceries, grub, hash, munga, munger, nosh, peck(s), scoff, scran, tack, tuck, tucker; spec. junk food (fast food)

2. *bad food:* crap, dog's dinner, dog vomit, garbage, glop, gunge, slop(s), shit, vom; spec. burnt offering (burnt food)

3. *bread:* needle and thread, Uncle Fred (rhy.sl.), tommy

4. *sandwich:* butty, sango (Aus.), sarnie

5. *meat:* beemal (backsl. = lamb), cold (frozen meat), delock (backsl. = cold), feeb (backsl. = beef); kayrop (backsl. = pork), piano (US black, spare ribs), teekay (TK = town killed); spec. Kate and Sidney (rhy.sl. = steak and kidney)

6. *sausages:* snorker, snags, swags; spec. red-hots (frankfurters with chilli)

7. *poultry:* elwoff (backsl. = fowl)

8. *stew:* Mulligan stew (tramp's assembly of available foods)

9. *mince:* shit on a shingle (minced meat on toast)

10. *spreads:* marj (margarine), stammer and stutter (rhy.sl. = butter)

11. *potatoes:* murphies, praties,

spuds, taters; spec. bimps (french fries)

12. *cake:* Joe Blake, Sexton Blake (rhy.sl.); spec. sinker (doughnut)

13. *mayonnaise:* mayo

14. *watermelon:* African golf ball, culture fruit

15. *cheese:* bended knees, stand at ease (rhy.sl.)

16. *sugar:* sand

17. *breakfast cereals:* burgoo, soggies

18. *vegetables:* veggies; spec. prison use: has-beens (rhy.sl. = greens)

19. *kipper:* Jack the Ripper (rhy.sl.)

20. *pizza:* za

21. *pickles:* Harvey Nichols (rhy.sl.)

22. *pasta:* spag bol (spaghetti bolognese)

23. *gravy:* army and navy (rhy.sl.)

24. *salad:* rabbit food

25. *soup:* loop-the-loop (rhy.sl.)

26. *foreign food:* (an) Indian, (a) Chinese, Chink chow

27. *egg dishes:* Adam and Eve, – on a raft (of toast), – on a raft and wreck 'em (scrambled eggs on toast), two looking at you (two fried eggs), sunny side up (eggs fried on one side only), two down, – with their eyes closed, over easy, (eggs turned over), two on a slice of squeal (two eggs on fried ham)

28. *prison tea:* diesel

29. *ice cream:* scream

30. *chilli:* red

87. Beverage: Drink (non-alcoholic)

n. 1. *coffee:* java, joe

2. *tea:* brew, cuppa, Rosy Lea, – Lee (rhy.sl.), splosh, you and me (rhy.sl.)

3. *cocoa:* ki (RN use)

4. *milk:* cow, Grade-A

5. *lemonade, soda, etc.:* pop

v. 6. *to drink:* chugalug, dip the beak, gargle, inhale, knock back, put away, wet the whistle

88. Preparing and Serving

v. 1. chase up, dish up, rustle –, scare –, fix; spec. shackle up (tramp use, cooking lunch), brew up (to make a pot of tea)

2. *to serve food:* hash, jump tables, sling hash

3. spec. spud-bashing (peeling potatoes)

4. *to boil:* Conan Doyle (rhy.sl.)

89. Eating

n. 1. *daily food:* three squares

2. *catered food:* take away, take out

3. *breakfast:* brekker; spec. Mexican breakfast (a cigarette and a glass of water)

4. *dinner:* din-din, Jimmy Skinner, Lilley and Skinner (rhy.sl.), Tommy Tucker (rhy.sl. = supper)

5. *feast:* beano, blow-out, bust-out, gross-out, grubfest, nosh-up, spread, tuck-in; pig heaven (gross over-eating)

v. 6. *to eat:* chow down, feed one's face, get one's eating tackle around, gnaw a bone, grab a bite, grub up, hook down, lower (it), peck, put away (the groceries), put on the feed bag, – the nosebag, spoon, stoke up, stow away, tie on the feed-bag, – nosebag

7. *to eat greedily:* blow (oneself out), cram, dig in, eat like a horse, fill one's face, gross out, go for the groceries, grub it up, guzzle, hog it (down), ibble out, knock (it) back, lay into, mac out, pig out, pitch in, pork out, scarf (up), scoff, shovel (it) down, slop (it) up, stack (it) away, throw (it) down, wade into, whack (it), back; spec. guzzle (choke)

8. *to eat a small meal:* catch a bite, tear off a bite

phr. 9. *calls to eat:* chow down!, come and get it!, dig in!, pitch in!, grub('s) up!

abbrev. 10. FHB (family hold back)

90. Appetite; Thirst
n. 1. inner man
2. *hunger:* spec. munchies (cannabis-induced cravings for food)
3. *lack of appetite:* spec. chuck horrors (loathing of food that follows withdrawal from heroin)
mod. 4. *hungry:* peckish

91. Cooking and Dining Utensils
n. 1. *eating utensils:* Duke of York (rhy.sl. = fork), eating irons; sunbeam (Aus. a clean item of cutlery on the table); drugstore (the cutlery trolley in a restaurant)
2. spec. doggie-bag (a bag provided in some restaurants to take away leftovers)

LIQUOR: PERSONS
92. Liquor Dealers and Drinkers
n. 1. *alcohol seller:* mine host
2. *barman:* apron, barkeep, mixologist
3. *drunkard:* barfly, booze artist, – hound, boozer, bottle baby, dredge-head, jarhead, jickhead (US black), jughead, juice-freak, – head, lush, piss artist, pisspot, plonky, rum-dum, rummy, rumpot, sauce hound, soak, souse, tosspot; spec. bottle-a-day man, two-bottle man, etc.
phr. 4. *free:* on the house

93. Abstainers and Prohibitionists
v. 1. to go to the wagon
mod. 2. TT (teetotal)
phr. 3. off the bottle, on the wagon

LIQUOR: ALCOHOL
94. Liquor (general)
n. 1. alky, bevvy, booze, the creature, eel juice, gargle, grog, hooch, juice, jump steady (US black), neck-oil, oil, piss, sauce, shicker, swag (US black), tea; spec. hard stuff (spirits as opposed to beer, wine)
2. *superior liquor:* (just) what the doctor ordered, a little of what you fancy, the (real) goods, the real McCoy, – stuff
3. *inferior liquor:* cat's pee, – piss, dishwater, gnat's pee, – piss, rat's pee, – piss
4. *illegal liquor:* jungle juice, kong, moon, moonshine, nigger-pot, panther piss, potato jack, white lightning
5. *effects of liquor:* bang, boot, buzz, jolt, kick, lift, oof, oomph, pep, powee, punch, smack, sock, wham, zing, zip, zowie
6. *measure of liquor:* shot

95. Varieties of Liquor
n. 1. *beer:* amber fluid, – liquid, – nectar, apple fritter (rhy.sl. = bitter), beevos, brew, brewski, Crimea (rhy.sl.), greenie, joy juice, jug, oh my dear (rhy.sl.), reeb (backsl.), road brew, skimmish, stage fright (rhy.sl. = light ale), suds, wallop; spec. Nigerian lager, photo finish (rhy.sl.), plain (Guinness stout)
2. *wine:* berries (US black), plonk, pluck (US black), schoolboy scotch (US black), smash, vino
3. *cheap wine:* red Biddy, dago red, muski (muscatel), railroad whisky, sixteen-year-old after-shave, smoke, sneaky Pete
4. *champagne:* boy, bubbly, champers, fizz, poo, pop; spec. the Widow (Veuve Cliquot)
5. *whisky:* brownie, the creature, gay and frisky (rhy.sl.), gold watch, pimple and blotch (rhy.sl. = scotch)
6. *cheap spirits:* dog juice, redeye, rotgut
7. *brandy:* fine and dandy, Jack-a-dandy (rhy.sl.)
8. *gin:* mother's ruin, Vera Lynn (rhy.sl.)
9. *port:* didn't ought (rhy.sl.); spec.

WPLJ, shake-'em down (white port and lemon juice)
10. *rum:* Tom Thumb (rhy.sl.)
11. *abnormal drinks:* blob (Aus. mix of brandy, wine and hot water); corporation cocktail (coalgas in milk), metho, smoke, white lady (Aus. metholated spirits)

96. Mixed or Adulterated Drink
n. 1. spec. bloody (bloody Mary)
phr. 2. on the rocks (with ice), back (on the side, ie: 'soda back')

LIQUOR: DRINKING
97. Drinking (general)
n. 1. boozing, hitting the bottle, lushing (it up), swilling, tying one on, wetting one's whistle
2. *a drink:* bracer, drop (of the creature), gargle, hit, jag, jolt, liquid lunch, night-cap, rosiner (Aus.), shot, slug, snifter, snort, squirt game, tincture, tonic, turps (Aus.), wet; spec. eye-opener, phlegm-cutter (first of the day); leg opener (drink when used for seduction); hair of the dog (an anti-hangover drink); one for the ditch, – for the road (a farewell drink); pick-me-up (invigorating drink)
v. 3. *to drink:* bend one's elbow, booze, – it up, chug, chug-a-lug, crack a bottle, – tube (Aus.), dip the bill, – the snoot, farm, gargle, get a load on, get a snootful, get an edge on, – one's nose painted, – one going, hit the booze, – the bottle, – the jug, – the sauce, hoist one, inhale (a snort), irrigate the tonsils, knock (one) back, lush, – it around, – it up, oil the tonsils, put one/a few back, – down, shicker (Yid.), slop (some) down, sneeze, splice the mainbrace, suck the bottle, swig, swill, take a drop, – a few, – one, – a wet, etc., throw (one, a few, etc.) down, tie one on, tip, wet

one's whistle; spec. brownbag (to drink from a 'hidden' bottle when public drinking is banned); fall off the wagon (to resume drinking after a period of abstinence); wet the baby's head (to celebrate by drinking)
adv. 4. *drinking:* on the bash, on the bottle; D&D (drunk and disorderly)
phr. 5. it's the beer talking (an excuse for breaking wind)

98. Spree; Party
n. 1. bat, batter, bender, binge, blind, booze-up, bout, gig, shitface, shindig, shindy; spec. down to Larkin (free drinks); BYO (Aus. 'Bring Your Own' drink to a party); beer bust, beer fest (beer-drinking only)
v. 2. *to go drinking:* cut up, go on a bat, a bender, etc., hell around, raise hell, paint the town red, pull to a set (US black)
adv. 3. *on a party:* on a bat, – a batter, – a bender, – a bust, – a toot, on the lush, – the piss, – the randan, – the razzle, – the tiles, – the tipple

99. Toasts; Drinking Invitations
phr. 1. best of luck!, bottoms up!, bung-ho!, cheerio!, cheers!, chin-chin!, down the hatch!, good luck!, here's how!, here's looking at you!, here's mud in your eye!, more power to your elbow!
2. *invitations to drink:* get them in, it's your corner, what's your poison?, your shout, you're in the chair

100. Temperance; Abstinence
v. 1. to get straight, go on the wagon

LIQUOR: EFFECTS
101. Drunkenness
n. 1. affliction, blind staggers, edge, glow, skinful, snootful, staggers, thick head

v. 2. *to be drunk:* to be addled,
– afflicted, – afloat, – basted,
– blasted, – bevvied, – bowsered,
– boxed, – canned, etc. (see 101.3),
bet one's kettle, burn with a low
blue flame, – one's shoulder, get a
jag on, – one's shoes full, go
Borneo, – for veg, – to Mexico,
hang one on, have a buzz on, – a
few too many, – a heat on, – a
skinful, – one's back teeth afloat,
– one's pots on, kill one's dog, lay
(US black), lose one's rudder,
pepper 'em up (US black), show it,
squiff out, tank, walk on one's
cap-badge, – on rocky socks, watch
the ant races

adj. 3. *drunk:* about right, addled,
afflicted, afloat, aled up, alkied, all
at sea, all mops and brooms, – wet,
arseholed, arse on backwards,
awash, awry, back teeth afloat,
bagged, basted, belly up, below the
mahogany, belted, bevvied, blasted,
bleary, blind, blitzed, boiled,
bombed, boozed, – up, bottled,
bowsered, boxed, Brahms and Lizst
(rhy.sl. = pissed), bug-eyed, bullet
proofed, bummed, buoyant,
buzzed, canned, can't find one's
arse with both hands, – hit the
ground with one's hat, – see through
a ladder, carrying a load,
chateaued, clobbered, cock-eyed,
comboozelated, commode-hugging
(drunk), corked, corned, crocked,
crocko, cross-eyed, cut, damaged,
damp, decks-awash, dizzy, drunk as
a bastard, – a bat, – a beggar, – a
besom, – a big owl, – boiled owl,
– brewer's fart, – a cook, – a coon,
– coot, – a cooter, – a dog, – a
fiddler, – a fiddler's bitch, – a fish,
– a fly, – a fowl, – a Gosport fiddler,
– a hog, – a king, – a little red
wagon, – a log, – a lord, – a
monkey, – a Perraner, – a pig, – a
piper, – a poet, – a rolling fart, – a
sailor, – a skunk (in a trunk), – a
sow, – a swine, – a tapster, – a tick,
– a top, – a wheelbarrow, – to the
pulp, elephant's trunk (rhy.sl.),
elevated, embalmed, exalted, faced,
fallen off the wagon, far gone,
feeling funny, – good, – high, – no
pain, – right royal, fired (up),
flaked, flako, flummoxed, flushed,
flying blind, foxed, fractured, fried,
full, full as a boot, – a bull, – an
egg, – fairy's phonebook, – a
fiddler, – a goat, – googy egg, – a
lord, – as a pig's ear, – a seaside
shithouse on Boxing Day (Aus.),
– a state school hatrack, – the family
po, – a tick, – two race trains, – to
the gills, gaga, gassed, geed (up),
giffed (from TGIF: Thank God Its
Friday), ginned (up), glad, globular,
glowing, goofy, groggy, half-cut,
– gone, – seas over, – slewed,
– shot, – the bay over, hammered,
high (as a kite), hit and missed
(rhy.sl. = pissed), iced to the
eyebrows, inked (Aus.), in one's
cups, – orbit, – the bag, – the tank,
– the wrapper, jarred, jiggered,
John Bull (Aus. rhy.sl. = full),
juiced, laced, laid out, lame, legless,
likkered, listing to starboard, lit,
– to the gills, lit up, – like
Broadway, – a Christmas tree,
– Main Street, – a store window,
– Times Square, – London, loaded,
loaded to the barrel, – the earlobes,
– the gills, – the guards, – the
gunnels, – the hat, – the muzzle,
– the Plimsoll mark, – the tailgate,
looped, low in the saddle,
lubricated, lushy, maxed (out),
melted, mizzled, mulled (up),
muzzy, newted, not all there, off
nice, oiled, on a brannigan, – a
skate – a tipple, on the booze, – the
floor, – the fritz, – the grog, – the
piss, – the sauce, one over the eight,
out of one's head, out of one's mind,
out to lunch, over the top, paralytic,
petrified, pickled, pie-eyed, pissed,
– as a fart, – as a newt, – as a
rat, – to the ears, – up, pixillated,

plastered, polluted, pop-eyed, potted, primed, putrid, ratted, reeking, rigid, ripe, ripped (to the tits), roaring, rolling, rotten (Aus.), saturated, sauced schizzed, seeing double, – bats, – the bears, – pink elephants, etc., shellacked, shickered, shitfaced, skulled, skunked, skew-whiff, slewed, slopped, sloshed, smashed, snockered, snootered, soaked, sodded, soused, sozzled, spifflicated, squashed, squiffy, stewed, – as a prune, – to the eyebrows, – the gills, stiff, stinking, stinko, stoked, stoned, stonkered, stretched, stung (Aus.), swacked, swacko, tanked (up), teed up, teeth under, three sheets to the wind, tiddly, tipsy, tired, tired and emotional, top heavy, topped up, totalled, trashed, tubed, tweeked, twisted, under the influence, under the table, under the weather, vegetable, wasted, wazzocked, well away, well-oiled, whazood, wollied, woozy, wrecked

102. Hangover
n. 1. DTs, head, Joe Blakes (Aus. rhy.sl. = shakes), morning after (the night before), pink elephants, shakes
v. 2. *to feel ill:* have a mouth like the inside of an Arab's underpants, – the bottom of a bird's cage, – a Turkish wrestler's jockstrap
3. *a drink to recover:* hair of the dog

LIQUOR: MANUFACTURE; SALE
103. Manufacture and Sale
n. 1. spec. wash (WI: mash used in home-distilleries)
v. 2. *to work in a bar:* behind the stick

104. Drinking Establishment
n. 1. battle-cruiser (rhy.sl. = boozer), booze joint, boozer, dive, drinkery, filling station, jack (rhy.sl. = jack tar = bar), jinny, juice house, leeky store, LIQ (US black), rescue station, rubbidy, rub-a-dub (rhy.sl. = pub), scatter, vineyard
2. *illicit establishment:* blind pig, blues (WI), shebeen, slygrog (Aus.)

105. Drink Container
n. 1. *liquor container:* perch (pint), trophy (half a gallon), puppy (small bottle)
2. *wine bottle:* crop (fifth of a gallon), mickey, short dog
3. *beer:* frosty, minnow, stubby, tinnie, tube
4. *empty bottle:* dead, – man, marine, soldier

TOBACCO
106. Tobacco
n. 1. baccy, salmon (and trout) (rhy.sl. = snout), snout
2. *cigarette:* burn, butt, ciggie, coffin nail, dub, dubber, fag, gasper, Harry Wragg (rhy.sl. = fag), oily (rhy.sl. oily rag = fag), rette, straight, weed
3. *end of a cigarette:* bumper, butt, dog-end, fag-end, short, shorts, snipe
4. *hand-made cigarette:* roll-up, roll-your-own
5. *cigarette papers:* papers, skins
6. *cigarette lighter:* flint
7. *cigar:* la-dee-dah (rhy.sl.), stogie; spec. guinea stinker (a cheap cigar)
v. 8. *to pass cigarettes:* flash the ash, toss the squares (US black)
9. spec. defug (to get fresh air into a smokey room)

107. Tobacco Using
n. 1. *a puff of a cigarette:* drag
v. 2. *to smoke:* take a drag, – puff,

– pull, suck on; spec. bog, niggerlip (to wet the end of a cigarette when smoking)

3. *to light a cigarette:* spec. match me!

4. *share a cigarette:* do a twos (WI)

Animate Existence

LIFE
108. Life
n. 1. school of hard knocks, university of life; spec. good run, long innings (long life)

109. Pregnancy
n. 1. pudding club
2. *foetus:* little stranger
v. 3. *to make pregnant:* knock up, put in the family way, – in the club, – up the duff, stork; spec. break an ankle, cheat the starter (to become pregnant out of wedlock)
mod. 4. *pregnant:* a bun in the oven, clucky (Aus.), egg in the nest, fat (US Black), in pig, in the (pudding) club, in the family way, infanticipating, knocked up, on the hill, – the nest, poisoned (US black), preggers, priggling, pu the elop (backsl. = up the pole), the rabbit died, up the creek, – the duff, – the flue (Aus.), – the pole – the spout

110. Birth
n. 1. blessed event

111. Age
n. 1. *old age:* anno domini
v. 2. *to be old:* be over the hill, – past it, have whiskers, make old bones, seen better days; spec. senior out (to abandon the young lifestyle)
adj. 3. *young:* wet behind the ears
4. *old:* no chicken, one foot in the grave, over the hill, past it, seen one's best days; spec. on the shelf (of an ageing woman, still unmarried)

DEATH
112. Death
n. 1. big sleep, (big) chill, (final) curtain, curtains, end of the ball game, fadeout, kickoff, kiss-off, last farewell, – goodbye, – muster, – roundup, long goodbye, (final) pushoff, the (grim) reaper, send off; spec. Roman candle (milit. use: death when a parachute fails to open)
2. *corpse:* cold meat, dead –, goner, rags and bones, stiff, wormbait
3. *cemetery:* bone yard; spec. Davy Jones' locker (a watery grave)
4. *coffin:* six-foot bungalow, pine overcoat, wooden kimono, – overcoat
v. 5. *to die:* answer the last roll-call, – the last muster, – the last round-up, be thrown for a loss, bite the dust, buy the farm, call it a day, – quits, cash in one's chips, check out, come to a sticky end, conk out, crap out, croak, curl up one's toes (and die), cut one's cable, drop off the twig, – the cue, feed the worms, get (as in 'get yours, get his', etc.), get it in the neck, give up the ship, go belly up, – for a Burton, – west, go for one's tea, go to the races, hand in one's dinner pail, hang up one's harness, – one's hat, have one's chips, – one's number come up, join the great majority, jump the last hurdle, keel over, kick off, – the bucket, – up daisies, – up dust, lay down one's knife and fork, pass in one's dinner pail, peg out, push up the daisies, put one's checks in the rack, quit, slam off, snuff it, strike out, take the big jump, throw

in one's cards, – one's hand, – the sponge, turn one's face to the wall, – up one's toes, weigh out

6. *to drown:* go feed the fishes, go to Davy Jones' locker, turn into fish food

7. *kill oneself:* do the Dutch, do oneself in, take a Brodie, – the easy way out; spec. gorge out (leap from a high cliff), bump oneself off, put out one's lights, take a powder, top oneself, turn off one's lights, wipe oneself out

8. *bury:* to plant, put six feet under, send home in a box

9. *to be dying:* on one's last legs, one foot in the grave, (have) one's number come up, pegging out

adv. 10. *dead:* across the river, all bets are off, all up, belly up, checked out, counting worms, croaked, dead as a doornail, done for, gone for a Burton, – west, kicked the bucket, – off, one's hash is settled, – number is up, – race is run, out for the last count, – of the picture, – of one's misery, pegged out, popped off, pushing up daisies, rubbed out, shuffled out of the deck, stiff, through, (all) washed out, – washed up, wasted; spec. KIA (milit. abbrev. killed in action)

113. Killing; Murder

n. 1. the business, – big chill, – kiss-off, the bump (off), the chill, hit, one way ticket, rub-out, wipe out, the works; spec. one-way ride, slay-ride; necktie party (a hanging or lynching); contract (a killing arranged for a fee)

2. *death by shooting:* lead poisoning

v. 3. *to be executed:* spec. burn, fry, sit in the hot seat, take the juice (die in the electric chair); swing (for it) (to be hanged)

4. *to kill:* biff, blast, blow away, brush off, bump (off), cancel one's ticket, chill, clean up, croak, cut loose, erase, do in, do the business

on, – the job (on), drop, fog, give the business, – the chop, – the rap, – the works, get shot of, grease, hit, ice, knock (US black), knock off, – out, – over, let one have it, make cold meat of, off, plaster, polish off, put away, put out one's lights, – to sleep, rain on, rip off, rub out, send up the river, snipe (US black), snuff (out), spifflicate, squib off, stop one's clock, take care of, – for an airing, – for a ride, – off the count, – out, top, waste, whack out, zap; spec. DX (milit. euph: direct exchange); make one's bones (Mafia use: perform one's first murder); reimburse (murder some who will not pay debts)

5. *to shoot:* lead down, plug; spec. gutshoot (to shoot in the belly)

6. *to mark for death:* put a notice on, – the cross on, take out a contract on

---

PLANTS

114. Plants

n. 1. April showers (rhy.sl. = flowers)

2. spec. carnies (carnations, Aus.), glads (gladioli, Aus.)

ANIMALS

115. Animals

n. 1. *dogs:* bow-wow, goddie (backsl.), mutt, pooch, tyke; spec. dachsie, sausage dog (dachshund)

2. *chicken:* chook (Aus.)

3. *birds:* bow and arrow (rhy.sl. = sparrow)

4. *insects:* clinch (bedbug), cooties, creepy crawly, taxi-cabs (rhy.sl = crabs)

5. *dog excrement:* dog, doggy-do, hocky; spec. pooper-scooper (implement for cleaning up after dog)

6. spec. alderman's nail (rhy.sl. = tail)

7. spec. BEM (Bug-Eyed Monster)
8. *donkey:* burro, donk, moke
9. *elephant:* heffalump
10. *horse:* critter, dobbin, dog, gee-gee; spec. screw (an inferior horse); trotter (racehorse)

THE BODY
116. Parts of the Body
n. 1. *the body:* bod, chassis, frame; spec. shaft (the female body considered purely for sex)
2. *hair:* barnet (fair) (rhy.sl.), righteous moss (US black)
3. *mind:* gourd, thinker, upstairs
4. *head:* attic, bean, belfry, biscuit, block, boko, bonce, chump, coco, conk, crust of bread (rhy.sl.), deache (backsl.), dome, loaf, napper, noggin, noodle, nut, pimple, scone (Aus.), swede, topknot, top storey, wig
5. *face:* airs and graces (rhy.sl.), beezer, boat (rhys.sl. boat-race = face), chevy chase (rhy.sl.), clock, dial, esaff (backsl.), frontage, Jem Mace (rhy.sl.), kisser, lug, map, mug, mush, pan, phiz, phizog, puss, smiler
6. *jaw:* jackdaw, rabbit's paw, (rhy.sl.); spec. glass jaw (boxing use: a fragile jaw)
7. *mouth:* bazoo, cakehole, chops, flapper, gob, hole, kisser, maw, north and south (rhy.sl.), puss, smush, trap, yap
8. *teeth:* choppers, eating tackle, Hampsteads (rhy.sl. Hampstead Heath), laughing tackle, pearlies, toothy pegs
9. *nose:* beak, beezer, boko, bugle, conk, honker, hooter, horn, I suppose (rhy.sl.), konk, schnozzle, schnozzola, schnoz (Yid.), snitch, snoot, snout, snoz, snozzle
10. *beard; moustache:* face fungus, fungus, mouser, muff, stache, tash; spec. bum-fluff (light beard of a teenager)
11. *ears:* flaps, lug, lughole; spec. cauliflowers (ears deformed through boxing); tin ear (no ear for music)
12. *eyes:* babyblues, bins, daylights, headlights, minces (rhy.sl. mince pies), optics, peepers; spec. luggage (bags under the eyes); mouse, shiner (a black eye)
13. *stomach:* Auntie Nelly (rhy.sl.), breadbasket, Darby Kelly (rhy.sl.), elly-bay (backsl.), gizzard, kishkes (Yid.), Ned Kelly (rhy.sl.), Newington Butts (rhy.sl. = guts), tum (-tum), tummy, yellib (backsl.)
14. *ribs:* slats
15. *hands:* deenach (backsl.), German bands, hooks, lunch-hooks, Mary Anns (rhy.sl.), maulers, mitt, paw
16. *fist:* bunch of fives, dukes, maulers, meathooks
17. *fingers:* bell ringers (rhy.sl.), forks, lean and lingers (rhy.sl.), lunch hooks; spec. presents (US black: lucky white spots on fingernails)
18. *legs:* bacon and eggs (rhy.sl.), doog gels (backsl. = good legs), drivers, drumsticks, gams, ham hocks, hammers, pegs, pins, Scotch pegs (rhy.sl.), shanks' pony, stumps, timbers
19. *shoulder:* redloch (backsl.)
20. *knees:* biscuits and cheese (rhy.sl.)
21. *neck:* Gregory Peck, bushel and peck (rhy.sl.)
22. *feet:* hoff, mud flaps, plates of meat (rhy.sl.), puppies, trotters
23. *chin:* button, Errol Flynn, Gunga Din (rhy.sl.)
24. *heart:* pump, raspberry tart, ticker
25. *womb:* kidney
26. *skin:* hide, pelt
27. *freckles:* angel kisses
28. *bodily fluids:* claret (blood), axle grease, cream, come, emok (backsl. = come), gissum, gizzum, jam, load, love juice, melted butter,

sugar, water of life (US black), whipped cream (semen); spec. crud (dried semen on sheets or clothes); cheese, crotch cheese, jelly baby (secretions around the penis or vagina)

29. *anus:* arsehole, asshole, backeye, – slice, – slit, blot (Aus.), brown-eye, brownie, bucket, bumhole, bung, – hole, cornhole, date (Aus.), deadeye, dinger (Aus.), dirt chute, – road, freckle, gazoo, gripples (US black), jacksie, jampot, kazoo, keester, keister, leather, poop-chute, quoit, ring, satchel, shit chute, shitter, stank (US black), winker-stinker

30. *buttocks:* arse, ass, batti (WI), bottle and glass (rhy.sl.), BTM, bum, buns, butter (US black), caboose, can, chips, Daily Mail (rhy.sl. = tail), date, dinger (Aus.), elephant and castle (rhy.sl. = arsehole), fanny (US), heinie, kab edis (backsl. = backside), kazoo, keel, keister, Khyber Pass (rhy.sl. = arse), labonza, North Pole (rhy.sl. = arsehole), parking place, poop, pratt, quoit (Aus.), rusty-dusty, seat, sit-me-down, sit-upon, squatter, tail, tooshie, toches, tuches, tushie (Yid.)

31. *female breasts:* apples, balloons, bazoom, bazoomas, brace and bits (rhy.sl. = tits), Bristol City (rhy.sl. = titty), Bristols (rhy.sl. Bristol bits = tits), BSHs (British Standard Handfuls), bumpers, cakes, cats and kitties (rhy.sl. = titties), charlies (Aus. rhy.sl. Charlie Wheeler = Sheila = female, thus breasts), chichi (Mex.), cupcake, dairies, diddies, dubbies, dugs, gazungas, gib tesurbs (backsl. = big breasts), grapes, grapefruits, hangers, headlights, jugs, knobs, knockers, lollies, lungs, mams, maracas, Mary Poppins, milkers, mountains, nay-nays, ninnies, norks, pumps, rack, T and A (tits and ass), tits, titty, TNT (two nifty tits), top bollocks, tremblers, wallopies; spec. eyes (nipples)

32. *genital area:* down there, genials, naughty bits, rude parts, sweet potato pie (US black), you know where

33. *male genitals:* accoutrements, basket, crown jewels, equipment, family jewels, gear, kit, marriage gear, necessaries, nick-nacks, rig, string and nuggets, three-piece set

34. *penis:* acorn, almond (rhy.sl. almond rock = cock), arm, baby maker, bald headed hermit, bazooka, beef (US black), beef bayonet, big bird, big foot Joe, bird, blue-veined piccolo, – steak, – trumpet, blow stick, box, candy stick, cannon, cherry splitter, chopper, cock, colleen bawn (Irish), creamstick, dagger, dangler, derrick, dibble, dick, dickory dock (rhy.sl.), dingaling, ding-dong, dingus, dinosaur, dirk, do-jigger, dong, doodle, doover, dork, driving post, end, enob (backsl. = bone), ferret, flapper, four-eleven-forty-four (US black), gigglestick, goober, good time, gun, gutstick, hammer, Hampton rock (backsl.= cock), Hampton Wick (backsl. = prick), hog, honker, horn, ice cream machine, ID ('let's see your ID'), inch, Irish root, jigger, jock, joint, JT, John Thomas, joy prong, – stick, kidney wiper, knob, lob, lunch, maggot, member, middle leg, mole, mouse mutton, – dagger, nimrod, nob, one-eyed brother, – trouser snake, peacemaker (US black), pecker, peenie, percy, peter, piece, pillock, pipe, pistol, plonker, pole, pooper, pork sword, prick, prod, prong, pud, putz, rabbit, ramrod, reamer, rod, root, schlong, shitstick, short arm, skinflute, stalk, stick, string, stump, swack, swipe, tadger, thing, third leg, todger, tommy, tool, tubesteak, tummy

banana, Uncle Dick (rhy.sl. = prick),
turkey neck, wand, wang, wanger,
wang-tang, weapon, weenie, wienie,
willy, winkle, wire, wood, woofer,
worm, ying-yang, yoyo, yutz; spec.
IBM ('itty bitty meat' = small
penis); donkey-rigged, hung (having
a large penis); puppy (small penis);
stringbean (US black: thin penis)
35. *erect penis:* Bethlehem steel (US
black), blue vein, bone, colleen
bawn, Marquis of Lorne (rhy.sl. =
horn), prong, scope; spec. dead
rabbit (penis that remains limp)
36. *testicles:* ballocks, balls,
bollocks, cobs, cods, cojones (Sp.),
eggs in the basket, flowers and
frolics (rhy.sl. = bollocks), frick and
frack (US black), goolies, grand
bag, knackers, nerds, Niagara Falls
(rhy.sl = balls), nuts, orchestra
stalls (rhy.sl. = balls), pills, rocks,
sack o'nuts, slabs (backsl. = balls),
tommy rollocks (rhy.sl.)
37. *foreskin:* lace curtains, snapper;
spec. blind, cavalier, near-sighted
(uncircumcised penis)
38. *circumcised penis:* clipped, low
neck and short sleeves, roundhead
39. *pubic hair:* area, brush, bush,
cotton, Fort Bushy, garden, grass,
lawn, squirrel, wool
40. *vagina:* apple, bacon sandwich,
barge, beaver, bite, boat, booty,
box, butcher's window, canyon,
catty-cat, central cut, chasm,
chopped liver, chuff, cock (US
South), cono, cooch, coot, cooze,
crack, cranny, crevice, cunt, damp,
Dead End Street, diddly pout,
ditch, down there, drain, fanny
(UK), fig, finger pie, fish, fluff,
front bum, – door, fud, fur,
furburger, furrow, furry hoop, futy,
futz, fuzzburger, fuzzy cup, G
(goodies), gap, gape, garden, – of
Eden (US black), gash, gib teenuck
(backsl. = big cunt), ginch, glory
hole, golden doughnut (Aus.),
groceries, grumble and grunt

(rhy.sl. = cunt), gulf, gully (hole),
gutter, hair pie, hatchi, hole,
honeypot, Irish fortune, jam,
jellybox, jing-jang, joxy, joy trail,
kennel, kettle, kitty, kitty-cat, little
sister, lucky bag, lunch box,
Maggie's pie (US black), magpie's
nest (US black), maw, met,
middle-cut; minge, mink, monkey,
muff, muffin, mutton, nasty, nest,
notch, passion pit, PEEP (perfectly
elegant eating pussy), penocha
(Sp.), placket, pole hole, poon,
poontang, poozle, prime cut, pta
(US black: pussy, titties and
armpits), puss, pussy, pussycat,
quiff, quim, rag box, rattlesnake
canyon, red lane, rubyfruit, scat,
second hole from the back of the
neck, sharp and blunt (rhy.sl. =
cunt), slice of life, slit, slot,
snapper, snapping turtle (puss),
snatch, split beaver, stank, stench
trench, stink, stinkpot, tail, that
there, toolbox, trench, trim, trout,
tuna, twat, vag, where the monkey
sleeps, you know where; spec.
cherry (maidenhead), horse collar
(large vagina)
41. *female pudendum:* ace of spades
(US black), fern, ha'penny, hide,
jelly roll, moneymaker, rubyfruit,
you know where; spec. cuffs and
collars (pubic hair the same colour
as head hair)
42. *clitoris:* boy in the boat, button,
clit, clitty, dot, joy buzzer, little
man, (little) man in the boat, nuts
(US black), taste bud
43. *labia:* beef, curtains, flange,
Hottentot apron, piss flaps
44. *throat:* red lane
45. *arm:* Chalk Farm (rhy.sl.)

117. Physical Characteristics
1. *of the weight:* bagels, beer belly,
– gut, broad in the beam, fat city,
hipsters, love handles, Milwaukee
goitre, spare tyre, taff (backsl.),
zaftig (Yid.)

2. *skin problems:* Conan Doyle (rhy.sl. = boil), custards, goob (small spot, fr. goober = peanut), zit hickey (love bite)

3. *scars:* glassed (cut in the face), stripe, tram line

4. *of the eyes:* eyes like pissholes in the snow

5. *having a large penis:* hand-reared, straps it to his ankle, well-hung

6. *naked:* bare-ass, (in one's) birthday suit, bollock naked, bollocko, in the altogether, – the buff, – the rude, laid to the natural bone (US black), nuddy, starkers, stripped to the buff

7. *of the fingernails:* in mourning (dirty)

8. *of the face:* fish-faced, poker-faced, sour-pussed; spec. more chins than a Chinese laundry (fat-faced)

9. *of the hair:* bottle blonde (dyed hair)

10. *bald:* chrome-dome

11. *having a good figure:* built, best-built, stacked

12. *large:* built, built like a brick outhouse, built like a brick shithouse, hunky

13. *having good legs:* leggy, legs up to her arse

118. Bodily Functions

n. 1. *menstruation:* beno (Aus. 'be no fun'), curse, monthlies, on the rag, red dog on a white horse, red Mary (US black) wallflower week

2. *breaking wind:* beast, breezer (Aus.), fart, guff, raspberry tart (rhy.sl.), thumper

3. *mucus:* dewdrop, lunger, oyster, snot

4. *an erection:* boner, hard (on), stand, touch-on; spec. piss proud (early morning erection); brewer's droop (impairment of erection by alcohol); muddy waters (US black: loss of erection)

5. *orgasm:* big O, come

6. *vomiting:* school lunch rerun, technicolour rerun, technicolour yawn

v. 7. *to menstruate:* be on the rag, have a little visitor, – the flag out, – the painters in, – the rag on, put the flags out, ride the rag (US black), stub one's toe

8. *to break wind:* backfire, cheese, drop a beast, – a thumper, drop one's guts, fart, repeat; spec. he who smelt it dealt it (cp)

9. *to spit:* gob

10. *to sneeze:* bread and cheese (rhy.sl.)

11. *to achieve erection:* crack a fat (Aus.), flood (US black), get a boner, – a hard (on), etc. (see 118.4)

12. *to achieve orgasm:* cheese, come, get one's gun off, – rocks off, light off, pop one's nuts, shoot (off) one's load, – wad

13. *to vomit:* barf, blow one's cookies, – doughnuts, – groceries, – lunch, boot, buick, call for Hughie, – Ralph, cat, chuck, chuck a dummy, chunder, cry Hughie, – Ralph, – Ruth, drive the big white bus, drive the porcelain bus, dump one's load, feed the kippers, flash, go to instant boot camp, go the big spit, – big split (Aus.), hack, have a liquid laugh, have a technicolour yawn, heave, hug the porcelain, hurl, kak, kiss the porcelain god, kneel before the porcelain throne, lose one's doughnuts, – groceries, – lunch, park a custard, pray to the porcelain god, puke, ralph, shoot a cat, spew, – one's guts, – one's ring, spill one's breakfast, spread a technicolour rainbow (Aus.), throw one's cookies, – one's voice (Aus.), throw up, Tom and Dick (rhy.sl. = to be sick), toss one's cookies, – one's tacos, Uncle Dick (rhy.sl.), upchuck, vom, woof

14. *to masturbate:* beat off, – one's dummy, – one's hog, – one's meat,

bring oneself off, choke the chook (Aus.), get one's nuts off, jerk off, play pocket billiards, play with oneself, pull one's joint, – one's pud, – one's pudding, – one's wire, rub off, – up, sew (US black), stroke one's beef, tickle one's pickle, toss off, twang one's wire, wank, whip off, – one's wire, whack off, whank; spec. catch a buzz (to masturbate with a vibrator) (see also 360:19)
15. spec. Barcoo salute (Aus. = brushing flies away from the face)
phr. 16. spec. looks like a wet weekend (Aus.: menstruation will make sex impossible)

119. Defecation
n. 1. business, call of nature
mod. 2. *urination:* gypsy's, jimmy (riddle), Johnny Bliss (Aus. rhy.sl. = piss), little jobs, slash, wazz
3. *ordure:* big hit (Aus.), – jobs, boom-boom, crap, crash (Aus.), diddley-poo, dookey, dukie (US black), honey, job, kak, ka-ka, lemon (rhy.sl. lemon curd = turd), number twos, pony (rhy.sl. pony and trap = crap), poo, edopie-plops, Richard the Third (rhy.sl. = turd), shit, tomtit (rhy.sl.), turd; spec. dog, horse apples, road apples (animals); dags, clinkers, dingleberries (adherent excrement); skid marks (stains on underwear)
4. *urine:* little jobs, number ones, pee, piddle, piss, Robert E. (rhy.sl. = Robert E. Lee = pee), snake's hiss (Aus. rhy.sl. = piss), wee-wee, widdle; spec. golden shower (urolognia)
5. *diahorrea:* Aztec twostep, Cairo crud, Delhi belly, GIs, Gyppy tummy, Hong Kong dog, Montezuma's revenge, Rangoon runs, ringburner, runs, scoots, shits, toms (Aus. rhy.sl. = tomtits = shits), touristas, trots

v. 6. *to visit the lavatory:* (go and) see a man about a dog, powder one's nose; spec. caught short, taken short (desperate to visit the lavatory)
7. *defecate:* cramber, crap, choke a darkie (Aus.), dump, shit, take a crap, – dump, – shit, sit on the throne; spec. ride the porcelain bus, – porcelain Honda (to have diahorrea)
8. *urinate:* bleed the liver, drain the dragon, get rid of the bladder matter, have a gypsy's (rhy.sl. = gypsy's kiss = piss), – a jimmy (rhy.sl. jimmy riddle = piddle), – a piss, – a slash, make pee-pee, pee, piddle, piss, point percy at the porcelain, see a dog about a man, see a man about a dog, shake hands with an old friend, shake hands with the wife's best friend, shake the dew off the lily, spend a penny, splash the boots, strain the potatoes, strain the spuds, syphon the python, take a leak, – a pee, – a piss, – a slash, tap a keg, tinkle, visit Miss Murphy, wee-wee, widdle
phr. 9. who cut the cheese (who farted?), SBD (silent but deadly)

THE BODY: CARE
120. Toilet; Hygiene; Grooming
n. 1. *hairstyle:* afro, 'fro, DA (duck's arse), duck's arse, cowlick
2. *parts of the hair:* bugger's grips, sidies (sideburns)
3. *straightened black hair:* fried, dyed and swooped to the side, konk, process
4. *comb:* rack pick (a comb for curly black hair)
5. *wig:* Irish jig (rhy.sl.), rug, syrup (rhy.sl. = syrup of figs)
6. *shave:* dig in the grave (rhy.sl.)
7. *cosmetics, etc.:* axle grease (hair oil), BO juice (deodorant)
8. spec. grease (gay use: KY jelly)
v. 9. *to straighten black hair:* conk,

konk, fry one's hair, press one's
hair, process, wig bust
10. *dress one's hair:* have a hair-do,
rat one's hair (backcomb hair)
11. *to shave:* dad and dave (Aus.
rhy.sl.), mow the lawn
12. *apply cosmetics:* put on one's
face, – warpaint; spec. flame
(homosexual use)
adj. 13. *natural black hair:* nappy
14. *long-haired:* sheepish

121. Physical Exercise
n. 1. *strength and ability:* fire power
2. *exercising:* pumping iron, pushing
iron, throwing iron, working out
3. spec. the burn (in aerobics: the
pain barrier)

HEALTH
122. Health; Physical Condition
n. 1. feather, fig, form, kilter,
shape, way, whack
2. spec. million dollar wound
(milit.: wound that does not kill but
invalids out of war)
phr. 3. *enquiries as to health:* how
are they hanging? how are you
doing?, – going?, how's by you?,
how's your head?

123. Good Health
n. 1. fine fettle, – feather, – form,
– shape, – whack, tiptop form
v. 2. *to feel well:* feel one's oats, go
strong, run on all cylinders
adj. 3. *healthy:* aces, alive and
kicking, all there, – to the good,
A1, bobbish, bully, chipper, clever
(Aus.), feeling one's oats, – right
(royal), fit as a butcher's dog, fit as
a Mallee bull (Aus.), full of beans,
– piss and vinegar, hitting on all
four/six/eight (cylinders),
hotsy-totsy, hunkydory, in fine
fettle, – form, – whack, in good
shape, – good trim, in the pink,
keen, primo, one hundred per cent,
ripper (Aus.), rosy about the gills,

sharp, skookum, slap-up, top hole,
– notch, topping, the tops, up to
par, – scratch, – snuff, – the
mark
4. *replying to enquiries as to health:*
can't complain, could be worse, fair
to middling, not so bad, nothing to
brag about, – write home about, still
here, – (alive and kicking)

124. Poor Health
v. 1. *to be ill:* feel a bit green, feel
bum, – crook (Aus.), – like hell,
– lousy, – off colour, – ratshit,
– under the weather, have one foot
in the grave, not feel like anything,
– too hot, not feel up to scratch,
– up to snuff, etc. (see 123.3)
2. *to become ill:* break down, conk
out, crack up, fold up, go on the
blink, get out of commission, – of
sorts, – of whack
3. *fake illness:* come the old soldier,
pull an act, swing the lead, work
one's ticket
adv. 4. *ill:* below par, blah, bunged
up, butcher's (Aus. rhy.sl. =
crook), crook (Aus.), crummy,
down at heel, in bad shape, – the
shit, not so dusty, – so hot, off
colour, – form, out of commission,
– of sorts, peakish, peaky, punk,
putrid, ratshit, run down, seedy,
sick as a dog, under the weather,
wonky, yucky
5. *dying:* bought and sold and done
for, done for, on one's last legs,
(with) one foot in the grave, seen
better days, – one's best days, (all)
shot, through
6. *exhausted, run down:* beat,
burned out, dead-beat, dead on the
vine, frazzled, fucked, gone smash,
wrecked
7. *delirious:* bats (in the belfry),
batty, cuckoo, dippy, dotty, gaga,
loony, loopy, nuts, nutty, off one's
bean, – chump, – head, – nut,
– onion, out of one's head, – gourd,
– chump, etc., screwy

125. Ailments; Diseases

n. 1. *stomach ache:* bellyache, collywobbles, gutache, tummyache
2. *headache:* a head
3. *cold:* snotty nose
4. *cramp:* Charlie horse
5. *bad breath:* jungle mouth
6. *hepatitis:* hep
7. *cough:* strep throat
8. *cancer:* Big C
9. *cystitis:* honeymoon cystitis
10. *venereal disease:* band in the box (rhy.sl. = pox), clap, cold in the dong, dose, drip, dripsy, gleet, horse (rhy.sl. = horse and trap = clap), jack (Aus.), Nervo and Knox (rhy.sl. = pox), pox, syph, sypho (Aus.); spec. full house (both syphilis and gonorrhoea); nine day blues (incubation period for gonorrhoea); blue balls (testicular swelling)
11. *haemorrhoids:* hems, Nuremburgs (rhy.sl. Nuremburg trials = piles)
12. *fit:* wingding, wobbler
13. *backache:* shagger's back (Aus.)
14. *deaf mute:* D & D (deaf and dumb)
v. 15. *to catch venereal disease:* be jacked up (Aus.), be one of the knights, cop a dose, (get) dosed up, piss broken glass, ride the silver steed, take the bayonet course
16. *to catch a cold:* catch one's death
17. *to faint:* throw a seven (Aus.)
18. *body odour:* BO, the pits

126. Physical Injury

n. 1. *scars:* Mars bars (rhy.sl)
adj. 2. *lame:* gammy, gimpy
3. *injured:* buggered up, out of commission, – whack
4. *wounded:* fucked up

127. Physical and Mental Breakdown

v. 1. *to have a nervous breakdown:* blow it, – up, come unglued, – unstuck, crack up, fall apart, go smash, go to pieces, – pot
adj. 2. *mentally unstable:* cracked, off one's hinges, (all) shot, all to fuck; spec. Shrinksville (a state of mind that may require professional aid), (see also 138.3 and 147)
3. *disorientated:* spaced out

128. Recovery

n. 1. comeback
2. *spec. medicine:* op (operation), plastic job (plastic surgery), short-arm inspection (inspection of genitals), scrape (abortion); dust-off (milit: medical evacuation)
3. *pills:* apples, daily-daily (US milit. anti-malaria pills)
v. 4. *improve, recover:* buck up, perk up, on the up (and up)

SENSATION

129. Sensation; Touch

n. 1. *odd feeling:* creeps, jim-jams, shivers, willies
v. 2. *to touch:* goose

130. Taste

mod. 1. *tasty:* scrumptious, scrummy, yummy
2. *distasteful:* icky, yucky

131. Smell

n. 1. niff, phew, pong, whiff
2. *spec. sexual odour:* funk, wolf-pussy (US black)
v. 3. *to smell:* get a noseful, niff, phew, pong, whiff
4. *to be smelly:* pen and ink (rhy.sl. = stink)
adj. 5. *smelly:* loud, niffy, noisy, pongy, sniffy, whiffy

SIGHT

132. Sight; Look; Glance

n. 1. butcher's (rhy.sl. = butcher's hook = look), Captain Cook, Charlie Cooke (rhy.sl.), darry,

decko, dekko, gander, gig (Aus. =
a glance), glaum, glom, look-see,
lookism, measure, once-over, pipe,
shot, shufti, shufty, slant, squizz,
up-and-down; spec. coke stare (US
black = aggressive stare); glad
eye, goo-goo eyes (amorous
glance); hard eyes (unpleasant
look)
2. *view:* spec. flash, flash of light
(rhy.sl. = sight), free show; theatre
use: Mickey Mouse (rhy.sl. = house
= audience)
3. *spectacles:* bins, cheaters,
gig-lamps, glims, goggles,
headlights, -lamps, peepers, specs;
spec. shades (dark glasses)
4. *maps:* comics
5. *assessment:* recce
v. 6. *to look at:* book (the joint),
cast one's optics (at), – peepers (at),
clock, cop a decko, – gander, – sight
(of), eeson (backsl.), eevach a kool
(backsl. = have a look), eyeball,
gander, gawp, geek, get a load of,
get an eyeful, give a going-over,
give the eye (to), – the once-over,
glaum, glom, goggle (at), have a
decko, – a looksee, key in, lamp,
orb, pan, peg, pipe, run the eye
over, size up, take a flash at, – a
gander (at), – a hinge (at), – a
measure (of), – a shot at, – a slant
at, – a squint at, twig; spec. watch
the birdie, – the dickey-bird
(admonition from photographer to
subject); shoot the squirrel (glimpse
a girl's underwear or genitals)
7. *to spy on:* get a line on,
gumshoe, snoop, tail
8. *to stare:* double-o, gander, gawk,
gawp, gig (Aus.), goggle, rubber,
rubberneck, scope, screw, take a
screw at
9. *to disappear:* do a vanishing act,
go disappearo
10. *show, reveal:* exhib, flash, trot
out, uncork
11. *to assess:* case over, check out,
have one mapped, keep tabs on,
orb, pan, peep one's hole card (US
black), pin
12. *to appear before:* front (Aus.)

133. Light
v. 1. *turn off lights:* douse the
Edisons, kill (the lights), pull the
juice

SOUND
134. Hearing
n. 1. earwigging, the Earie, the Erie
v. 2. *to hear:* catch, earhole, get a
load of, get an earful, peg, take in
3. *listen:* be all ears, bend one's ear,
catch a listen, cop –, earwig, get an
earful, grab a listen, give (it) the ear
4. *eavesdrop:* be on the earie, – the
Erie, have big ears, – long ears
adj. 5. *deaf:* Mutt and Jeff
(rhy.sl.)
phr. 6. *loud and clear:* lumpy
chicken (milit.)

135. Sound
n. 1. *solid noise (of a blow, or
falling object):* bam, bash, biff,
blam, blop, bong, bop, cachunk,
etc., chunk, dab, flop, flump,
kerbam, kerboom, kerchunk, etc.,
pam, phut, pom, pomp, powie,
slam-bam, slambang, smack,
smacko, sock, socko, swack,
swacko, whack, wham, whammo,
whang, zam, zap, zoom, zowie
2. *light, splashing noise:* burble,
guggle, slap, slip, slop, slosh,
squelch, squidge, squish
3. *loud noise:* biff-bang, biff-boom,
racket, slam-bang
4. *sheet music:* maps
5. *records:* discs, plates, platters,
sides, slices, sounds; spec. box (tape
recorder, record player), wheel (of
steel) (record deck)
6. *instrument:* box (guitar)
v. 7. *to play the piano:* tickle the
ivories
8. *play records:* spec. toast (WI: for

a DJ to add his lyrics to a backing track), spin discs

136. Silence
n. 1. shush
vt. 2. *to quieten:* put down the soft pedal, – the lid on, turn off
3. *to be quiet:* hush one's mouth, – up, (be like dad and) keep mum, put a sock in it, put the lid on, stow it, – the gab
excl. 4. *be quiet!:* can it!, chuck it!, enough!, hold it down!, hush up!, lay off (the racket)!, pipe down!, pull in your ears!, stow it!, take it easy!

Personality

CHARACTER
137. Character; Disposition
n. 1. bag, the likes (of), number, (one's) size, (–) speed
2. *personality:* dope, goods, merchandise, oil, (the old) this and that, what it takes
v. 3. *to be characteristic:* be that way, built that way, be one all over, (about) one's speed, (just) one's speed, right in one's bag, – up one's alley, – down one's street
4. *to have charm:* be on the ball, have it (right) down, have (plenty of) what it takes
adj. 5. *charming:* ducky
phr. 6. where one is at, – one is coming from

138. Idiosyncracy; Eccentricity
n. 1. idiosity
2. *eccentricity:* bats in one's belfry, bee(s) in one's bonnet
v. 3. *to be eccentric:* have a bee in the bonnet, – a screw loose, – bats in the belfry, – bugs in the brain
adv. 4. *eccentric:* barmy, bats, batty, bourbon, cracked, crackers, daffy, doofus, doolally, dotty, funny (in the head), half-cracked, – crazy, kinky, loopy, nutty, off-beat, off-brand, off the wall, on the edge, out of left field, potty, queer as a coot, – as a nine-bob note, screwy, weird (see also unintelligence 145–147)

REPUTATION
139. Repute
n. 1. front, rep; spec. it (US black:

the quintessence of Blackness); bell (US black: personal notoriety)
v. 2. *to have a good reputation:* be in, – in good, count, keep one's nose clean, rate
3. *be important:* (see Greatness: 18), be on top of the heap, make a noise in the world
4. *gain importance:* feature, grab one's fifteen minutes (fr. A. Warhol's dictum 'Everyone will be famous for 15 minutes'), headline, hit it big, hit the headlines, make it big, make the front page, pick up brownie points
adv. 5. *reputable:* aces, all wool and a yard wide, kosher, straight, waxed (US black: anyone who is well known), white
6. *eminent:* (see Greatness: 18), big deal, – cheese, stuff, etc., high-up, high muckamuck, swell
7. *famous:* big-named, (a) celeb, having one's name in lights; spec. glitterati (international social-literary circles)

140. Disrepute
n. 1. bad rep, – smell
2. *loss of reputation:* climb-down, nose-dive
v. 3. *to lose reputation:* be brought down a peg (or two), blow up, come down a peg, – a notch, get a black eye, go down the chute, – the tubes, – on the skids, have one's nose put out of joint, hit the skids
4. *to put into disrepute:* smear
adv. 5. *disreputable:* low-down, lowest of the low, low-life, no-hoper, ornery, past praying for, wouldn't tell you the time of day

6. *obscure, insignificant:* (see Smallness: 19), bottom of the heap, lightweight, low rent, no great catch, – shakes, not amounting to a piss in the ocean, small beer, – change, – potatoes, – time

---

BREEDING

141. Gentility; Culture
adj. 1. *genteel, well-bred:* aristo, blue-blood, blue-book, glitzy, high-hat, high-tone(d), nobby, posh, ritzy, slick, smooth, swanky, tony, upper crust, uptown; spec. Sloane (Ranger), county (UK upper bourgeoisie)

142. Ungentility; Vulgarity
v. 1. *to live in squalor:* pig it
adj. 2. *vulgar:* all dressed up like a pox-doctor's clerk, brassy, flash, – as a Chinky's horse, – as a rat with a gold tooth, jumped up, lairy (Aus.), not backward in coming forward, out of order, over the top, poncy, smart-ass
3. *rustic:* billyjack (US black), cornball, corny, folksy, jungly
4. *affected:* artsy-crafty, arty-farty
5. *rough:* hard-boiled, leather-necked, rough-and-ready, rough-necked, tin-arsed, wild and woolly
adv. 6. *living in squalor:* pigging it, pig style (US black)

Intellect

INTELLIGENCE
143. Intelligence; Intellect
n. 1. brains, (little) grey cells, grey matter, gorm, gumption, horse sense, nous, savvy, smart money, smarts
2. *an intellectual:* long-hair, pointy-head
v. 3. *to be clever:* be on the ball, have all one's marbles, – what it takes, know a hawk from a handsaw, know a shilling from sixpence, know a thing or two, know enough to come in and out of the rain, know how many beans make five, know one's age, know one's anus from one's ankle, – one's arse from a hole in the ground, – one's arse from one's elbow, know one's boxes, know one's eccer (Aus.), know one's kit, – one's onions, know one's stuff, know one's way about, – something, – up from down, – what's what, – what's happening, know what time it is, know where one's arse hangs, know whether one is Arthur or Martha (Aus.), know whether it's pancake Tuesday or half-past breakfast time, – which way is up, use one's loaf; spec. to know where the bodies are buried (to have knowledge which gives leverage over others)
4. *to be wise, shrewd:* be bright as a new pin, – nobody's fool, – not as daft as one looks, – as stupid etc., have a head on one's shoulders, know what time it is, use the old bean, – chump, – noggin, turnip; spec. graduate (US black: to gain knowledge)
adj. 5. *intelligent:* all there, not so

dumb, – dusty, on the beam, there with the goods, smart
6. *wise, shrewd, aware:* (be) down (US black), cool, culture, first cab off the rank, fly, half-wide, hardcore, hep, hip, jerry, long-haired, necklaced, (US black), no flies on . . ., quick on the trigger, ready (US black), ready-eyed, savvy, sharp, spunko, streetified, street smart, street wise, swift, switched on, tasty, together, triple hip (US black), turned on, with it
phr. 7. must have swallowed the dictionary, who slept in the knife box? (and is thus 'sharp')

144. Knowledge
n. 1. dope, know-how, nitty-gritty, savvy
2. *identity:* ID; spec. P Check (UK milit. personality check); Wilkie Bard (ID card)
v. 3. *to be aware of, know about:* (be) hep, – hip, – jerry (to), – on the inside track, – posted, – up on (one's stuff), – wise (to), have a line on, – the inside track, – the goods on, – the stuff on, – dead to rights, – down cold, – down pat, – its number, – it pegged, – it straight, – it sussed, know it backwards, – it down to the ground, – one's stuff, – the ropes, – what time it is, what's happening, etc. (see Intelligence 143), sus out
4. *to recognize:* burn, get a line on, – next to, – on to, give (it) a tumble, make (it for), peg, rumble, tumble (to)
5. *see one's own interest:* blow wise, get hep, get smart, – wise, – next to

oneself, – one's head screwed on, – one's mind right, – straight (to oneself), smarten up, wise up
6. *see through:* be jerry (to), – on one's wavelength – wise (to), blow wise (to), have down, – pegged, – cold, – one's measure, – one's number, – one sussed, know what makes one tick, know where one is at, – is coming from, – where one's head is at, – one's wavelength
7. *to ask for identity card:* card
8. *to prophesy:* Kreskin
adv. 9. *intelligent, aware:* down, fly, hep(ped), hip(ped), jerry, next to, on the ball, on to, smart (to), sussed (out), up to, wise (to)

UNINTELLIGENCE
145. Stupidity
n. 1. numbskullery
v. 2. *to be stupid:* be boneheaded, sapbrained, etc. (see adj. 145), to be a dickhead, dorkbrain, dumbo etc. (see Disreputable: 433), couldn't find one's way to first base, – find his arse with both hands, doesn't know a mule's ass from a lemon, – his ass from a double-barrelled shotgun, – his ass from a hole in the ground, – his ass from his elbow, – his ass from third base, – his butt from a gourd, doesn't know – owl-shit from putty without a map, – sheepshit from cherry-seed, doesn't have a clue, – the foggiest, doesn't know enough to come in out of the rain, – to pound sand in a rathole, doesn't know shit from Shinola, – know from Adam, – know from the man in the moon, – know t'other from which, – know up from down, have one's head up one's arse, – shit for brains, isn't ready for people, thinks it's just to pee through
adv. 3. *stupid:* (see 433: Stupid Person); blockheaded, blubberbrained, boneheaded,

bonkers, chuckleheaded, clueless, cuckoo, daffy, daffydown dilly (rhy.sl. = silly), daft, dead between the ears, – from the neck down, dumb, dumbarse, dingy, dopey, dorky, fatheaded, flaky, foggy, goofy, goopy, green as owl-shit, half-baked, jugheaded, King Dick (rhy.sl. = thick), lame, lamebrained, lunchy, lunkheaded, muttonheaded, nitwitted, not all there, – ready for people, off one's trolley, old enough to know better, ossified, out to lunch, pig ignorant, sap-headed, silly as a two-bob watch (Aus.), so dumb he couldn't find his ass with two hands at high noon, – he couldn't piss out of a boat, – he couldn't piss without a button hook, soft (in the head), slow on the trigger, thick, untogether, wet behind the ears, young in the head (US black); spec. addict (one who falls for confidence tricks)
phr. 4. *of the stupid:* some mothers do have 'em
5. *admitting ignorance:* ask a silly question . . ., ask me another, damned if I know, don't ask me, God knows, I haven't the foggiest, I pass, I give up, it's (all) Greek to me, your guess is as good as mine, what's that when it's at home?

146. Foolishness; Nonsense
n. 1. funny business, monkey business, mug's game, shenanigans; spec. scream (ludicrous idea)
2. *nonsense:* ackamaracka, all my eye and Betty Martin, applesauce, apple butter, ballocks, bollocks, bollox, balls, baloney, boloney, bologna, banana oil, bilge, blatherskite, booshwah, borax, bosh, bushwa, bughouse, bull, bullcrap, bullsh, bullshit, bullshine, BS, bunk, bunkum, claptrap, cobblers (rhy.sl. = cobblers awls = balls), cock, cods, codswallop, cowyard confetti, crap, crock (of

shit), duck soup, eyewash,
fiddle-faddle, fiddlesticks, flannel,
flapdoodle, flubdub, gammon,
garbage, guff, hogwash, hokum,
hooey, hoo-ha, horsefeathers,
horseshit, jiggery-pokery, krazin,
(a) load of applesauce, balls, etc.,
load of reg, – (old) madam,
magoozlum, malarkey, mishegaas
(Yid.), mumbo-jumbo,
phonus-balonus, phooey, piffle,
pigshit, poop, poppycock,
rannygazoo, rhubard, rollocks, rot,
strunz, toffee, tommyrot, tosh,
trash, tripe, twaddle
3. *foolish talk:* air, ballyhoo,
baloney, blah, blather, bull, gas,
guff, hooey, hot air, jive, wind
v. 4. *to play the fool:* arse about,
– around, bugger about, fart about,
– around, fuck about, – around,
grab-arse, piss about, – around,
silly-arse about, – around, sod about
5. *do something stupid:* (see 146.4);
do the crazy act, fuck up, make a
bloomer, – a dumb play, – a prick of
oneself, screw up,
6. *to talk nonsense:* blah (on), bull,
bullshit, crap (on), dish the bull,
– the crap, etc. (see 146.2), flannel,
go off at the mouth, run off at the
mouth, hand (out) a line, – of bull,
– of crap, etc., let off hot air,
ratchet-mouth, rot, shoot the bull,
talk balls, crap, guff, etc., talk
through one's arse(hole), – one's
hat, – the back of one's neck, talk
shit, – trash, tommyrot, wank (on)
phr. 7. *stop being stupid:* act your
age, be your age, cut it out, – the
comedy, – the crap, get your arse in
gear, – yourself together, grow up,
stop arsing around, – buggering
about, etc. (see 146.4)
8. *to make a fool of:* make a
monkey of, – a sap of, etc. (see 433:
Stupid Person)
adv. 9. *foolish:* (see 145: Stupid)
phr. 10. GIGO (garbage in, garbage
out)

excl. 11. *that's absurd!, don't be
absurd!:* applesauce!, are you
kidding!, arseholes!, bagpipe it!,
balls!, blooey!, bull!, bullshit!,
coffee and cocoa! (rhy.sl. = I
should cocoa), come off it!, crap!,
cut it out!, – that out!, – the crap!,
did I fuck!, don't be funny!, – fuck
about!, – give me that!, – make me
laugh!, fiddlesticks!, forget it!,
fucking Ada!, fuck that (for a lark)!,
gag me with a spoon!, gertcha!, get
away (with you)!, – along (with
you)!, get wise!, go chase yourself!,
– run up a drain!, – shit in your hat
(pull it over your ears and call it
feathers)!, – take a flying fuck!, I
should cocoa! (rhy.sl. = I should
say so), in a pig's arse!, knickers!,
later (for that)!, leave it out!, leave
off!, – over!, less of it!, like fuck!,
my eye!, my foot!, never happen!,
no way!, nothing doing!, not much
you wouldn't!, pull the other one
(it's got bells on it)!, quit fooling!,
says you!, screw it!, shut your
mouth and give your arse a chance!,
skip it!, stick it!, stroll on!, tell it to
the marines!, – me another!, turn it
up!, up your arse!, – your gazoo!,
– kazoo!, up yours!, walk on!, what
else is new?, who do you think
you're kidding?, you must be
joking!, you've got a nerve!

147. Insanity; Craziness
n. 1. barminess, bats in the belfry,
lame brains, looniness, (a) screw
loose, space case
2. *mental hospital:* bin, booby
hatch, bughouse, crazy house, funny
farm, loony bin, nut hatch, nut
house
v. 3. *to be insane:* be all over the
board, – around the bend,
– bananas, etc. (see 147.5); have a
screw loose, – a tile loose, – one's
wires crossed, – bats in the belfry,
not be all there, – have all one's
marbles

4. *to become insane:* blow a fuse, – one's cork, – lid, – mind, – top, crack up, flip one's lid, – wig, get out of gear, go balmy, – bananas, – batty (see adj. 147.5), go off one's bean, – one's chump, – one's gourd, – one's nut, – one's onion, go out of one's bean, – one's chump, etc., go off one's rocker, – the rails, – over the edge, lose one's marbles, shoot one's marbles (US black), wig out

adj. 5. *insane, crazy:* all over the board, around the bend, asiatic bananas, balmy, barmy, bathouse, batty, bats, batshit, bats in the belfry, boho, bourbon, bughouse, cuckoo, cracked, crackers, cracko, crazy-arse, cruising with one's lights on dim, daffy, dippy, doofus, doolally, dopey, dorky, dotty, freaky, gaga, gone, half-cracked, – gone, – there, harpic ('clean around the bend'), has a few of his pages stuck together, kooky, lakes (of Killarney) (rhy.sl. = barmy), lamebrained, loco, loony, loopy, loose up top, mental, meshugge (Yid.), neuro, non compos, not all there, – quite there, (not having) both oars in the water, not playing with a full deck, not the full quid (Aus.), nuts, nutso, nutty (as a fruitcake), off-beat, off-brand, off one's bean, out of one's box, – cake, – chump, – gourd, – nut, – onion, – rocker, off the beam, – the wall, out of left field, out of one's head, – mind, – onion, – tree, out of whack, out to lunch, plumb loco, potty, only eighty pence in the pound, queer as a coot, – as a nine-bob note, rum, schitzi, screwy, (one) shingle short (Aus.), sicko, squirrelly, stark staring bonkers, troppo (Aus.), two bricks short of the load, two pence short of a bob, toey (Aus.), twisted, unglued, whack-a-doo, whacked out, whacko, whacky, weird, wig city, wigged out, wiggy, wild, wild-arse, (living in a) worm farm, wired, yarra (Aus.)

phr. 6. keep taking the tablets

ATTENTION
148. Attention; Heed

v. 1. *to be alert:* be all there, – fly, – on the job, get down (US black), keep one's eye on the ball, know what's what, – what the time is, look alive, – sharp, – slippy, not miss a trick, – take any wooden nickels

2. *to become alert:* brace up, buck up, get on the case, – on the job, get with it, jump to it, snap (it) up, snap out of it, stand point

3. *to notice:* catch

4. *to point out:* finger, put the cross on

5. *make an obscene gesture (at):* give the finger, flip the bird, make a V-sign

6. *to be involved:* get in deep

adv. 7. *alert:* alive and kicking, all there (with the goods), chipper, hot to trot, Johnny on the spot, live, (up), on one's toes, on the ball, – the hop, – the job, sharp

8. *engrossed, obsessed:* behind, crazy for, have a ring through one's nose (US black), hot for, head over heels, into, up to the neck (in), right in (it), from soup to nuts, – the ground up

149. Care

n. 1. caginess, leariness

v. 2. *take care of:* keep tabs on, ride herd (on), ride shotgun; spec. look out for number one (take care of oneself first)

3. *be careful:* keep one's eyes peeled, – one's head down, not stick one's head out, – stick one's neck out, – take any wooden nickels, watch one's arse

4. *be alert:* be on the job, stay on the job, cock a weather eye, keep

one's eyes peeled, look sharp,
– slippery, watch it
5. *keep watch:* give jiggs, keep cave,
– KV, – chickie, – nit, – one's ear to
the ground, lie doggo
excl. 6. *be careful:* be cool!, don't
take any wooden nickels!, get wise!,
hang tight!, stay loose!, take it
easy!, watch it! – your step!, don't
do anything I wouldn't (do)

INATTENTION
150. Inattention; Neglect
v. 1. *to neglect, ignore:* brush off,
drop (it), fake on (one) (US black),
give (it) the go-by, – (it) a miss, let
(it) go, – (it) ride, – (it) slide,
– it sweat, not to give a damn, – a
fuck, – shit, – a tumble (for), skip
it
adv. 2. *absent-minded:* asleep on the
job, blank, dead from the neck up,
– to the world, not all there, – on
the job, somewhere else

151. Carelessness; Recklessness
n. 1. slapdashery, sloppiness
2. *careless work:* cheap and
cheerful, lick and a promise, quick
and dirty, quickie
v. 3. *to perform carelessly:* bang out,
hack –, knock –, slam –, slap –,
whack –, do any which way,
– everywhichway, knock off, not
give a damn (for), – a fuck (for),
etc. (see 150.1)
4. *to be reckless:* ball the jack, break
a leg, go off half-cocked, – like a bat
out of hell, – like hell on wheels,
– hell-for-leather, – hell('s)-bent
(for), rip, tear arse
adj. 5. *careless:* slapdash,
what-the-hell, who-gives-a-damn,
– a-fuck, etc.
6. *reckless:* chancy, iffy
adv. 7. *carelessly:* all anyhow,
everywhichway, half-arsed,
half-cocked, slam-bang, slap-bang,
slap-dab

8. *recklessly:* harum-scarum,
hell('s)-bent, hell-for-leather, (like)
hell on wheels, like crazy, over the
top
phr. 9. fubis (fuck you buddy I'm
shipping out), I could care, I don't
give fuck

REASON
152. Reason
n. 1. *argument:* argy-bargy,
free-for-all, gabfest, set-to, splang
(US black), tangle
2. *conclusive argument:* knockout
v. 3. *to argue:* argy-bargy, chew the
fat, chinwag, fatmouth, go to the
mat, go head-to-head,
– mano-a-mano, – one-on-one,
scream some heavy lines, slug it out,
weigh in
prep. 4. *why?:* how-come?, why in
the name of hell?, – the hell?
– heck?

153. Thinking
n. 1. brainwork
2. *idea, thought:* brainchild,
brainstorm, brainwave, hot one,
wheeze, wrinkle; spec. skulldrag
(taxing thought)
3. *opinion:* two cents'
worth
v. 4. *to think:* bear down on, beat
the brains, chew the cud, figger,
figure, hammer away at, have
something on one's head beside
one's hat, – one's hair, pound
(one's) brains, put on the thinker,
– thinking cap, run down, skulldrag,
use the (old) bean, – brainbox,
– chump, – noggin, – thinker,
– turnip, use one's loaf, zero in on;
spec. run it up the flagpole (and see
if anyone salutes) (to put forward an
idea)
5. *to think again:* get back (US
black)
adj. 6. crackerbarrel (homespun
philosophy)

7. *intellectually demanding:* thick (US black)

8. *spontaneous thought:* off the top of one's head

adv. 9. *lost in thought:* dead to the world, – the wide, elsewhere, out to lunch

10. *thinking about:* on one's chest, on the brain, under one's hat

excl. 11. *think about:* bite on that!, chew on that!, stick that in your pipe (and smoke it)!, stick that in your hat!

12. *what do you think (of that)?:* how does that grab you?, – do you like them apples?, like it?

INQUIRY

154. Interrogation

n. 1. *question:* draw, feeler, sounder

2. *cross-examination:* going over, grilling, hot seat, roasting, third degree, workover

v. 3. *to interrogate:* give a going-over, – a roasting, – a workover, go over, go to town on, – to work on, grill, open up on, pump, put in the hot seat, put the cosh on, put the screws to, – the squeeze on, – through the grinder, shake down, sweat, throw the hook into, turn inside out, work over; spec. put the feelers out (to pump for facts)

phr. 4. what's biting you?

155. Inquisitiveness; Curiosity

v. 1. have a stickybeak, – big ears, – long ears, poke one's nose in, Paul Pry; spec. study (gay use: to observe a possible pickup)

adj. 2. long-nosed, nosy, sticky(beak), snoopy

phr. 3. what's it (all) in aid of?

156. Investigation; Examination

n. 1. eye, look-see, measure, once-over, the tape; spec. tale of the tape (boxing use: rival boxers' vital statistics)

2. *test, trial:* go, shot, tumble, workout

v. 3. *to investigate:* check out, – over, dig into, figure, line up, size –, give the eye, – the once-over, have a look-see, take a decko (at), – a shufti (at), root about – around, run the tape over, see how the cat jumps, – the land lies, – the wind blows, – which way the wind is blowing; spec. case the joint (cant: to inspect a place that may be robbed)

4. *experiment:* fool (with), fuck around (with), futz around (with), mess (with), play around (with), try it on the dog

5. *to study:* hit the books, oil it

157. Search

v. 1. *search for, hunt:* be after, – on the prowl for, grubble (around), go gunning for, gun for, look all over the shop, peel the eyes for, scout (around), scout out, sniff out, take a gander (for), turn upside down; spec. declare open season on (to hunt with intent to kill or harm)

POSSIBILITY

158. Possibility; Probability

n. 1. hope, shot

2. *Impossibility:* Chinaman's chance, Chinese chance, dead pigeon, dog's chance, fat chance, longshot, no-no, some chance, – hope, sweet chance

v. 3. *to be possible:* be on the cards, – in the running, can do, run, stands fair to, worth a punt

4. *to be impossible:* be out of the running, not have a hope (in hell), not have a dog's chance, – Chinaman's chance, etc. (see 158.2), not stand a cat's chance in hell, – a snowball's chance in hell

adv. 5. *impossible:* done for

6. *possible:* on the cards
phr. 7. *that's impossible:* forget it,
forget you, no dice, not a hope in
hell, not an earthly, no soap, no
fear, no way I should be so lucky,
– I should live so long, not on your
Nellie
8. *in emergency:* at a pinch

159. Certainty
n. 1. blue-chip(s), cert, cinch, dead
cert, good thing, lead-pipe cinch,
monte, a moral, moral certainty,
nice one, shoo-in, sure thing
v. 2. *to be certain:* bank on, bet
one's life, go bail on, put money
on
adj. 3. *certain:* bang to rights, dead
sure, dead to rights, (down) cold,
in like Flynn, no ifs and buts, no
two ways (about it), open-and-shut,
stoneginger, sure as eggs is eggs,
– God made little green apples
adv. 4. *certainly:* abso-bloody-
lutely, abso-fucking-lutely, and
how!, as sure as eggs is eggs, – as
God made little green apples, def
(definitely), fair dinkum (Aus.), for
sure, natch, no shit, poz, pozzy
(positively), sho' 'nuff

BELIEF
160. Belief; Credence
n. 1. cred, sell, slant, twist, wrinkle
v. 2. *to believe:* Adam and Eve
(rhy.sl.), buy, buy the (whole) farm,
fall (for), figure, go for, have,
swallow
3. *to be credulous:* be an easy mark,
– easy, – green (as grass), – raw,
bite, go for (it), gobble (it) down,
lap (it) up, take the hook, tumble
(for), walk into
4. *to be confident:* bank on, bet
one's life, – one's bottom dollar,
– the lot, – the wad, go bail
on
adj. 5. *plausible:* unsus
6. *gullible:* sold, sold on

161. Disbelief; Suspicion
v. 1. *to disbelieve:* not see (it), – go
for (it), – swallow (it)
2. *to be suspicious:* be leary, – sus,
hawk, rumble, smell a rat, tumble
3. *to act suspiciously:* fancy pants
adj. 4. *suspicious:* fishy, hincty,
leary, sus, sussy, wet (US black)
adv. 5. *incredible:* bit steep, – tall,
– thick, – thin
excl. 6. *I don't believe it!:* (see
Nonsense 146); all kidding aside,
are you for real?, are you kidding?,
can it, come off it!, the hell you
say!, don't give me that!, don't kid
yourself!, – make me laugh!, – shit
me!, get along (with you)!, – away!,
fuck off!, I ask you!, I don't believe
this!, I don't buy that!, I'll eat my
hat!, in a pig's eye!, – arse!, my
(giddy) aunt!, my eye!, my foot!, no
kidding!, no shit!, says who?, sez
who?, – you!, tell it to the marines!,
tell me another!, there (just) ain't
such an animal!, you must be
joking!, you've got to be joking!

SOLUTION
162. Solution; Discovery
n. 1. *evidence:* dope, goods (on),
lowdown (on), nitty-gritty, stuff
v. 2. *to solve:* blow wise, break,
crack, crack wise (to), get outside
of, – a line on, – a slant on, have
taped, – by the tail, – down, knock
over, size up
3. *to discover:* catch up with, clap
eyes on, cop, get a line on, – next
to, – onto, – wise to, give a rumble,
– tumble, glaum, glom, make, nab,
nail, nick, nip, peg, slap the peepers
on, sniff out, rumble, tumble (to),
twig
4. *to meet with, happen on:* barge
into, bump into, connect, hit up
with, knock into, run into
5. *to catch, catch out:* bust, catch
bending, – cold, – on the hop,
– with one's pants down, – trousers

down, do up (like a kipper), do up
right, have bang to rights, – by the
short and curlies, – by the short
hairs, – the dope on, – the goods on
6. *to be caught:* be bowled out,
– caught bending, – cold, etc. (see
162.5), dead to rights
adv. 7. *solved:* bang to rights,
cinched, cracked, doped out, down
cold, nailed, sussed out, taped

163. Judgement; Conclusion
n. 1. at the death, bottom line,
clincher
2. *result:* come-out, curtain, end of
the line, payoff
3. *estimate:* guesstimate
v. 4. *estimate:* angle, dope (out), get
a line on, – the hang of, – the lay of,
size up
5. *to deal with:* square away
adv. 6. *estimated:* by guess and by
gosh

ACCURACY
164. Accuracy; Truth
n. 1. *facts:* brass tacks (rhy.sl.), nuts
and bolts, nitty-gritty, rodge,
runabout, (US black), score,
strength, ticket
2. *truth:* the goods, gospel, inside
track, legit, straight dope, – goods,
– poop, – shit
3. *essentials:* brass tacks, cases,
name of the game, nuts and bolts,
nitty-gritty, real grit (US black)
4. *real thing:* aces, cheese, goods,
legit, real McCoy, – McKay, stuff,
ticket
v. 5. *to be correct:* be right there,
– (right) on the ball, hit the spot,
have (it) down, – bang to rights,
– dead to rights, hit it, nail
it
6. *tell the truth:* come across,
– clean, lay it on the line, shoot
straight, tell it like it is
7. *promise the truth:* bet one's
boots, – bottom dollar, – life (on it),

cross one's heart (and hope to die),
swear blind, – to God.
adj. 8. *genuine, true:* aces, all wool
and a yard wide, as large as life (and
twice as natural), blowed in the
glass, dinki-di (Aus.), dinkum,
eighteen-carat, for real, – sure,
legit, no ifs or buts, on the level,
– the up and up, pukka, sure
enough, sho' 'nuff, solid, straight up
adv. 9. *precisely:* bang on, – up, in
the groove, on the button, – the
line, – the nail, – the spot
10. *correct:* bang to rights, dead –,
bang on, jake, righteous, rodge,
(just) what the doctor ordered
11. *directly:* bam, bang, blam, blap,
blip, blop, caplump, caplunk,
casmack, dap, slap-bang,
smack-dab, smack, sock, spang,
wham
phr. 12. *you're right:* AOK, ain't
that so, – a fact, – the truth, and no
mistake, back of the net, check and
double check, don't I know it, hole
in one, 'nuff said, I'll say she does,
– you do, no shit, now you're
cooking, – talking, righto, Roger,
seen (WI), that's telling them, that's
the stuff, you ain't just whistling
Dixie, you bet, you can say that
again, you don't know the half of it,
you got it, you know it is, you're
dern tootin', you're telling me,
you've got me there, you've got
something there, you've said it

165. Error; Mistake
n. 1. bad break, balls up, blue
(Aus.), bloomer, boob, boob play,
boo-boo, bum steer, bust, cropper,
dumb play, – trick, fluff, foulup,
fuckup, howler, miscue, misfire,
plumb, rick, ricket, wrong'un
v. 2. *to be wrong:* back the wrong
horse, be all wet, have another
guess coming, not hold together,
– hold water
3. *to make an error:* ball up, blot
one's copybook, boob, bugger (it)

up, cock (it) up, cock up, come a cropper, drop a brick, fluff, foul up, fuck (it) up, goof, go off the rails, louse up, make a bloomer, – boo-boo, etc. (see 165.1), put one's foot in it, – in one's mouth, put on a black, screw up, step on one's dick, – one's prick, zeke (US black)

adv. 4. *mistaken, wrong:* barking up the wrong tree, cuckoo, daffy, (a) mile wide, off (the) beam, – (the) line, – the tack, screwed up, way off, – out

excl. 5. *you're wrong:* (see 146); are you kidding!, don't kid yourself!, – make me laugh! in a pig's eye!, – arse!, like fuck!, – fun!, – hell!, etc.

UNDERSTANDING
166. Intelligibility
n. 1. savvy

v. 2. *to understand:* blow wise, crack wise, catch (on), colly (US black), connect, cop, dig, earwig (rhy.sl. = twig), figure (out), get a line on, – next to, – outside of, – the message, – the picture, – with it, glaum, glom, grok, have a line on, – a slant on, – pegged, – it down, – the goods on, know the score, – the number, – the ropes, – the words and music, latch on (to), make, make the scene, nail, peep one's hole card, spot one out (US black), sus out, tumble (to), tune in, twig; spec. flash on (to have a sudden moment of comprehension)
3. *to be understood:* talk one's language
adv. 4. *understanding:* into, onto, up one's alley
phr. 5. *I understand:* (see 164.12); AOK, check, – and double check, gotcha, got it, got you, reet, seen (WI), you said it
6. *do you understand:* are you with me?, comprenny? (Fr. comprenez?),

dig?, do you read me? – get me?, get it?, you get my drift?, – my meaning?
7. *to read:* crack the books

167. Unintelligibility
n. 1. double Dutch, Greek
v. 2. *cannot understand:* can't figure, – sus, etc. (see 166), don't know from, no can see, no savvy, not have the foggiest, – the first idea
adv. 3. *incomprehensible:* above one's head, over –, beyond one, clear as mud, geechie (US black)
excl. 4. *what?:* er?, huh?, says which?, sorry, what in the hell? – Sam Hill? etc., what you say?, whatta whatta, you what?
phr. 5. *I don't understand:* beats me, – the hell out of me, beyond me, don't ask me, fucked if I know, God knows, (I) can't get that together, it's got me, sod that (for a lark), you've got me (there), your guess is as good as mine

168. Bewilderment; Perplexity
n. 1. botheration, backward thinking (US black)
2. *problem:* bamboozler, curly one, facer, handful, Harvey Nichol (rhy.sl. = pickle), headache, queeb, (bad) shit, shit on a string, teaser
v. 3. *to confuse:* bamboozle, floor, flummox, get (one) going, keep (one) guessing, stump, throw (for a loop)
4. *to be confused:* don't know one's arse from one's elbow, – from a hole in the ground, – whether one is coming or going, get one's head up one's arse, go into a flat spin, need a foghorn, up a gumtree, – a stump
adv. 5. *confused:* all at sea, – at sixes and sevens, between a rock and a hard place, hot and bothered, on one's beam ends, up against it, up shit creek (without a paddle); spec. on the fence (undecided)

169. Bewilderment; Confusion; Disconcertion
n. 1. *muddle:* dopiness, dottiness, fuddleheadedness, fuziness, grogginess, muzziness, wonkiness, wooziness
v. 2. *to be disconcerted, muddled:* (all) balled up, be like a chicken with its head cut off, run around in circles, not know whether you're on your head or heels, walk on one's head
3. *to disconcert, muddle:* discombobulate, drive up a pole, – out of one's brain, – gourd, – skull, etc., faze, flabbergast, flummox, jive, make one's head swim, put all at sea, put at sixes and sevens, – in a flat spin, – on the hop, – on a crosstown bus (US black), spifflicate
adj. 4. *bewildered:* all behind like a fat woman, all to shit, cockamamie, discombobulated, dusty (US black), fazed, gimped up, in a (right) two and eight (rhy.sl. = state), in a flat spin, paranoid, up in the air
5. *muddled:* addled, addle-pated, adrift, arsed up, at sixes and sevens (all) at sea, dopey, dotty, frazzled, goofy, in a loop, in a spin, jingled, muzzy, not all there, – with it, screwy, twisted, (having) one's wires crossed, woozy

RECOLLECTION
170. Memory
v. 1. *to stay in the mind:* get under one's skin, – in one's hair
2. *to reminisce:* cut up old scores
3. *refresh the memory:* beat the brains, pound the brains, jog the brains, polish up, sharpen, shine up, wise up
4. *to remember:* wake up
5. *to learn:* mug up
6. *to remind:* ring a bell

171. Forgetfulness
v. 1. *to forget:* bury (it), draw a blank, let slide in one ear and out the other, lose the combination, wipe (Aus.)
adj. 2. *forgetful:* foggy, rusty, with a head like a sieve, with a hole in the head

EXPECTATION
172. Expectation; Anticipation
n. 1. *presentiment:* hunch
v. 2. *to expect:* feel in one's bones, figure, reckon
adv. 3. *expectant:* (all) hopped up, hot (to trot), raring (to go)
4. *as expected:* nothing to write home about, par for the course

173. Inexpectation; Surprise
n. 1. bombshell, jar, jolt, knockout, turn, turn-up
v. 2. *surprise:* catch asleep at the wheel, – bending, – flat-footed, – off-base, – with one's pants down, – trousers down, give one a (nasty) jolt, – turn, etc., jump
3. *to astonish, amaze:* blindside, blow away, – one away, blow one's mind, knock for six, knock dead, – cold, – down with a feather, – for a loop, – make one's hair curl, – head swim, psych out, smoke out (US black), strike all of a heap, – one blind, – dead, – dumb, – pink, wow, zap, zoom one out
4. *to be surprised:* take the knock
adv. 5. *unexpected:* out of the blue; spec. unbuttoned (unprepared)
6. *astonished:* all of a heap, blown away, buggered, flabbergasted, jiggered, on the ropes, reelin' and rockin'
excl. 7. *what a surprise:* are you ready!, are you prepared!, as I live and breathe!, blow me down (with a feather)!, blow my nose!, bugger me!, can you beat it!, can you feature that!, – you hack it!, did

you ever!, for crying out loud!, for a motherfucker! (US black), for days!, heavens to Betsy!, – to Murgatroyd!, hell's bells!, – teeth!, holy smoke!, (well) hush my mouth!, if that doesn't beat the band!, (well) I'll be a monkey's uncle!, (well) I'll be fucked, lumme!, my word!, shit a brick!, shit, eh!, (Aus.), sock it to me!, starve the lizards!, stiffen the lizards! (Aus.), (well) strike me blind!, – me pink!, – a light!, (well) strip my gears!, shiver my timbers!, stone me!, stone the crows!, swipe me!, this'll pin your ears back!, that's news!, that too much!, fuck!, too fucking much!, what a turn-up!, who (the hell) would've thought it!, yikes!, yipes! you could have knocked me down with a feather!, you wouldn't read about it, (see Oaths 194); spec. Mercy Mary! (homosexual use)

8. *imagine!:* fancy!

9. *really!:* do say!, do tell!, don't tell me!, go on!, he/she did!, he/she didn't!, izzatso!, no shit!, say it ain't so!, the hell you say!, you did!

SUPPOSITION

174. Supposition; Conjecture

n. 1. *guess:* potshot, shot (in the dark), stab –; spec. guesstimate (informed guess)

v. 2 *to predict:* call it (right), call one's (best) shot, dope out, figure, hit (it) on the head, – the nose,

3. *to guess:* go it blind, take a shot (at), – stab (at), make a stab (at), whistle in the dark, – in the wind

175. Imagination; Fantasy

n. 1. pie in the sky; spec. thousand-yard stare (the 'lost' look of a combat soldier)

v. 2. *to imagine:* moon around, space out

adv. 3. *fantasising:* moony, spaced (out), sanpaku (fr. Zen), T-zoned (T = transcendental)

Communication

LANGUAGE
176. Language; Speech
n. 1. chat, -ese (language peculiar to a person or profession)
2. *jargon:* gobbledegook, Morkrumbo (journalese)
3. *slang:* slanguage
phr. 4. as she is spoke

177. Word; Letter
n. 1. dickybird (rhy.sl.), peep (as in 'not a peep'), verbals
2. *hard word, big word:* jawbreaker, mouthful, two-dollar word
3. *introductory word:* er, like, look, you know, now, right, say, well
4. *printed character:* dog's cock, – bollocks, screamer (exclamation point)

NAME
178. Name
n. 1. handle, label, monicker, tab, tag, trademark
2. *title:* his nibs, hizzoner
3. *general forms of address:* boyo, boysie, bub, bubby, buddy, buster, cock, cocky, cuz, dad, daddy-o, dearie, digger (Aus.), ducks, ducky, guv, guvnor, hon, honey, Jim (US black), John, Jack, love, lovey, mac, mate, mister, momma, moosh, mush, my man, pal, squire, toots, tosh, wack; spec. Miss (homosexual use)

179. Nickname
n. 1. *UK football team:* Addicks (Charlton Athletic), Brough (Middlesbrough), Canaries (Norwich), Cestrians (Chester), Dons (Wimbledon), Fifers (East Fife), Filberts (Leicester), Forest (Nottingham Forest), Gills (Gillingham), Glaziers (Crystal Palace), Grecians (Exeter City), Gunners (Arsenal), Hammers (West Ham), Imps (Lincoln City), Latics (Oldham), Lions (Colchester), Moorites (Burnley), Orient (Leyton), Owls (Sheffield Wednesday), Paraders (Bradford), Pilgrims (Plymouth), Rangers (Queen's Parks Rangers), Reds (Manchester Utd, Liverpool), Robins (Bristol City), Saddlers (Walsall), Seasiders (Blackpool), Shakers (Bury), Spurs (Tottenham Hotspur), Trotters (Bolton Wanderers), Villains (Aston Villa)
2. *commercial:* Coats and 'Ats (C&A), Freds (Fortnum and Mason), Rods (Harrods), Gucky (Gucci), Moss Bross (Moss Brothers), M&S, Marks (Marks & Spencer), Woolies (Woolworths); spec. Chucks, Cons (Converse basketball boots)
3. *military:* The Andrew (RN), big Deuce (WW2), Kate Karney (rhy.sl. = the army), looey (lieutenant)
4. *US college courses:* blabs in labs (linguistics), shocks for jocks (basic engineering), stones & bones (prehistory), darkness at noon (art history slide show), slums and bums (urban sociology), rocks for jocks (introduction to geology), stars for studs (basic astronomy), chokes and croaks (first aid and safety education), sounds and tunes (campus songs), clapping for credit

(music appreciation), physics for poets (basic physics of arts graduates), jock major (physical education), holes and poles (sex education classes), nuts and sluts (abnormal psychology); spick (Spanish), number-cruncher (involving complex maths), nudes for dudes (art), Plato to NATO (European civilisation), monkeys to junkies (anthropology), gods for clods (comparative religion), Monday Night at the Movies (film school)

5. *UK newspapers:* Daily Excess, – Getsmuchworse (Daily Express), Thunderer (The Times), News of the Screws (News of the World), Grauniad, Garudnia, Grudian, etc. (The Guardian – from its many misprints)

6. *racial:* (see Persons: Nationalities 385); Johnny- (as in Johnny-Chinaman, Johnny-Pathan, etc.)

7. *first names:* Del (Derek), Tel (Terence)

8. *'inevitable' nicknames:* Agony (Paine, Payne), Betsy (Gay), Blanco (White), Bodger (Lees), Bogey (Harris), Bomber (Harris), Brigham (Young), Buck (Taylor), Busky (Smith), Chalkie, Chalky (White), Charlie (Peace), Chats (Harris), Chatty (Mather), Chippy (Carpenter), Cock (Robins, -son), Dan (Coles), Darky (Smith), Dickie (Bird), Dixie (Dean), Dodger (Green), Dolly (Gray), Doughy (Baker), Dusty (Miller, occ. Jordan, Rhodes, Smith), Dutchy (Holland), Edna (May), Fanny (Fields), Flapper (Hughes), Foxy (Reynolds), Ginger (Jones, Smith), Granny (Henderson), Gunboat (Smith), Happy (Day), Hooky (Walker), Iron (Duke), Jack (Sheppard, -erd, -herd), Jesso (Read), Jigger (Lees), Jimmy (Green), Johnny (Walker), Jonah (Jones), Jumper (Collins), Kitty (Wells), Knocker (Walker, Wright), Lackery (Wood), Lefty (Wright), Lottie (Collins), Mouchy (Reeves), Muddy (Waters), Nobby (Clark, -e, occ. Ewart, Hewart, Hewett, Hewitt), Nocky (Knight), Nutty (Cox), Pedlar (Palmer), Peeler (Murphy), Piggy (May), Pills (Holloway), Pincher (Martin), Pony (Moore), Rabbit (Hutchins, -son), Rattler (Morgan), Sandy (Brown), Shiner (Black, Bright, Bryant, Green, White, Wright), Shoey (Smith), Shorty (Wright), Slinger (Woods), Smoky (Holmes), Smudger (Smith), Snip (Parsons, Taylor), Snowy (Baker), Spider (Kelly), Spikey (Sullivan), Spokey (Wheeler, Wheelwright), Spud (Murphy), Taffy (Davis, -ies, Jones, Owen and other Welshmen), Timber (Wood), Tod (Hunter, Sloan), Tom (King), Topper (Brown), Tinkle, Tinker, Tottie (Bell), Tubby (Martin), Tug (Wilson), Wheeler (Johnson), Wiggy (Bennett)

9. *rhyming nicknames:* Charlotte the Harlot, Dennis the Menace, Even Stephen, Flo the Chro (Aus.), Giggling Gertie, Hairy Mary, Harriet the Chariot, Harry the Horse, Merv the Perv, Myrtle the Turtle, Nola the Bowler (Aus.), Peter the Poof (Aus.), Phil the Dill (Aus.), Randy Mandy, Roger the Lodger, Terry the Ferry (Aus.), Dizzie, Tizzie Lizzy

10. *of strong men:* Buck, Bull, Butch, Spike

11. *of hair:* Darky; Blondie; Bricktop, Carrots, Ginger, Red; Curly; Baldy

12. *of a slim person:* Daddylonglegs, Lanky, Lofty, Spider

13. *of a fat person:* Chubby, Chubs, Fats, Fatso, Fatty, Jumbo, Tiny, Tub, Tubby, Tubs

14. *of a short person:* Half-Pint,
Pee-Wee, Shorty, Tiny, Titch
15. *of one who wears glasses:*
Four-eyes
16. *of a foolish person:* Dizzy,
Dopey, Goofy, Sappy, Simp
17. *of a conceited person:* (Mr, Mrs,
etc.) Knowitall, – Smartarse,
– Smartypants
18. *BBC:* Auntie, Beeb, Corp
19. *popular black use:* T-bone

180. Pet Name
n. 1. *names of affection,
endearment:* angel, -face,
apple-dumpling, babe, baby,
babycakes, birdie, blossom, booful,
buggins, buggle, bunny, buttercup,
chick, -adee, chicken, chicky,
cutems, cutesie, -pie, dear heart,
diddums, duck, ducks, ducky, fruit
pie, honey, – bunny, -child, -pie,
-suckle, izzum, -kins (general
suffix), lamb, -chop, -pie, little one,
– thing, love, lovey, lovey-dovey,
oodlum, oozit, peach, pearl, pet,
– lamb, piggy, poopsy, precious,
– heart, pretty, pudding, pussums,
rabbit, snooks, snookums,
squidlums, sugar, -bun, -pie, -plum,
sweet, sweetie, – pie, sweetness,
sweets, toots, tootsie, – wootsie,
turtle-dove, ums, wootsie

SIGN
181. Sign; Symbol
n. 1. *badge:* buzzer, potsy; spec.
pips, stripes (milit. use)
2. *certificate, etc.:* union card (US
certificate of one's degree)
3. *medal, award:* gong, ruptured
duck; spec. leather medal, wooden
spoon (metaphorical award for
coming last)

182. Signal
n. 1. flash, high sign, nod, office,
tipoff, wink
2. spec. Maggie's drawers (US milit:

on a firing range, the flag that
denotes a miss)
v. 3. *to signal:* flash, give the high
sign, slip the ink, tip the nod,
– wink

SPEECH
183. Speech; Talk
n. 1. blab, broadcasting, bunny,
crack, gab, gaff, gas, guff, jaw,
jaw-jaw, kaylack (backsl.), (mouth)
music, noise, patter, rabbit, (rhy.sl.
= rabbit and pork), rap,
tongue-wagging, wind, yap; spec.
ji-jibe (US black: unimportant
chatter); fat lip (US black:
unpleasant talk); blooper
(embarrasing public verbal error);
beef (complaint)
2. *smooth talk:* applesauce, banana
oil, blarney, bull, bullshit, BS,
bunk, bunkum, chat, (the) con,
come-on, eyewash, flannel,
gammon, line, (old) oil, riff, soap,
spiel, snow (job), speeching (WI),
spit-bit (US black); spec. sob stuff,
– story (stories intended to persuade
through pity)
3. *complaining:* beating the gums,
going on (at), wanking (on)
4. *remark:* capper, crack, whammy,
zinger; spec. (the) liquor's talking
(to talk unrestrainedly or
embarrassingly)
5. *articulacy:* gift of the gab
6. *voice:* pipes
v. 7. *to talk:* beat the gums, bat the
breeze, blab, blow, break one's
chops, bunny (= rabbit), burble,
cackle, chew (the fat), dish, gab,
gas, go (as in 'I go ... and he goes
...'), jaw, jib (US black), rabbit,
rap, shoot a line, – the breeze,
sound off, spiel, spill a line, warble,
yap
8. *whisper:* blow down one's ear,
talk out of the side of one's neck;
spec. deadpan (to speak without
expression)

9. *talk loudly:* ballyhoo, blart, blat, bloviate, blow hard, blow off (at the mouth), broadcast, loudmouth, sound off, talk big

10. *to remark:* crack, cut loose (with) dish, let loose (with), out with, shoot (one's wad), sing one's song, spew (it out)

11. *to become abusive:* curse out, get down dirty (US black), slag off; spec. rub in (to emphasise maliciously)

12. *to talk sincerely:* be one hundred per cent, come flat out (with), get down to brass tacks, let oneself go, pull no punches, make no bones (about), put one's cards on the table, rap on the real (US black), shoot straight (from the shoulder), show one's (hole-) card, take no prisoners, take the gloves off, talk turkey, touch base with; spec. on one's say-so (on trust); put the bee on (air one's obsessions)

13. *to talk cleverly:* come the smart arse, crack wise, deliver the goods, say one's stuff, spritz (Yid.), talk like a book

14. *to start talking:* fire away, out with (it), shoot; spec. break squelch (milit: break radio silence)

15. *interrupt:* butt in, chip in, pick up fag ends; spec. pull one's coat (to draw attention)

16. *to talk aptly:* hit the button, say a mouthful, strike home, touch base

17. *offer an opinion:* cop an attitude, put in one's two cents, say one's piece, sound off (about)

18. *speak foolishly:* go off half-cocked, put one's foot in it, – in one's mouth, shovel (the) shit; spec. foot in mouth disease (constant stupidities)

19. *to talk smoothly:* apply the oil, blarney, bull, bullshit, BS, feed a line, hand (out) a line, pour on the oil, soft soap, schmooze, shoot the bull, snow (under)

184. Talkativeness

n. 1. *chatter:* babble, blarney, blather, bosh, burble, cackle, dribble, gas, gift of the gab, guff, gush, hot air, jabber, jive, natter, schmoose, tosh, wind, yackety-yak

v. 2. *to chatter, talk idly:* bang on, beat one's chops, – one's gums, bend one's ear, blow (off), blow off steam, break one's chops, burble, chew the rag, flap at the jibs (US black), gab, gabble, gas, go off (at the mouth), go on, jaw, jawbone, natter, pop off (at), run off at the mouth, schpritz, shoot blanks (US black), shoot off (at one's mouth), spout (off), spruik (Aus.), talk a blue streak, – the hind leg off a donkey, waffle, woof (US black), yackety-yak, yak, yawp; spec. work the room (chatter at a party)

3. *to tell a secret:* blow the gaff, let the cat out of the bag (see also 202)

adj. 4. *talkative:* full of it, gabby, gassy, gobby, mouthy, yappy

185. Grandiloquence

n. 1. blah, gas, hot air, jazz, wind

v. 2. blah, lay it on, pile it on, splash it on, swallow the dictionary, swank; spec. do a Melba (announce one's retirement, glean the publicity, then continue working)

3. *to boast:* sell a wolf ticket (US black)

186. Conversation; Discussion

n. 1. bull sesh, – session, chinwag, confab, dialogue, gabfest, frank and fearless, pow-pow, rap, sound; spec. commo (US milit: communication); stiffin' and jivin' (US black: an unreal, false conversation); spec. bad talk (US black: politically unsound talk)

2. *'line', 'pitch':* mack (US black), riff, snow job, spiel, stuff (as in 'do your stuff')

3. *conference:* confab, huddle, pow-wow

4. *explanation:* rundown
5. *response:* comeback, feedback
v. 6. *to discuss:* bat (it) around,
chew the fat, – the rag, kick (it)
around, pow-wow, run down some
lines (US black), splish and splash
(US black); spec. say something
(US black: to make a profound
statement)
7. *to 'shoot a line':* come on (to),
crack (something) up, give one a
song and dance, give (one) the old
boracic, run down some lines (US
black), scream some heavy lines
(US black)
8. *to communicate:* keep the lines
open
9. *to discuss again:* rehash
phr. 10. talk to the engineer, not
the oily rag (talk to the boss)
excl. 11. get this!, what's it to you?

187. Public Speaking
n. 1. bitch box (US milit: Tannoy),
PA (public address system)
2. *publicity:* ballyhoo, hype, promo
v. 3. spec. belt (it) out (to sing
loudly)

188. Call; Cry; Shout
n. 1. bleat, boola-boola, hog-caller,
holler, squawk, whoop, yawp, yip
v. 2. barrack, bleat, holler, squawk,
whoop, yawp, yell blue murder, yip
3. *summon:* bell (by telephone), hoy
(Aus.)

189. Cursing; Profanity
n. 1. effing and blinding, four-letter
words, toilet talk
2. *curse:* hex
v. 3. *to swear:* cuss, Lord Mayor, rip
and tear (rhy.sl.); spec. excuse my
French, pardon my French
(apologies for swearing)
adj. 4. *cursed:* all-fire(d),
blame(d), blankety, blasted,
bleeding, blessed, blinking,
blithering, bloody, blooming,
blowed, buggering, cocksucking,

consarn(ed), corksacking, cussed,
dad-blasted, dad-gasted,
dadgummed, damnation, dang(ed),
dashed, dern, deuced, doggone,
dratted, effing, fizzing, flipping,
freaking, frigging, fucking,
God-blasted, gd, goddam,
goldarn(ed), goldurn(ed),
gosh-damned, – danged, – dern,
hell-fired, mammy-jamming,
mammy-ramming, mammy-tapping,
mollyfocking, motherflunking,
motherfouling, motherfucking,
mothergrabbing, motherhugging,
mother-jiving, mother-jumping,
motherless, motherloving,
mother-raping, pissing, plaguey,
shitting, sodding, stinking
excl. 5. *damn!:* balls!, barf!, barf me
out!, begorra!, bejabers!, bejazus!,
bless me!, – my heart!, – my soul!,
blimey!, blow (it)!, botheration!,
bugger!, bugger me!, by George!,
– golly!, – gosh!, – gorry!, – gum!,
– jimminy!, – jingo!, – jove!, – the
great horn spoon!, Christ!,
– Almighty!, – on a crutch!,
Christmas!, Christopher Columbus!,
chuck you Farley!, cor!, cracky!,
crikey!, criminy!, cripes!, crumbs!,
damnit!, – to hell (and back)!, damn
my stars!, – sakes!, darn!, dash!,
dash it (all)!, dern!, doggone!, drat!,
ferchrissakes!, for Christ's sake!,
– crap's sake, – cripes' sake, for
crying out loud!, – a mother-fucker!
(US black), – gosh sake!, etc.,
– God's sake!, – heaven's sake!,
– landsakes!, – the love of Mike!,
– of Peter!, fuck a duck!, – this for a
lark!, – for a game of soldiers!,
fudge!, gee whillikens!, – whillikers!,
– whiz!, glory (be)!, goddam!,
goldarn!, goldern!, etc., golly!, gor
blimey!, Gordon Bennett!, gosh!,
gosh-almighty, gosh-darn!, etc.,
great Caesar's ghost!, great Scott!,
– snakes!, etc., heavens to Betsy!,
– to Murgatroyd, heck!, hell!, hell's
bells!, Hogan's ghost! (Aus.), holy

cats!, – cow!, – cripes!, – mackerel!, – Moses!, – smoke!, Jesus!, – H. Christ!, Jiminy Cricket!, Judas Priest!, jumping Jehosaphat!, landsakes, Lawd(y)!, lawks!, Lord love a duck!, Mary!, mercy!, motherfuck!, mollyfock!, etc., my (holy) aunt!, my sainted aunt, – eyes!, – gosh!, – hat!, – stars (and garters), nerts!, nuts!, pigs!, pigshit!, radishes!, rats!, sheet!, shit!, shit and derision!, shoot!, shucks!, strewth!, suffering cats!, sugar!, sweet (bleeding) Jesus, tarnation!, the hell with it!, to hell with it!, what the hell!, – the fuck!, – shit!, ye gods! – and little fishes!, your mother!
6. *I'll be . . .!:* I'll be a Chinaman!, – a Dutchman!, – a dirty word!, – a monkey's uncle!, – a (lowdown) son of a bitch!, etc.; I'll be blowed, – consarned!, – darned!, – jiggered!, etc. (see 194.5); I'll be hanged, – shot
7. *curses:* bugger you!, fuck –!, sod –!, damn your hide, go to hell!, rot your bones, the hell with you, – fuck with you, get fucked, – knotted, (go), take a flying fuck!, – a run up yourself!, you piece of crap!, – of shit!, you SOB!, you son-of-a-bitch!, you whoreson bastard!, you scumsucking shit-for-brains!, etc., etc.

WRITING
190. Writing
n. 1. hacking (it out), inkslinging, knocking it out, pen-pushing, pencil-pushing, whacking it out
2. *ticket:* bat and wicket (rhy.sl.), ducat, ducket; spec. Annie Oakley, chinee, Chinese ducket (free, complimentary ticket)
3. *signature:* handle, John Hancock, mauley
4. *handwriting:* fist; spec. chicken

scratchings, poultry –, pothooks and hangers (bad writing)
5. *typewriter:* typer
6. *paper:* repap (backsl.)
7. *book:* Captain Cook (rhy.sl.)
v. 8. *to write:* crank it out, hack (it out), knock it out, sling (some) ink, whack it out
9. *to study:* book it, book up, bone up (on), hack (it)

191. Correspondence
n. 1. *letter:* line (as in 'drop a line'), pc (post-card)
2. *invitation:* stiff, stiffie
3. *thanks:* bread and butter letter, thank-you letter, – note
4. *bureaucracy:* bumf, red tape
5. *lovers' codes on envelopes:* SWALK (sealed with a loving kiss), SWAK (sealed with a kiss), SWANK (– a nice kiss), NORWICH (knickers off ready when I come home), SWALCAKWS (sealed with a lick 'cos a kiss won't stick), BOLTOP (better on lips than on paper – next to an X for a kiss), ILUVM (I love U very much), ITALY (I trust and love you), BURMA (be undressed, ready, my angel), HOLLAND (here our love lives and never dies), EGYPT (eager to grab your pretty tits)
6. *love letter:* mash note; spec. Dear John (ending an affair)
v. 7. *to send a letter:* drop a line

INFORMATION
192. Information (inside)
n. 1. dope, goods, hot poop, – stuff, info, line (up), lowdown; spec. beat, scoop (exclusive newspaper story);
2. *inside information:* buzz, hot poop, – steer, – stuff, – tip, inside dope, – stuff, – tip, lowdown, etc. (see 192.1)
3. *reliable information:* cinch, good thing, (the) goods, lead-pipe cinch,

real thing, straight goods, – poop, sure bet, – thing; Mister Ed (unimpeachable inside source), deep throat
4. *false information:* bum steer
v. 5. *to inform:* dish (the lowdown), – the dirt, dope up, give the dope on, – the goods on, etc. (see 192.1), let (one) in, – on the ground floor, put a word in one's ear, put in the know, put next to, put on to something good, – something hot, smarten (up), wise (up); spec. kibitz (to offer unwanted information, esp. to a card-player)
6. *to teach:* larn, learn, show the ropes, – a thing or two, smarten up, wise up
7. *to give false information:* bum steer
8. *to become informed:* get a line on, get alongside, get behind, get the hang of, get into, get next to, get onto, get on the inside (track), get wise to, get with (it), sus out
9. *to be uninformed:* not know the score
adj. 10. *of inside information:* hot off the presses
11. *reliable:* blue-chip, gilt-edged

193. Disclosure

n. 1. finger-pointing, (dead) giveaway, let-on, top-off (Aus.), whistle-blowing
2. *rumour:* sniff
v. 3. *to disclose, reveal:* blab, come across (with), come clean, cough, ding, get (it) off one's chest, – (it) out of one's system, give, – (it) a name, go the hang-out route, lay (something) on, loosen up, make a clean breast (of it), open up, put up one's hand, put out, show one's cards, sing, – like a canary, sneeze (it out), spill (one's guts) – the beans, – the works, spit (it out), stand up, unbutton (one's lip), unload
4. *to betray, inform on:* blab, blow the gaff, – the whistle (on), bubble (rhy.sl. = bubble and squeak = speak), deep throat, dob in (Aus.), finger, fink (on), grass (up), nark (on), pin on, put a name up, put one in (Aus.), put the whisper on, rat on, rat one out, shop, snitch, squeal, stool, tip in, tom out (US black), top-off (Aus.)
5. *to expose:* blow the whistle (on), muckrake, stir up
6. *to reveal one's intentions:* stand up, stick one's chin out, – neck out, tip one's hand, – hole-card
7. *to disillusion:* knock the props from under, pull the rug from under, let down easy, puncture one's balloon
adv. 8. *betrayed:* bubbled, fingered, grassed (up)

194. News; Newspapers

n. 1. dope, gen, griff, info, (hot) poop, SP (starting price); spec. kicker (problematical information)
2. *privileged information:* beat, lowdown, scoop
3. *spec. newspapers, etc.:* bladder, book, funnies, funny pages, – papers, glossy, heavy (serious paper), linen, scream sheet, tab (tabloid), sheet; spec. hatched, matched and dispatched (births, marriages and deaths columns in The Times); bread and butter column (column based on rewritten PR handouts); bulldog (first edition)
4. *'men's magazines':* one-hand magazine, stroke book, tit mag; spec. eight-pager, Tijuana bible (small pornographic comic book)
5. *pin-ups:* beefcake, cheesecake, leg art
6. *journalistic technique:* baby-sitting, body-snatching (hiding away the human source of a big story); door-stepping (waiting outside the house of a possible interviewee); spoiling (ruining a rival paper's story)

v. 7. *to appear in a paper:* get some ink
8. *for a story to happen:* break

195 Television; Telephony, etc.
n. 1. *television:* boob-tube, box, custard and jelly (rhy.sl. = telly), gobble box, goggle box, idiot box, Nervo and Knox (rhy.sl.), tube; spec. God slot (religious programmes), sit. com. (situation comedy), soap opera (very long-running drama series); idiot board (cue board), idiot girl (cue board operator)
2. *film:* flicks
3. *porno film:* cock movie, snuff movie (spec. death), trick flick
4. *still picture:* Beecham's (rhy.sl. Beecham's pill), X-ray
5. *telephone:* blower, dog and bone (rhy.sl.), hook, Molly Malone (rhy.sl.), seven digits (US black)
6. *rehearsals, etc.:* Acton Hilton (BBC rehearsal studios); mug book (casting directory)
7. *film types:* ear-jerker (featuring the score); weepie (sentimental/ romantic); oater (Western)
8. *film director:* lenser, megger
9. *photographer:* shutterbug; spec. blinker (camera)
10. spec. sleeper (media use: slowly developing success)
v. 11. *to telephone:* bell, buzz, give (one) a bell, – (one) a buzz, tinkle, tootle
12. *to watch TV:* tube it
13. *to direct a film:* lens, meg

196. Gossip
n. 1. buzz, Daily Mail (rhy.sl. = tale), dirt, dish, furphy (Aus.), jazz, scuttlebutt, whisper
2. *collective gossip:* bull session, bush telegraph, (the) dirt farm, galah session (Aus.), grapevine
v. 3. *to gossip:* bad-mouth, bad-rap, barber, bat the breeze, bum-rap,

clean up the walls (US black), dish the dirt, get down dirty, – shitty (US black), hardmouth, put it on the street, put (one's business) on front street (US black), put in the poison, set mouth (US black), shoot the breeze, – the bull, – the regular, – the shit, shovel shit, slay, smartmouth (US black), stir (it up), talk out of school, – that talk, – trash, throw some dirt (on)
adv. 4. *gossiping:* on the wire

197. Description; Explanation
v. 1. *to explain:* break down (US black), clue (one) in, daylight (US black), dope out, fill (one) in, fold one's ears, give, hip (to), lay (the scene) on, light (US black), mark one's card, run (it) down, school (US black), whip it on (one), wire up (US black); spec. kick apart (analyse); knock into (one's skull), – through (one's skull) (to explain to the dull)

198. Story
n. 1. Daily Mail (rhy.sl. = tale), spiel, tell, yarn
2. *unlikely story:* cock-and-bull story, con, fairy story, fish story, song-and-dance, tall story, wind-up; (see Lie 312)
3. *depressing story:* hard-luck story, Newgate gaol (rhy.sl. = tale), sob story, tearjerker
4. *exciting story:* chiller, cliffhanger, shocker, snorter, spine-tingler, thriller; spec. potboiler (story written purely for cash, not art)
5. *romantic story:* bodice-ripper, gay gothic, hysterical historical, sweet savagery; spec. confessional (religious romance)
v. 6. *to tell a story:* spin a yarn, yarn
7. *to tell an unlikely story:* feed (one) the bull, hand a (cock-and-bull) story, – a line, shoot a line, spin a line

8. *to exchange stories:* cut up touches (with)

AFFIRMATION AND DENIAL

199. Assertion

v. 1. *to assert:* lay down the law, – it on the line, take no shit, tell it like it is

2. *to believe absolutely:* eat one's hat, – one's head, hope to die, swear till one's blue in the face, bet one's bottom dollar, etc. (see 160)

excl. 3. A!, ain't that a fact!, – so!, – it the truth!, all kidding aside!, all reet!, all right!, and don't you forget it!, and that's a fact!, AOK!, awright!, believe me!, betcha!, bet your boots!, blood oath! (Aus.), Bob's your uncle!, check!, – and double check!, damn right!, darn right!, dern right!, etc. (see 164), did I ever!, does a bear shit in the woods?, – the Pope shit in the woods?, fucking A!, go on twist my arm, harbour light! (rhy.sl. = all right), honest injun!, I ain't just whistling (Dixie)!, I don't mean maybe!, I hear you!, I'll say!, I'll eat my hat!, – my head!, etc., I mean!, I should say so!, Isle of Wight (rhy.sl. = all right), is that ... or is that? (insert subject as to context), is a bear a Catholic?, is the Pope a Catholic?, lahteeache (backsl. = all right), left off!, lovely grub!, naked!, natch!, no kid(ding)!, no risk! (Aus.), no shit!, OK, okey-dokey, on the level!, right arm!, righto!, right on!, scotia! (US black), see (backsl. = yes), seen! (WI), (you can) take it from me!, that's the shot! (Aus.), – the ticket!, way to go!, word!, word up!, would I shit you! (you're my favourite turd!), you bet!, you can say that again!, you don't know the half of it!, you('ve) got it!, you know it (is)!, you're dern tootin'

200. Negation

n. 1. blank, KB, knock-back, nix, no-no

v. 2. blank, give the thumbs-down (to), KB, knock-back, nix, no-no

excl. 3. don't make me laugh!, fat chance!, fuck off!, I don't think!, I'll be damned if!, – fucked if!, like fuck!, – fun!, – hell!, nerts!, nix!, no dice!, – sale!, – soap!, – way!, not bleeding likely!, not on your Nellie!, not on your tintype!, nothing doing!, no siree (Bob)!, nope!, not fucking likely!, nuts!, on! (backsl.), some chance!, – hope!, you must be joking!

UNCOMMUNICATIVENESS

201. Muteness

v. 1. *to be quiet, silent:* button one's lip, – up, clam up, dry up, dummy up, freeze, hold one's noise, – water, keep mum, – stum(m), – the cap on the bottle, put a sock in it, shut one's cakehole, – face, – gob, – hole, – trap, zip one's lip

2. *to make quiet:* choke off

3. *to withhold information:* clam up, dummy up, freeze up, hold one's breath, – out (on), keep the cap on the bottle, – the lid on, – them guessing, – it on one's chest, – under one's hat, keep stum(m), save one's breath, stonewall

adj. 4. mum, stum(m)

excl. 5. *stop talking!:* bag your face!, belt up!, button your lip!, button up!, can it!, cheese it!, cut the chat!, – the crap!, – gas!, – the noise!, drop it!, dry up!, dummy up!, enough said!, forget it!, get back in the knife box!, give your face a rest!, hit me and cut the crap!, hold it!, hold it down!, hold your noise!, hush your mouth!, keep mum!, – stum(m)!, knock it off!, nark it!, nit-nit, 'nuff sed!, put a sock in it!, – the stopper in it!, save it!, – your breath!, shut it!, – your face!,

– gob!, – hole!, – trap!, shut your mouth and give your arse a chance!, stow it!, wrap up!, zip it up!
6. *don't interrupt!:* butt out!, who pulled your chain!

202. Secret
n. 1. cover-up, family jewels, hole card, whitewash
v. 2. *to keep a secret:* clam up, close up, dummy up, hush up, keep it dark, – it down, keep a stiff lip (US black), – mum, – on the strict q.t., – under one's hat, not let the cat out of the bag, not peep, not spill the beans, play the dummy, put the lid on, tell no tales (out of school)
3. *to suppress:* blue-pencil, put the lid on
4. *to confide in:* blow in one's ear, pull one's coat, put wise (to), wise up
adj. 5. *secret:* closet, hole and corner, hush-hush, inside, on the quiet, – the q.t., stum(m) and crumm, under the table, – one's hat, under wraps
adv. 6. *secretly:* on the quiet, – the q.t.

203. Concealment
n. 1. cover-up, smoke screen, whitewash
2. *hiding place:* funk-hole
3. *cache:* drop, slaughter (burglar's storeroom), stash
4. *disguise:* front
v. 5. *to hide* **vt:** bag, drop, dump, law away, plant, stash
6. *to hide* **vi:** dive, duck-out, hole up, keep on the q.t., lay low, lie doggo, – low, lie dead, play dead, – possum, sit quiet, – tight
7. *disguise* **vt:** cook up, doctor (up), fake (up), ring
adv. 8. *in hiding:* holed up, lying low, on the lam, playing possum etc.
9. *disguised:* cooked up, doctored (up), etc., incog

Volition

RESOLUTION; DETERMINATION

204. Resolution

n. 1. balls, guts, stones

v. 2. *to be determined:* barrelass, be out for blood, – for business, do the full sesh, get behind, – down, – into, – (it) on, – one's head down, – some respect (US black), – stuck in, give one's best shot, go for broke, – (for) the whole shot, – nap on, – overboard, – the limit, mean business, play hardball, put one's head on the block, – foot down, run with the ball, shit or bust, shoot one's bolt, shoot to kill, stand pat, step fast (US black), stick one's neck out, take care of business, TCB, take no prisoners, take one's best shot, wade in

3. *to make determined:* psych (oneself) up

4. *to determine:* allow, figure, fix (to), reckon

adj. 5. *determined:* ballsy

adv. 6 *determined:* behind, dead set, hell-bent, hells-bent, hot for, into, psyched up, set

excl. 7. *I mean it:* honest (injun)! I ain't just whistling Dixie!, no kidding!, no shit!, would I shit you? (you're my favourite turd)

205. Perseverance

n. 1. stick-to-itiveness

v. 2. *to persevere:* bang away (at), buck (for), bust a gut, bust one's arse, go down the road (for), hammer away (at), hang in (there), – tight, hit for six, keep the ball rolling, – the show on the road, make the fist (US black), not give up the ship, plug away at, run down one's best game (US black), shag ass, shoot from the hip, – one's best mack (US black), show the flag, sit tight, steam in, stick one's neck out, stick to (it), sweat (it) out, throw one's hat in the ring, tough it out

adv. 3. *persevering:* shovin' and pushin' (US black)

205. Obstinacy

v. 1. *to be obstinate:* have one's head up one's arse, put one's foot down, run into the ground, take no shit

adj. 2. *uncompromising:* bloody-minded, bullnecked, cussed, dog in the manger, hard-assed, hard-nosed, mulish, pig-headed

adv. 3. spec. accidentally on purpose

phr. 4. it's my story and I'm sticking with it

IRRESOLUTION; EVASION

207. Irresolution

n. 1. fence-sitting; spec. touch of the seconds (second thoughts)

v. 2. *to be irresolute:* beat about the bush, – around the bush, fart around, fuck about, hum and haw, piss about, – around, pussyfoot, seesaw, shilly-shally, stall

adj. 3. *irresolute:* betwixt and between, half and half, ho-hum, on the fence

208. Caprice

n. 1. *whim:* bee in the bonnet, wheeze

v. 2. *to act madly:* rally
adv. 3. *acting irresponsibly:* triflin'
(US black)

209. Abandonment; Relinquishment
n. 1. chuck, heave-ho, push, shove
v. 2. *to relinquish, abandon:* axe,
call it a day (give up), chuck (it)
(up), cut loose, ditch, dump, fold,
give (it) the (old) heave-ho, – it the
chuck, – the elbow, – the E, – the
toss, give up the store, hang (it) up,
jack (it) in, junk, kiss goodbye,
– one's arse goodbye, knock on the
head, knuckle down, – under, pack
(it) in, put on ice, sack it up, (US
black), scrub (it), throw in one's
hand, – the sponge, – the towel, top
up, wash out, wind up; (see also:
Discard 25.4)
3. *to retract one's words:* back down,
– out, bow out, call all bets off,
chicken out, clam up, crawfish, eat
dirt
4. *to alter an opinion:* change one's
tune, draw in one's horns, pull in
one's horns
5. *to desert, abandon:* break it off
(with), cut (out), ditch, do a fade
(on), give the brush-off, – the
go-around, go bent (on), kiss
goodbye, – off, lay down on,
leave flat, play the chill (for),
take a powder, – a runout
powder on, throw overboard, toss
overboard (see also v. 2)

210. Evasion
n. 1. dodge, duck, E, elbow,
go-around, run-around; spec.
AWOL, French leave (absence
without leave)
v. 2. *to evade:* back off, bob and
weave, buck, cock a deaf 'un, duck
(out), get cold feet, give the go-by,
– the runaround, go AWOL, go
cold on, lose one's bottle, oil out,
play the duck, – hide-and-seek
(with), plead the Fifth, punt off,

shake; spec. beat the rap (avoid
punishment)
3. *to play truant:* flick (US black),
hop the wag, play hookey, wag off
4. *to avoid:* fight shy (of), give a
wide berth, give the go-by, – the
runaround, – the miss, steer clear
(of)
5. *to avoid work:* come the old
soldier, – the tin soldier, dodge the
column, flick (US black), goldbrick,
goof off, lay down on the job,
soldier, swing the lead
6. *to absent oneself:* go AWOL, take
French leave

211. Flight; Escape
n. 1. bunk, disappearing act,
vanishing act, el disappearo,
powder, skip
2. *narrow escape:* close call,
– shave, narrow squeak, near
squeak, – go
v. 3. *to escape:* amscray (backsl. =
scram), beat it, blow, bunk, buzz
the nab, cheese it, cop out, crash
out, cut out, do a runner, – a fade,
– the disappearing act, – the
vanishing act, duck out, fade, fly the
coop, fuck off, get out, – the fuck
out, – the hell out, go on the lam,
go walkabout, have it away, head
for the hills, – the tall timber, – the
tall trees, – the woods, hightail it,
make a break, pull a runner, save
one's bacon, Scapa (rhy.sl. = Scapa
Flow = go), scarper (= Scapa
Flow), show one's heels, skip (it),
sod off, take a (runout) powder,
– the air, take it on one's toes, take
it on the lam, vamoose; spec. flick
(US black: to play truant, to avoid
work)

CHOICE
212. Choice; Option
n. 1. bag, bet, cup of tea, cuppa,
druthers, fave, – rave, scene, thing
2. *alternative:* any old, between hell

and high water, betwixt and
between, or else, no two ways
about it
v. 3. *to choose:* do one's thing, go
for; *spec.* you pays your money and
you takes your choice
phr. 4. *after a decision:* when the
chips are down

213. Freedom; Independence
n. 1. open slather (unlimited
situation, Aus.), Rafferty's rules
(Aus.); *spec.* indie (entertainment
use: an independent TV/film/record
company)
v. 2. *to be free, independent:* cut
one's own throat, do as one damn
well pleases, – one's own thing,
footloose and fancy-free, go it
alone, go one's own (sweet) way,
hoe one's own row, keep oneself to
oneself, look after number one,
– out for number one, paddle one's
own canoe, roll one's own, take
care of number one, write one's
own ticket
3. *to give freedom:* cut loose, get off
one's case, give enough rope, let off
the hook
adv. 4. *free:* footloose and
fancy-free, on the loose
5. *without rules:* anything goes, no
holds barred, no punches pulled, no
strings (attached), the sky's the limit
6. *solo:* (all) on one's lonesome, on
one's Jack (rhy.sl. = Jack Jones =
alone), – one's Pat (Aus. rhy.sl. =
Pat Malone = alone), – one's Tod
(rhy.sl. = Tod Sloan = alone),
under one's own steam

CHANCE
214. Chance; Opportunity
n. 1. breaks, fling, go, hope, main
chance, shot, show, slant
2. *good chance:* aces, cinch, clean
shot, fair go, fair pop, good thing,
natch, runner
3. *poor chance:* crapshoot, longshot

4. *no chance:* on a hiding to
nothing, not a Chinaman's chance,
– a dog's chance, – an earthly
(chance), – a hope in hell, – cat's
chance in hell, – a hope, – a
snowball's chance in hell
v. 5. *to take a chance, to risk:*
chance one's arm, – one's luck,
give it a go, have a fling (at), – a
shot (at), lead with one's chin,
odds (it), play a hunch, punt
(around), punt it (up), sail close to
the wind, stick one's neck out, take
a stab (at), wing it
6. *to bet:* bet one's bottom dollar, go
the whole bundle, – the whole pile,
– the whole wad, put one's shirt on
7. *to have a good chance:* have a
look-in, – a hope, stand pat
8. *to have little or no chance:* to be
on a hiding to nothing, to have a
Chinaman's chance, etc. (see 214.4)
9. *to use one's chances:* not to miss a
trick, play one's hand
adv. 10. *at risk:* on spec
excl. 11. *no chance!:* don't make me
laugh!, you must be joking!

215. Luck
n. 1. beads, breaks, Dame Fortune,
dice, ins and outs, joss, Lady Luck,
ups and downs
2. *good luck:* break, mazel (Yid),
mozzle, muzzle, turnup (for the
book)
3. *bad luck:* tough break, – shit,
– titties, tzuris (Yid. = problem)
4. *a bad luck totem:* hoodoo, Jonah
v. 5. *to be lucky:* be in clover, – in
fat, – on a roll, – on a winner, break
the bank, get the breaks, get hot,
luck into, luck out, turn up trumps;
spec. born with a silver spoon in
one's mouth (to be born to riches)
6. *to be unlucky:* be down on one's
luck, be fucked, screwed, etc., crap
out, draw a blank, on the outs, not
to have the breaks; *spec.* sizzle (US
black = to be unusually prone to
arrest)

7. *to cause bad luck:* hoodoo, jinx, Jonah
adv. 8. *lucky:* hot, in clover, in the fat, on a roll, on a winner
9. *unlucky:* behind the eightball, born under a bad sign, cold, jinxed, hoodooed, fucked, screwed, etc.
10. *destined:* in the cards, – the dice, – the stars

CONTROL
216. Authority
n. 1. clout, final cut, juice
2. *order:* say-so
v. 3. *to have authority:* to be in the chair, – in the driving seat, etc. (see 216.4), call the punches, – the shots, come on strong, crack the whip, have (it) covered (US black), – one's act together, – one's act down, – one's game uptight, – shit together, – shit down, – it knocked, hold the can, keep ahead of the game, ramrod, ride herd (on), run a tight ship, sit down, toughen (up) one's game (US black), wear the trousers; spec. go under one's neck (Aus. to usurp another's position)
4. *to give orders:* lay down the law, put one's foot down
5. *to lose control:* blow it, jump the rails
adv. 6. *in authority:* ahead of the game, in the box seat (Aus.), in the chair, in the driving seat, in the saddle, on one's game (US black)
7. *strict:* death on
phr. 8. don't just stand there, do something, if it moves salute it, if it doesn't, paint it

217. Force; Compulsion
n. 1. screws, squeeze, third degree; spec. habe (abbr. habeas corpus)
v. 2. *to compel:* blackjack, clobber one with, dump on, put the screws to, – the squeeze on, scare up, strongarm, twist one's arm

3. *to be forced:* like it or lump it, toe the line, walk the plank

218. Restraint; Curb
n. 1. clamp, crimp, damper, freeze, lid, squelch
v. 2. *to restrain:* bottle (up), clamp (down) (on), crimp, put the clamp on, – a crimp into, sit on; spec. dock (to cut wages)
3. *to subdue:* buffalo, bust, take down a peg (or two), take the frills out of
4. *to restrain oneself:* hold one's horses, pull one's punches, slow one's row (US black), soft pedal
adv. 5. *restrained:* in bondage (US black), over a barrel

INFLUENCE; INDUCEMENT
219. Influence
n. 1. clout, drag, fluence, juice, mojo, pull, strings, wires
v. 2. *to use influence:* pull strings, pull wires, railroad, tickle palms
3. *to have influence:* draw (a lot of) water, have clout, drag, etc., know where the bodies are buried
4. *to persuade:* do a number (on), get around, grind down, hassle, hook in, pressure, put something over, sell (on), sell a bill
5. *to deceive:* ballyhoo, bamboozle, bullshit, con, get at, get one's hooks on, – one's hooks into, pull the wool over one's eyes, set up, take to the cleaners, three-sheet, wind up
6. *to urge:* ding, drum up, egg on, kack up, kid (along), talk (something) up
7. *to influence emotionally:* get to, put through changes

220. Enticement; Allurement
n. 1. come-on, draw, sucker bait
v. 2. *to entice:* give the come-on (to), pull, smoke out, throw out a line, work (on)
3. *to attract:* bring down

adj. 4. *enticing:* come hither

WILLINGNESS
221. Willingness
adj. 1. *willing:* game
adv. 2. *willingly:* at the drop of a
hat, like a shot
phr. 3. I don't mind if I do

222. Consent; Assent
n. 1. go-ahead, green light, OK,
thumbs-up
v. 2. *to consent:* give a nod (to), give
the go-ahead, – the green light (to),
– the OK, – the thumbs up (to), go
with, – the flow, hang loose, lay
down (for), roll with the punches,
stand still (for), stand up, tip the
wink (to); spec. swallow (it) (to
accept – often knowingly – lies);
choke (it) down (accept reluctantly)
excl. 3. spec. bags I! (schoolboy: yes
please!)

UNWILLINGNESS
223. Unwillingness
excl. 1. *I refuse!:* the hell you say!,
the hell I will!, the fuck I will!, don't
make me laugh!, you must be
joking!, in a pig's arse I will!, I'll be
damned, – danged!, – dashed!,
– hanged!, – shot (if I will)!, I'll see
you in hell first!, like fuck I will!,
– fun I will!, – shit I will!, etc.,
include me out!, kiss my arse!, ring
the other one (it's got bells on it)!,
get fucked!, on your bike!, no deal!,
– dice!, – go!, – soap!, – not on your
life!, not on your tintype!, try and
make me!, you've got another think
coming!; spec. bags I (baggy) no
par! (schoolboy: not me!)

224. Refusal; Rejection
n. 1. big E, elbow, nix, red light,
thumbs-down
2. *dismissal:* boot, brown envelope,
sack

v. 3. *to reject:* blank, blow out, ding,
give the E, – the elbow, – the hard
word, give the thumbs-down, – the
red light (to), kiss, kiss goodbye,
kiss off, turn one's nose up at
4. *to chase away:* hunt (Aus.)
5. *to dismiss:* give the boot, give the
brown envelope, give the sack

225. Prohibition
v. 1. *to prohibit:* nix, thumbs-down,
zero
adv. 2. *forbidden:* verboten
excl. 3. *no!:* (see 'Stop it' 11.10);
forget it!, ixnay!, nix!, – on that
(stuff)!, no way!

CUSTOM
226. Habit
n. 1. (daily) grind, nine-to-five,
same old same old
adj. 2. *habituated:* hooked, hung up
(on) (see also Drugs 510)

227. Convention
n. 1. done thing
v. 2. *to be conventional:* follow
one's nose (US black), get in line,
mind one's Ps and Qs, toe the line,
watch one's lip, – step
adj. 3. *conventional:* burbed out,
button-down, grey

228. Unconventionality
n. 1. spec. the Revo (Revolution)
v. 2. *to behave oddly:* to get away
with murder
adj. 3. *bizarre:* craze-o, out of
left field, OTT, over the top, way
out, weird (see also Insanity 152.5)

229. Fashion
n. 1. *glamour:* pizzazz, Tate and
Lyle (rhy.sl. = style)
2. spec. nigger fronts (US black,
very smart clothes)
v. 3. *to be unfashionable:* have
whiskers
adj. 4. *fashionable:* glitzy, happening,

high-tone, keen, mod, ritzy, sharp, snazzy; spec. early (US black)
5. *unfashionable:* dead as a dodo, joanie, lunchy, the pits
6. *ostentatious:* flash as a Chinky's horse, – as a rat with a gold tooth (Aus.)

BEHAVIOUR
230. Behaviour; Conduct
n. 1. (where one is) at, bag, (where one is) coming from, doings, goings on, (one's own) thing
v. 2. *to conduct one's life:* do one's own thing, keep one's end up, – one's nose clean, – one's pants zipped, – on the straight and narrow, set to rights, shape up, stack up, wise up; spec. CYA, cover your arse (look after yourself)
3. *behave yourself!:* act your age!, be yourself!, cut the comedy!, – the crap!, – the funny business!, don't fuck about!, – muck about!, – piss about!, get yourself together!, – your act together!, – your shit together!, – your arse in gear!, lay off!, quit fooling (around)!

231. Misbehaviour
n. 1. carry-on, cold shot (US black), ego trip, shenanigans, to-do
2. *set-to:* big how-de-do, randan, razzle-dazzle, ruckus, shindy; spec. knock-down-drag-out (extremely rough)
3. *social error:* floater
v. 4. *to misbehave:* carry on, come it, – the old acid, – the raw prawn (Aus.), create, cut up rough, – up rusty, draw the crabs (Aus.), hell around, jump bad, kick up hell, raise Cain, – hell, – a racket, – a ruckus, – sand (US black), throw one's weight about, turn the set out (US black), trash around, whoop it up; spec. tart about (for a female to act like a tart)

adj. 5. *unpleasant:* boldacious (US black), bucko
adv. 6. *misbehaving:* all over the board, off the track, out of pocket (US black), out of order, over the top, OTT

PLAN
232. Plan; Method
n. 1. angle, big idea, gag, hustle, lay, moves, racket, ropes, scam, schmeer, wangle, wheeze
2. *schedule:* layout, lineup, sked, set-up
v. 3. *to plan:* angle, figure, honcho, hustle, plot up, promote, wangle
4. *to plot:* be up to (something) (US black), cook up, fake up
adv. 5. *anyhow:* all ways to hell, – to shit, anywhichway, everywhichway
excl. 6. *how?:* how (in) the devil?, – (in) the fuck?, – (in) the heck?, – (in) the hell?, – the deuce? the blazes? the shit? etc.
7. *what's happening?:* how about it?, how's about it?, what do you (whaddya) say?, what's the deal?, what's up?, where do we go from here?

233. Prearrangement
v. 1. *to prearrange:* fake (up), fix, put in the bag, – on ice, ready up, set up, sew up, tie-up, wrap up
2. *to reveal a plan:* spring (it)
3. *to succeed in a plan:* click
4. *to go wrong:* blow (it), duff (up), gum things up, – up the works; spec. go in the tank, take a dive (to lose deliberately)
5. spec. back to the drawing board (to replan after a failure)
adv. 6. *arranged:* bagged, boxed, fixed, in the bag, in one's pocket, in the tank, on ice, open-and-shut, sewed up, sewn up, stacked up, tied up, wrapped up; spec. accidentally on purpose

UTILITY
234. Use
n. 1. *useful part:* business end
v. 2. *to use:* cash in (on), keep on
tap, play (it) for all its worth
3. *to make useful:* doctor (up), rejig,
rev, revamp
adv. 4. *available:* on tap, up for
grabs

235. Uselessness
n. 1. *useless object, idea:* crock (of
shit), dead duck, – rabbit, washout,
write-off
2. *rubbish:* crap, drack (Aus.),
junk, leavings, schlock, tripe; spec.
honey (human extrement); round
file (waste paper basket); airmail
(rubbish tossed out the window)
3. *waste of time:* boondoggle,
undertaker job
4. *to waste:* blow, fiddle-faddle
away, fool away, footle (away),
piddle away, piss away
5. *to waste time:* hack around, piss
around
6. *to be worthless:* suck
adj. 7. *spare:* gash
adv. 8 *useless:* crook (Aus.), crude
(US black), down the drain, duff,
4-F, gonzo, no account, on doog
(backsl. = no good), sunk, washed
up; spec. rumour (irrelevant)
9. *third-rate:* crappy, half-arsed,
icky, junky, tacky
phr. 10. ain't worth wiping your ass
on, don't amount to a fart in a
whirlwind, don't amount to a
pisspot full of crab-apples, (as
useless as) a spare prick at a
wedding, – tits on a bull, not worth
a fart in a noisemaker, – a light, – a
pisshole in the snow

ACTIVITY
236. Activity; Liveliness
n. 1. game (US black), goings-on,
hustle, jump, lark, play (US black),
-tripping, trot

2. *spirit, energy:* bang, bounce,
flash, ginger, go, hotcha, hustle,
kick, oof, oomph, pep, piss and
vinegar, pizzazz, punch, snap,
socko, steam, zap, zing, zip, zowie
3. *enthusiasm:* get-up-and-go,
hustle, push, spunk, what it takes
v. 4. *to rush around:* bang around,
buzz around (like a blue-arsed fly),
– like a one-armed paper-hanger,
come on (like gangbusters),
shazzam
5. *to enliven:* crank (up), hop up,
jazz up, pep up, punch up, put some
pep, punch, etc. into (it), snap (it)
up, stir the possum (Aus.), stoke
the fires, zip (it) up
6. *to draw attention:* draw the heat
adv. 7. *lively:* chipper, chirpy,
feeling one's oats, feisty, full of
beans, – of go, – piss and
vinegar, hopped up, on one's toes,
offish, on the go, peppy, zappy,
zingy, zippy
8. *ambitious, enthusiastic:* full of go,
– of pep, – of what it takes,
go-ahead, hard-charging, hungry,
Johnny on the spot, not backward in
coming forward, on the make,
pushy, spunky

237. Preparation
n. 1. once-over
v. 2. *to prepare:* clear the decks,
gear up, get set, pepper 'em up (US
black), prep, ready (up)
3. *to train:* lick into shape, sharpen
up, wise up
4. *to rear:* drag up
adv. 5. *prepared:* armed for bear,
fired up, good and ready, hot to
trot, loaded for bear, up to scratch
6. *unprepared:* half-cock(ed), not
cut out for, not up to scratch

238. Undertaking
n. 1. (tall) order
2. *attempt:* crack, dab, fist, fling, go,
hack, jab, lick, shot, shy, smack,
stab, try-on, whack; spec. good shot

(best, if useless effort), darnedest, Sunday punch (best effort)

v. 3. *to try:* balloon, give it a burl, – it a fling, – it a fly (Aus.), – it a go, – it a tumble, – it a whirl, go for it, have a see who salutes, take a pop (at), – a shot (at), etc., try it on

4. *to undertake:* bog in (Aus.), get into, get one's arse in gear, go out for, go to bat, motivate, put on the front burner, take the plunge

5. *to try hard:* be in there pitching, – slugging, break a blood-vessel, – one's neck, buck for, bust a grape (US black), – a gut, – one's arse, – one's hump, – one's nuts, get cracking, get down (US black), get one's act together, – one's finger out, – one's shit together, lean over backwards, pull one's socks up, turn on the heat

6. *to do one's best:* do one's level best, – one's darnedest, give (it) all one's got, go for broke, – the limit, shit or bust

7. *to go to excess:* come it, – on strong, run (it) into the ground

239. Performance; Accomplishment

n. 1. schtick, shtick, shtik (Yid.), stunt

v. 2. *to do:* cut loose with, hit, pull, talk talk and walk walk (US black); spec. go ahead up (US black: to do something together); do it like Mommy (act domestically)

3. *to do roughly:* bang out, knock out, toss off

4. *to do well:* blow fire (US black), deliver, – the goods, fire on all cylinders, do it up (right), do one's stuff, do the works, – the whole bit, go great guns, go the route, have (it) knocked, hit for six, fire on all cylinders

5. *to accomplish:* bring home the bacon, come through (with), cut it, cut the mustard, get away with, get it together, get outside of, hack it, lift one's game (US black), play past

(US black), pull a stroke, pull it off, pull one's finger out, put (it) across, – (it) over, put one's money where one's mouth is, score, swing (it), turn a trick

6. *to complete, finish:* be through (with), call it a day, – it quits, drop the curtain, hang up one's tools, knock it on the head, pack (it) in, polish (it) off, put (it) away, – (it) in cold storage, – (it) on ice, – the lid down, – the lid on it, top (it) off, wash up, wind up

7. *to work out:* crack (it), lick (it)

8. *to entertain:* do a bit

phr. 9. *completion:* when all's said and done

240. Production

v. 1. *to creat, concoct:* bodge (up), – together, cook up, hammer out, hash up, kludge, lash up, rustle up, toss off, whip up

adv. 2. *spontaneous:* off the cuff, – the top of one's head

phr. 3. damned clever these Chinese

241. Work; Employment

n. 1. fag, graft, grind, hang (US black), nine-to-five, racket, slave (US black), yakka (Aus.); spec. shit detail, shitwork (unpleasant work)

2. *a job:* meal ticket, spot; spec. chump job (US pimp: any 'straight' work); undertaker job (a hopeless job); foreigner (an illegal second job)

3. *work shift:* swing (4pm–12 midnight), graveyard (midnight to 4am), lobster (early morning), golden hours (overtime)

v. 4. *to work:* be in harness, graft, punch the clock, sock the clock; spec. go around the block (gain work experience); moonlight (to work two jobs, one at night); stooge (to work as an assistant)

5. *to start work:* dig in, fire away, get cracking, – going, – moving, – off one's arse, – the lead out, – the

show on the road, hit it, hop to (it),
jump to (it), knuckle down (to), lay
into, let rip, light into, pile in, pitch
in, plough into, rip into, sail into,
snap (in)to, turn it up, up and at
'em, wade into
6. *to work hard, keenly:* bat (it) out,
battle (Aus.), break one's arse,
– one's neck, bust a grape (US
black), bust one's arse, – one's
hump, – one's nuts, fire, go at it hot
and heavy, hammer ass, pour it on,
root hog or die, shake a leg, sweat it
out, work like a black (derog.),
work like anything, – like billy-o,
work one's arse off, – one's butt off,
– one's tail off; spec. gut it (US
college: to work all night); spec.
nigger-driving (US black: white
exploitation of black workers)
7. *to endure tedious work:* bang
away, grind, hammer away, peg
away, whack (it) out
8. *to end work:* call it a day, – it
quits, clock off, down tools, hang
(it) up, knock off, punch out; spec.
chuck (it) up, go south, jack (it) in
(leave a job)
9. *to defy union rules:* blackleg, fink,
rat, scab, scissorbill
adj. 10. *busy:* at it, at bat, busy as a
one-armed paper-hanger (with the
itch), hard at it, on the ball, – the
hop, – the jump, – the trot, snowed
under, tied up, up to one's eyes,
– one's ears, – one's elbows, – one's
neck, etc.
phr. 11. *work hard or don't waste
time:* fish, or cut bait, piss, or get off
the pot, shit, or get off the pot
12. spec. no rest for the wicked;
spec. why keep a dog and bark
yourself (use the available labour
force); illegitimis non carborundum
('Latin': don't let the bastards grind
you down)

242. Hiring
n. 1. *employment bonuses:* golden
handshake (payoff at dismissal or

retirement), golden hello (financial
inducement to a new recruit),
golden parachute (a long-term
contract that must be paid in full
even if one is fired)
2. *dismissal:* boot, elbow, heave-ho,
sack, tin-tack (rhy.sl. = sack)
v. 3. *to hire:* sign up
4. *to promote:* spec. kick upstairs (to
promote into inactivity)
5. *to demote:* bump, bust, kick
downstairs
6. *to fire:* can, give the bullet
7. *to be fired:* get one's cards, – the
boot, – the slingers
adj. 8. retired: spec. bowler-hatted
(retired from the Services)
excl. 9. *I want work!:* gissa job!

243. Fatigue
v. 1. *to collapse:* blow up, burn out,
– down, crap out, curl up (and die),
drag one's arse, keel over, peg out,
peter out, poop out, rock out (US
black), tucker out
2. *to work to excess:* have too much
on one's plate
3. *to tire out, exhaust:* beat, blow
one out, burn out, do in, do over,
fag (out), run ragged, tucker out
adj. 4. *exhausted:* all in, – shot, at
the end of one's rope, beat, blown
out, burned out, – down, bushed,
crapped out, creased, dead, dead to
the wide, done in, – up, euchred
(Aus.), fagged (out), fit, flaked out,
flat (Aus.), fuckfaced, jiggered,
kerried (rhy.sl. = Kerry Packered =
knackered), knackered, muzzy,
one's get-up-and-go got up and
went, on one's last legs, out of it,
out like a light, – on one's feet,
played out, pooped, racked, rooted
(Aus.), rusty, shagged out, shot,
stoked out, stroked (out), sparkers,
tuckered, washed up, zoned

INACTIVITY
244. Inactivity; Idleness
n. 1. *to idle, waste time:* arse

around, bum around, dog around,
– it, duff around, fart about,
– around, – off, fartarse around,
fiddlefart around, footle about,
freeload, fuck off, futz about, ghost
(US milit.), goldbrick, goof off, half
step (US black), horse around, jerk
off, keep banker's hours, layin' and
playin' (US black), let one's game
slip (US black), lollygag, mess
about, muck about, piddle about,
– around, play ring a rosie, ponce
around, razzle-dazzle (US black),
screw around, scrimshank, shuck
and jive, skive (off), sod about,
swing the lead, veg out, work one's
ticket; spec. punt (US campus: to
abandon work)
2. *to remain:* hang about, – around,
satellite, stay put, stick around
adj. 3. *inactive:* dead as a doornail,
– as a dodo
adv. 4. *unemployed:* at liberty, in
dock, on the beach, – the loose,
pattin' leather, resting (esp.
theatrical)
phr. 5. *you're idle:* don't strain
yourself; you'll be a long time dead

245. Laziness
adj. 1. *lazy:* bone idle, born tired,
doggy, drag-assed, niggerish
(derog.), rum-dum

246. Rest
n. 1. lay-off, lay up; spec. five, ten
(as in 'take five' or 'take ten'
minutes break)
v. 2. *to rest:* ease it, hole up, lay
back, – dead, – up, take five, take
ten
3. *to lie or sit down:* flop, park one's
carcass, – one's frame, plant
oneself, take a pew

247. Sleep
n. 1. beddy-bye, Bo Peep (rhy.sl.),
horizontal exercise, kip, rack
monster, sack time, shuteye, winks;
spec. rack attack (desire to sleep)

2. *nap:* forty winks, zizz
v. 3. *to go to bed:* bunk down,
crash, doss down, fall out, flop, get
one's head down, go beddy-bye,
– bye-bye, – nighty-night, hit the
hay, – the sack, hop in the hay, – in
the sack, spark out, turn in
4. *to sleep:* bag (some) Zs, cop
(some) Zs, crash (out), get some
shuteye, kip, pound one's ear, rack,
rack out, sack out, pile up some Zs,
Z; spec. do skippers, skipper (sleep
in derelict houses, etc.)
5. *to take a nap:* catch forty winks,
cop a snooze, grab a little shuteye
6. *to get up:* hit the deck, rise and
shine, show a leg
adj. 7. *asleep:* crapped out, flaked
(out), on flake, sacked out, Z'd out;
(see also Tired: 243)
excl. 8. *get up!:* hands off your cocks
and on your socks!, let's be having
you!, rise and shine!, shake a leg!,
show a leg!

248. Delay; Postponement
n. 1. hang-up, stand-off
v. 2. *to delay vi:* hold the phone, put
on the back burner, take a rain
check, – the scenic route, wag (US
black)
3. *to delay vt:* let (it) ride, put on
hold, – on ice, stall
4. *to be impatient:* bite the carpet,
chomp at the bit, foam at the
mouth, froth at the mouth, sweat it
out
excl. 5. *wait:* half a mo!, hang
about!, hold everything!, – it, – the
phone!, keep your hair on!
6. *stop it:* ock it

INTERFERENCE
249. Interference; Meddling
n. 1. back-seat driving, flak, horning
in, kibitzing, nosing around
v. 2. *to interfere:* barge in, cut off at
the pass, dip in one's business (US
black), horn in, mess with, monkey

with, muscle in, nose around, play one too close (US black), poke one's nose in, shove one's oar in, – one's nose in, stick one's bib in (Aus.), stick one's nose into, snoop 3. *intrude in a conversation:* breeze in, put in one's two cent's worth, – two pennorth, mouth in, -off
excl. 4. *don't interfere!:* butt out!, fuck off!, go bark up another tree!, – blow you own nose!, – chase yourself!, – fish!, – fly a kite!, – fry an egg!, – bag your head!, – join the navy!, – jump in a lake!, – jump off a cliff!, – lay an egg!, – peddle your fish!, – roll your hoop!, – soak your head!, – stick your head in a bucket!, – take a running jump (at yourself)!, – take a walk!, keep stum(m)!, – your nose out!, m.y.o.b.!, pull in your neck!, sit on it and rotate!, slip it where the monkey slipped the nuts!, shove it where the rhino got the javelin!, shove it where Moby Dick got the old harpoon!, what's it to you?

250. Hindrance; Obstacle
v. 1. *to hinder, cause trouble:* ball up, cook one's goose, crab (one's act), cramp one's style, dish, fuck around, – over, gum up, – the works, knock the bottom out of, lumber, put the bag on, – the block on, – the freeze on, – the kibosh on, – the mockers on, – the mozz on (Aus.), – the screws to, queer the pitch, shanghai, throw a spanner in the works; spec. corpse (theatre use: to cause another actor to forget lines)
adv. 2. *hindered, in trouble:* (all) balled up, (all) gummed up, (all) screwed up, up against the wall

FACILITY
251. Facility; Ease
n. 1. blow off, breeze, (dead) cert, cinch, cushy number, doddle, duck shoot, – soup, easy game, – ride, – stuff, free ride, gravy train, gut, money for jam, – for old rope, picnic, piece of cake, – of piss, pushover, snap, snip, soft number, tit, tough stuff (US black), velvet; spec. featherbedding (giving 'jobs to the boys'); sitter (sporting use: an easy catch – cricket; an easy target – hunting)
v. 2. *to make easy:* grease the wheels
3. *to have an easy life:* have it soft, sit pretty
4. *to do easily:* do (it) on one's dick, – on one's head, – on one's prick, have a field day (with), piss it, waltz it
adv. 5. *easy:* as easy as ABC, – as cake and ice cream, – as falling off a log, – as kiss my arse, – as one-two-three, – as pie, – as shooting fish in a barrel, – as taking candy from a baby, – as taking money from a child, – as winking, cheesecake, cushy, easy-peasy, in the bag, pie, pimpsy, plain sailing, right up (down) one's alley, skate, sweet (as a nut), under the odds
6. *easily:* hands down, in a walk, on one's dick, – one's prick, like a house on fire, no sweat, right off the bat
7. *out of trouble:* off the hook

252. Difficulty; Trouble
n. 1. *problem:* bad news, bind, bother, facer, hang-up, hassle, headache, hot potato, hot seat, jam, kick in the pants, Queer Street, screamer, sharp end, skulldrag (US black), sweat, Tom Mix (rhy.sl. = a fix), TS, tough shit; spec. bear (hard college work)
2. *unpleasant situation:* can of worms, drag, (the) devil to pay, – hell to pay, holy mess, – muddle, jive hand (US black), (a) nice how-d'you-do, pain in the arse, pretty mess, – muddle, – pickle,

rainy days (US black), (a) right
how-d'you-do, shit city, shithouse,
(a right) two and eight (rhy.sl. =
state), when the shit hits the fan,
when the solids hit the air
conditioning
3. *unfair treatment:* bumps, hard
lines, iron cross (US black), jack
job, more kicks than ha'pence, raw
deal, rough end of the pineapple
(Aus.), shaft, short end of the stick,
static, tough tits, – titty
4. *something difficult:* bastard,
bitch, bother, brute, bugger, pain
(in the arse), SOB, sod, son of a
bitch, tall order, tough nut to crack
v. 5. *to be in trouble:* (be) for it, – in
for it, – in the shit, – in the soup,
– in shtuck (Yid.), – up shit creek
etc. (see: adj. 11 below), catch a
cold, catch one's (big fat) tit in a
wringer, get one's arse in a sling, go
a million (Aus.), have one's cock
caught in a zipper, hit some shit,
scoff fishheads, scramble for the
gills
6. *to cause trouble:* mix (it), put the
mozz on (Aus.), shit on from a
great height, signify (US black), stir
(it up)
7. *to get into trouble:* get in a hole,
– in the shit, – in shtuck, – one's
arse in a sling; (be) in a pickle, – a
holy mess, etc. (see n. 2 above);
spec. it's your little hip pocket (US
black = you're in bad trouble)
8. *to get into trouble:* dob in (Aus.),
hit the shit
9. *to avoid, escape from trouble:*
beat the rap, crawl out from under,
hang tough, land on one's (own)
two feet, play it cool, save one's
bacon, slide out (of)
10. *to make trouble for:* crap
around, do over, fuck around,
– over, – with, have against the
ropes, put (up) against the wall, – in
shtuck, – on the spot, etc. (see 7
above), screw
adj. 11. *difficult:* bread and lard

(rhy.sl. = hard), no picnic, no
laughs (laffs), shitty, sketch,
tough
adv. 12. *in trouble:* between the
devil and the deep blue sea, – the
rock and the hard place, buggered,
caught by the short and curlies,
cruising for a bruising, done up (like
a kipper), floored, fucked, in
bother, – a bind, – a jam, – a pickle,
– a spot, – a tight hole, – Dutch, – it
(for fair), – it (for real), – Queer
Street, – Shit Street, – shtuck, – the
doghouse, – the shit, – the soup, on
offer, on the chopping block,
– one's beam end, – the ropes, – the
spot, out on a limb, riding for a fall,
screwed, shafted, sunk, stymied,
under the cosh, – the gun, up
against it, up a gum tree, up shit
creek (without a paddle), up the
creek, up to one's neck, up against
the wall, well fucked and far from
home
excl. 13. *what's the matter?:* what's
eating you?, what's biting you?,
what's got into you?, what's the
bitch?, what's the beef?, what's up,
Doc?, what's with you (him, her,
etc.)?

253. Skill; Ability

n. 1. goods, gumption, naus, savvy,
smarts, street smarts, what it takes;
spec. mileage (experience)
2. *cunning:* curves, fast one, good
one, nifty
v. 3. *to be able, skilful:* be all there,
– on the ball, – up to snuff, – wised
up, come up to snuff, cut it, cut the
mustard, hack, have it knocked,
– something on the ball, – what it
takes, know all the answers, – how
many beans make five, – one's arse
from one's elbow, – one's onions,
– one's stuff, – the ropes, – what
time it is, – what's happening, know
where it's at
4. *to do well:* be death on, be the
berries (at), have a (good) head for,

have its number, – it knocked, piss it, stride (US black), waltz (it)
5. *to be suitable:* hit (it) on the head, – on the nose, – between the eyes, – the bull's eye, fill the bill
6. *to take care of, to deal with:* square, swing (it), TCB, take care of business; spec. hold the baby (to be left to deal with a problem)
adj. 7. *experienced, efficient:* bonified (US black), fly, hip, hot stuff, keen, keeno, no flies on (him, her, etc.), plugged in, sharp, slick, snappy, up to snuff, wicked
8. *suitable:* about one's speed, just one's speed, right up (down) one's alley, right up one's street, etc.

254. Unskilfulness; Awkwardness
n. 1. butterfingers, muffishness
v. 2. *to be unskilful, make a mess of:* arse about, – around, – up, bollix up, bollocks up, bitch up, bugger up, cack-hand, cock (it) up, cods up, foul up, fuck up, gum up, gum up the deal, – the play, – the works, etc., make a cods of, – a cobblers of, – a hash of, put one's foot in, screw up, stub one's toe
adj. 3. *incapable:* can't cut it, – cut the mustard, – hack it (see Facility 253) half-arsed, lame, no can do, not all there: playing with a full deck, etc. (see Unintelligence: 145ff), – up to snuff, out of one's (own) league, playing with the big boys (now)
4. *unsophisticated:* down-home, on fire, square, – to the wood
5. *inexperienced:* amateur hour, green (as grass), half-baked, uncool, unhip, wet behind the ears
6. *clumsy, gauche:* all thumbs, – fingers and thumbs, arsy-versy, gimpsy
phr. 7. *of incompetence:* couldn't run a piss-up in a brewery; couldn't organise a fuck in a brothel

SECURITY
255. Safety; Protection
n. 1. twirl (skeleton key)
2. *to protect:* mind
v. 3. *to protect oneself:* cover your ass, CYA, look after number one, save one's bacon
4. *to stand watch:* give jiggs, keep cave, keep decko, – KV, – jiggers, play chick, – chicken
adj. 5. *safe:* copasetic, in the clear
adv. 6. *secure:* dry land (US black = all clear), home and dry, on a good wicket

256. Danger
n. 1. bad news, – scene, heat, heavy scene, hassle; spec. trick bag (US black = unpleasant situation)
2. *warning:* high sign, tip-off, whisper, (the) word
v. 3. *to warn:* tip (off), put the word about, – out
4. *to endanger:* put in the middle, – on the spot; spec. put in the frame (to frame up)
adj. 5. *dangerous:* heavy, iffy, sus, uncool
excl. 6. *look out!:* heads up!, Hey Rube!, nonnus! (backsl. = someone!), kool toul (backsl. = look out) there'll be blue murder if, watch it!
7. *be careful:* don't do anything I wouldn't do, – take any wooden nickels

ATTAINMENT
257. Success
n. 1. fat city, gorilla, hole in one, killing, numero uno, result, score, smash, smasherino, smasheroo, smashola, sock, sockeroo, sockerino, socko, sockola, three-bagger
v. 2. *to succeed:* ace, beat the game, box clever, break the bank, bring down the house, bring home the bacon, click, come through,

connect, cop a packet, – the lot, crack it, cream, cut the mustard, do (it) up right, get across, get a guernsey (Aus.), get a result, get clear, get it together, get it to the T, get over (US black), get places, go over (big), go over like a house on fire, – like a ton of bricks, go great guns, go to town, hack it, have it dicked, – it taped, – it knocked, hit it (off), knock dead, – cold, KO, make a go (of), make a killing, make (it), – it big, – the grade, make out, mop up, play one's cards right, put it all together, register, score, – big, – heavy, sew up, strike it rich, – paydirt, – oil, take the biscuit, – the cake, turn up trumps, whup the game (US black)

3. *to do successfully:* clean up on, come through, cut it, – the mustard, deliver (the goods), fill the bill, get away (with it), get down, go to town with, hack it, knock for a loop, make a go of, – it stick, – the grade, put (it) across, – (it) over, – over big, wrap (it) up, have it big, wrap (it) up

4. *to be successful:* be there, – the guvnor, – the boss, – number one, get to the top of the heap, – the top of the tree, have it big, wrap (it) up, have it dicked, set the world on fire

adv. 5. *successful:* ahead of the game, doing a hundred (US black), going full blast, – great, great guns, – over big, on the make, – the up and up, on top of the heap, – of the tree, on – velvet, quids in

258. Failure

n. 1. bad job, blow-out, blow-up, brodie, bum deal, – trip, bummer, bust, crackup, crapout, crash, croak, cropper, dive, dud, fadeout, fall, fizzle, flash in the pan, flat tyre, flop, floperoo, flopola, flunk, fold, fold-up, frost, fuck-up, goner, lemon, let-down, mess, miss, muff, no dice, – go, – soap, – sale,

nose-dive, not a bite, – a hope, – a nibble, poop, raw deal, smash, turkey, washout, wipe-out

v. 2. *to fail:* be all up (with), – all washed up, bite the dust, bomb, – off, – out, cave in, cock off, come to grief, come undone, – unstuck, – a cropper, conk out, crap out, crash (out), die, – on the vine, draw a blank, fall down on the job, fall flat, fizzle out, flop, flunk (out), fold (up), fuck up, go all to shit, – all to hell, – all to smash, – all to fuck, – all to buggery, – bluey, – bung, – flooey, – down in flames, – down the pan, – the plug (hole), – down for the third time, – down like a lead balloon, – the drain, – down the tubes, – hang, – phut, – sour, go to pieces, – to the dogs, – to the pack (Aus.), – under, – up the spout, have two left shoes (US black), lay an egg, lose out, lose the ball, miss the boat, – the bus, not cut it, – hack it, etc. (see Success: 257), not get past first base, not hit a lick (US black), peg out, poop out, pull a brodie, score an own goal, shovel shit against the tide, strike out, stub one's toe, suck wind, take a bath, – a fall, – a header, – a nose-dive, – it on the button, – it on the chin, take the count, tube, wipe out; spec. go in the tank, – in the water, take a dive (to fail deliberately)

adv. 3. *failing:* at the end of one's rope, – one's tether, on one's last legs, on the fritz, – kibosh, – skids, riding for a fall

4. *failed:* at the bottom of the heap, blooey, buggered, cold, cooked, cracked, done for, done up, down the pan, – the plug, fizzled out, gone phut, – under, – to hell, – to the dogs, – down the drain, etc., on the rocks, thrown for a loss, upgefucked, up shit creek, up the spout, washed up, wiped out

phr. 5. *resignation:* can't win them all

259. Advantage
n. 1. ace in the hole, – up one's sleeve, beat, card up one's sleeve, drop, edge, hook, inside track, long suit, pull, scoop, set-up, something on one
v. 2. *to have an advantage:* be in on the ground floor, – on the inside, have an ace up one's sleeve, – the inside track, hold all the cards
3. *to put at a disadvantage:* catch bending, come (it) over, do like a dinner, – to a turn (Aus.), fade, have by the short and curlies, – by the short hair, – by the balls, – the edge over, – the drop on, – the jump on, – it over, – cold, – dead to right, – bang to rights, – on toast, – on the run, – one over a barrel, – the drop on
4. *take advantage of:* come something over, give the double-shuffle, put something across, – something past (one), put something over (on), sting, work
adv. 5. *at a disadvantage:* naked

Emotion

FEELINGS
260. Emotion
n. 1. attitude, groove, soul; spec. tude, vibes (one's emotional 'style')
2. *spec. black sensibility:* ebony (US), soul
v. 3. *to undergo emotions:* feel funny, go through changes

261. Sentimentality
n. 1. flapdoodle, goo, gush, hearts and flowers, milk and water, schmaltz (Yid.), slop, slush, sob stuff, sweetness and light, tear-jerking
2. *sentimental talk:* dribble, drool, goo, gush, slobber
v. 3. *to become sentimental:* dribble, drool, gush (over), moon over, slobber
4. *to become mawkish:* give a sob story, go ga-ga, moon about, turn on the water-works
adj. 5. *sentimental:* ga-ga, icky, moony, mushy, sappy, schmaltzy, soppy

---

EXCITABILITY
262. Excitement
n. 1. fireworks, flap, heat, hoopla, kerfuffle, lather, panic stations, shemozzle, stew, stink, streak, sweat, tizzy, to-do, two and eight (rhy.sl. = state), wind-up
2. *a stimulant:* bang, shot in the arm, turn-on
v. 3. *to be excited:* come in one's pants, cream one's jeans, get a bee in one's bonnet, – one's bowels in an uproar, – one's knickers in a twist, – one's shit hot, – steamed up,

go hog-wild, hit the ceiling, – the roof, make a Federal case (out of), run around like a chicken with its head off, wail, work up a circulation, – up a lather, zeek out; spec. let it all hang out (to abandon inhibitions)
4. *to live excitingly:* pace (US black)
5. *to shock:* blow one out, – one's mind, freak one out
adj. 6. *exciting:* hairy, hairy-assed, smoking (US black)
7. *excited:* (all) fired up, (all) hot and bothered, all of a doodah, – of a tiswas, – of a tizzy, hepped up, het up, hopped up, in a lather, – a sweat, – a tizzy, – a twitter, on the hop, psyched (to death), rattled, (all) steamed up, up in the air
excl. 8. tonight's the night! (excited expectation)

263. Nervousness
n. 1. ants in (one's) pants, collywobbles, creeps, edge, heeby-jeebies, jimmies, Jimmy Britts (Aus. rhy.sl. = the shits), jitters, jumps, needle, screaming abdabs, shakes, shim-sham, West Hams (rhy.sl. = West Ham reserves = nerves), willies, wim-wams, yikes; spec. flopsweat (stage-fright); yips (golfer's nerves)
v. 2. *to be nervous:* climb the walls, get the jitters, – shakes, – willies etc., get the wind up, have the breeze up, shizzout
3. *to make a fuss:* do a number, throw a moody, – a wobbler
adj. 4. *nervous:* antsy, busting, edgy, froggy (US black), hyper, jittery, screaming blue murder,

spare, under house, under the cosh,
– the gun, windy
5. *unnerved:* climbing the walls,
cracked up, frazzled, in a frazzle, on
the edge, shattered, shot (to hell, to
pieces), up in the air, uptight
6. *intense:* heavy

264. Impatience
n. 1. lather, stew, sweat
v. 2. *to be impatient:* (to be)
champing at the bit, – hot to trot,
hurt to, in a lather, – sweat, raring
to go, etc. (see adv.)
adv. 3. busting, champing at the bit,
hot to trot, hurting, in a lather, – a
stew, – a sweat, on tiptoe, raring to
go

INEXCITABILITY
265. Calmness
n. 1. cool
2. *emotional freedom:* slack, space
v. 3. *to remain calm:* bite the bullet,
chill out, cool down, – it, hang
loose, keep a tight asshole, – one's
cool, – one's hair on, – the cork on,
lay tight (US black), not turn a hair,
stay cool, taken one's best hold (US
black), track
4. *calm down:* cool, – down, – it,
– off, – the rock, get one's head
together, go off the boil, lighten up,
mellow (out), pull in one's horns,
simmer down
5. *to calm one down:* cool (off), get
someone's head together, mellow
out, tune off
adj. 6. *calm:* laid back, mellow, off
the boil, on a tight leash, Swiss
excl. 7. *calm down!:* cool it!, don't
get your bowels in an uproar!, – get
your knickers in a twist!, – get your
shit hot!, – make a Federal case (of
it)!, keep your hair on!, – your shirt
on!, lighten up!, no muss no fuss!,
pull in your horns! quit racing your
motor!, simmer down!, steady the
buffs!

266. Patience
v. 1. *to be patient:* cool it, hold one's
horses, – one's water, – it down
2. *to endure, tolerate:* go (for), hang
in (there), keep a stiff upper lip,
– one's pecker up, like (it) or lump
(it), not let it get to one, – get one
down, stand still for, stay the pace,
stick with it, take, – it, – it on the
chin, – the nose, etc., tough it out
3. *not tolerate:* take no guff, – no
shit
excl. 4. *be patient:* hang on!, hold
your horses!, hold your water!,
don't shoot the pianist he's doing his
best!

INTEREST
267. Interest
n. 1. hots
v. 2. *to be interested:* fall for, flop
for, go for, give a tumble, – the time
of day, have big eyes for, make a
dead set for, rush, tumble for
3. *to interest.* grab, tick (one)
off
adv. 4. *interested·* all for, hot for,
into, strong on, struck on

268. Desire
n. 1. itch, yen
v. 2. *to want:* choose, do with, go
for, have a yen for, hurt for, spoil
for, want the worst way
3. *to be selfish:* look after number
one, pig it
adj. 4. *desirous:* bursting (for),
crazy (for, to), hopped up, hot
(for), hung for, hurting (for), itchy,
nuts about, nutty, raring (to),
screaming (for), sold on, spoiling
for, steaming, wild (for, to)
5. *greedy:* grabby, piggy
phr. 6. what's in it for me?

269. Ambition
n. 1. get-up-and-go, pizzazz,
stick-to-it-iveness, what it takes (see
Initiative: 236)

v. 2. *to be ambitious:* to have what it takes
adj. 3. *ambitious:* (see Enterprising: 236)

270. Enthusiasm
n. 1. full scream (US black), go, hotcha, oomph, pep, zap, zing, zip, zowie
2. *craze, fad:* bee in the bonnet, bug, -itis, -mania
v. 3. *to be enthusiastic:* be bugs about, carry on (about), crack on (about), flip for, get it up (for), get stuck into, give a shit, go for, – nap on, – on about, – overboard, – to town (on), max out
adj. 4. *enthusiastic:* cooking, full of beans, gung-ho, hung up, jumping, overboard, skied
adv. 5. *enthusiastic about:* as a (Aus.), as a bean (Aus.), bats about, batty about, crazy for, daffy about, gone on, het up over, hot for, – on, hung up on, (all) in a lather about, – a sweat about, etc. (see Excitement: 262), like a good 'un, like crazy, nuts about, rapt (Aus.), shook on (Aus.), stuck on, tiger (for) (Aus.), up in the air over, wild about, worked up (about), wrapped (Aus.)
6. *fanatically:* bugs about, nuts about

DISINTEREST
271. Indifference
n. 1. what-the-hell
v. 2. *to be indifferent:* go off the boil, not give a damn, – a darn, – flying fuck, – a shit, – a tuppenny fuck, – a good goddam, – a hoot, – a monkey's, – give a rap (for), – a stuff, – a tinker's cuss
3. *to act indifferently:* play it cool, sit on the fence
4. *to make no difference:* cut no ice
adj. 5. *indifferent:* deadpan, on the fence, sniffy, stoneface

6. *nonchalant:* flip
excl. 7. *I don't care:* big deal, break my heart, FIGMO (fuck it, got my orders), fuck you Jack I'm all right, I should care, – worry, it's not my funeral, no skin off my arse, – off my nose, see if I care, so what? that's your bad luck, – funeral, – problem, tough tits, what's the percentage?, who gives a damn?, – a fuck?, etc. (see v. 2), what do I do now, cry? beats me, don't ask me, I don't know, – dunno, – wouldn't know, no biggie, three tears and a bucket (US black), your guess is as good as mine, you reckon

272. Dullness; Tedium
n. 1. drag, full tour, snooze job, three-hour tour
2. *something tedious:* corn, fag, history, old hat, – stuff, pain (in the arse), yawn
v. 3. *to bore:* bore stiff, – to tears, – the pants off, have a stick up one's arse
4. *to be bored:* cool off, get jack of (Aus.), (see Disinterest: 271)
adj. 5. *boring:* dead as a doornail, – as a dodo, – from the neck up, – on the vine, dopey, drag-ass, gutty, ho-hum, tired
adv. 6. *bored:* bored stiff, – to tears, drug, fed up with, to have a bellyful of, – skinful, – snootful, jack of (Aus.), sick and tired (of), up to here
excl. 7. *I'm bored:* here we go again, ho-hum, that finishes me, what a life, – a pain

---

PLEASURE
273. Pleasure; Delight
n. 1. bang, buzz, charge, kick, knockout, thrill, turn-on, wallop
2. *pleasant situation:* bee's knees, hot stuff, humdinger, lollapaloosa; spec. sight for sore eyes (a welcome appearance)

v. 3. *to please:* be up one's alley, click with, go down, go over (good), hit the (right) spot, make a hit, score, turn on, turns one's crank
4. *to thrill:* bowl over, give a bang, – buzz, charge, etc. (see n. 1), go over strong, – in a big way, – like a house on fire, – like a million dollars, hit for six, knock dead, – out, – the pants off, lay one out, mow one down, send out of this world, slaughter, slay, throw, tickle (pink), tickle to death, wow
adj. 5. *pleased:* all over oneself, fit to bust, happy as a dog with two tails, – as Larry, – as a sandboy, (see also 274), over the moon, pleased as the devil, – as heck, – as hell, – as punch, stoked, tickled, – pink, -- to death, – to pieces
adv. 6. *pleasant:* ace, bully, cute, daisy, darling, divine, ducky, fantabulous, fucking-A, hotsy, jammy, keen, peachy-keen, the tops, too-too, TF much
excl. 7. *I feel happy:* ain't love grand, – that something, – we got fun, and how, baby, boy, boy-oh-boy, (oh) brother, cowabunga!, daddy, diggety damn, – dog, fucking-A, hey, hotcha, hot-cha-cha, hot damn, – diggety, – diggety dog, – shit, love it to death, man, man oh man, oh mama

274. Happiness; Cheerfulness
n. 1. hoopla, hoot, whoopee
2. *a laugh:* boff, gag, yok, yuk
3. *smile:* spec. shit-eating grin (smug smile)
v. 4. *to laugh:* be in stitches, break up, burst, crack one's face, – up, crease up, fall about, – out, goof on, haw-haw, hee-hee, hoot, laff, piss oneself, roll in the aisles
5. *to make laugh:* bowl over, break up, bring the house down, convulse, get a laugh, hand a laugh, kill, knock them in the aisles, paralyze, put away, put in stitches,

slaughter, slay, tickle the funny bone
6. *to become happy:* brace up, buck up, chirp up, come out of it, drop it, pep up, pull oneself together, snap out of it
7. *to cheer one up:* brace up, buck up, pep up, perk up, pull together
8. *to be happy:* be full of beans, – full of pep, – Mr Laffs, pop
adj. 9. *happy:* bobbish, breezy, chipper, chuffed, grooved, happy as a pig in shit, – as a king, – as Larry, – as you-know-what, high wide and handsome, in the pink, lunchy, nice (US black), one hundred per cent, over the moon, perky, rorty, wrapped tight; spec. slap-happy (slightly eccentric); spec. paralytic, spastic (convulsed with laughter)
10. *merry:* feeling one's oats, feisty, full of beans, larky, on the razzle

275. Contentment; Satisfaction
n. 1. *comfort:* easy street, velvet
v. 2. *satisfy:* cut the mustard, fill the bill, go down one's alley, hold (one's), keep (one's) cool, – sweet, play one's tune, sing one's song, talk one's language, walk on one's side of the street
3. *to be satisfied:* have no beef, – no kick, – no squawk
adj. 4. *satisfactory:* ace(s), all reet, AOK, bang on, can't complain, hunky-dory, (right) in there, jake, jerry, kosher, OK, OK by me, – for my dough, okey-doke(y), okay, a (little) bit of all right, no kick, no squawk, no sweat, on the ball, – the beam, – the button, slap-up, solid, up to snuff
5. *comfortable:* cushy, soft
6. *contented:* all the way live, joint-joint (US black)
phr. 7. *that's satisfactory:* AOK, everything's cool, – hotsy-totsy, – jake, – OK, etc. (see adj. 4), righto, roger, that's affirmative, – a big ten-four, we have lift-off

276. Enjoyment; Fun
n. 1. barrels of fun, barrels of laffs, juice, loads of fun, – of laffs, (a) laugh a line, more fun than a barrel of monkeys

2. *a good time:* (see also Party: 361) action, ball, goof bender, high old time, hot time, shit stopper; spec. the life of Riley (an easy, enjoyable life)

3. *a celebration:* (see also Spree: 98) bat, beano, bender, binge, blast, blow-out, Bushey Park (rhy.sl. = lark), bust, cutup, hi-de-hi, let-go, shindig, shindy, tear, toot, whoopee

v. 4. *to enjoy:* dig, eat up, gas, get down with (US black), – one's thing off (US black), – a bang out of, – a kick out of, etc. (see Thrill: 273), get off on, groove (on), – behind, have a high old time, – a hot time, live it up, – the life of Riley, love it to death, party, rally, swing with, tear up (US black), wig out

5. *to have a good time, celebrate:* bat around, boogaloo, boogie, break loose, cut loose, get one's rocks off, – one's jollies, go bananas, go on a bust, – a shindy, – the razzle, hell around, high-step (it), hit the high spots, jive and juke (US black), kick ass, – up one's heels, let her rip, – one's hair down, make whoopee, paint the town red, raise a hullaballoo, – a racket, – a ruckus, – Cain, – (merry) hell, – sand (US black), skylark, step high wide and handsome, swing, whoop it up

6. *to play the fool:* act up, carry on, clown around, cut up, horse around, kick up one's heels, loon about, play funny buggers, play silly buggers; spec. score yoks (to get laughs); mug (make funny faces)

adj. 7. *playful:* feeling one's oats, feisty, full of beans, etc. (see Animation, Lively: 236)

8. *enjoyable:* hot

adv. 9. *for fun:* for kicks, – laughs, – the hell of it, – trips

phr. 10. *it's been fun:* it's been a slice

277. Wit and Humour
n. 1. *joke:* boff, boffola, crack, fast one, gag, good one, hoot, laff, laff riot, nifty, scream, shit stopper, shriek, yell, yok, yuks; spec. horse laugh (a bad joke); pisser (a very funny joke)

v. 2. *to amuse:* cop the laughs (laffs), crack (one) up, crease (one) up, tickle one's funny bone

3. *to tease:* hack around, josh

4. *to tell jokes:* crack (wise), gag, pull a fast one, – a nifty, etc. (see n. 1)

5. *to play practical jokes:* come it over, horse around with, put over a fast one (on), send for a left-handed monkey wrench, whip the cat

6. *to pull funny faces:* mug

adj. 7. *funny:* killing, rich, ripe wacky

phr. 8. *that's funny:* that's a good one, that's a laugh; spec. funny peculiar or funny ha-ha? (do you mean humorous or not?)

DISPLEASURE
278. Displeasure; Disagreeableness
n. 1. *something unpleasant:* barf city, damper, downer, Motel Hell, nowhere, – city, outers, pain (in the arse), – in the neck, piece of crap, – of shit, pit city, pits, puke, stinker, stinkeroo, tack city

2. *unpleasant time:* dog's life, thin time, tough tittie

v. 3. *to act unpleasantly:* play the heel

4. *to displease:* be hard to take, curdle one's guts, get in one's hair, – up one's arse, – up one's nose, give one a headache, – a pain, – a pain in the arse, – in the neck, stick on one's craw, turn one's stomach, – one's tum

adj. 5. *unpleasant:* bit thick, creepy,

crumby, crummy, deadly,
gut-wrenching, heavy-duty, icky,
icky-poo, jive-ass, low-life,
low-rent, no-hope, on the nose
(Aus.), outers, out of order, putrid,
ratshit, ratty, stinking, stinko,
tacky, ucky, vomitous
adv. 6. *displeased with:* had it
(with), out with, pissed off (with),
up to there with
excl. 7. *of displeasure:* bugger off!,
can you stand for that!, don't give
me that!, drop dead!, fiddlesticks!,
fooey!, fuck off! (out of it), fuck
that for a bowl of cherries!, – for a
lark!, how do you like them
apples?, how does that grab you?, it
shouldn't happen to a dog, nuts!, of
all the . . . !, on your bike!, piss off!,
pull the other one it's got bells on
it!, shit!, shoot!, shucks!, sod off!,
that's just too bad!, the hell with it,
tough shit!, ts, up your arse!, – your
brown!, what's the big idea?, who're
you screwing!, you and who's army,
you would!

279. Sullenness; Depression

v. 1. long face, misery-guts,
sourpuss
2. *depression, misery:* black dog,
blues, dumps, Edgar Britts (Aus.),
glooms, grumps, hump, jimjams,
jimmies, Jimmy Britts (Aus.),
mulligrubs, pits, the pip, red arse
v. 3. *to be sullen, depressed:*
bellyache, come the old moody,
drag one's tail, feel like death
warmed up, gripe, grizzle, grump,
gutache, shit and wish (US black
– 'shit in one hand, wish in another,
see which fills up first'), throw a
moody, wear the dog (US black)
4. *to feel miserable:* be down in the
dumps, – among the wines and
spirits, – in a bad shape, – in the
cellar, feel blue, – ratshit, – sick, get
the hump, get up on the wrong side
of the bed, have (a fit of) the blues,
– the glooms, – the jimmies, etc.

(see n. 1), have one's heart in one's
boots
5. *to depress:* bring down
adj. 6. *sullen:* grouchy, grumpy,
long-faced, mopey, root-faced,
sourpussed, strung out, tight-assed
7. *depressed:* black, blue, brought
down, bummed out, cheesed off,
choked, down, down in the mouth,
drug, fit to bust, hurting, in the
dumps, lower than a snake's belly,
off one's feed, shafted, shot down,
sick as a parrot, torn down (US
black), with one's tail between one's
legs; spec. solitary as a bastard on
Father's Day (Aus. use: lonely)
8. *depressing:* depresso, pit city

280. Temper; Anger

n. 1. bate, peeve, red ass, red pants;
spec. slow burn (gradually rising
temper)
2. *explosion of rage:* blow-up,
carry-on, conniption fit, fireworks,
flare-up, lather, stew, sweat, tizzy
3. *to lose one's temper:* boil over,
blow a fuse, – a gasket, – off steam,
– one's cool, – one's cookies,
– one's cork, – one's gasket, – one's
stack, – one's top, blow it, blow off,
blow up, bust a blood vessel, – a
gut, climb the rigging, – the walls,
create, do one's block, – one's nut,
– the lolly (Aus.), flip, – one's lid,
– one's wig, – out, fly off the
handle, foam at the mouth, get a
hair up one's arse, – hot under the
collar, – mad, – sore, etc. (see adv.
6), – one's dander up, – one's
knickers in a twist, – one's shit hot,
– one's bowels in an uproar, etc.
(see Excitement: 262), – one's back
up, – one's nose out of joint, – the
ass, – the red ass, – the mohawk,
get up on one's hind legs, go ape,
– apeshit, – bananas, – haywire,
– off one's chump, – off one's nut,
– off the deep end, – spare, – up in
the air, – up the wall, grow horns,
have a bellyful (of), – it up to here,

– kittens, – the (dead) needle, – the rag on, hit the roof, kick up a racket, jump down one's throat, jump salty, jump the rails, lose one's cool, – one's hair, – one's marbles, – one's rag, make a (great) to-do, – carry-on, make the fur fly, – the sparks fly, nut up, poke one's mouth off (US black), pop off, – one's cork, raise a ruckus, – (merry) hell, – Cain, – the roof, reach boiling point, run around like a chicken with its head off, see red, simmer, sizzle, smoke, steam (up), throw a fit, – a wingding, trip out, work up (a head of) steam, zeek out, zoon out
4. *to make angry:* burn, get a rise out of, get one's dander up, – one's back up, – one's nose out of joint, – one's mad up, – one going, needle, piss off, rub up the wrong way, ruffle one's feathers, team up
5. *ill-tempered:* crusty, feisty, gritchy, grouchy, in a snit, mean, niggly, ornery, out of sorts, peevish, salty, snappy, sour
adv. 6. *angry:* apeshit, burned (at), fighting mad, (all) fired up, fit to be tied, gutted, hacked, het up, hopping (mad), hot, (all) hot and bothered, in a lather, – a pet, – a peeve, – sweat, jacked (Aus.), leery, loaded for bear, mad, – as a cut snake (Aus.), – as a wet hen, miffed, on one's hind legs, on the muscle, peeved, pissed off, POed, pushed out of shape, raving (mad), sore, steamed (up), uptight, wild

281. Grief
n. 1. hurting dance, pit city, sob stuff
2. *crying:* jag, weeps
v. 3. *to cry:* blub, boohoo, pipe one's eye, squawk, turn on the waterworks

282. Disappointment
n. 1. bring-down, choker, dud, false alarm, frost, lemon, let-down, misfire, no dice, – joy, – soap, sickener
v. 2. *to disappoint:* bring down, burn, dish, fall down on, let down, puncture one's balloon, piss on one's parade, stand up, sting; spec. let down easy (to soften the blow)
3. *to be disappointed:* draw a blank, get left, land with a (dull) thud, lose out, miss the boat, take it on the chin
adj. 4. *disappointed:* burnt, dished, let down, screwed, stood up, stung, taken for a ride
phr. 5. *disappointed:* all dressed up and nowhere to go, looks like he/she lost a pound and found sixpence

283. Anxiety; Worry
n. 1. butterflies (in one's stomach), freak-out, joes (Aus.); spec. all points bulletin (plea for help)
v. 2. *to be worried:* be in a lather, – a stew, – a sweat, drop one's bundle (Aus.), fall apart, freak, give a shit, have a bee in one's bonnet, have kittens, – one's heart in one's boots, piss blood, sweat; spec. feel a draught (US black: to sense racism)
3. *to reveal one's worries:* get it off one's chest, – out of one's system, let down one's hair, spill the beans, take the load off one's mind, unload
4. *to worry:* discombobulate, give one the creeps, mess one's mind, throw one for a loop
5. *to worry about:* have a hard-on for
adj. 6. *worried:* (all) hot and bothered, at the end of one's tether, bitched, buggered and bewildered, blue around the gills, charlie, down, fucked up and far from home, hot pants, in a mucksweat, – a sweat, – stew, – the pits, jacked up, jumpy, sick, uptight, wired
adv. 7. *worrying:* eating (someone), heavy

phr. 8. I can't handle this

284. Annoyance; Vexation
n. 1. bitch, burn, needle, pain, pain in the arse, – the neck, (the) pip; spec. slow burn (increasing rage); aggravation (UK: mutual grievances between police/criminals)
v. 2. *to annoy, vex:* be on one's arse, bitch off, bite, brass off, brown off, bug, burn, burn up, cheese off, drive one nuts, – around the bend, – through the roof, – up the wall, get across, – in one's hair, – one's back up, – on one's wick, – on one's goat, – on one's tits, – one going, – under one's skin, – up one's nose, give one a pain (in the neck, arse), give the needle, – the pip, grief, jerk around, – one's chain, make ignorant, miff, nark, needle, peeve, piss off, put one's back up, – one's nose out of joint, rub (up) the wrong way
3. *to be annoyed:* get the hump, – the needle (with), have a mad on with, – ants in one's pants, – a flea in one's ear, – something biting one, – something eating one, jump salty, steam
4. *to be offended:* get on one's high horse
adj. 5. *irritated:* brassed off, browned off, cheesed off, fed up, had it (with), jacked out, miffed, narked, nettled, on the rag, peeved, pissed (off), ratty, salty, stroppy, teed off, twisted, up a tree; spec. OT&E ('over-tired and emotional' – of an irritable child)
6. *sensitive:* tetchy
7. *perfectionist:* finicky
excl. 8. *of annoyance:* buggeration!, come off it!, don't get funny!, – get smart!, don't mind me I only live/work here!, forget it!

APPROBATION
285. Approval
n. 1. the all-clear, the go-ahead, the nod, the OK, nod and a wink, thumbs-up
2. *recommendation:* blurb, boost, build-up, plug, write-up
v. 3. *approve:* be (all) for, – behind, give the all-clear, – go ahead etc. (see n. 1), have a soft spot for, OK
4. *to recommend:* front for, go to bat for, – to the mat for, go for, – overboard for, put in a (good) word for, stand up for
excl. 5. *of approval:* all the way!, attaboy!, attagirl!, beaut! (Aus.), (God) bless you!, bully (for you)!, dandy!, death!, fair dos! (Aus.), fair enough!, fairy snuff!, for sure!, fucking-A!, good on you! (Aus.), great!, hubba! hubba!, I should be so lucky!, is that good or is that good!, keen, keeno, nice one Cyril!, no sweat!, not half!, not to be sniffed at!, – to be sneezed at!, now you're cooking!, – you're talking!, solid!, swell!, tasty!, that's it!, that's the stuff (to give the troops)!, – telling them!, – the way!, too Irish stew! (rhy.sl. = too true), too right!, what a boy!, – a man!, – a star!, wicked!, you're a pal!, – a peach!, – a prince!, you're darn tootin!, – singing my song!, you tell them!, you wrote the book!

286. Praise
n. 1. boost, plug, puff, push, rap (Aus.), rave; spec. log-rolling (mutual praise)
v. 2. *to support, enthuse:* beat the drum for, bang the drum for, boost, come on strong (for), crack on, go on about, hype, lay it on (heavy/thick), pile it on (heavy/thick), puff, push, root (for), sell (up), talk (it) up
phr. 3. *spec. praise of a passing woman:* I could do that a favour, whap that thing! (US black), whacko the diddle-a (Aus.)

287. Flattery
n. 1. applesauce, banana oil, blarney, build-up, bull, eyewash, flannel, grease job, guyver (Aus.), hokum, oil, soft soap; SEG (abbr. shit-eating grin)
v. 2. *to flatter:* blarney, bull, bullshit, butter up, con (along), dish out the applesauce, – the oil, – a line, feed a line, grease, hand a line (of bull), jolly (along), kid (along), kiss the blarney stone, lay it on (thick), – with a trowel, pat on the back, plaster, pour it on (heavy/thick), shmeer (Ger. = grease), shoot the bull, – the shit, – a line, soft soap, spread it on (thick)
3. *to toady:* arse-lick, back-slap, bootlick, brown-nose, creep, get in (solid) with, – next to, kiss-arse, make up to, pal up to, play up to, polish the apple, roll over for, schmooze (Yid.), stooge for, suck around, suck-arse, suck hind tit, suck up to, wax up, wipe one's arse, – one's nose, yes, yessir

---

DISAPPROBATION
288. Disapproval
n. 1. frost, nix, the no, thumbs-down
2. *disapproving look:* dirty look, old-fashioned look
v. 3. *to disapprove:* be down on, corrode, give the no, – the thumbs-down, nix, not go for, put the thumbs down, turn up one's nose at
adv. 4. *disapproving:* down on, on the coat (Aus.)
phr. 5. *of disapproval:* all yours!, bobkhes! (Yid. anything absurd or insulting), count me out!, no way!, perish the thought!, that's so ill!, you've got to be joking!, yuck!
6. *spec. disapproval of passing girl(s):* don't fancy yours, I wouldn't touch it with a (ten-foot) barge-pole, I wouldn't touch it with yours

289. Objection; Complaint
n. 1. beef, bellyache, bitch, crab, kick, kvetch (Yid.), moody, squawk, yip
v. 2. *to complain:* ballsache, bellyache, beef, beat the gums, bitch, bleat, blow great guns, buck (against), crab (about), go on (about), gritch, grizzle, howl, kick (about), kick up a fuss, – a racket, kvetch, made a Federal case (out) of, – a great how-do-you-do (out of), pitch a bitch, pull one's joint, raise Cain, – a racket, rattle one's beads (gay use), sound off (about/over), squawk, yell blue murder
adv. 3. *complaining:* crooked on (Aus.), on at, po-faced, snippy

290. Censure; Criticism
n. 1. knock, putdown, roasting, slam, slash; spec. hatchet job (journalism); sledging (cricket: on-field barracking)
v. 2. *to criticise:* come down on, come down fonky (US black), come down hard, come down heavy, crab, cut up, go for, go to town on, hack up, hammer, haul over the coals, knock, pull to pieces, put down, roast, rub (US black), savage, slam, slash (up), slice up, take a swipe at, – to pieces; spec. give the duke (to slow handclap)
phr. 3. some people!

291. Scolding
n. 1. bawling out, bit of one's mind, bollocking, calling down, cussing out, dressing down, earful, flea in one's ear, going over, jaw, kick in/up the arse, piece of one's mind, roasting, rocket, rucking, scorcher, serve (Aus.), shakeup, stick, talking-to, toco, what-for, wigging
v. 2. *to scold:* bawl out, – the

(living) hell out of, bear down (on), blow the daylights out of,
– sky-high, bollick, bring one up (US black), carpet, chew one's balls off, chew out, climb all over, come down on, cuss out, cut down to size, dress down, drop on, eat one's arse off, get down dirty, – fonky (US black), give (one) a piece of one's mind, – a (good) talking to, etc. (see n.1.), – one some curry (Aus.), – one some stick, give it hot and heavy, – one the business, – it the works, go after (right and left), go for, go to town on, haul over the coals, jump all over, – up and down on, – on with both feet, lay down the law, lay into, let (one) have it, light into, lower the boom on, make it hot for, pin one's ears back, pull one's coat, put a flea in one's ear, – one through it, – the fear of God into, – through the mill, – the blast on, raise hell with, – the dickens with, – the devil with, etc., read the riot act, – the Rocks and Shoals, ride ragged, roast, rollick, say a mouthful, sit on, slag (off), smack down, take a jab at, – a smack at, talk to like a Dutch uncle, tear off a strip, – a piece (or two), tear one's arse, tell a thing (or two), – what is what, – one where to get off, – where to go, throw the book at, vamp on, wade into; spec. read one's beads (gay use)

3. *to be in trouble:* be on the carpet, – on the mat, catch hell, catch it (hot), get it in the neck

4. *to nag:* break one's balls, go on at, hassle, henpeck, stay on one's case

adv. 5. *nagging:* at the micks, on one's case

292. Disparagement

n. 1. knocking, panning, razzing, (big) razoo

2. *sarcastic remark:* crack, dig, raspberry, razz, shot, shy, slam, slant, slap, sock, swipe

v. 3. *to disparage:* bag, base, blow a raspberry, fire on (US black), give the big razoo, – the finger, knock, pan, pin one's ears back, put the hammer on, razz, shoot down, slam, slap, slash (US black), take a shot, shy etc. (see n. 2), vamp on, weigh into

4. *scorn:* bucket (Aus.), chump off (US black), need like a hole in the head

adj. 5. *sarcastic:* sarky

adv. 6. *scorned:* stuffed

excl. 7. *sarcastic comment:* and you!, (the) answer is a lemon!, back in the knifebox!, be your age!, – yourself!, big deal!, bite the ice!, blow it out (your arse)!, bully for you!, butt out!, cost ya!, does your mother know you're out?, don't ask me, I only work here!, drop dead!, eat it!, eat my shorts!, – shit!, fag your face!, famous last words!, get!, get fucked!, – her!, – him!, – knotted!, – onto yourself!, – out of my way!, – stuffed!, give over!, go (and) bark at the moon!, – boil your head!, – jump in a lake!, – take a long walk off a short pier!, go fuck a dead horse!, – fuck yourself!, – fuck yourself in the ass and get some brains!, – fuck yourself with a rubber wienie!, – piss up a rope (and play with the steam)!, – shit in a pot and duck your head!, – to blazes!, – shit in your hat pull it over your head and call it curls!, go to buggery!, half your luck! (Aus.), stick it up your jumper!, stop moing me!, suck it and see!, sucks to you!, take a flying fuck!, – a running jump!, thanks a bunch, – a million, TS!, tough shit!, up your arse, – your brown, – your jacksie, – yours!, with knobs on!, you'll be sorry!, you slay me!, your mama!; spec. shall I put a bit of hair on it? (to an inept workman); were you

born in a barn? – in a tent? (to
someone who has left a door open)
8. *contempt:* be hanged, blah!, fuck
you!, huh!, nuts to you!, phooey!,
pooh!, screw you!, the hell with it!,
– with you!

293. Ridicule; Banter

n. 1. Bronx cheer, hee-haw, horse
laugh, panning, raspberry, razz, rib,
roast
2. *teasing:* codology, kidology,
joshing, kidding, ragging, taking the
Michael, – the mickey, – the piss
3. *gesture of derision:* the finger,
two fingers of scorn, V-sign
v. 4. *to ridicule:* cast nasturtiums,
give the bird, needle, pan, razz, rib,
roast
5. *to tease:* bull, extract the Michael,
get gay with, get one at it, – going,
give one the business, – the leg,
haze, howl, jack around, josh, kid,
move one, piss-take, pull one's leg,
– one's pisser, put on, rag, rib, send
up, shoot on, sling off (Aus.),
sound, stick it to, take the Michael,
– the mickey, – the piss, wind up
6. *to make a rude gesture or noise:*
flip the bird, give a Bronx cheer, – a
raspberry, – the finger
phr. 7. *you silly fool:* (now you've)
been and gone and done it

294. Vilification; Slander

n. 1. spec. dozens, dirty dozens,
momma's game (US black: ritual
'games' of insult)
2. *slander:* dirt, muck, mud,
mudslinging, poison, shit-stirring,
smear
3. *abuse:* bullyrag, (the) hard word,
rough edge of the tongue, verbals
v. 4. *to vilify:* slag off, talk trash;
spec. play the dozens, shoot the
dozens (see n. 1)
5. *to slander:* bad-mouth, crap on,
dish the dirt (about), poormouth,
put the bad word on, – the hard
word on, – out the poison, rank,

sling dirt, – mud, – shit, smear, stir
shit, stab in the back
6. *to abuse:* bullyrag, call (one) out,
chew out, curse out, give the hard
word, – rough edge of one's tongue,
lay into, let loose on (see Scold:
291), put down, rubbish, schpritz
(Yid.), snipe on (US black)

COURAGE

295. Courage; Confidence

n. 1. Aristotle (rhy.sl. = bottle),
arry, balls, bottle (rhy.sl. = bottle
and glass = arse = 'bottom'), brass
balls, cojones, face, grit, guts, hair,
heart, intestinal fortitude, moxie,
rocks, rooks (US black), spunk, stiff
upper lip, stones, what it takes;
spec. Dutch courage (liquor-induced
bravery)
v. 2. *to be brave:* be a man, have
(plenty of) what it takes
3. *to encourage:* brace up, buck up
4. *to encourage oneself:* keep a stiff
upper lip, – one's chin up, – one's
pecker up
adj. 5. *brave:* ballsy, game (for
anything), gutsy, nervy, spunky
excl. 6. *of encouragement:* buck up,
it will all come out in the wash,
don't make a production out of it,
worse things happen at sea, (keep
your) chin up!, don't let the
bastards grind you down, keep your
pecker up, the first hundred years
are the hardest, cheer up – the
worst is yet to come!, it's a great life
if you don't weaken!, be a devil!, go
for it!, snap out of it!, stay with it!,
hang in there!, up there Cazaly!
(Aus.); spec. break a leg!
(theatrical)

296. Cowardice

n. 1. dog, funk, yellow streak; spec.
edge city (at one's emotional limits)
2. *fear.* blue funk, cold feet, creeps,
horrors, white-knuckler
v. 3. *to be a coward:* bottle out,

chicken out, cop out, get cold feet, have a yellow streak (right down one's back), lose one's bottle, punk out; spec. can dish it out but can't take it (usually of a weak bully) 4. *to be afraid:* get the wind up, have one's heart in one's mouth, pack 'em (Aus.), piss (in) one's pants, shit a brick, – bricks, – oneself, wear brown trousers, wet one's pants
5. *to frighten:* freak out, give a bad moment, – a turn, make one's hair curl, psych out, put the fear of God into, – the frighteners on, rattle, scare stiff, – the bejazaus out of, – the pants off, – the shit out of, spook, throw a scare into, wierd out
adv. 6. *cowardly:* chicken, CS, chickenshit, chicken-hearted, dripping, gutless, nervy, weedy, wet, wimpy, yellow, yellow-bellied
7. *afraid:* freaked (out), in a blue funk, packing 'em (Aus.), pissing oneself, scared shitless, – stiff, shit-scared, shitting bricks, – oneself, spooked, white about the gills

---

PRIDE
297. Pride; Conceit
n. 1. high-hatting, (old) acid, snippiness
v. 2. *to be conceited, arrogant:* be too big for one's britches, come it, get a swelled head, – above oneself, have one's nose in the air, high-hat, put on dog, strong it, think one is 'it', throw one's weight around, upstage
adj. 3. *arrogant:* all over oneself, boasie (WI), cocky, dickty (US black), flash, Flash Gordon (US black), highfalutin', high-toned, hincty, hoity-toity, la-de-dah, on one's high horse, smart-ass, smartypants, snobby, snooty, snotty, stuck-up, stuck on oneself,

stuffy, toffee-nosed, too big for one's britches, uppish, uppity
adv. 4. *arrogant:* on one's high horse
excl. 5. *don't be so conceited:* come down off your high horse, – off your perch, come off it, who do you think you're fooling?
phr. 6. more front than Brighton beach, more hide than Jessie (Aus.)

298. Ostentation
n. 1. dog, frills, high-sidin' (US black), high-steppin' (US black), side, splash, splurge, swank
v. 2. *show off:* act the nigger (US black), come on strong, cut a swath, fan, flame (gay use), flash (it about), grandstand, lay it on (thick), peddle one's wares, ponce about, put on (the) dog, put on jam (Aus.), spread it about, strut one's stuff, tart about, show boat, style, throw one's weight around; spec. put on the guiver (to affect a smart accent)
3. *to ornament:* ponce up, tart up
4. *to put on airs:* high-side, high-step (US black), get on one's high horse, put on the ritz, put on frills, – one's high hat, put on the dog, put on jam (Aus.), swank
adj. 5. *ostentatious:* flash, – as a rat with a gold tooth, flossy, jazzy, nouveau, piss elegant, saddity, screaming, sidity, swanky, tarty

299. Boasting
n. 1. ballyhoo, blatherskite, bosh, BS, bull, bullshit, flapdoodle, gas, hot air, six-sheeting, three-sheeting, tall talk, wind
v. 2. *to boast:* advertise, ballyhoo, blow black (US black), blow hard, blow heavy, blah, blow one's own trumpet, broadcast, BS, bull, bullshit, come on like gangbusters, come the big note (Aus.), crack on, crap on, fiend on (US black), gam (US black), gas, give it all that,

grand (US black), high-side (US black), lairize (Aus.), let off some hot air, loudmouth, loudtalk, mouth off, lip off, pop off (at the mouth), put the bee on, run a line, scream some heavy lines (US black), sell a wolf ticket (US black), shoot off at the mouth, shoot the bull, shovel shit, skite (Aus.), spread the bull, swank, talk shit (US black), three-sheet,

adj. 3. *boastful:* all mouth and trousers, – piss and wind, mouthy, smart-arse

excl. 4. *boasting:* did I ever!, is the Pope a Catholic!, does the bear shit in the woods!, is the bear a Catholic, does the Pope shit in the woods, watch my dust!

HUMILITY
300. Humility; Meekness
n. 1. back seat
2. *humiliation:* bring-down, climb-down, come-down, crow, putdown, take-down
v. 3. *to be humble:* be on the (strict) QT, eat crow, fly low, keep a low profile, lie low, take a back seat
4. *to humiliate:* bring down, burst one's bubble, come down on, jump on (with both feet), knock (down), – off one's perch, knock the bottom out of, – the stuffing out of, – the kibosh out of, – off one's high horse, puncture one's balloon, put (one) down, put one where they belong, – the skids under, – one's nose out of joint, settle one's hash, squash, squelch, take the wind out of one's sails, – down a peg, – a few pegs, – the starch out of, tell where to get off

5. *to be humiliated:* come down to earth, – a peg, – a few pegs, land on one's arse, lower one's flag, take a fall, tuck in one's tail

301. Embarrassment
v. 1. *to embarrass:* burn, get, put in the hot seat, – on the spot
2. *to be embarrassed:* be in the hot seat, – on the spot, feel like a horse's arse, – like nothing on earth, – like hell, – like two cents, wilt
3. *to hurt one's feelings:* get one (where it hurts), get one where they live, step on one's corns, touch a soft spot
excl. 4. *of embarrassment:* I could have died!, I didn't know where to put myself!, was my face red!

302. Submissiveness
n. 1. back seat, cave-in, climb-down, second fiddle
v. 2. *to give in:* back down, break, break it down (Aus.), call all bets off, – it a day, – it quits, chuck it (in), chuck up the sponge, crack, cry uncle!, give up as a bad job, give it a miss, go under the table!, – in the tank, knuckle under, take the count, throw in the towel, – the sponge, – one's cards, – one's hand
3. *to be subservient:* crawfish, dep (act as deputy), eat crow, kiss arse, play second fiddle, play the Tom (US black), take a back seat, Tom (US black)
adj. 4. *subservient:* whipped; spec. hincty (US black derog. ref. to blacks who ape whites)
excl. 5. *of resignation:* if you can't beat 'em join 'em, that's the ball game, that's the way the cookie crumbles

Morality and Religion

INTEGRITY
303. Morality
n. 1. straight and narrow; spec. Brownie point (an award for 'goodness')
adj. 2. *moral:* tallawah (WI), white
3. *self-righteous:* pi, prissy, stuffy

304. Obligation
n. 1. *responsibility:* load
2. *to be responsible:* pay one's dues, pick up the tab, put one's money where one's mouth is, stand up, stick one's neck out
3. *to make responsible:* wish on, – upon
4. *to deserve:* be in line for, get one's come-uppance, have it coming
adv. 5. *due:* down to

305. Honesty
n. 1. fair go (Aus.), fair shake (Aus.), the handsome thing, no stuff (US black), square shake, straight poop, – goods, – shit, – shooting
2. *blamelessness:* clean nose, – sheet
v. 3. *to be honest:* act on the square, be on the level, – on the legit, – on the up-and-up, etc. (see adj. 6), lay (it) on the line, – one's cards on the table, play it square, – with a clean deck, shoot straight, – square, toe the line, walk the line
4. *to treat fairly:* be one hundred per cent with, do the handsome thing, give a fair crack of the whip, – a fair shake, – a square shake, play it straight (down the line), – the game, – the white man
5. *to be blameless:* have a clean nose, – a clean sheet, keep one's

nose clean, – in the clear, stay kosher
adj. 6. *honest:* clean, dinkum (Aus.), for real, kosher, (on the) legit, on the level, outfront, ridgie-didgie (Aus.), righteous, straight, up and up, upfront, white
7. *frank:* straight from the shoulder, – down the line
8. *trustworthy:* A1, aces, all wool and a yard wide, blowed in the glass, dinkum (Aus.), kosher, the (real) McCoy, the (real) McKay, on the level, – the legit, – the square, one hundred per cent, regular, right, solid, sure-fire, sure-as-shit
excl. 9. *honest!:* fair crack of the whip!, fair dinkum! (Aus.), fair shake of the dice!, on my life!, stand on me!, straight up!, strictly!, you know me Al!

IMPROBITY
306. Immorality; Evil
n. 1. bad news, backmark (US black), no-no
v. 2. *to become immoral:* crack up, go blooey, – downhill, – down the chute, – down the tubes, – haywire, – smash, – to the dogs, – to the bow-wows, – to hell (on a rocket), – to pot, – to shit, – to the devil, hit the rocks, – the skids, smash up
adj. 3. *immoral:* alias (WI), as bad as they come, – as they make them, left-handed, low-down, low-rent
4. *tough:* hard-boiled, heavy-duty, mean
5. *risqué:* adult, blue, hot, juicy, ra+uncy, spicy, strong

307. Dishonesty
n. 1. dodge, emag (backsl. = game), funny business, graft, lurk (Aus.), racket; spec. payola (bribery to gain publicity)
v. 2. *to be dishonest:* fall down on, go back on, lay down on (see also Crime: 460 ff)
adj. 3. *dishonest:* bent, – as a nine bob note, fishy, funny, iffy, off, sneaky
4. *untrustworthy:* bent, cronky (Aus.), lurky, wrong
phr. 5. *of distrust:* I wouldn't trust him/her as far as I could throw him/her

308. Unfairness
n. 1. carve-up, dirty deal, dirty pool, dirty work (at the crossroads), funny business, not cricket, raw deal, the dirty, the shaft
v. 2. *to treat unfairly:* do one dirt, do the dirty (on), hit below the belt, play (one) dirty, pull off some funny business, – off
adj. 3. *unfair:* below the belt, crummy, low-down, low-rent
adv. 4. *treated unfairly:* shafted, screwed

309. Dissoluteness; Dissipation; Self-Indulgence
n. 1. the life of Riley, the Life (US black underworld), the fast lane, – track
v. 2. *to live 'fast':* fly high, go for broke, go it, – the pace, hit the high spots, kick up one's heels, play the giddy goat, rip it up, run in the fast lane, – the fast track, step high (wide and handsome), tear it up, whoop it up
3. *to indulge oneself:* bust loose, kick over the traces, let oneself go, let loose, loosen up, take the lid off
adj. 4. *dissolute:* fast, sporty

DECEPTION
310. Deception; Deceit
n. 1. bill of goods, bull, bullshit, bunk, bunkum, con, crap, eyewash, hanky-panky, jiggery-pokery, jive, kidology, moonshine, put up job, shuck, snowfall, snow job, window dressing
2. *trick:* all done by mirrors, bunco, dirty pool, dodge, fast one, gaff, gag, okey-dokey (US black), old moody, (one's) little game, racket, ramp, ripoff, sucker trap; spec. crib (examination aid); long con (long-term con trick), short con (short-term con trick) (see also Confidence Trick: 491)
3. *hoax, swindle:* cod, con, dry shave, fast shuffle, fiddle, gyp, hook, job, mace, number, put-on, shakedown, sell, skin, touch
v. 4. *to deceive:* bamboozle, blag, blow past, chi-ike, chump, con, criss-cross (US black), deal them from the bottom of the deck, do brown, – down, – in the eye, drop one in it, flimflam, flummox, get the drop on, give (one) a fast shuffle, give (one) the business, hand a lemon, have on toast, have one on, lead up the garden path, play for a sucker, play the con, – the nut role, pull an act, – a fast one, put down a routine, put it across (on), – the shuck on, – one over (on), rat fuck, RF, ring it on, rip off, rope in, run one way and look another (US black), sam, scale (Aus.), sell a bill of goods, sham on (US black), show out, shuck, snow, string along, suck, take for a ride, – for a sucker, two-time, work
5. *to fool:* cod, goose, jive, josh, kid, pull one's leg, – the wool over one's eyes, send on a humbug trip (US black), throw a curve (to), – dust in one's eyes
6. *to defraud:* ace, – out of, beat for, beat (one) out of, burn, chisel, chizz, diddle, do, – a job on,

– brown, – over, flim-flam, fuck out of, game, get the fat off (Aus.), gazump, gessump, gyp, give a fucking, – a screwing, hook for, lay for, take for, jip (out of), half-ounce (rhy.sl. = bounce = short-change), have, have one over, – one on, Jew (derog.), knock, mace, milk, nail, pluck, promote, ring the changes, rip off, roll, rook, scale (Aus.), screw, sell (one) a pup, send to the cleaners, shake down, shanghai, shave, skin, stick it up, sting, take to the cleaners, trim, tuck up, weed; spec. gas and run (fill up without paying); walk the check (leave without paying)
7. *to hoax:* BS, bull (along), bullshit, cod, feed a line, – load of baloney, have on a string, hand a linc (of bull, baloney, etc.), hokum, jolly (along), josh, keep (one) on a string, kid (along), lay it on thick, pile it on (thick), play (along), shoot the bull, – a line, string along, toss a line
8. *to be tricked:* be bamboozled, – done up brown, – given a fast shuffle, had, etc. (see v. 4, 6), fall for, get a haircut, – it in the neck, – suckered, go for, jump at, play out of the pocket (US black), swallow (hook, line and sinker), tumble for
adj. 9. *deceitful:* full of shit, leery, near the mark, snaky
10. *cheating:* macing, stuffing (US black)
11. *cheated:* done, x-ed out (US black)
phr. 12. *warning:* don't take any wooden nickels

311. Falsification; Sham
n. 1. bunkum, dud, phony, phonus balonus, ringer, Sexton Blake (rhy.sl. = fake), snide; spec. Oliver (rhy.sl. = Oliver Twist = fist = false entry in a ledger); slum (fake jewellery)

2. *pretence:* act, blind, front, put-on, smoke screen
v. 3. *to falsify:* cook (the books), pad (a bill), ring, sell a pup
4. *to pretend:* come it, come the old soldier, drum up, fake it, go through the motions, make like, play dumb, pull an act, swank; spec. pass (for a Jew to act as a Christian, a gay to act as a heterosexual, etc.)
adj. 5. *false:* brummagem, bent, bum, cheesy, cooked (up), doctored (up), dud, hokey, jive, not all that it seems, phony, snide
adv. 6. *faked:* ain't holding no air (US black)

312. Falsehood; Lie
n. 1. ackamaracka, balls, BS, bull, bullshit, crap, fanny, fib, fish story, get up, good one, jiggery-pokery, jive, likely story, moody, one (US black: one big lie), pitch, porky (rhy.sl. = pork pie), sell, snow, snow job, straight shit, tall story, – tale, whopper
v. 2. *to lie:* blow smoke up one's arse, BS, bull, bullshit, cluck a daffy (S.Afr.), crap, draw a long bow, feed one a line, – one stuff (US black), fib, fudge, fly a kite, give a little leg, jive, lumber, pile it on (thick), play stuff (US black), prop up, shit through one's teeth, three-sheet
adj. 3. *exaggerated:* gross, howling, thumping, thundering, whacking, whopping
phr. 4. *am I lying?:* can you see green in my eyes? (S.Afr.), would I shit you (you're my favourite turd)?

313. Treachery
n. 1. dirty work (at the crossroads), funny business, the shaft
v. 2. *to be treacherous:* dingo (Aus.), give one some funny business, – the shaft, play (one) dirty, stab in the back

3. *double-cross:* cross, cross up, two-time
adj. 4. *treacherous:* two-faced, two-timing

314. Betrayal
n. 1. squeal, tipoff
v. 2. *to betray:* do the dirty (on), fink (on), front one off (US black), play Judas, put the finger on, rat on, sell down the river, sell out, spill the beans on, turn in (see also Crime: 481, Crime: 501)
3. *to turn against:* go back on, go sour on, lay down on, poop out on

315. Entrapment
n. 1. fit up, fix, frame up, put up job, set-up
v. 2. *to entrap:* drop (right) in, fit up, frame up, put in the frame, set up; spec. plant (to 'discover' false evidence); (see also Crime: 497)

CULPABILITY
316. Accusation; Blame
n. 1. beef, knock, rap
v. 2. *to accuse:* call the turn on, drop on, finger, hang something on, knock, pip (something) on, put the finger on, – the shoe on the right foot (US black), shift the weight, throw down on (see also Crime: 481)
3. *to blame unfairly:* bark up the wrong tree, put the shoe on the left foot (US black), smear
4. *to take the blame for:* be left holding the baby, – holding the bag, carry the can (for), take the rap (for)

317. Vindication
n. 1. let-off, let-out
2. *excuse:* blind, (load of) flannel, song-and-dance, stall
v. 3. *to acquit:* give an out, slide; spec. spring (to free a prisoner); (see also Crime: 504)

4. *to make an excuse:* alibi out of, clean up (US black), give a song and dance, stall along
5. *to apologise:* eat crow, – dirt, – one's words

318. Punishment
n. 1. rap
2. *chastisement:* dose, dressing-down, going over, shellacking, trimming, what-for
3. *beating:* anointing, basting, clouting, fanning (one's arse), hiding, larruping, lathering, leathering, licking, polishing, seeing-to, shellacking, strap oil, swishing, tanning (one's arse/hide), toco, welting, whacking; spec. kneecapping (IRA punishment)
v. 4. *to punish:* attend to, bear down on, bust loose on, come down on, crack down on, do, – for, go after, – for, fix, get on one's arse, – one's case, – one's tail, give a dose, – a dressing-down, etc. (see n. 2), give (merry) hell, – it to, – the business, – the works, – one Larry Dooley (Aus.), hang one to the wall, have one's guts for garters, let one have it, – it in the neck, – have what-for, go at, – to town on, jump on (with both feet), knock it out of, land on, lay on, light into, make it hot for, pour (it) on, nail to the wall, put through the grinder, – the mill, – through it, – through the hoop, – under the cosh, raise Cain with, – merry hell with, settle one's hash, skin alive, spifflicate, turn inside out, walk into (see Crime: 502, Crime: 503)
5. *to beat:* anoint, bash, baste, beat the daylights out of, – the devil out of, – the hide off, beat up, dust one's coat, fan, give a basting, – a clouting, etc. (see n. 3), hammer, knock the stuffing(s) out of, larrup, lather, lay into, leather, lick the hell out of, – the tar out of, – the pants off, – to a frazzle, nail to the wall,

pan, shellac, sock, swack, swish, tan (one's arse/hide), tickle one's tail, wallop, whale the shit out of, – the tar out of, whop
6. *to be punished:* cop it, draw the crow (Aus.), eat shit, get it in the neck, take it on the chin, – one's lumps, – the fall, – the gas, – the knock, catch (merry) hell, catch it, get it (good and hot), get toco; spec. have it coming and going (be punished twice) (see Crime: 502, Crime: 503)
7. *to accept one's punishment:* face the music, get what's coming to one, – one's come-uppance, pay the piper, stand up and take it, take it (like a man), – one's medicine, – the rap
8. *to deserve punishment:* be riding for a fall, be for it, – in for it, – on the spot, have it coming, let oneself in for it
9. *to escape punishment:* beat the rap, duck the rap (see Crime: 504)

REPARATION
319. Confession
n. 1. come-across, cough (up), squawk, squeak
v. 2. *to confess:* come across (with the goods), come clean, – one's cocoa, – one's fat (Aus.), – one's lot, cough (up), fess up, get (it) off one's chest, – (it) out of one's system, – (it) off one's mind, level (with), open up, out with (it), put up one's hand, sing, spill (it), spill one's guts, – the beans, – it out, squawk, squeak, talk, unload (see also Crime: 481, Crime: 501)
3. *force to confess:* break (down), crack, – wide open, make one sing, put the arm on, third degree

320. Reform
n. 1. clean-up; spec. Black justice (black self-determination)

v. 2. *to reform:* clean up, clean up one's act, go legit, – square, – straight

RELIGION
321. Religion
n. 1. spec. fish-eater, Taig (derog: Roman Catholic); God slot (compulsory religious hour on UK TV)
adv. 2. *religious:* holier-than-thou, nearer-my-God-than-thee, pi

322. Religious Activities
v. 1. *spec. take a collection:* pass the hat

323. Religious Person
n. 1. bible-banger, bible-basher, bible-puncher, Holy Joe
2. *spec. Salvation Army:* Sally Ann, Salvo (Aus.)
3. *preacher, priest:* Holy Joe, sky pilot
4. *charlatan:* mitt man

324. Religious Buildings and Organisations
n. 1. *church:* Godbox
2. *YMCA:* Y
3. *Salvation Army:* Sally Ann, Salvo (Aus.)

325. Supernatural Beings
n. 1. *euphemisms for God:* dad, gad, gawd, golly, gor, gorra, gorry, gosh, gor, gum, Lawd, lawdy, lawks, laws, lor, Lordy
2. *euphemisms for Christ:* Christmas, Christopher (Columbus), crikey, criminy, cripes, gee, geez, jayzus, jeez, Jesus H. Christ
3. *the Devil:* deuce, dickens, divil, Old Bendy, – Billy, – Blazes, – Boots, – Boy, – Cain, – Clootie, – Dad, – Driver, – Gentleman, – Gooseberry, – Harry, – Horny, – Lad, – Ned, – Nick, – One,

– Poger, – Poker, – Roger, – Ruffin,
– Scratch, – Serpent, – Toast, Sam
Hill
4. *ghost:* bogeyman, boogieman,
spook

326. Afterlife
n. 1. *heaven:* happy hunting
grounds, harp farm
2. *hell:* blazes, blue blazes,
Hades

327. Sorcery; Magic
n. 1. hocus-pocus
v. 2. *to put a spell on:* hex, hoodoo,
put the hex on

Human Relations

FRIENDLINESS
328. Friendship
n. 1. *welcome:* glad hand
v. 2. *to make friends:* buddy up, chum up, get next to, get one's feet under the table, hit it off, pal up (with)
3. *to get on with:* click (with), knock along with
4. *to be popular with:* be in good with, – on the right side of, – in with, etc. (see adv. 9), rate, stand good with, sit right with
5. *to be overfriendly:* glad hand; spec. press flesh (for a politician to shake hands)
6. *to associate with:* hang around with, hook up with, mob up with, run with, tie in with, – up with
adv. 7. *friendly:* buddy-buddy, chummy, down with, hope-to-die (US black), in one's corner, one on one, pally, palsy-walsy, running with, thick with, tight with
8. *intimate:* on speakers; spec. just quietly (Aus. between you and me)
9. *popular with:* aces with, in good with, in solid (with), in with, into, next to, on the right side of
excl. 10. *terms of friendship:* ace, amigo, baby, babes, babycakes, bless your little cotton socks, buggerlugs, diddums, ducks, love, lovey, sunshine

329. Kindliness; Consideration
n. 1. TLC (tender loving care)
v. 2. *to be kind:* have one's heart in the right place
3. *to be lenient:* ease up on, let down easy, let up on, pull one's punches

adj. 4. *kind:* big hearted, soft
excl. 5. don't worry it may never happen, upsidaisy, worse things happen at sea, you can't win them all

330. Reconciliation
v. 1. *to reconcile:* square up
2. *to be reconciled:* bury the hatchet, get clear with

HOSTILITY
331. Estrangement
n. 1. break-up, bust-up, splitsville
v. 2. *to become estranged:* break it off, – up, – with, bust up, call it a day, – it quits, chuck, ditch, dump, give one the brush(-off), part brass rags, split (with), throw over, wash one's hands of (see also Reject: 224, Jilt: 353)

332. Enmity; Disfavour
n. 1. frost, hard word; spec. shit list (black list); spec. Jim Crow laws (racist laws in US)
v. 2. *to dislike:* be down on, – off, go off, – sour on, have a down on, have a hard-on for, – a hate on, – it in for, – no love lost for, not go nap on (Aus.)
3. *to earn disfavour:* get in bad with, – on the outs with; spec. one's name is mud (to be unpopular)
adv. 4. *on bad terms:* in bad (with), in Dutch (with), – the doghouse, – wrong (with), off of, on the outs, on the outer (Aus.), out with, washed up with, went down like a pork chop at a Jewish wedding

333. Jealousy
v. 1. *to be jealous:* eat one's heart out
phr. 2. *of jealousy:* all right for some, I should be so lucky, nice work if you can get it

334. Malice
n. 1. cussedness, shenanigans ·
2. *grudge:* axe to grind, bitch, bone to pick, down, peeve
v. 3. *to cause trouble for:* louse (one) up, mess over, put the mockers on, rubbish, trash; spec. put the black on (blackmail); set up (place in a vulnerable situation)
4. *to provoke trouble:* gee up, head-hunt (US black)
5. *to hold a grudge:* be down on, have an axe to grind, – a bone to pick, – a down on, – a peeve with, – it in for
adj. 6. *malicious:* mean, mean-hair, ornery, shitty

335. Retaliation; Revenge
n. 1. comeback, paybacks (US black)
v. 2. *to take revenge:* come back at, even the score, fix, settle one's hash, settle up, square (it), stuff
3. *to seek revenge:* be out for blood

336. Intimidation
n. 1. big stick, frighteners, screws
v. 2. *to intimidate:* buffalo, bulldoze, bullyrag, come down on, come down fonky (US black), – heavy, hang tough, hard-talk, heavy, lean on, put the arm on, – the bull on, – the cosh on, – the frighteners on, – the screws on, – the squeeze on, – the wind up, stand over (Aus.), weird out; spec. kneecap (IRA punishment) (see also Cowardice: 300)
excl. 3. *threats:* or else!, I don't mean maybe!, I'll knock your block off!
4. *counter to threats:* oh yeah!, sez who!, you and whose army!

337. Rough Treatment
n. 1. muscle, rough-house, rough stuff, strong arm stuff (see also Kill: 118); spec. heading, nutting; knuckle sandwich
2. *a blow:* backhander, bang, haymaker, lick, old one-two, one (ie 'fetch him one'); spec. Christmas hold (on the testicles), king (Aus. kinghit = knockout punch)
v. 3. *to manhandle:* be rough on, bounce, cut up rough, – up rusty, hand out punishment, – a bit of stick, get tough with, rough up, tough up
4. *to hit:* banjo, barrel (Aus.), bash, bean, belt, boff, boot (around), burst, bust (one) up, clip, clobber, clock, clunk, conk, crown, dance on one's lips, deck, dish it out, do a job on, do over, drive on (US black), duff over, duff up, duke, dust (one), flatten, get in one's eye (US black), give a fourpenny one, give one the leather, go down on, go the knuckle (Aus.), go upside one's head (US black), grunge, hang one on, jam one up (US black), job (Aus.), kick (one's) arse, kick the stuffing out of, knee, knock one's block off, knock the bejazus out of, – the stuffing out of, lump, nut, paste, pepper one up (US black), plaster, pop (in the eye), put a hurting on (US black), put one on, – one's arse in sling, – the boot in, – the leather in, ring one's bell, roak (US black), run over, run sets on (US black), run up the side of one's head (US black), scone (Aus.), scrag, slosh, slug, sock, spank, stick one on, stomp, take a pop (at), tan one's hide, throw a punch, throw hands (US black), tump over, whack, whale the piss out of, – the shit out of, – the tar out of, whap, whup, wooden (Aus.), work over

5. *to knock out:* cold-cock,
cold-deck, drop, kayo, knock cold,
KO, lay out, put (one) away, put
one's lights out
6. spec. chive, let the daylights into,
stick (stab); skullneck (decapitate);
stripe (slash)
7. *to shoot:* bang off, blast, blow
away, blow one's head off, chop,
drill, give it to, – (one) lead
poisoning, let have it, nail,
perforate, plug, put the blast on,
shoot the daylights out of, take a
crack at
8. *to wound, hurt:* hurt, nip; spec.
mark up (bruise)
9. *to kick:* give the leather, leather
adv. 10. *hit on the head:* boned

338. Attack; Assault
n. 1. *a fight:* aggro, barney, bovver,
confusion (WI), ding-dong,
donnybrook, dust-up, fair, fist
junction (US black), kick-up (WI),
knock-down drag-out, knuckle,
mash-up (WI), pasting, punch-up,
rashing (US black), ruffle (US
black), rumble, scrap, spillin' (US
black), stoush (Aus.), thumb (US
black), up-and-downer; spec. shin
battle (a fake battle); spec. queer
bashing, Paki-bashing,
nigger-bashing (attacks on gays,
Pakistanis, blacks)
2. *rape:* drumstick case (US black)
v. 3. *to fight:* bop, duke it out, get
down from the Y (US black), give
the works (to), go from the Y, go
from the fists, go from the
shoulders, gunzel (US black), kick
(some) ass, lay into, lock arseholes,
mess up, mess with, mix it, rain on,
rough-house, shuffle, snap
arseholes, sort out, straighten
4. *to attack:* beat up (on), blaze on
(US black), do, do up, get tore in,
get stuck into, go down, go round
with, jack up, make a pass at,
muscle in, rip into, sail into,
sandbag, sic onto, snag, tear into,

tear one a new arsehole, vamp on
(US black)
5. *to beat, defeat:* beat the can off,
– the pants off, – the shit out of,
boff, bop, break in half, brown-slice
(WI), cream, crease, do over, do to
a turn, do up (brown), donkey-lick
(Aus.), dough-pop, eat up, flatten,
floor, give it to (one) good, give
lumps, give the chop, give the works
to, hang one out to dry, have one's
guts for garters, jam one up (US
black), jump all over, knacker,
knock bowlegged, – for a loop,
– hell west and crooked, – into the
middle of next week, – one's socks
off, – one's teeth down his throat,
– silly, leave for dead, lick, make
mincemeat of, mogador (rhy.sl. =
floor), mullah, paste, push one's
face through the back of one's neck,
put (one) away, shove one's fist
down his throat, smear all over the
map, take to the cleaners, wax one's
tail, wax, whale the shit out of,
– the tar out of, whip one's arse,
wipe out, work over good; spec.
mummy (US black: beat to death)
6. *to rape:* gorilla, jam one up (US
black)
7. *to ambush:* jap, jump, snag
adv. 8. *beaten up:* done over, done
up (like a kipper)
9. *aggressive:* scrappy

CO-OPERATION
339. Co-operation
n. 1. cahoots, get-together,
hook-up, tie-in, tie-up
v. 2. *join in:* case out, hook up with,
lock into, muck in, play ball (with),
tie up with, tie into; spec. re-up (US
milit: to re-enlist)
3. *to involve:* get one in (on an act),
ring in, rope in
4. *to do one's share:* do one's bit,
keep one's end up, pull one's
weight, weigh in
5. *to make a deal:* cut up the cake

adv. 6. *united:* crewed up, in cahoots, hooked up, mob-handed, solid, team-handed, tied in, – up
phr. 7. *let's co-operate:* you scratch my back and I'll scratch yours

340. Agreement
n. 1. click, hook-up, tie-up
v. 2. *to agree:* be on, get behind, go a bundle on, go for, go (along) with, swing with, tumble for
3. *to sign a contract:* ink, pact
phr. 4. *agreement:* put it there!, shake!
5. *agreed:* and how, aren't we all, bags I, check, check and double check, count me in, don't mind if I do, I'm on, I'll go for that, I'll say, I'm with you, me and you both, 'nuff said, put it there, shake, same here, that's (for) me, you're on

341. Assistance
n. 1. boost, leg-up; spec. log-rolling (mutual aid)
v. 2. *to help:* boost, chip in, give a leg-up, pinch-hit, reach (US black)
3. *to support, back up:* boost, front for, go overboard for, get behind, get one's back (US black), go to the mat for, stooge for
4. *to defend oneself:* throw a punch
5. *to give a chance to:* give a break, – half a chance, – a squeeze
6. *to let someone get on with:* let the dog see the rabbit
7. *to do a favour:* do a solid (US black), lemon (rhy.sl. = lemon flavour = favour)

OPPOSITION; CONFLICT
342. Opposition
n. 1. spec. needle match
2. *litigation:* Sue City
v. 3. *to oppose:* thumb the nose at, throw one's hat in the ring
adj. 4. *rebellious:* bolshy, uppity

343. Disagreement
v. 1. *fail to agree:* get out of line

adv. 2. *in disagreement:* no deal, – dice, – go, – sale, – soap, – way, nothing doing

344. Contention
n. 1. *argument, quarrel:* argy-bargy, barney, blow-up, blue (Aus.), bull and cow (rhy.sl. = row), ruck, ruckus, run-in, shoot-out, spat, to-do; spec. demo (demonstration); Mexican stand-off (no-win situation); sporting encounter: blinder
v. 2. *to pursue, compete:* breathe down one's neck, duck-shove (Aus.), go for pinkslips, have a hit on, jockey, lock assholes, tangle assholes
3. *to argue:* have it out, pick a bone with, weigh in
4. *feel aggressive:* feel froggy (US black)
5. *to challenge:* buy a (wolf) ticket (US black), call (one) out, choose off (US black), step out on the green (US black)
adv. 6. *in contention:* head up, mano-a-mano, one-on-one
7. *aggressive:* bad-ass, chippy, hard-boiled
phr. 8. *challenges:* leap and you will receive (US black), want to make something of it?, who (are) you screwing?

COURTESY
345. Courtesy; Politeness
n. 1. spec. cool (street gang peace)
excl. 2. *social remarks:* age before beauty, be my guest, bully for you!
3. *thank you:* ta, ta muchly, thanks a bunch, – a million
4. *you're welcome:* forget it, keep the change, no sweat, skip it, that's cool
5. *no thank you:* I'll freeze, that's cool

346. Greeting
n. 1. howdy, howdydo; spec. dap,

soul shake (ritual black palm-slapping)
v. 2. *to greet with mutual palm-slapping:* give some skin, – spli, give the drummer some, high-five, slap, – five, – the plank (US black)
excl. 3. *hello:* bhani ghani (US black), cop a squat, getting any?, Hello, John (got a new motor?), hi-de-hi! (response: hi-de-ho), how's it hanging?, how're they hanging?, how's tricks?, lay some on me! (US black), long time no see, look what the cat's brought in, – the wind's blown in, park your carcase, roll your own (US black), skin me! (US black), what can I do you for?, what gives?, what's cooking?, – going on?, – happening?, – new?, – shaking?, – the deal?, what sup?, wotcher; spec. Miss Thing (homosexual use)
4. *goodbye!:* Abyssinia!, (see you later) alligator, catch some rays, – you later, cheerie-bye, cheerio, chin-chin, don't call us, we'll call you, don't do anything I wouldn't do, – spend it all at once, – take any wooden nickels, hooroo (Aus.), oh reservoir, pip-pip, seeya, seeyabye, see you in church, – in court, – the funny pages, so long, stay loose, ta-ta, TTFN (ta-ta for now), teuf-teuf, toodle-bye, toodle-oo, toodle-pip

---

DISCOURTESY
347. Impudence; Audacity
n. 1. *cheek:* brass, chutzpah (Yid.), crust, face, neck, lip, moxie, once a week (rhy.sl. = cheek), piss and vinegar, sass, stalk
2. *cheekiness:* guff, jaw, lip, mouth, sauce, sass
v. 3. *to be impudent:* cock a snoot (at), have a brass neck; spec. gross out (to shock); spec. take tea with (to outwit)

adj. 4. *impudent:* bold, bold as brass, faastie (WI), fresh, leery, lippy, more front than Brighton beach, mouthy, pushy, rumbunctious, rumbustious, smart-arse, smart-alecky, snotty, wise-ass
excl. 5. *don't be cheeky!:* can you beat that!, what a nerve!, less of it!, of all the . . ., don't be smart!

348. Slight; Snub
n. 1. brush (off), cold shoulder, frost, frozen mitt, go-around, kick in the pants, run-around, smack in the eye (see also Ejection: 62)
v. 2. *to slight, snub:* freeze on, give one the belt, – the brush (off), – the cold shoulder, – the freeze (out), – the frost, – the go-around, – the runaround, have a shot at (Aus.), high-hat, see off, send away with a flea in one's ear, shoot down, shine on (US black), upstage; spec. cold-cunt (lesbian use: ignore)
phr. 3. *of ignorance:* don't know one from a bar of soap (Aus.)
excl. 4. *of contempt:* in your eye!

LOVE
349. Love
n. 1. *infatuation:* crush, pash
v. 2. *to be in love:* be stuck on, fall for (like a ton of bricks), go for, have a thing for, – eyes for, – one's nose open (US black), – a ring through one's nose, – the hots (for), rush, take a shine to, wear the ring (US black)
3. *to fascinate:* get under one's skin
adv. 4. *in love with, obsessed:* after, bitten, crazy for, cuckoo over, dead set (on), gooey about, – over, goofy about, gone on, head over heels, in a bad way, in deep, lovey-dovey, mad about, moony (over), nuts about, smitten, snowed over, soft on, sweet on, on a tight leash, wild about

350. Courtship
n. 1. dating, macking, nanny-goating (rhy.sl. = courting); spec. basket picnic (gay use: looking over prospective pickups)
2. spec. heavy date (very important date)
v. 3. *to pick up:* chat up, give the business, hoopdie-swoop (US black), mack, pluck (US black)
4. *to appraise sexually:* give the glad eye, make a dead set for, – a play for, prop up, pull a quick park (US black), put the hard word on, scope (on); spec. cruise (gay use)
5. *to go out:* spec. double (double-date), sit (a woman) (US black)
6. *to steal someone else's date:* cut out, snake
7. *to interfere with courtship:* (play) gooseberry

351. Caressing
n. 1. (bit of) slap and tickle, bush patrol, finger pie, groping, lovey-dovey, parking, PDA (public display of affection), pecking and necking (US black), stink(y)-finger; spec. first base (initial sexual contact); ga-ga, jam (gay use)
2. *a kiss:* French kiss, kissyface, hit (rhy.sl. = hit and miss), soul kiss (US black), smacker, tongue sushi
v. 3. *to caress:* canoodle, climb all over, cock pluck (US black), cop a feel, dry-fuck, feel up, finger-fuck, get to first base,
4. *to kiss:* chew face, mug, poof, suck face, swap spit
adv. 5. *physically affectionate:* H^2 (hot and heavy)
phr. 6. *rejection of caresses:* not tonight Josephine

352. Flirtation; Philandering
n. 1. *philandering:* catting (US black); spec. little black book (bachelor's address book)
2. *a flirt:* cock-teaser, cunt-teaser, prick-teaser
3. *flirtatious glance:* bedroom eyes, come-hither look, glad eye, goo-goo eyes
4. *flirtatious talk:* chat, line, lyricising (WI)
v. 5. *to philander:* cat around, cruise, fan one's ass, – one's pussy (US black), flag (gay use), fool around, give up rhythm (US black), hit and run, jack around, jazz around, perv about, play around, play the field, put it about, shoot the thrill (US black), tomcat; spec. basketeer (gay use: to size up possible conquests); play checkers (gay use: to move around a cinema looking for sex)
6. *to flirt:* play hard to get
7. *to approach for sex:* bumchat, hit on, jeff (US black), mack on (US black), make a pass, pick up, sweet-talk, shoot a line, talk business (US black); spec. front one off (US black: to seduce for gain, not lust)
8. *to frustrate:* cocktease, pricktease
9. *gay use:* have kidney trouble (solicit in public lavatories)
10. spec. red-light, shell-road (to throw a girl out of a car if she refuses to have sex)

353. Jilting
n. 1. air, brush, chuck, dump, freeze, frost, kiss-off, let-down, push
v. 2. *to interfere in a relationship:* bird dog, cock block, gigolo, play chicken, rank one's style (US black)
3. *to cheat:* burn, chippie, chippy on, two-time
4. *to have an affair:* carry on, tip out (US black)
5. *to end an affair:* chuck, dump, give the air, – the brush, etc. (see n. 1), kiss off, run out on, throw over, tip (US black), unload (see also Reject: 224)

6. *to miss a lover:* carry a torch, torch for
adv. 7. spec. on the rebound

354. Engagement
n. 1. spec. bottom drawer
v. 2. *to be engaged, go out with:* date (Aus.), get it together, go steady, have something going
3. *to propose:* pop the question
adv. 4. *engaged:* dropped, taped up (US black)

355. Marriage; Living Together
1. ball-and-chain
2. *living together:* LTR (living together relationship), shack job, shack-up
3. *uncertain relationship:* see-saw (US black)
4. *marrying someone younger:* baby-snatching
v. 5. *to marry, be married:* be spliced, – hitched, have papers (US black), make the legal move, tie the knot
6. *to live together:* bungalow, knock on together, shack (up)
adv. 7. *married:* cash and carried, cut and carried (rhy.sl.), hitched, spliced
8. *unhappily married:* hen-pecked, pussy-whipped

356. Divorce; Parting
n. 1. bust-up, splitsville
v. 2. *to divorce, part:* blow one out, bust up, call it a day, – quits, split
3. *to repel:* turn off

SEX
357. Sexuality
n. 1. *desired object:* cookies
2. *desire, passion:* hard-on, load (US black), hot nuts, – pants, zazzle (US black); spec. blue balls (frustration)
3. *to desire:* be hot for, go for, gun for, have hot pants for, – hot nuts

for, honk for, lech (after), feel one's oats
4. *to excite:* get one going, – get one's nose open (US black), (this will) put lead in your pencil, prime one's pump, turn on
5. *to be sexually active:* have some rabbit, put it about
6. *to expose the genitals:* flash
7. *to be bisexual:* swing both ways
adj. 8. *sexy:* foxy, hot, raunchy, rude, warm
9. *bisexual:* AC/DC, ambidextrous, bi, half-and-half
10. *pornographic:* adult, blue, hard, strong
adv. 11. *excited:* begging for it, dripping for it, fruity, horny, hot (for), hot to trot, randy, sexed up
phr. 12. as the actress said to the bishop; nudge nudge wink wink know what I mean say no more

358. Sexuality: Homosexual
n. 1. spec. debut (first gay experience); mother-love (gay male's relationship with a heterosexual woman); talking (lesbian use: a relationship when one partner is in jail); bambi effect (for a young gay male to turn to heterosexuality); second closet (an admission of homosexuality); squelch (sex without affection)
v. 2. *to hide one's homosexuality:* pass, stay in the closet, wear a mourning veil; spec. lose one's gender (to abandon homo- for heterosexuality); wear a cut-glass veil (fail to hide one's homosexuality)
3. *to reveal one's homosexuality:* come out, discover one's gender, drop one's beads, – one's hairpins, lay it out, learn a new way, wear one's badge; spec. be brought out (to be initiated into the gay life); turn the tables (for a homosexual to blackmail a heterosexual)

4. *to act effeminately:* camp, foop, poof about, ruin, swish, wreck
5. *to become homosexual:* turn the corner
adj. 6. *effeminate:* la-di-dah
7. *homosexual:* bent, camp as a row of tents, chichi, having a dash, lavender
8. spec. longwinded (taking a longtime to reach orgasm)
9. spec. on the fence (ambivalent about homosexuality)
10. spec. enthroned (soliciting in a public lavatory), dethroned (ejected from a public lavatory)

359. Intercourse
n. 1. ball, bang, bit of how's-yer-father, – of the other, bunk-up, bush patrol, dash in the bloomers, dead shot (US black), Donald Duck (rhy.sl. = fuck), fickey-fick, fratting, fucking, fucky-fucky, fugging, ground rations, horizontal jogging, – rumble, horry (Aus.), hot fling (US black), indoor sledging, interior decorating, Jack in the box (US black), jig-a-jig, lay, legover, nasty, naughties, naughty, nobbing, nookie, oats, parallel parking, roll in the hay, root, rub-a-dub, seeing-to, thrill and chill (US black), turking, Ugandan discussions, wellington (Aus. rhy.sl. wellington boot = root), you know what; spec. knee-trembler (intercourse while standing up); straight shot (intercourse without contraception)
2. *spontaneous intercourse:* bip bam thank-you ma, bump, fast-fuck, quicke, wham bam thank-you mam
3. *lunchtime intercourse:* afternoon delight, funch, nooner
4. *place of intercourse:* killing floor, whip shack (US black)
5. *coitus interuptus:* getting off at Redfern (Aus.), – out at Gateshead, leaving before the gospel

6. *to have intercourse:* ball, bang, beanbag, biff, bust some booty (US black), cha-cha, charver, chingazo (Sp.), cut a side (US black), cut a slice off the joint, dance on the mattress, dip it, dip one's wick, – the fly (US black), dive into the dark (US black), do, do a kindness, do the do (US black), – the nasty, – the natural thing, – the pussy (US black), drill, drop one's load, empty one's trash (US black), exercise the ferret, feature with (Aus.), fill one up (US black), frig, fuck, fug, fugh, futz, gee, get a shot of leg (US black) , – into one's pants, – into, – on top of, – one's ashes hauled, – one's cookies, – one's end away, – one's greens, – one's jollies, – one's leg over, – one's oats, – one's rocks off, – some big leg, – some cock, – some pussy, – some tail, – some, give her a length, give her one, – one a tumble, – some body, – the dog a bone, go all the way, go with, grind, have a cut off the joint, have a dash in the bloomers, have a shag, – a slice off the joint, – a tumble, – it away (with), – it in, – one's greens, – one's oats, hide and salam, hide the salam, honeyfuck, honeyfuggle, hop on a babe, hump, jack up, jazz, jump, jump up and down, knock it off, knock it out (US black), – off a piece, lay, lay some pipe, make it (with), mash the fat (US black), meddle, mess around, mount, off, pile (US black), plank, play mothers and fathers, – mummies and daddies, – night baseball, plonk, plough the back forty, plough poke, pole, pork, prod, punch, ride, roger, root, rout, rump, schtup (Yid.), score between the posts (Aus.), scrape (Aus.), screw, see the King, shaft, shag, skeet (US black), skin the cat, slip her a length, slip it to, snag, spear the bearded clam (Aus.), stick it to,

stoop, stroke (US black), stuff, take a turn on Shooter's Hill (US black), throw, tom, tonk, tumble, twang; spec, roof it (to have sex on the roof); spec. talk fuck (to talk obscenely during intercourse); come across (surrender to seduction)

7. *to copulate enthusiastically:* bang like the shithouse door in a gale, go in out like a fiddler's elbow, go up her like a rat up a drain, rip her guts down (US black), screw the arse off, shag like a rattlesnake

8. *to have an orgasm:* come, come one's cocoa, – one's fat, cream, pop one's cork; spec. have a double shot (ejaculate twice)

9. *to give an orgasm:* ring one's bell, – one's chimes

10. *to have many sexual partners:* climb trees to get away from it (Aus.), get more arse than a toilet seat, have more pricks than a second-hand dart-board, have to swim underwater to get away from it (Aus.), hump 'em and dump 'em, so busy I've had to put a man on to help (Aus.), swing

11. *to deflower a virgin:* cherrypop, cop a cherry, crack a cherry, cut the cake, pop a cherry, split the cup (US black)

12. *to seduce:* Georgia, Georgy (US black), get across, – off with, – next to (US black), – one's leg over, go case with, have, – it away with, have one over, make, nail, prong, race off (Aus.), reel in the biscuit; spec. strike out (fail to seduce); are you saving it for the worms (an attempt to persuade an unwilling girl)

13. *to lose one's erection:* mess with nature (US black)

adj. 14. *promiscuous:* fast

15. *seduced:* had

16. *having intercourse without contraception:* bareback

adv. 17. *having intercourse:* at it, firkin, frigging, fucking, in the saddle, on the job, – the nest, – top of; spec. been there (referring to a previous sexual partner); spec. dog-knotted (for partners to be locked together during intercourse through muscle spasm)

18. *satiated:* plucked (US black)

phr. 19. it takes two to tango

20. *sexual distaste:* don't fancy yours, I wouldn't fuck her with your prick, – with a borrowed prick, I wouldn't touch it with yours, – with a ten-foot barge-pole

360. Varieties

n. 1. *oral sex:* head, lunch, sixty-nine, soixante-neuf; spec. rubbernecking (auto-fellatio)

2. *fellatio:* blow-job, deep throat, face-fucking, gob-job, head, lunch, sixty-eight ('you suck me and I'll owe you one'); spec. punishment (gay use: taking on an extra-large penis); glory hole (a hole in a public lavatory – the penis is pushed through for fellation)

3. *cunnilingus:* box lunch, dining at the Y, dipping in the bush, head, mouth music, punch in the mouth, sack lunch, skull (US black); spec. red wings (Hell's Angel use: cunnilingus with a menstruating woman)

4. *anilingus:* felch, reaming, ream job, rimming, rim, rim-job; spec. black wings, brown wings (Hell's Angels use)

5. *sodomy:* arse fucking, back jump (US black), brown-eye, browning, going up the arse, – the chute, – the tan track etc. (see Parts of Body: 121), Greek culture, hoop, ring, trip to the moon (gay use)

6. *group sex, orgy:* all in one, bunch punch, daisy-chain, gang-bang, gang-shag, group grope, team cream (gay use), threesome, three-way deal, triangle; spec. sloppy seconds (a girl moving from one partner to the next)

7. *fringe sex:* B&D, English culture (bondage and discipline) bagpiping (intercourse under the armpit), freak fuck, leg work (intercourse between the thighs), S&M (sado-masochism), Swedish culture (rubberwear); tightbuck (gay use: foetal position used for S&M or bondage)

8. spec. collegiate fucking, Princeton rub (gay use: body-to-body rubbing); flat-fucking (lesbian use: body rubbing)

9. *masturbation:* J. Arthur (rhy.sl. = wank), five-finger Mary, four sisters on Thumb Street, hand job, hand shandy, J/O scene, jerking the gherkin, Jodrell Bank (rhy.sl.), Lady Five Fingers, mother fist and her five daughters, Mrs Palm and her five daughters, Onan's Olympics, one-legged race, – off the wrist, one stick drum improvisation, pocket pool, slaking the bacon, wank, whizzing the jizzum; spec. circle jerk (group masturbation); playing chopsticks (gay use: mutual masturbation)

10. *coprophilia:* scat

v. 11. *to have oral sex:* eat, fress (Yid. = eat), give up one's face, go around the world, – down (on), – down south, gobble, take it any way (gay use)

12. *to fellate:* bite one's crank, blow, blow one's cookies, – one's glass, – the skin flute, cop one's bird, – one's joint, deep throat, eat one's meat, feed one's face, french, gam, give cone, – head, gnaw the 'nana, go down on, gobble, – the goo, kiss, – the worm, lay the lip, plate (rhy.sl. = plate of ham = gam), play hoop-snake with (gay use), smoke, suck off, swing (gay use), tongue lash; spec. ride a blind piece (gay use: to fellate an uncircumcised penis); spit out of the window (gay use: to spit out semen); spray the

tonsils (ejaculate in the mouth); bag (US black: swallow semen)

13. *to practise cunnilungus:* blow some tunes (US black), brush one's teeth (US black), clean up the kitchen (gay use), dine at the Y, dip in the bush, dive, – in the canyon, drink at the fuzzy cup, eat, – hair pie, – out, face the nation (US black), go way down South in Dixie, gorilla in the washing machine (US black), go under the house (US black), grin in the canyon, have a moustache, scalp (US black), sip at the fuzzy cup (US black), sneeze in the cabbage, – in the canyon, tongue (gay use), yodel, – in the canyon (of love) – up the valley; spec. sit on one's face (cunnilingus with the female superior)

14. *to practise anilingus:* eat jam, eat pound cake, go way down South in Dixie, rim (out)

15. *to sodomise:* ask for the ring, ass-fuck, brown, bunghole, burgle, butt-fuck, buy the ring, cornhole, dive into the sky, go up the old dirt road, get some brown, – some brown sugar, – some duke, go Hollywood, hose (gay use), lay the leg, leather (gay use), pack peanut butter, plug, punk, shoot one's star, throw a buttonhole on (US black); spec. use the English (wriggle the buttocks during penetration)

16. *to permit sodomy:* duck, flopover, pick up the soap for, pratt for, take it up the arse, – up the butt, – up the (poop-) chute, etc. (see also Parts of Body: 121), take on some backs (US black)

17. *to have group sex, an orgy:* gang bang, gang shag, line up on, make a sandwich, turn out; spec. run a double train (for two men to penetrate a woman simultaneously); pull a train (to suffer gang-rape)

18. *to molest:* diddle, touch up

19. *to masturbate (male):* bang the bishop, beat one's little brother,

– one's meat, beat off, – one's dummy, – one's hog, – one's meat, belt one's hog, bring oneself off, burp the worm, butter one's corn, choke the chicken, – the chook (Aus.), clean one's rifle, consult Dr Jerkoff, crank one's shank, dinky one's slinky, do oneself off, do a dry waltz with oneself, feel in one's pocket for one's big hairy rocket, file one's fun-rod, fist fuck, fist one's mister, flex one's sex, flick one's Bic (US black), flip oneself off (Aus.), flog one's mutton, – the dolphin, – the dog, – the log, get one's nuts off, grease one's pipe, hack one's mack, hand-gallop, haul one's own ashes, hump one's hose, jack off, jerk off, Levy (rhy.sl. = Levy and Frank = wank), milk the chicken, pack one's palm, paint one's ceiling, play a flute solo on one's meat whistle, play pocket billiards, – the male organ, – with oneself, please one's pisser, point one's social finger, polish one's sword, pound one's pork, – one's pud, – one's flounder, prompt one's porpoise, prime one's pump, prune the fifth limb, pull one's joint, – one's pud, – one's pudding, – one's taffy, – one's wire, – the pope, rub off, – up, run one's hand up the flagpole, sew (US black), shake hands with the guy who stood up when I got married, shine one's pole, shoot the tadpoles, slam one's hammer, slam one's spam, slap one's wapper, spank the monkey, – the salami, – with the wife's best friend, stir one's stew, strike the pink match, stroke one's beef, – one's poker, – the dog, talk with Rosy Palm and her five little sisters, thump one's pumper, tickle one's pickle, toss off, twang one's wire, tweak one's twinkie, unclog the pipes, varnish one's pole, walk the dog, wank, watch the eyelid movies, wax one's dolphin, whip off, whip one's dripper, – one's wire, whack off, whank, whip it, wonk one's conker, yang one's wang, yank the yam, – one's crank; spec. catch a buzz (to masturbate with a vibrator)
20. *to masturbate (female):* beat the beaver, buttonhole, clap one's clit, cook cucumbers, grease the gash, hide the hot dog, hit the slit, hose one's hole, make waves, pet the poodle, slam the clam, stump-jump
21. spec. fist, fist-fuck (gay use: to insert the fist into the anus)
22. spec. pick up the vibrations (gay use: watch a gay sex-show); take one's meat out of the basket (gay use: to reveal the genitals to another man)
adv. 23. *aberrant:* geared

SOCIAL LIFE
361. Sociability
n. 1. *'good life':* life of Reilly, sporting life
2. *invitation:* stiffy
v. 3. *to lead a social life:* get around, put oneself about; spec. sit eggs (US black: overstay one's welcome)
4. *to visit:* blow by, fall by, knock up, pop in, slide by, stop by
adj. 5. *sociable:* chummy, pally, palsy(-walsy)

362. Social Engagement
n. 1. *meeting:* date, meet, one to meet
2. *a meeting place:* hang-out; spec. cottage (gay use); meat market (student use)
3. *to meet:* bump into
4. *to break a date:* duck out, give one a miss, stand up
5. *to have a date broken:* be shafted, stood up
6. *to stay at home:* bing it (US black)

363. Social Entertainment; Party
n. 1. bash, bean-feast, beano, beer bust, beer-up (Aus.), blast,

bunfight, bust, do, gang-shag (US
black), get-together, heller,
knees-up, racket, rave, ruckus, rug
beat (US black), shake, shindig,
shindy, thrash, turn (Aus.),
wing-ding; spec. hen party (all
women); stag party (eve-of-wedding
men-only party); be-in (hippie
gathering)
v. 2. *to go out:* creep, hit the high
spots, night-club; spec. party-hop
(to move from party to party); get
home with the milk (return after a
night's revels)
3. *to have a good time:* cut it up,
juke, party, whoop it up
4. *to entertain:* do the honours,
throw a party, – a bash, – a beano,
etc. (see n. 1)

364. Dancing
n. 1. bopping, boogying, cutting the
rug, juking; spec. breaking,
hip-hop, hoofing
2. *a dance, ball:* bollock, clutch
v. 3. *to dance:* boogaloo, boogie, cut
the rug, juke, shake a leg, shake it,
strut one's stuff

POSSESSION: ACQUISITION
365. Acquisition; Gains
n. 1. goodies, killing, pickings,
rake-off, take
v. 2. *to obtain:* bag, collar, come in
for, cop, freeze onto, get one's
hooks on, glom, gobble up, land,
load up on, mop up, nab, nip, pull
down, rope in, rustle up, scare up,
snag, sneeze, whistle up; spec.
trouser (to pocket)
3. *to take everything:* go the whole
hog, sweep the board
4. *to obtain by fraud:* chisel out of,
ease out of, promote for, wangle out
of, work for (see also Influence: 219)
adv. 5. *gaining:* on a roll
phr. 6. *I want!:* bags I!, dibs on!

366. Possession; Property
n. 1. traps; spec. dead man's shoes

(property of a dead person); OPs
(other people's property)
2. *luggage:* bindle, keister
v. 3. *to have plenty:* be cochealed,
– lousy with, pack, reek with, roll
in, stink of, swim in
adj. 4. *supplied:* cochealed, stinking
adv. 5. *well-supplied:* crummy with,
filthy with, loaded, long on, lousy
with, rolling in, stinking with,
swimming in
6. *lacking:* clean out of, fresh out of
phr. 7. *how much do you have?:*
how are you fixed?; spec. are you
holding? (do you have drugs)

367. Joint Possession; Sharing
n. 1. piece, rake-off, shake, slice,
split; spec. Dutch treat (both parties
share payment); even Steven (fair
shares); short end, – straw (the
lesser share)
v. 2. *to share:* chip in, cut up, divvy
(up), go Dutch, – fifty-fifty,
– halves, – splits, muck in with,
split; spec. deck up (drug use)
3. *to give a share:* cut in, deal in,
give a cut, – a piece, etc. (see n. 1),
ring in, split with
4. *get one's share:* come in for, cut a
piece, – a slice, etc. (see n. 1), get a
cut, – a piece, – a slice, etc. (see n.
1); spec. get in the ground floor (get
a share at the outset); hog, muscle
into (take an extra share)
5. *to share out:* dish out
adv. 6. *sharing:* even Steven,
fifty-fifty, going halves, – Dutch
7. *excluded from a share:* out of the
game, – the picture, – the running

368. Borrowing and Begging
n. 1. *a request for something:* bite,
hit-up, mooch, shakedown, tap,
touch
v. 2. *to beg:* bite one's ear, bludge
(Aus.), bot (Aus.), brace
up, bum off, coat and badge
(rhy.sl. = cadge), fang (Aus.), get
into one's ribs, grub, make a touch,

mump, ponce off, put the bee on,
– the bite on, – the lug on, – the
touch on, shake down, soak, stick
one for, tap, throw the hooks into,
touch; spec. work a crowd (beg
from an audience)
3. *to extort:* bleed (white), put the
bite on
adv. 4. *begging:* on the bot (Aus.),
– the coat and badge (rhy.sl. =
cadge)
phr. 5. *lend me some money:* let me
hold some change

369. Loss
n. 1. wipe-out; spec. losing streak
(continual losses)
v. 2. *to lose:* drop a packet, – a
bundle, – one's roll, – one's wad,
get the short end (of), kiss goodbye,
kiss off, lose one's shirt

POSSESSION: BESTOWAL
370. Giving
n. 1. *gift:* freebie, handout, pressie,
prezzie
v. 2. *to give:* chip in, come across
(with), come up with, cough (up),
deal out, dish out, dob in (Aus.),
eevige (backsl.), fork out, – over,
hand out, kick in, shell out, sub
(up); spec. give one the pink slip (to
cede something of value); mash it
on one (US black: to give someone
their dues)
3. *to contribute:* chip in, kick the tin
(Aus.), weigh in with
4. *to tip:* cross one's palm, grease;
spec. stiff (fail to tip)
5. *to treat:* blow one to, go for, pick
up the tab, shout; spec. my shout
(my round of drinks)
6. *to be generous:* spread oneself
adj. 7. *generous:* handsome

371. Reward
n. 1. payoff; spec. pie in the sky
(fantasy reward)
2. *deserts:* come-uppance

3. spec. leather medal, wooden
spoon (metaphorical prize for the
poorest loser)
v. 4. *to give one's deserts:* cook
one's goose, give one's come-
uppance
5. *to be rewarded:* bring home the
bacon, pick the plums, take the
cake; spec. get it coming and going
(get double rewards)

372. Bribery
n. 1. dash (Nigeria), fix, grease job,
kickbacks, payoffs
2. *a bribe:* backhander, bung, drink,
hush money, kickback, payoff,
straightener, take
v. 3. *to bribe:* bung, get to,
grease, – one's palm, juice, oil,
palm, patch (Canada), piece off, put
the fix in, schmeer (Yid. = grease),
sling (Aus.), square on off,
stiffen, straighten, take care
of
4. *to accept bribery:* be on the take,
dip one's beak, get one's hands
dirty, take

POSSESSION: ECONOMY
373. Extravagance
n. 1. splurging
v. 2. *to be extravagant:* blow one's
wad, flash one's dough – one's wad,
have a hole in one's pocket, live
high off the hog, ride high wide and
handsome, splash it about, splosh it
on, splurge, throw one's money
away

373. Thrift
n. 1 *something in reserve:* ace in
the hole, card up one's sleeve
v. 2. *to live on the cheap:* take the
bus
3. *to hide away:* keep on ice, put in
cold storage, rat-hole
adj. 4. *mean:* cheap, chinky, Jewy
(derog.), mingy, tight

POSSESSION: ESTATE
375. Wealth
n. 1. barrel of money, pot of dough
2. *funds:* bundle, pile, roll, wad
v. 3. *to be rich:* have money to burn, live high on the hog, ride the gravy train, roll in money
adj. 4. *wealthy:* cashed up, filthy rich, flush, in the money, loaded, made of money, rolling, stinking, stuffy, up in the dough, – in the money, well in, – away, well-fixed, – -heeled, – -lined
adv. 5. *comfortable:* high on the hog, in clover, in good shape, living off the tit, on a good wicket, on Easy Street, on the sunny side (of the street), on velvet, set, sitting pretty

376. Poverty
n. 1. Queer Street
2. *insufficient funds:* ain't long enough, not a bean, – a brass razoo (Aus.)
v. 3. *to be poor:* be down to one's bottom dollar, – in Queer Street, – in a hole, feel the pinch, have the wolf at the door, not have a pot to piss in, – have a prayer, – a red cent, rough it, scrape the bottom of the barrel, skate on one's uppers, touch bottom
4. *to lose money:* drop; spec. alley-whipped (unpaid for work performed)
adv. 5. *poor:* at the bottom of the barrel, – the end of one's tether, beat, boracic (rhy.sl. boracic lint = skint), bought and sold and done for, broke (to the wide), busted, clean broke, cleaned out, cold in hand (US black), dished, doesn't have a pot to pee in, done for, – up, down on one's luck, flat as a pancake, – broke, hard-up, heart of oak (rhy.sl. = broke), hung for bread, hurting, in a hole, – a tight corner, nigger-rich, on one's beam ends, – one's uppers, – the Rory (rhy.sl. Rory O'Moore = floor = poor), out (of pocket), poor as a church mouse, – as a shithouse rat, pushed (for), raggedy-ass, skint, stony (broke), strapped (for cash), touching bottom, up against it, washed up, wiped out; spec. beggar my neighbour (rhy.sl. visiting the Labour = Unemployment Office)
6. *indebted:* in hock

People

PERSONS: GENERAL
377. People
n. 1. *person:* article, artist, bastard, bim, bimbo, bird, bleeder, blighter, bloke, bozo, cat, civvie, critter, customer, dude, egg, face, fish, fuck (as in 'dumb fuck', etc.), guy, head, jamoke, Joe Blow, joker, Mr Average, momser (Yid.), nosper (backsl.), number, (ordinary) Joe, people, proposition, punter, scout, sort, stiff, ticket, whatshis(her)face, whatshis(her)name; spec. breeders (gay use: non-homosexuals); textiles (nudist use: non-nudists)
2. *self:* yours truly
3. *suffix:* -nik

378. Group; Crowd
n. 1. crew, idrin (WI: brethren), mob, outfit, pack, posse, push (Aus.), team; spec. slag (unpleasant people)
2. *everyone:* all and then some, all hands, – the world and his wife, – the world and his brother, every mother's son, every man Jack, every Tom Dick and Harry, whole kit and caboodle, – shbang, – shooting match, – works
3. *cults, clubs, etc.:* bodgies (Aus.), bopping club, – gang, Brussel sprouts (rhy.sl. = Boy Scouts), greasers, mods, rockers, punks, sharpies (Aus.), skinheads, Sloanes, Valley Girls, widgies (Aus.)

379. Men
n. 1. bloke, bozo, bugger, chap(pie), cock, cove, cuss, customer, dude, geezer, hombre, ice cream freezer (rhy.sl. = geezer), John, joker, meat, moosh, nam (backsl.), old bean, – boy, – chap, – cock, – horse, – top, omee, regular Joe, sport, wallah

380. Women
n. 1. apron, babe, band (US black), biddy, bim, bimbo, bird, bit of fluff, bitch, booty (US black), broad, butter (US black), chick, cock, cono (Sp.), cookie, coot, crack, crotch, cuddle and kiss (rhy.sl. = miss), cunt, dame, dish, doll, dolly (bird), filly, fish, fluff, fox, frail, gash, hairy, haybag, hen, jane, judy, kitty-cat, minge bag, moll, moo, mustang, mystery, nammo (backsl.), nemmo (backsl.), one good woman, oyster, piece, piece of ass, – of tail, polone, potato (Aus. rhy.sl. = potato peeler = sheila), pussy, quail, rag baby (US black), real woman (US black), sheila (Aus.), sister, skirt, slit, snatch, sort, squirrel, tart, totty, trout, tuna, twist, womon, wool; spec. -widow (a woman whose husband is occupied elsewhere)

PERSONS: BY AGE
381. Young Persons
n. 1. spec. youthquake
2. *baby:* ankle-biter, chickabiddy, crumb-crusher, – -snatcher, diddums, lambkin, little man, rug rat
3. *child:* dustbin lid (rhy.sl. = kid), gawdelpus, God forbids (rhy.sl. = kids), goober, kiddiwink, kiddo, nipper, pogue, shaver, short, sprog, sprout, snotnose; spec. moppet

(young girl); bub (young boy); drop (US black: orphan)
4. *young man:* bimbo, geepie, pup(py); spec. Queerbait (pretty young man); toy-boy (young boy pursued by older women)
5. *young woman:* bimbo, bint, bobby-soxer, bopper, bubble-gummer, bud, schoolie, teenybopper, yummy; spec. gaolbait, San Quentin quail (sexy underage girl); schlubette (stupid girl); little madam (self-opinionated)
6. *immature youngster:* candy-butt, cootie, poopbutt (US black), puppy dog, rootiepoot (US black), young blood
7. *virgin:* cherry, puppy, raw sole (US black)

382. Old Persons
n. 1. antique, buster, crumbly, dusty, fossil, geri, grunters, oldie, old coot, – timer, wrinkly
2. *old man:* buffer, codger, deelo nam (backsl.), gramps, joskin, mossyback, old buzzard, – cocker, – geezer, – sweat, pop(s), pot and pan (rhy.sl.); spec. DOM (dirty old man), sugar-daddy (provider for a younger girl), (see also Man: 379)
3. *old woman:* battleaxe, boiler, bunty, delonammon (backsl.), drago, leather, old bag, – biddy, – boiler; (see also Woman: 380)

PERSONS: INHABITANTS
383. Nationality
n. 1. *American:* septic (rhy.sl. = septic tank = yank), uncle, Uncle Sam, yank, yankee-doodle; spec. WASP (white anglo-saxon protestant)
2. *Australian:* Aussie, digger; spec. Alf, Fred, ocker (unsophisticated Australian); Roy (sophisticated Australian)
3. *Canadian:* Canuck

4. *Chinese:* Chink, Chinky, tiddley-wink (rhy.sl.)
5. *Dutchman:* butterbox
6. *Englishman:* John Bull, jumble, kipper (Aus.), limey, pom(my) (Aus.), pongo (NZ); spec. expat (expatriate English)
7. *Frenchman:* frog
8. *German:* boche, Fritz, Heinie, hun, jerry, kraut, Otto, squarehead
9. *Greek:* bubble (rhy.sl. = bubble and squeak)
10. *Hawaiian:* kanaka
11. *Indian (US):* spec. breed (half-breed)
12. *Irish:* bogtrotter, green nigger, harp, Mick, narrowback, Paddy, Patsy, tad; spec. lace-curtain Irish (genteel Irish)
13. *Italian:* dago, eyetie, ghinny, ginney, ginzo, guinea, guinzo, mountain wop, spag, spaghetti bender, wop; spec. moustache Pete (early Italian immigrants to US); paisan (fellow-Italian)
14. *Japanese:* nip
15. *Mexican:* bato, beaner, bean eater, chico, cholo, chuc, dago, greaseball, greaser, pachuco, spic(k), taco bender, – head; spec. wetback (illegal immigrant to US)
16. *New Zealand:* Kiwi
17. *Pakistani:* Paki, Pakki
18. *Philippino:* flip
19. *Russian:* Ivan, Russki; spec. commie, commo (Aus.), pinko, red
20. *Scot:* Jock
21. *South African:* rock spider (Afrikaaner)
22. *Welshman:* Taffy
23. *West Indian:* Bimi
24. *Yugoslav:* Yug
25. *foreigners:* ding (Aus.), reffo (Aus.), snow (Aus. Latins)
26. spec. PIGS (Poles, Italians, Greeks, Slavs: US 'ethnics')

384. Race and Religion
n. 1. *blacks (by whites):* boog, boogie, chocolate, chungo bunny,

coon, dark meat, darkie, dinge, egg and spoon (rhy.sl. = coon), eightball, groid, harvest moon (rhy.sl.), jig, jigaboo, Jim Crow, jungle bunny, Lucozade (rhy.sl. = spade), nigger, nignog, oogie, Rastus, razo (rhy.sl. = razor blade = spade), sambo, schvug (Yid.), schwartze (Yid.), shadow, shine, silvery spoon (rhy.sl.), smoke, smut-butt, soap dodger, spade, spearchucker, spook, stove lid, swartzer (Yid.), wog, zigaboo; spec. touch of the tar brush (black ancestry); pickaninny (black child); Afs, munt (S.Afr. use); boong (Aus. aborigine)

2. *blacks (by blacks):* all-originals, black 360°, bleed, blood, boot, brothers, homeboy, homegirl, member, original, skillet, speck, suede; spec. butterhead (US black: embarassing person); bungo (WI: fool); royal (WI: non-West Indian black)

3. *spec. dark complexioned black (by blacks):* black bird, – dust, inky-dinky, midnight, smokestack, zombie

4. *spec. light complexioned black (by blacks):* bright, buckwheat, casper, grey, lemon, pinkie; spec. high yaller, – yellow, yellow ass, – girl (mulatto)

5. *spec. rebellious black (by blacks):* bad boy, – nigger, bad-ass nigger, cut-throat, field nigger, hardhead; spec. John Henry (tough, hard worker despite odds); firsts (blacks who are first to invade white purlieus)

6. *spec. subservient or bourgeois black (by blacks):* Aunt Jemima, – Jane, Dr (Mr) Thomas, fade, faded boogie, handkerchief head, house nigger, HN (house nigger), oreo, seddity, shuffle, (Uncle) Tom, yard negro

7. *gypsy:* diddicoi, gyppo

8. *Jews (derog.):* abe, Abie

Kabibble, abie, bagel bender, eskimo, fast-talking Charlie (US black), five-to-two (rhy.sl.), four by two (rhy.sl.), front-wheel skid (rhy.sl. = yid), Goldberg (US black), goose, half-past two (rhy.sl.), hebe, hooknose, ikey mo, kangaroo (rhy.sl.), kike, lox jock, moch, mockie, quarter-to-two (rhy.sl.), Red Sea pedestrian (Aus.), saucepan lid (rhy.sl. = yid), sheeny, shonk, shonnicker, slick-'em-plenty (US black), three balls (US black), Yid, yiddle; spec. JAP (Jewish-American princess)

9. spec. Litvak, Polack (immigrant Jews from Lithuania, Poland)

10. *spec. non-Jews (by Jews):* goy, goyim, yoks; flour mixer (rhy.sl. = shikse), shikse (gentile girl)

11. *orientals (derog.):* chopstick, dink, gook, little people, ricer, slant, slit, slope, yellow peril

12. *whites (by blacks):* beast, blanco, chalk, Charlie, devil, fay, fey, gray, hay eater, honk(ie), hunkie, kelt, lily, man with fuzzy balls, Mr Charlie, – Cracker, – Peanut, ofay, paleface, peck, peckerwood, pink, rabbit, whitey, yacoo; spec. gringo (Mexican use); gub, Mr Gub (aborigine use); roundeye (oriental use); pepper and salt (US black: a mix of blacks and whites); superhonkie (ultra-authoritarian, possibly racist white)

13. *white females (by blacks):* bale of straw, Lady Snow, Little Eva, Miss Amy, – Ann, – Lillian, pinktoes, silk, snow, white meat; spec. gringa (Mexican use)

14. *subservient US Indians (by Indians):* apple (red on the outside, white inside), Uncle Tomahawk

385. Inhabitants

n. 1. spec. banana bender (Aus: Queenslander), brummy (inhabitant of Birmingham, UK), crow eaters (Aus: South Australians);

cornpone, cracker (US: poor Southern white), ethno (Aus: any immigrant, usually Italian, Greek, Yugoslav), fly-over people (US: 'middle America'), raddie (UK: Italian living in London), scouse (Liverpudlian), Wooloomooloo yank (Aus. one who attempts to ape US style); yellow-belly (inhabitant of Lincolnshire)

386. Townspeople
n. 1. slicker, townee; spec. town (student use; local residents, rather than 'gown' – students)
2. *neighbour:* Texan rude nam (backsl. = next door man)
3. *resident:* old identity (Aus.)
4. spec. blockbuster (first white or black family to live on a black or white block)

PERSONS: TYPES
387. Person of Importance
n. 1. big cheese, – chief, – deal, – enchilada, – fish, – gun, – noise, – pot, – stuff, – wheel, – wig, biggie, BMOC (big man on campus), Boss Charlie (US black), celeb, gaffer, guvnor, hammer man (US black), head cook and bottle-washer, headliner, heavyweight, (high) mucky-muck, high-up, high monkey-monk, his nibs, honcho, hook, hot-shot, kingfish, main man, men in suits, mensch (Yid.), Mr Big, pitch and toss (rhy.sl. = the boss), pooh-bah, sachem, shtarka (Yid.), shtarker, the cheese, – gorilla, – man, top cat, – dog, wheel; spec. higher-higher (US milit. use: high command); blue-eyed boy, fair-haired boy, white-haired boy (favourite)
2. *conceited person:* doll

388. Insignificant or Petty Person
n. 1. bebopper (US black), bit of fluff, crumb, dud, feeb, frip, half-pint, jobsworth, lightweight, Melvin, no big deal, – great shakes, nobody to write home over, one-eyed scribe (US black), pint-size, pipsqueak, piss-ant, slob, small change, stooge, tick, tinhorn, twerp, zero; spec. grunt (USMC use); shower (group of insignificant people)

389. Polished and Sophisticated Person
n. 1. cool cat, hipster, jumping cat (US black), Mr Cool, smart guy, smoothie

390. Unsophisticated Person
n. 1. booboisie, Great Unwashed, Johnny-come-lately, square, working stiff; spec. squaredom (world of 'squares')
2. *peasant:* apple-knocker, boonie, carrot cruncher, clod, farmer, hayseed, hick, honyok, hoosier, neck, red, redneck, rube, shitkicker, swede, woollyback
3. *lout:* ape, baboon, bohunk, boob, clunk, dumbo, dummy, geek, goop, honky, hunk(y), jibone, lob, lug, lump, lunkhead, ox, palooka, plug, swab, yahoo
4. *socially inept:* diddy-bop (US black), ditty-bop, flamer

391. Gullible Person; Dupe
n. 1. boob, chump, fall guy, gobshite, lollipop, loogan, mark, meal ticket, mug, pigeon, puppethead, pushover, sap, soft-cop, soft touch, square, steamer (rhy.sl. = steam tug = mug), sucker, Trick Willy (US black), turkey on a string (US black)
phr. 2. there's one born every minute

392. Ill-bred Person
n. 1. grunge, lowlife, sleaze, sleazo, yob(bo)
2. *snobbish abbrevs.:* NB (no

background), NQOCD (not quite
our class dear), SQPQ (suspiciously
quiet, probably queer)

393. Awkward, Careless Person
n. 1. baggage smasher,
butterfingers, mollydooker (Aus.),
shithook, spas(tic), stumblebum
2. *uncoordinated:* non (US black)

394. Superior, Admirable Person
n. 1. *admirable:* bottler (Aus.),
brick, cool head, curly wolf, good
news, killout (US black), natural
(born) man/woman (US black),
notch (WI), regular guy, straight
shooter, through and through (US
black); spec. soul child (US black:
high in black consciousness)
2. *superior:* big shot, high
mucky-muck, Mr Big, toff; spec.
OMCD (gay use: out of my class
darling)

395. Terms of Disparagement
n. 1. animal, ape, arsehole,
ball-buster, basket, beige,
butterhead (US black),
chippy-chaser, cocksucker, crud,
cunt, cunt-lapper, dickhead, dog,
dork, dos a reno (backsl. = sod),
douchebag, dratsab, (backsl. =
bastard), dub, dumb cluck, – fuck,
four-letter man, fuckwit,
granny-jazzer, horse's arse, J.
Arthur (rhy.sl. = wanker), kiss of
death, knucklehead, long thin
streak of piss, lug, lummocks,
mammy-jammer, – -rammer,
– -hugger, – -tapper, m.f.,
mollyfock, momma-hopper,
momser (Yid.), mooch, mother,
mother-fouler, – -flunker, – -raper,
– -fucker, – -grabber, – -hugger,
– -jiver, – -jumper, mug, naus,
nellie, nerd, out-and-out (US
black), peck, pheasant plucker,
piss-cutter, poppa-lopper, ponce,
poopbutt (US black), pootbutt (US
black), prick, pug(gy), putz (Yid.),

rat arse, – bastard, – prick, ratbag,
sap, schmo (Yid.), scumsucker, shit,
shit on a stick (US black),
shit-for-brains, slag, sleeping Jesus,
smartiepants, so-and-so, SOB, sod,
sonofabitch, sonofagun, stinker,
sucker, sumbitch, triple clutcher,
turkey, twat, twot; spec. REMF
(US milit: rear-echelon
mother-fuckers), SOHF (UK
'society': sense of humour failure);
(see also: Insignificant Person: 388,
Low-bred Person: 392,
Contemptible Person: 396,
Vexatious Person: 397, Selfish
Person: 399, Weakling: 403,
Effeminate Person: 404, etc.)
2. *thug:* ass-kicker, goombah, goon,
jibone

396. Contemptible Person
n. 1. bad egg, – hat, – lot, – penny,
bastard, beat off, Berkeley Hunt
(rhy.sl. = cunt), bitch, bitch's
bastard, blood claat (WI), bugger,
bum, cocksucker, creep, cunt,
dipstick, dipshit, droob (Aus.), fart,
flake, fuck, fucker, jel, lower than
the spots on a snake's ass, – than
whale-shit, merchant banker (rhy.sl.
= wanker), Mr Do-You-Wrong,
motherfucker, mucker, pain in the
arse, piece of crap, – of shit, poison,
prick, rat, shithead, shitheel,
skull-and-crossbones (US black), so
low he can look up a snake's asshole
and think its the North Star, sod,
tick, TL (Yid: tochus-lekker =
arse-licker), toe-rag, turd, wanker
(see also Insignificant Person: 388,
Ill-bred Person: 392, Terms of
Disparagement: 395, Vexatious
Person: 397, Selfish Person: 399,
Weakling: 403, etc.)

397. Annoying Person
n. 1. blister, crasher, gangster,
gawdelpus, god-help-us, pain in the
arse, – in the neck, PITA, pill,
poison; spec. mudcrusher (US

black: bully); jobsworth (petty
official)

398. Meddler or Inquisitive Person
n. 1. back-seat driver, buttinski,
finick, fleabag (US black), kibitzer,
stickybeak (Aus.), stirrer (see also
Talker: 422)
2. *obsessive:* neatnik

399. Selfish or Greedy Person
n. 1. *mean:* cheap Charlie, cheapie,
cheapskate, clam, crawfish, doggy
(US black), Jew (derog.) meanie,
meany, penny-pincher, piker,
skinflint, Scotchman (derog.), tick,
tight as Kelsey's nuts, – as
O'Reilly's balls, tightwad
2. *egocentric:* jackanape (US black),
jake flake (US black)
3. *greedy:* gannet, glut (glutton),
gross-out artist, guts, hog, pig; spec.
foodie (gourmet)
4. *obstinate:* cuss, donkey,
hardhead, hard nut to crack, mule,
'ornery cuss, pighead, tough
customer, – proposition

400. Unselfish, Helpful Person
n. 1. good thing, pussycat, softie,
soft touch, stand-up guy
2. *helper:* helping hand, meal ticket,
rooter; spec. angel (theatrical
backer)
3. *representative:* dep, double,
stand-in, sub
4. *go-between:* fixer, front
5. *advisor:* back-seat driver,
kibitzer, tipster, woppitzer

401. Vain Person
n. 1. *braggart:* all wind and piss,
– mouth and trousers, bigmouth, big
note artist (Aus.), bilge artist,
blatherskite, blowhard, bullshit
artist, ear-basher, fatmouth, man
with a paper ass (US black), smart
arse, – guy, swellhead, windbag,
wise arse, – guy, wisenheimer (see
also Talker: 422)

2. *show-off:* bit of a lad, diddy-bop
(US black), hot-dogger, Jack the
lad, lair (Aus.), teddy bear (Aus.
rhy.sl. = lair)
3. *self opinionated:* acts like shit
would melt in his/her mouth,
hard-on (derog.), thinks his/her ass
is icecream and everyone wants a
bite, thinks he/she shits lollipops,
– he/she is so nice his/her shit don't
stink
4. *snob:* Lady Muck, Lord Muck,
sadit (US black), stuffed shirt,
upways (US black)
5. *flashily dressed:* butterfly (US
black)

402. Brave and Reckless Persons
n. 1. chancer, fire-eater, redhot,
shtarka (Yid.)
2. *street fighter:* diddley-bop

403. Weakling; Coward
n. 1. baa-lamb, bottler, candy-ass,
Caspar Milquetoast, chicken,
chickenshit, copout, creampuff,
creeping Jesus, CS, div, drip, 4-F,
fraidy-cat, funk, funker, girl's
blouse, jellyfish, lightweight,
limp-dick, Mary Ann, microbe,
milksop, milquetoast, mollycoddle,
mother's boy, namby-pamby,
panty-waist, puss gentleman (US
black), pussy, rabbit, scaredy-cat,
sheep, snow (Aus.), softy, sook
(Aus.), sop, tired people (US
black), wanker, waterboy, weak
sister, wimp, wimp-guts, yellowbelly
2. *whining person:* creeping Jesus

404. Homosexuals
n. 1. *male homosexuals (derog.):*
arse bandit, bananas, battyman
(WI), bent, birdie, bitch, boy-ass,
brown artist, – family, – hatter,
browning family, sisters, bufu,
bugger, bum-boy, bunker, burglar,
butch, buttercup, buttfucker,
chutney ferret, cocksucker,
dead-eye dick, dicky-licker, dirt

tamper, Dorothy's friends,
dung-puncher, eye doctor, fag,
faggot, fagola, fairy, fancy-pants,
femme, flit, fooper, four-letter man,
fruit, funny man (US black), gay,
gender-bender, ginger (rhy.sl. =
ginger-beer = queer), grand
duchess, haricot (Aus. rhy.sl. =
haricot bean = queen) he-she,
homo, iron (rhy.sl. = iron hoof =
poof), jam duff, jocker, ki-ki, lily,
mouser, muzzler, nance, nancy-boy,
nellie, nelly, nola, off-colour,
omee-polone, one of those, pansy,
pillow biter, pixie, poof, poofta,
poofter, poove, (powder) puff,
quack (US black), queen, queer,
shandy (rhy.sl. = chandelier =
queer), she-man, shirt-lifter (Aus.),
sissy, skippy (US black), so, sweet
(US black), swish, tan tracker, that
way, three-letter man, tonk,
tooti-frooti (US black),
turd-burglar, – packer, Turk, waffle,
white liver, wind jammer, wolf,
yoo-hoo boy; spec. fats and fems
(overweight or effeminate gays,
barred from many clubs)
2. *female homosexuals (derog.):*
Amy-John, charlie, dike, dyke,
finger artist (US black), jasper (US
black), lady lover, les, lesbo, leso
(Aus.), lezzie, lezzo, malflor (Sp.),
nelly, pinky, Sappho, thespian;
spec. bluff (bisexual lesbian); spec.
beard (a man acting, for
appearances, as lesbian's husband)
3. *'masculine' lesbian:* bull, bull
dagger, bull-dyke, bumper, collar
and tie, daddy, dagger, diesel,
diesel-dyke, drag-dyke
horsewoman, jockey, mantee, pap,
top sergeant, truck driver
4. *'feminine' lesbian:* fem, femme,
fluff, mama, pinky, puss, ruffle,
twist; spec. sil (silly about = a
partner in a love affair)
5. *male homosexual types:* auntie,
chicken hawk, – queen, dirty
dowager, dowager, grand duchess,

john, mother, mother ga-ga,
Mother Superior, your mother
(older men); belle, bronco,
butterbox, chicken, cornflakes,
daughter, debutante, ga-ga, lamb,
pogue, poggler, tender box, tail,
twinkie (novice or youngster);
husband, pitcher ('masculine'
homosexual); bitch, wife ('feminine'
homosexual); peek freak, peer
queer, watch queen (voyeur);
church mouse (one who solicits in
churches); angel, cousin, gazooney,
gonsil, possesh (older man's young
lover), show stopper (particularly
attractive boy); body lover
(homosexual frotteur), rim queen
(one who practises anilingus), top
man, bottom man (dominant and
passive partners in a
sado-masochistic couple), privy
queen, tearoom queen (one who
solicits in lavatories), body queen
(one who prefers body-builders), ill
piece (unattractive man); brilliant
(ostentatious queen), drag-queen
(one who dresses as a woman), kiki
(an active or passive homosexual),
oncer (promiscuous male, never
repeating a partner); uniforms
(members of the armed or
uniformed services); sea food
(sailors); rough trade (genuine or
fantasising 'proletarian' sexual
partners); size queen (one who
prefers large penises); golden
shower queen (one who enjoys
urolagnia); toe queen (foot
fetishist), felch queen
(scopophiliac); angel with a dirty
face, closet case, – queen (one who
dare not reveal his homosexuality);
breeders (married homosexuals who
father children); kid simple, pee-pee
lover (one who prefers very young
boys); jam fag (one who is devoted
only to sex); sister-act (homosexual
couple, or a homosexual man
copulating with a heterosexual
woman); RFD (Rural Free

Delivery) queen (homosexual living in the country); payoff queen (one who prefers to pay for sex); jam, straight (a non-homosexual male); pretender to the throne (one who poses as homosexual for his own purposes)

405. Gloomy or Irritable Persons
n. 1. *gloomy:* crab, crag, fuddy-duddy, gloom, meanie, misery, misery-guts, party pooper, sad sack, sourpuss, wet blanket
2. *irritable:* carpet-biter, grassfighter (Aus.), grouch, hothead, sorehead

406. Humourist; Amusing Person
n. 1. bundle of laughs, card, caution, cutup, kidder, laugh riot, Mr Laffs, stitch; Carl Comedian (one whose jokes are not appreciated)

407. Stable, Conservative Person
n. 1. dodo, do-right man, eightball, grey, Mom-Dad-Buddy-and-Sis, mossyback, shell-back, square, square John, stick-in-the mud, straight; spec. heterosexual (gay use); spec. dusty bread (US black: conventional girl)
2. *unemotional:* iceberg

408. Unstable, Irresolute Person
n. 1. bug, jellyfish, man-a-hanging (US black), pussyfooter, shilly-shallyier, yoyo

409. Eccentric, Unconventional Person
n. 1. bat, card, cough-drop, crazo, dag (Aus.), dorf, flip-out, fruitcake, galoot, GB, geek, goof, goofball, half-saved, headcase, honker, nut, nutcase, odd stick, oddball, outfit, psycho, rum 'un, – customer, rummy, squirrel, wacko, weirdo, zod
2. spec. hippie, hipidity, mind-tripper

3. spec. little green man (extraterrestrial)

410. Enterprising, Energetic Person
n. 1. ball of fire, comer, eager beaver, fool (for), go-getter, heller, hotshot, Johnny at the rathole, Johnny on the spot, live one, – wire, mover, pisser, player, wheeler-dealer, zip; spec. -oholic (general suffix); buck private (US milit. use: a private who is 'bucking' for promotion)
2. *older (1):* battleaxe, warhorse
3. *hard worker:* grind, stayer, sticker

411. Lively or Passionate Young Woman
n. 1. goer, hot dish, – honey, – number, – one, – stuff, hotsy, piece, – of fluff, pushover, sassy box (US black)

412. Lazy or Unenterprising Person
n. 1 corner cowboy, dag (Aus.), deadbeat, dead duck, – 'un, drag-ass, feather-merchant, fuck-off, goldbrick, jerk-off lard-ass, layabout, lazybones, passenger, piker, poop-butt (US black), skiver, sleeper, slowcoach, sooner (Aus.), weary Willie
2. *dreamer:* wanna be (US black)

413. Successful Person
n. 1. big-timer, comer, hitter, hot-dog(ger), hotshot, it, jumping cat (US black), knockout, Mr Shit, natural, top dog; spec. butter-and-egg man (small-town success)

414. Failure
n. 1. also-ran, back number, blind Freddy (Aus.), bum, deadbeat, dero (Aus.), dud, dudley, duffer, flake, fuck-up, gimp, goner, jerk, nebbish (Yid.), no-hoper, pooch, ring-ding, schlemiel (Yid.),

schlepper (Yid), shmeggegge
(Yid.), trash, washout, yesterday's
papers, Z-bird (see also Terms of
Disparagement: 495, Contemptible
Person: 396, Weakling: 403)

415. Wealthy Person
n. 1. fat cat, green thumb (US
black), lobster (US black), Mr Big,
pound-note geezer, silvertail (Aus.),
silk stocking (US black), tall poppy
(Aus.), zillionaire; spec. nouveau,
nouvy (newly rich)
2. spec. cock (one on whom one can
sponge)

416. Poor Person
n. 1. broker, dosser (see also
Parasite, etc.: 417)

417. Parasite; Dependant; Beggar; Borrower
n. 1. *parasite:* bludger (Aus.),
crasher, freeloader, friend in need
(US black), goldbrick, leech; spec.
doley (Aus. one who draws the
dole)
2. *beggar:* dero (Aus.), glimmer,
mooch, mook, panhandler,
schnorrer (Yid.)
3. *tramp:* bag lady, bindle stiff,
bum, dino, dosser, hurricane lamp
(rhy.sl.), pikey, scat; spec. street
people
4. *lodger:* artful dodger (rhy.sl.)

418. Praiser; Flatterer
n. 1. apple-polisher, ass-kisser,
– licker, bootlicker, brown-noser,
bull artist, bum-sucker,
mealy-mouth, politician, shmooser
(Yid.), suck-up, tom, Uncle Tom
(US black), yes-man; spec. flack
(promo man); log-roller (one who
praises their friends)

419. Critic; Opposer
n. 1. Dutch uncle, knocker, Monday
Morning quarterback, yenta; spec.
crix (show business: critics)

2. *reformer:* bluenose, comstock,
killjoy, longnose, smuthound,
snoop(er), wowser (see also
Meddler: 399)
3. *arguer:* rucker
4. *nag:* ball-buster, – -tearer

420. Talker
n. 1. bag of wind, blowhard, gasbag,
gasser, loudmouth, spruiker (Aus.),
storefront preacher, tub thumper,
tummler (Yid.), windbag; spec.
barrack-room lawyer (self-taught
expert); (see also Vain Person: 401)
2. *gossip:* blabbermouth,
gatemouth, mixer, motormouth,
sack mouth (US black), shit-stirrer,
tattle-tale, whistle-blower; spec.
dish queen (gay use)
3. *user of obscenity:* garbage mouth,
sewer mouth
4. *barker, pitchman:* gee man
(Aus.), spruiker (Aus.)
5. *teller of tales, exaggerator:* bull
artist, bullshit artist, bullshitter,
slickster (US black), smoothie,
wind-up merchant
6. *one who reminds:* elbow shaker
(US black)

421. Listener
n. 1. spec. dummy (deaf mute)

422. Observer; Spectator
n. 1. spec. pinktea (gay use)

423. Eater; Drinker
n. 1. barfly, chow-hound, dustbin,
guts, gutso, sponge
2. *drunk:* one-pot screamer (Aus.)
3. *solo drinker:* Jimmy Woodser
(Aus.)

424. Traveller
n. 1. *'outlaw' motorcyclists:* biker,
easy rider, one percenter, ton-up
boy

PERSONS: PHYSIQUE
425. Attractive
n. 1. *attractive woman, girl:* angel, babe, banana (US black), beat, bit of all right, – crackling, – stuff, brickhouse (US black), butter baby (US black), candy, charmer, cheesecake, chick, classy chassis, cookie, creamie, crumpet, cupcake cutes, cutesie-pie, dish, doll, doll city, dollface, dolly, donah, dreamboat, eyeful, fleshpot (US black), frail, ginch, glamour puss, good-looking, grouse gear (Aus.), hamma, hammer (US black), honey, hot number, jam, (little) cracker, little pretty, looker, lovely, Mercedes (US black), mink (US black), nifty, – piece, page three girl, pancake, patootie, peach, pie, poodle (US black), Porsche, (US black), poundcake, real babe, scorcher, sexpot, sleek lady (US black), stallion (US black), star, sweet potato pie (US black), sweetie, talent, ten, thoroughbred black (US black), tomato, toots, tootsie, – roll (US black), yummy; spec. Barbie Doll (pretty and ultra-conventional); melted butter (US black: light-skinned girl); all tits and teeth (blatantly sexual)
2. *attractive male:* beefcake, buf, glamour-puss, hunk, little pretty, sexpot, smoothie

426. Unattractive
n. 1. face like a douchebag, – like a toilet seat, fright, grub, horror, picklepuss, pretty mess, sight, sourpuss
2. *unattractive woman:* BB head (US black), bad news, bag, bat, bear (US black), buzzard, chicken (US black), chromo, cow, crow, cull bird, dog, dogface, doggie, double-bagger, douchebag, drack (Aus.), grubber, hairbag, hedgehog, heifer, hog, mule, nailhead (US black), pitch, ragmop (US black), Ruth Buzzy (US black), scab, scuzz, skank, sleaze, snot, sweat hog, tackhead (US black), thunder chicken (US black), welfare mother (US black); spec. PTA (US black: pussy, tits and armpits – all smelly)
3. *unattractive male:* dick

427. According to Size
n. 1. *heavyweight:* bohunk, bozo, bruiser, brute, hunk(o), lug, lump, moose, ox, palooka, wham (US black)
2. *fat person:* barrel, blimp, chubette, dumpling, fat-arse, fatso, fatty, guts, gutso, hully (US black), lard-arse, pig, pudge, tick, tub of lard; spec. Miss Piggy (gay use: a fat homosexual)
3. *fat woman:* Bahama mama (US black), butterball, Judy with the big booty (US black), pig(ger), pigmouth, shuttlebutt, teddy bear (US black)
4. *small person:* crumb, feather merchant, half-pint, – portion, microbe, midget, peewee, pint-size, pipsqueak, sawn-off, shrimp, squirt; spec. lofty (as nickname)
5. *tall person:* beanpole, daddylonglegs, high-pockets, lofty; spec. shorty, tiny (as nickname)
6. *thin person:* bag of bones, broomstick, long (thin) streak of piss, string bean
7. spec. gallon head, pumpkin head (person with a large head)

428. According to Hair, Facial Look, etc.
n. 1. *redhead:* bluey, coppernob
2. *bald person:* skinhead, suedehead
3. *bearded person:* beaver, fuzzface, muff
4. *according to eyes:* boss-eye
5. *similar people:* dead fetch, – ringer, – spit, spitting image
6. *left-handed person:* lefty, southpaw
7. spec. Afro (US black: one

wearing such a hairstyle);
crinkle-top (US black: woman with
an Afro); duck's butt (US black:
woman with messy hair)
8. *spec.* long-hair (a hippie)
9. *with glasses:* four-eyes

429. Sick and Injured Persons
n. 1. *exhausted person:* burn-out,
crasher, crispy
2. *cripple:* basket case, gimp,
raspberry (rhy.sl. = raspberry
ripple)
3. *invalid:* cot-case (Aus.), gomer,
gork, vegetable
4. *alcoholics:* alky, dipso, wino
5. *corpse:* goner, stiff

PERSONS: MENTAL STATE
430. Intelligent; Experienced
n. 1. bear-leader, brain, egghead,
gallon head (US black), high-brow,
know-it-all, longhair, marv, maven
(Yid.), pointy-head, razor, smart
cookie, smartypants, wise guy,
wisenheimer; *spec.* old dog (US
black: expert in a given field);
culture-vulture, pseud (fake
intellectual)
2. *able person:* ace, clever dog,
crack hand, dab, good head, hot
stuff, natural, nobody's fool, no
slouch, (boss) player (US black),
sensation, the cheese, the tops,
up-and-comer, whiz, wizard
3. *experienced person:* old hand, old
timer, vet
4 *predictor:* crystal-gazer, dopester,
doper, steerer, tipster
5. *scholar:* spec. sponge (one who
learns easily)

431. Unintellectual; Stupid
n. 1. addlepate, airhead, ass,
asshole, BF (bloody fool), berk,
Berkeley hunt, Berkshire hunt,
birdbrain, blockhead, bonehead,
boob, boofhead, bozo, brenda,
bubblehead, bugs, busher,
cement-head, chowder-head,
chucklehead, clod, clodpoll, clown,
cluck, clunk, coot, crackpot,
crapbrain, deadhead, dickhead,
dildo, dill (Aus.), dingaling,
dingbat, diphead, dipshit, dodo,
dope, dork, dorkbrain, drongo
(Aus.), Dublin University graduate,
dum-dum, dumb-ass, dumb-bell,
dumbellina, dumb fuck, dumbhead,
dumbo, dummy, dumbski,
dunderhead, fathead, flipwreck
(Aus.), FNG (fucking new guy),
fruitcake, fuckhead, fuckwit, galah
(Aus.), get, gig (Aus.), gink, git,
goober, goof, gook, goop, greener,
greenhorn, hammerhead (US
black), head-banger, herbert,
horse's arse, – hangdown, ig man
(US black), ignant (US black),
Irving, klutz, kook, lame,
lamebrain, log, loogan, loon(y),
lug, lunchbox, lunk, lunkhead,
meathead, mental job, mo-mo,
momo, mug, mule, musclehead,
mutt, nana, ning-nong (Aus.), nit,
nitwit, nong (Aus.), no-no, noodle,
numbnuts, numbskull, nutcake,
nutter, pinhead, poon (Aus.), poop,
poophead, prat, prawnhead (Aus.),
pud, puddinghead, quashie (WI),
ring-ding, rookie, room to rent,
rube, schlemiel (Yid.), schlub
(Yid.), schmeggege (Yid.), schmuck
(Yid.), schnook (Yid.), screwball,
section eight, semolia (US black),
shitkicker, sickie, silly, silly-billy,
simp, spaz, squarebrain (US black),
stumer, stupe, stupe-head, stupid
fuck, thickie, thicko, three-dollar
bill, tool, toolhead, twit, veg,
wet foot, wethead (US black),
whacko, whizpop, wienie, wise,
zipalid; *spec.* schoolbook chump
(US black: one who is intellectual
but not intelligent); *spec.*
square-eyes (one who watches too
much TV)
phr. 2. one who looks like he
wouldn't piss if his pants were on

fire; (to a dullard) one of these days you'll wake up dead

PERSONS: MORAL STATUS

432. Good; Respectable

n. 1. baa-lamb, good time, real McCoy, regular guy, right guy, square John, – shooter, straight arrow, stand-up guy, white man
2. *'good girl'*: quandong (Aus.)

433. Disreputable

n. 1 alley cat, – rat, bad egg, – hat, – penny, baddie, bar steward, bugger, cloth-ears, face-ache, freak, fucker, hard, – case, heel, hood, lare (Aus.), lowlife, naus, oik, raas, raasclat, shitbird, shithead, shitheel, shit-for-brains, shtarka (Yid.), SOB, son of a bitch, sweep, wedgeass, wrong 'un, yob(bo)
2. *foulmouthed:* salty dog, trashmouth
3. *thug:* bruiser, bucko, goon, gorilla, hard case, hard egg, hatchet man, heavy, hood, husky, lowlife, muscle, plug-ugly, punch-out artists, SAN (stop-at-nothing) man, torpedo, tough guy, – nut, ugly customer; spec. goon squad (group of hired thugs)
4. *bodyguard:* heavy, minder, muscle
5. *rebel:* cowboy (US black)
6. *fugitive:* lamster, over the hill, runout man, skip(per); spec. draftnik (draft evader)
7. *freak:* geek
8. *assassin:* hitman

434. Dishonest

n. 1. chiseller, cowboy, gyp, hydraulic (Aus.), rip-off artist, rooker, shark, shicer, shyster, spiv, tealeaf (rhy.sl. = thief)

435. Deceitful; Untrustworthy

n. 1. actor, bad actor, Carl Rosa (rhy.sl. = poser), cross man, dreykop (Yid.) false face (US black), fly-by-night, four-flusher, grifter, high and goodbye (US black), merry-go-round (US black), PhD (piles it higher and deeper), real greek, sharpie, sly slick and wicked (US black), slyboots, snake, Spanish athlete (he 'throws the bull'), Turk McGurk, two-timer, welcher, wide boy, wrong guy, wrong 'un
2. *liar:* holy friar (rhy.sl.), one-eyed scribe (US black), Tom Pepper
3. *informer:* blab, blabbermouth, peach, snitch, squawker, squealer, stoolie (see also Crime: 481)
phr. 4. his guts are moving the wrong way, does a lot of shitting but his pants aren't down, doesn't know whether to suck or blow, – to shit or go blind, you need an ear scoop to filter his horseshit; don't pick up soap in his shower, he'd steal a rotten doughnut out of a bucket of snot, he'd fuck a snake if somebody would hold its head; you can't trust him further than you can throw a bull by the prick, – than you can see up an alligator's ass (in a dust-storm) (at midnight)

436. Sexual Choice

n. 1. *fellator:* barbecue (US black), face-artist, fluter, French active, – passive, Frenchman, icing expert, mouth worker; spec. glutton for punishment (one who continues to fellate after orgasm)
2. *one who performs cunnilingus:* cannibal, cuntlapper, fish queen, gash-eater, high diver, meat-eater, muff diver
3. spec. sandwich man (one male plus two females)
4. spec. butt-plunger (man who enjoys inserting a dildo into his own anus)
5. *child molester:* monster, nonce, perv, secko (Aus.)
6. *exhibitionist:* flasher

7. *trans-sexual, transvestite:* TS, TV
8. *bisexual:* double-life man, switch hitter
9. *masturbator:* jack-off, jerk-off, rod walloper, wanker
10. spec. cradle-snatcher (one who prefers much younger partners)
11. *celibate:* priest
12. *voyeur:* looker, peeper
13. spec. mystery mad (one who prefers stray young girls)

437. Promiscuous
n. 1. swinger
2. *promiscuous male:* alligator (US black), cock-hound, cocksman, come-freak, cum-freak, rooster (US black), saloon-bar cowboy, stud, swordsman
3. *promiscuous female:* baggage, bike, bimbo, broad, bum, carpenter's dream, charity girl, chippie, cooze, dead cert, dirty leg, easy lay, – ride, floosie, floozie, free for all, gash, gin-and-fuck-it, goer, knock, lay, leg, Little Miss Roundheels, lust dog, motorcycle (US black), mount, nymph(o), paraffin lamp (rhy.sl. = tramp), piece, piece of ass, – tail, pig, punch, pushover, quickie, quiff, right sort, screamer and a creamer, scrubber, shack job, shack-up, shagbag, slag, sleepy-time girl, steamer, stinker, tart, town bicycle, – pump, – punch, tramp, whore; spec. groupie, band rat; snow bunny (girls who specialise in rock groups, skiers); buttered bun (girl having sex with several men in succession); splash (the victim of gang-rape)
4. *promiscuous male homosexual:* fantail, glutton
5. *promiscuous lesbian:* clithopper
phr. 6. no better than he/she should be, one who's had more arse than a toilet seat, – more pricks than a second-hand dart-board

PERSONS: SOCIAL POSITIONS
438. Friends
n. 1. abc, ace, – boom boom, – boon coon, – coon poon, asshole buddy, blood (US black), bro (US black), brother, buddy, butty, china (rhy.sl. = china plate = mate), chum(my), cobber (Aus.), cutty, Dutch (rhy.sl. = Dutch plate = mate), family, good ole boy, home squeeze (US black), homeboy, homegirl (US black), landsman, main man, mate, mellow (US black), Mister Ed, mucker, off the block, pal, pard, PLU (people like us), road dog, running partner (US black), splib, splib-de-wib (US black), (main) squeeze, oppo, yardie (WI); spec. smiling faces (US black: false friends); sight for sore eyes (a friend in need)
2. *allies:* spec. cognoscenti, sisters (gay use); friendlies (military); crew (a gang); blue-eyed soul brother, paleface nigger (US black: white who is accepted by blacks); coon-lover, nigger-lover (derog.: a white who rejects racism)
3. *fan:* rooter

439. Hanger-on
n. 1. ligger
2. *fan:* celebrity fucker, grouper, groupie, star fucker
3. *spec. gay use:* fruit fly, fag hag, half-iron, scag hag
4. spec. walker (rich woman's male social companion)
5. *toady:* apple polisher, arse-kisser, – -licker, brown-noser, – -tongue, creep, suck-arse, yes-man

440. Stranger; Enemy
n. 1. *novice:* Johnny-come-lately, new fish, tenderfoot
2. *alien:* beastie, ding (Aus.), Queen's Park Ranger (rhy.sl. = stranger)

441. Lovers
n. 1. crush, dreamboat, flame, heart-throb, honeybunch, pash, sweetie, sweetie-pie
2. *male lover, boyfriend:* daddy one (US black), Lord Right, Mr Right, old man, sweet daddy
3. *female lover, girlfriend, mistress:* chick, dolly, frail, honey, jam tart (rhy.sl. = sweetheart), Lady Right, Miss Right, main bitch (US black), mat (US black), monotony, mum, old lady, ordinary (US black), Renee, Richard (the Third) (rhy.sl. = bird), steady, sweet patootie, sweetpea, toots, tootsie; spec. Mayfair Merc(enary) (using sex to succeed socially)
4. *adulterous lover:* back-door man, bit on the side, fancy man
5. *couple:* item, shack job
6. *'great lover':* fast worker, heaver (US black), makeout artist, stallion, stickman, stud, wolf; spec. 4-F club ('find 'em feel 'em, fuck 'em and forget 'em)
7. *former lover:* ex
8. *new lover:* fresh hide (US black)
9. *inter-racial lovers:* coal burner, gin-jockey (Aus.); spec. dinge queen (gay use); gin shepherd (man who attempts to keep races apart)
10. *physical preference:* arse man, chubby-chaser, leg man, tit man
11. *casual partner:* it, one-night stand, pick-up, trick
12. *flirt, teaser:* cunt-teaser (male), cock-teaser, prick-teaser (female)

442. Sentimentalist
n. 1. sopcan; spec. moon-ass, puppy (infatuated person)

443. Flirt; Philanderer
n. 1. *flirtatious woman:* cock-teaser, dick-teaser, gold-digger, man-eater, prick-teaser, vamp
2. *male philanderer:* chippy chaser, Jody (US black), hard-leg (US black), lady-killer, letch, masher, plumber, sharp-shooter, skirt-chaser, slugger, sport, steed, swordsman, tomcat, wolf
3. spec. MTF (must touch flesh), NSIT (not suitable in taxis) (UK 'society' use)

444. Relatives
n. 1. *family:* Mom-Dad-Buddy-and-Sis
2. *father:* my old guvnor, old boy, – fellow, – man, pop(s), sorry and sad (rhy.sl. = dad)
3. *mother:* ma, mam, mum(s), mumsie, old lady
4. *husband:* hubbie; spec. weekend man (US black: one who sees his family only at weekends)
5. *wife:* ball and chain, better half, carving knife (rhy.sl.), Dutch, Duchess of Fife (rhy.sl.), her indoors, old Dutch (rhy.sl.), – lady, trouble and strife (rhy.sl.)
6. *sister:* skin and blister (rhy.sl.)
7. *illegitimate child:* bachelor's baby
8. *grandparents:* gramps, nan(a)
9. *widow:* sod widow (as opposed to 'grass widow', whose husband is only absent)

445. Single Person
n. 1. loner, lone wolf, stag
2. *unattached girl:* bit of spare
3. spec. fishing fleet (girls who look abroad for husbands)

446. Sociable
n. 1. cookie-pusher, drugstore cowboy, lounge lizard, raver, stage-door johnny, wildcat (US black)
2. *uninvited guest:* crasher

447. Hedonist; Pleasure-seeker
n. 1. cutup, funster, good-time Charlie, hell-raiser, Mr Laffs; spec. nightstick (US black: one who enjoys night-life)
2. *tourist:* boing-boing, rubberneck

448. High Society; Elite
n. 1. blue-blood, carriage trade, high-hat, nob, swell, toff
2. spec. glitterati (fashionable academe); preppie (student at a US prep – UK public – school); Wellies (upperclass members of Exeter University, UK); hooray, Hooray Henry (boorish upperclass UK youth)
phr. 3. *an excess of leaders:* all chiefs and no indians

449. Masses; Rabble; Proles
n. 1. Joe Public, John Q. Public, the Great Unwashed

450. Fashionable; Chic
n. 1. clotheshorse, fancy pants, Mr Firstnighter, shoe, slicker, supersoul (US black), swing daddy (US black); spec. zubber (one dressed in top hat, tails, etc.)
2. spec. made (US black: one who has their hair straightened)
3. spec. glitterati (fashionable academe), preppie (member of US prep – UK public – schools), Sloane Ranger (British upperclass female), yuppie (young upwardly mobile professional)

451. Unfashionable
n. 1. boojie, boogie, cull, fish 'n' chip mob, gape (US black), geek, goose, greaser, grockle, ham and egger, jello squad, MCM (middle class monster), Nashville (US black), nerd, nerk, puck, rag head (US black), Santa Claus (US black), slummy, wally, zonko; spec. nubian (US campus: black students)
2. *badly dressed:* caution sign (US black)

452. Unsociable
n. 1. homeboy, homegirl, stay-at-home
2. *social failure:* clunk, creep, drag, drip, dumbell, dumbo, dummy,

feeb, iceberg, lemon, pain in the arse, – in the behind, – in the neck, pill, schmo, schnook, stick-in-the-mud, stiff, washout, wet blanket; spec. tired woman (US black: unsophisticated)

WORKERS
453. Worker
n. 1. jockey, wage-slave, working stiff
2. *assistant:* dogsbody, gofer, gopher, off-sider (Aus.), tickler; spec. candy-striper (US hospitals: voluntary workers); spec. head cook and bottle washer (general factotum)
3. *hard worker (at school, college):* cereb, conch, egg, gome, grub, hack, pencil geek, schoolbook chump (US black), spider, squid, swot, throat, tool, wonk
4. *hard worker:* eager beaver, grafter, workoholic
5. *strike-breaker:* blackleg, fink, goon, – squad, scab
6. *privileged worker:* IDB (abbrev. in Daddy's business)

454. Unskilled Worker
n. 1. *beginner, novice:* butterboy, greener, greenhorn, new fish, rookie, wet foot; spec. boot, yardbird (US military: recruit); prospect (recruit to an 'outlaw' bike club); fresher (freshman at university, college)
2. spec. pearl diver (washer-up)
3. *labourer:* ape, humper, roughneck, roustabout; spec. shovel stiff (one who digs); McAlpine fusilier (worker for a construction firm); lump (freelance unskilled workers, esp. in construction industry)

455. Domestic; Servant
n. 1. biddy, daily, flunky, keep-up (US black), shikse (Yid.)

456. Specialist

n. 1. *military:* boonie rat, dogface, doggie, doughboy, eleven-bravo, GI, grunt, swaddy, tommy (soldier); gyrene, leatherneck (US Marine), swab jockey (sailor), point (head of patrol), drag (last man), slackman (2nd man in patrol), Band-aid (corpsman); black gang (naval engine room crew); padre (chaplain); flyboy (pilot); deck ape (deck hand); grape (deck hand on carriers); early out (serviceman due for retirement); gunny (US: gunnery sergeant); bird dog (air spotter); lifer (career soldier), looie (lieutenant)
2. *medical:* croaker, medico, quack (doctor), butcher, sawbones (a poor surgeon), gynae (gynaecologist), headshrinker, looney doctor, nut doctor, shrink, trick cyclist (psycho-analyst); cock doctor (venerealogist)
3. *media:* sob sister, agony aunt (advice columnists), hack, journo, pencil pusher, scribe (writer), stringer (local correspondent); newsie (paper-seller)
4. *law:* ambulance chaser, brief, legal eagle, loudmouth, mouthpiece (lawyer), silk (Queen's Counsel); Barnaby Rudge, smear and smudge (rhy.sl. = judge); garden gate (rhy.sl. = magistrate); dick, gumshoe, shamus (private detective); repo man, skip tracer (debt collector)
5. *entertainment:* bouncer, chucker-out, wollyhumper (steward); hoofer (dancer); red (Butlins redcoat); carney (carnival worker); DJ, jock (disc jockey); muso (musician); combo (group of musicians); roadie (rock music road manager); lenser, megger (film director); gabriel (trumpeter); canary (singer)
6. *bureaucracy:* flak catcher (complaints officer), paper pusher, pencil pusher, red-taper (lowest form of civil servant); spec. sniffer (DHSS investigator)
7. *social:* walker (rich woman's companion)
8. *craftsman:* chippie (carpenter); sparks (electrician); mush faker (umbrella repairer); brickie (bricklayer); retchub (backsl. = butcher)
9. *political:* politico, flesh-presser, palm-presser; spec. lefty, parlour pink, pinko, Trot (left-wingers); lame duck (US politican who has lost office but still serves out time); libber (feminist activist)
10. *education:* chalkie (Aus.), schoolie (teacher); lollipop man/lady (road safety supervisor)
11. *travel:* hostie, stew (air hostess); clippie (bus conductress)
12. *scientists:* back-room boys, boffins
13. *taxis:* hack(er), hackie, mushie, musher (drivers); brown coat, white coat (inspectors at London Cab Office)
14. *cleaner:* garbo (Aus.), honey-dipper, sanno (Aus.); Mary Ellen (dockyard, boat cleaners)
15. *docker:* wharfie (Aus.), yardbird
16. *business, commerce:* drummer (salesman); uncle (pawnbroker); hired gun (expert); Collins Street farmer, Pitt Street farmer (Aus.: absentee rural landlords)
17. *chemist:* druggie
18. *sportsman:* jock; slugger (boxer), tanker (boxer who deliberately loses); jock (jockey)
19. *petrol station:* pump jockey
20. *farming:* cowpoke (cowboy)
21. *oil rigs:* roughneck, roustabout (labourer)
22. *services:* milko (Aus. = milkman); saw (US black: rooming house owner)
23. *spy:* spook
24. *general specialist:* artist, merchant, pro

25. *cook:* babbling brook (rhy.sl.)

**457. Superintendent; Manager
n.** 1. boss, bossman, Edmundo
(rhy.sl. = Edmundo Ros = boss),
gaffer, guv, guvnor, master-dog (US
black), pitch and toss (rhy.sl. =
boss), skip(per), top dog

2. *military:* brass hats, white
hats (officers); full bird (full
colonel); topkick (first sergeant);
Shake and Bake (graduate of US
NCO school); mustang (officer
promoted from the ranks); first skirt
(senior officer in WAC); -pipper
(lieutenant)

Specialist Jargons

CRIME: PERSONS
458. Persons

n. 1. *criminal:* babbler (Aus.), babbling brook (rhy.sl. = crook), bandit, body, buck, face, hardhead (Aus.), merchant, perp; spec. good people (former criminals); mooner (US: 'moonstruck' – a pathological lawbreaker); operator, the Man (major criminal); rounder (Can. sophisticated criminal); Ten (FBI's Ten Most Wanted Criminals list) (see also Persons, Disreputable: 435, Dishonest: 436, Deceitful: 437)
2. *gang:* crew, firm, mob, push (Aus.), team; spec. the Mob, the wise guys (US Mafiosi); made man (US: member of Mafia); coolie (street gang use: an unaffiliated youth); deb (street gang member's girlfriend)
3. *small-time criminal:* cruncher (Aus.), heel, international milk thief, meter thief, parking meter bandit, pie-eater (Aus.), tearaway; spec. soldier, button man (US: lower echelon Mafioso)
4. *young or novice criminal:* JD (juvenile delinquent), schoolboy, virgin; spec. MINS (US jail use: Minors in Need of Supervision); CHINS (Children In Need of Supervision); gunsel, gonsil (criminal's young – poss. homosexual – accomplice)
5. *violent criminal:* dropper, hatchet man, hit man, stick-up artist, trigger man
6. *sex criminal:* spec. player (pimp); junior jumper (US: underage rapist); diddler, monster, short eyes, shut eyes (child molester)
7. *thief:* blagger, jump-up merchant, – man, second-storey man; spec. in-and-out man (spontaneous thief)
8. *swindler, con-man:* alias man (WI), ginnal (WI), illywhacker (Aus.), ringer, samfie (WI); spec. bait (attractive girl used to lure victims); hedge (the crowd that gathers around a street con-man); ringer (one who steals, improves, then sells cars)
9. *arsonist:* firebug; spec. blanket man (arsonist's assistant)
10. *receiver:* buyer, fence; spec. placer (middleman between thief and receiver)
11. *planner:* set-up man
12. *go-between:* bag man, bird dog
13. *look-out:* earwig
14. *pickpocket:* dip, hoister, knockabout man (Aus.), legshake artist (Aus.), whiz, wire
15. *shoplifter:* booster, hoister, (US black), blockerm, stickman
16. *gambler:* KG (known gambler); spec. digits dealer (numbers racketeer); operator (controller of gambling game); subway dealer (US: card sharp)
17. spec. seducer (US black: one who provides means of making illicit cash)
18. *court personnel:* spec. beak (judge, magistrate); interrupter (interpreter); penitentiary agent (inadequate defence lawyer)
19. *legitimate person:* pop corn
adj. 20. spec. -handed (number: three-handed, four-handed, team-handed, etc.)

CRIME: PHYSICAL
459. Health
n. 1. spec. crush-out (the
obliteration of a corpse by crushing
it in a junkyard metal crusher)
adv. 2. *dead:* DOA (dead on
arrival), slabbed and slid, tits up

CRIME: PLACES
460. Locality
n. 1. *police station:* bill shop, cop
shop, factory, pig heaven, – sty
2. *police divisions:* ground, manor,
patch, toby
3. *storage enclosure:* flop, slaughter;
spec. Aladdin's cave (UK: a thief's
home or the hideaway for his loot)

461. Establishments; Resorts
n. 1. spec. clip joint, gyp joint
(swindling night-clubs)

CRIME: PROPERTY; BOOTY
462. Money
n. 1 (see Commerce: 516); spec.
California roll (US), flash (UK),
(large roll of low-denomination
notes, wrapped in a high-value note
to give illusion of wealth)
2. spec. case dough (limited funds);
drops (money hidden away); earner
(high-paying criminal enterprises;
bribe); fall money (funds set aside
for legal fees); indoor money (daily
expenses)
v. 3. *to profit from crimes:* earn,
score

463. Valuables
n. 1. red (gold), tom (rhy.sl. =
tomfoolery = jewellery); spec.
groin, groyne (UK: any ring)
2. *fake jewellery:* fool's gold,
patacca; spec. mug's ticker (dud
watch)
3. *safe:* can, crib, damper, peter

464. Booty; Illicit Goods
n. 1. goods, good stuff, hot stuff,
swag; spec. drop (delivery of booty,
money, etc.); five-finger discount
(proceeds of shoplifting); LF
gear (UK: proceeds of 'long firm'
fraud); overs (booty yet to be
disposed of); carve-up, cut, taste (a
share)
v. 2. spec. mash it on (one) (US
black: pass on contraband)
3. *to share out:* cut up touches

CRIME: IMPLEMENTS
465. Implements; Devices
n. 1. spec. autograph (blank paper
used to obtain victim's signature);
billy, Mr Wood, rosewood,
shit-stick (billy-club, truncheon);
stonicky, swailer (cosh); car key
(screwdriver used to break into
cars), can opener (safe-breaking
tool); combo (combination lock);
bracelets, cuffs, darbies (handcuffs);
come-along (manacle); flash case
(US black: case holding drugs,
contraband); happy bag (case
carrying a shotgun); HBI
(house-breaking implements);
jemmy, jimmy, tool (crowbar);
jigglers (skeleton keys); keister,
peter (bag of tools); jumper
(jump-lead); loid, Lloyd
(celluloid lock-pick); monkey
(padlock)

466. Weapons; Explosives
n. 1. *gun:* equaliser, Roscoe; spec.
crowd pleaser (US policeman's
weapon); sawed off, sawn-off
(sawn-off shotgun); Chicago piano,
– typewriter (machine-gun)
2. *knife:* shank; spec. shin (US jail
use)
3. *explosives:* dinah (nitroglycerine);
jelly (gelignite)
v. 4. *to be armed:* carry, hold
adv. 5. *armed:* CCW (US: carrying
a concealed weapon), carrying,
holding, rodded
6. *unarmed:* clean

CRIME: FOOD; LIQUOR, ETC.

467. Food
n. 1. spec. CNR strawberries (Canadian prison-issue prunes)

469. Tobacco
n. 1. burn, snout; spec. tailormade (factory-produced cigarette)

CRIME: COMMUNICATION

469. Communication; Correspondence
n. 1. spec. batphone (UK: police radio); dep (UK: deposition); squawk (UK: petition to authorities); stiff (UK: illicit jail communication)

470. Speech
n. 1. spec. toast (US jail: long epic poem)
v. 2. spec. cut up touches (reminisce over crimes, etc.)
adv. 3. *agreed verbally:* on a promise
phr. 4. spec. on the earie! (be quiet! someone is listening); Edna! (UK: rhy.sl. = Edna May = on your way!)

471. Signals; Symbols
n. 1. spec. show out (UK: signal between policeman and an informer who meet in public)

472. Information
n. 1. bubble (rhy.sl. = bubble and squeak = speak), dope, scream, squeal, the score, tickle, tip; spec. hooking (attempting to smear the police through false information); crude (US: informer's rather than public's tip-off)
2. *informer:* backmark (US black), canary, car park (rhy.sl. = nark), cheese-eater, dog (Aus.), dog's nose, finger, fizgig (Aus.), guinea pig, grass (rhy.sl. = grasshopper = shopper), mule mouth, nark, noah's ark (rhy.sl. = nark), nose, pig

brother (US black), rat, singer, slim, snitch, snout, stool-pigeon, stoolie, Tom Slick (US black), tout (IRA use); spec. narc (narcotics informer); supergrass (major informer)
v. 3. *to inform:* blow one's nose, cop out (on), copper, cough, give the man the play (US black), grass, holler cropper, put the bubble in, QE (turn Queen's Evidence), scream, spill, – the beans; blow through (phone in information); put it around (circulate rumours); turn one around (to persuade a criminal to turn informer)
adj. 4. *untrustworthy:* copper-hearted

473. Betrayal; Accusation
n. 1. spec. fix, frame-up (concoction of evidence)
2. *informer:* budgie, snitcher, squealer; spec. faded boogie, pig brother (US black: black informer to white authorities)
v. 3. *to betray:* blab, blow the gaff, – the whistle on, drop a dime on, – a quarter on, – a dollar (US black: cash sums vary as to degree of betrayal, all refer to using the telephone), finger, go bent, lolly, pin on, put a body up, – a name up, – away, – in the acid, – one in (Aus.), – the nigger on, – the whisper on, rat on, rat one out, shop, snitch, squeal, tip in, tom out (US black), top off (Aus.); spec. narc one over (betray to the drug squad)
4. *to concoct evidence:* frame, frame up, fit up, fix (up)
adv. 5. *betrayed:* bubbled, grassed up, etc. (see also Information: 472), lollied (rhy.sl. = lollypopped = shopped)

CRIME: OBSERVATION

474. Guarding
n. 1. *guard, lookout:* dogger out (US), six-man (Can.)

adv. 2. *on guard:* on the earie

CRIME: TRAVEL
475. Transportation Methods
n. 1. *driver:* wheelman; spec. skid artist, stoppo driver (UK: getaway driver)
2. *police car:* black and white, blue and white, blue dangers, hurry-up, salt and pepper; spec. nondescript, Q-boat (UK: unmarked police cars); noddy (UK: police motorcycle)
3. *'Black Maria':* cattle car, go-long, hurry-up wagon, meat wagon, paddy wagon

---

CRIME: TRAMPING
476. Vagrancy
n. 1. *vagrant:* wag; spec. vag (vagrancy charge)

477. Begging
adv. 1. on the bow, on the earhole

CRIME: CRIME AND PUNISHMENT
478. Crime
n. 1. caper, job; spec. across the pavement (UK: any street crime); back-alley deal (US black); rackets (underworld); the Life (US black: the underworld); MO (modus operandi: a given criminal's 'trademarks'); ways (US: ethos and style of the Mafia); aka (false name)
v. 2. *to commit crime:* do a job, get one's feet muddy, make one, perform, pull a caper, – a job; spec. put one together (plan a crime); chip (US: carry out petty crimes); have an in (have useful contacts); make one's rep (to establish one's criminal status); row in (to enrol in a criminal plan)
3. *to give up crime:* go straight
adj. 4. *criminal:* naughty

adv. 5. *involved in crime:* at it

479. Theft
n. 1. heist, hist, screwer; spec. B&E (breaking and entering); high-wall job, second-storey job (theft involving climbing); sneak job (house-breaking); sticksing (WI: pickpocketing); boosting, hoisting (US: shoplifting); snow-dropping (stealing from washing lines); creaming, the weed (stealing from one's employer's tills); Black Power dance (looting); cartnapping (stealing supermarket trolleys); matchbox (anywhere easily robbed)
2. *thief:* gazlon (Yid.), gonef, gonnif, macer, tealeaf (rhy.sl.); spec. nighthawk (specialist in night work)
3. *specialists:* bumper, cannon, fork, hooker, nudger, stall, pick (pickpockets); moll buzzer (pickpocket who prefers female victims); jack roller, lush worker, roller (one who robs drunks); breaker, crib-man, screwsman, second-storey man (house-breaker); pete-man, peterman (safe-breaker); booster, lugger, skin worker (shoplifter); creep(er) (sneak thief); git-'em-up-guy (hold-up man); reader, slow walker (US: one who follows postmen to rob them); dunnigan worker (one who robs in public lavatories); shitter (one who excretes where he has stolen)
v. 4. *to rob:* blag, clout, fleece, half-inch (rhy.sl. = pinch), kipe, knock off, – over, liberate, pinch, skank (WI), skulk, swipe; spec. dance (from upper floors); do a crib, jack in the box (to house-break); boost, hoist (to shoplift); drag, gleep a cage (US), make a car (US) (to steal from cars); work the hole, – the well (to pickpocket on public transport); drop sticks (WI), fan (to pickpocket); kiss the dog (to

pickpocket face-to-face); case (the joint) (to appraise a location prior to a robbery)

adj. 5. *larcenous:* sticky-fingered

adv. 6. spec. at the wash (stealing from public lavatories); creeping and tilling (US black: robbing from shop tills); on the bottle, on the whiz, at the push-up (working as a pickpocket); swagging (US prison: stealing prison property)

phr. 7. spec. it fell off the back of a lorry, they give them away with a pound of tea

480. Swindling

n. 1. bunco, con, flim-flam, FP (false pretences), high game, grift; spec. big con (large-scale confidence tricks); short con, – stuff (small-scale confidence tricks); slow con (slowly matured trick); fonfen (Yid. the 'line' used by a con-man); hit-and-get (moving quickly from town to town); pitch (site of a three-card monte game); bucket gaff, – job (fraudulent company); market (bait that lures the victim); donah ('the lady' in a three-card monte game)

2. *confidence tricks:* double-dooring (hotel fraud); drop game (using planted wallets); drumming (posing as a 'salesman'); the Hype, the Bill, twenties (confusing shopkeepers over change); LF, long firm (credit fraud); murphy (game) (beating and robbing of a prostitute's client); smack (coin-tossing fraud); tat (tricks using dice); tweedling (selling allegedly 'stolen' goods)

3. *confidence trickster:* bunco artist, con artist, grifter, megsman; spec. amster (Aus. rhy.sl. = Amsterdam = ram); bunco-steerer, buttoner, inside man, ram (Aus.) (con-man's confederate); broadsman (card-sharp); thrower, slide (members of a three-card monte team)

4. *victim:* flop, live one, mark, mug, percher, pigeon, punter

5. *to swindle:* con, take (for a ride)

6. spec. chop the clock (turn back a mileometer); do the party (lure victims in a three-card monte game); fly a kite (pass dud cheques); reload (permit the sucker to win); cook the mark (calm down the fleeced victim)

adv. 7. spec. at the switch (swindling shops); on the knocker (posing as a salesman); on the plastic (using stolen credit cards); at the mark-up (taking an excessive share of loot or profits)

481. Illicit Business

n. 1. dodge, lay, put up job, racket, scam; spec. shakedown (blackmail, extortion); corner, lawing (confidence tricks based on selling supposedly 'stolen' goods); brooming (UK cabbies: refusing all but profitable fares); mule (amateur smuggler)

2. *false appearance:* front

3. *illicit businesses:* spec. granny (business used as a front); laundromat (a business used to 'launder' money)

v. 4. spec. launder, wash (to 'decriminalise' illicitly acquired funds); scalp (to work as a ticket tout)

adj. 5. *illicit:* moody

phr. 6. *justifying possession of stolen goods:* it fell off the back of a lorry; they give them away with a pound of tea

482. Corruption

n. 1. *corruption:* graft

2. *bribe:* bung, drink, grease

3. spec. grass-eater (US: policeman who is satisfied with the bribes he is offered), meat-eater (one who demands higher payments)

v. 4. *to take bribes:* cop, cop a drop, drink

adj. 5. *corrupt:* a bit swift, bent, dodgy, wide
adv. 6. *accepting bribes:* mumping, on a pension, – contract, – the take, – the wrist; spec. on the tin (US: free meals, gifts offered policemen)
phr. 7. spec. can I speak to you? (UK: asking a policeman: can you be bribed?)

483. Counterfeiting and Forgery
n. 1. *counterfeit money:* funny money, slush (UK)
2. *counterfeiter:* cobbler, penman, scratcher; spec. lay-down merchant, slinger (one who passes forged banknotes); kitcr, paper hanger (one who passes dud cheques)

484. Kidnapping
n. 1. snatch
v. 2. snatch, sneeze

485. Violence; Coercion
n. 1 (see Rough Treatment: 337, Assault: 338); GBH (grievous bodily harm), push-in job (mugging on the victim's doorstep), RWV (robbery with violence); spec. cement kimono, – overcoat (the hiding of a corpse by burying it in cement); father and mother stuff (street gang use: attacking 'civilians')
2. spec. juice man (collector for a loan-shark); minder (bodyguard); sledge (one who carries a sledgehammer)
v. 3. *to hurt:* do a mischief (to), give it to, muscle, strongarm
4. *to rob with violence:* knock over, mug, stick up
adv. 5. *violent:* on the muscle
6. *marked for death:* on the spot

486. Evidence; Suspicion
n. 1. dope, goods, stuff (on); spec. dirty dishes (planted evidence); dabs (fingerprints); frame (general situation regarding suspicions); wild prints (prints as yet unidentified)
2. *surveillance:* ob(b)o, plant, stake-out; spec. blinker (police helicopter)
3. *identification:* ID, make; spec. mug shot (identifying photo of criminal)
4. *a suspect:* chummy
v. 5. *to suspect:* measure one's dick (for), row in
6. *to identify:* ID, make (for); mug (to take identifying photos)
7. *to plant or fake evidence:* fit up, flake, frame, plant, stitch up
8. *to hide evidence:* wax up
9. *to exonerate:* drop one out, row out
10. *to divert suspicion:* take the dairy off
adv. 11. *under surveillance:* pegged
12. *'framed up':* jobbed
13. *under suspicion:* hot, in the frame

487. Evasion
n. 1. fade, lam, powder, runout powder
2. *hiding place:* slaughter, stash
3. *escapee:* runner, take-off artist, trotter
4. spec. outfit (prison escape kit); outers (any means of escape)
v. 5. *to escape:* cop a heel, – a moke, cop and heel, do a runner, go over the hill, have it away (on one's toes), make one, make one out, take off; spec. jump bail (break one's bail conditions and flee)
6. spec. spring (to help one escape)
phr. 7. spec. one away! (UK prison officers cry of alarm)

488. Search; Pursuit
n. 1. *raid:* swoop
2. *search warrant:* brief, ticket, W
3. *to stop and search:* fan, frisk, jack up, pat (one) down, pull, rumble, turn over; spec. spin, – a drum (to search premises)

4. spec. go out poncing (UK: to search for working pimps); house (UK: to trace a suspect to a given place)
phr. 5. the heat's on!

489. Apprehension; Arrest

n. 1. bail up (Aus.), bounce (US), bust, capture, clear-up, collar, hook, jam, pinch, pull, tug; spec. accommodation collar, flake (US: arrest simply to fill a quota); lay down (UK: remand in custody); humbug, hummer, swift 'un (false arrest)
v. 2. *to arrest:* bail up (Aus.), book, borrow, bounce, bust, capture, claim, collar, drop the hook on, feel a collar, grab, have (it) off, hook, jam, life, nab, nick, pinch, pull, put the sleeve on, run in, scoop, spear, swag, swamp, toss in the bucket, toss in the can, tug; spec. railroad (to arrest unfairly); scratch for work (UK: to need an arrest)
3. *to be arrested:* get a capture, – a tug, – one's collar felt, fall, take a fall
adv. 4. *arrested:* bagged, captured, collared, hooked, etc. (see n. 1.), done up (like a kipper), nicked, popped, tucked up; spec. on the pavement (arrested in the street)
5. *caught red-handed:* bang to rights
6. *due to be arrested:* due
phr. 7. spec. it looks like rain (an arrest is imminent)

490. Examination of Prisoners

n. 1. line-up; spec. beef (court case)
2. *hard interrogation:* heat, third degree; spec. Mutt and Jeff ('good' and 'bad' role-playing by interrogators)
3. *statement:* verbal; spec. dock asthma ('surprised' reactions of the accused on hearing their confessions in court)
4. *charge:* rap; spec. bad rap (serious or unfair charge)

v. 5. *to interrogate:* strap (interrogate harshly); spec. verbal (for police to fake a confession)
6. *to confess:* come clean, – one's cocoa, – one's fat, – one's lot, – one's guts, cough, dob in (Aus.), sing, – like a canary, sneeze (it out), spill one's guts, stand up; spec. hold the bag, take the rap, wear it (confess to another's crime)
7. *to plead innocent:* plead
8. *to withstand interrogation:* beat the rap, stand up
adv. 9. spec. very swift (of corrupt police methods)
phr. 10. *charge him!:* stick him on!

491. Sentence

n. 1. bit, bird (rhy.sl. = bird lime = time), lagging, porridge, time
2. spec. chuck (US: 'not guilty' verdict); toothbrush day (the day of sentencing: one should take a toothbrush to court)
3. spec. baby life (US: 6 yrs, 4 mths); big bit, – time, lagging, long bit, nice bit (long sentences, 3 years+); carpet (UK: 3 mths); double carpet (6 mths); fin up (US: 5 yrs to life); haircut (UK short sentence); half a stretch (UK: 6 mths); handful (UK: 5 yrs); leggner (UK: 12 mths); maximum, minimum (US: longest/shortest times that must be served in an indeterminate sentence); nickel (US: 5 years); dime (US: 10 years), pontoon (UK: 21 mths); pound (US: 5 yrs); rofe (backsl. = 4 yrs); short time (short sentence, end of sentence); SS (UK: suspended sentence); stretch (UK: 12 mths); two (UK: 2 yrs); beggar's lagging, tramp's lagging (UK: 90 days); weekend (UK: very short sentence); woodener (UK: 30 days); zip-five (US: maximum 5 yrs)
v. 4. *to imprison:* send away, – down, – up, weigh off; spec. dish

out gravy (sentence harshly); cop a plea, cop out (plea bargain)
5. *to be imprisoned:* go away, – down, pull time
6. *to be found 'not guilty':* beat the rap
adv. 7. *on trial:* standing on the top step, up the steps, – stairs

492. Capital Punishment
n. 1. *electric chair:* chair, hot chair, – seat, – squat
v. 2. *to electrocute:* bake, fry
3. *hang:* stretch (one's neck)

493. Commutation and Release
n. 1. *bail:* Royal Mail (rhy.sl.)
2. *parole:* jam roll (rhy.sl.); back door parole (UK: dying in jail)
3. *rejection of parole:* blank, flop, knockback
4. *parolee:* early riser; spec. PV (parole violator)
5. spec. bleat (petition for repeal); lifeboat (pardon)
6. *release:* blue papers (UK), walking papers (US) (official statement of release date); get-up (release date); gate fever (pre-release nerves)
v. 7. spec. carry a case (to be freed on bail); on the count (US black: walking the streets); recoup (US black: to start post-prison life afresh); feed the bears (pay a parking fine)

494. Prison Life
n. 1. big house, boob, brig, bucket (Can.), calaboose, chokey, clink, college, coop, cross-bar hotel, glasshouse, hoosegow, Joe Gurr (rhy.sl. = stir), joint, jug, lagging station, pen, pokey, quod, slammer, sneezer, stir, tank, Texas steel; spec. drunk tank (lockup for drunks); the Island (Parkhurst, IOW); juvie (US: juvenile prison); the Moor (Dartmoor), outhouse (US: hostel) outside (the free world); Q (San Quentin); the Scrubs (Wormwood Scrubs); upstate (prisons in New York State); the Ville (Pentonville)
2. *places in prison:* range (US/Can. open areas outside cells); block, chokey, cooler, damper, Florida (US), hole, Siberia (US) (solitary confinement); crazy alley, paddy, pads (padded cells); limbo room (Can.: corporal punishment room)
3. *cell:* cheder (Yid.), flowery (rhy.sl. = flowery dell), slot (Aus.), peter, slams; spec. Rory (rhy.sl. = Rory O'Moore = cell door)
4. *prisoners:* con, gaolbird, (old) lag, yardbird (US black), spec. (new) fish (new inmate); flipflop (US: recidivist); short (nearing release); aces high, real man, right guy (US: popular prisoner); centreman, jointman (Can. sycophant to guards); stoolie (informer); red band (UK: trusty); atlas, OBC (one brutal convict) (strong convicts) baron, carvie (UK: tobacco trader); sweet kid (young homosexual); prison wolf (older homosexual); bug pass (Can. insane prisoner); politician (one who secures privileges); gaolhouse lawyer (one who studies law); wallflower (UK: one who plans an escape); lifer (serving life); three-time loser (US: serving mandatory life after a third conviction); recluse (a long-term prisoner with no outside contacts); lugger (Can. smuggler of contraband); knight of the golden grummet (US: prison homosexual); star (UK: first offender); daddy (UK Borstal use; powerful prisoner)
5. *prison officers:* flue (rhy.sl. = screw), hack, herder, screw, twirl; spec. bully beef, screwdriver, white shirt (senior officer); bitch's bastard, caser (severe officer); bent screw, safe screw (corrupt officer); light of love (rhy.sl. = guv = governor);

dep (deputy governor); particulars (US: external authorities); tube (UK: officer who eavesdrops on prisoners), zombie (UK: sour, surly officer); Gabriel (chapel organist); convictitis (paranoid fear of prisoners)

6. *imprisonment:* porridge, time; hard bit, – time (difficult sentence); first bird (first sentence); good time (remission); dead time (US: imprisonment that does not diminish the sentence); cons, jacket, mileage, PC (previous convictions); previous, rap sheet, sheet, yellow sheet (criminal record)

7. spec. bingo (Can.: riot); blanket party (US: initiation rite); break (an escape); cell task (UK: pin-up); cobitis (UK: dislike of jail food); duffer (UK: pudding, US: bread); fall money (US: legal fees); friend form (US: visiting order); grab (UK: pay); hominy gazette (Aus.: rumours); joey (UK: contraband); jo-jos (Can.: overcoat); jug-up (Can.: mealtime); bug juice, liquid cosh (Can./UK: major tranquilisers used for restraint); outfit (escape kit); pussy in a can (US: sardines); rim slide (US: fart); reader (UK: any reading matter); rower (UK: argument); scratcher (UK: match); whodunnit (UK: meat pie); wicked lady (cat o'nine-tails); kit (contraband communication; any prison paperwork); bug (Can.: homemade water-heater); KB (UK: knockback – rejection); full sheet (UK: prisoner's complaint against an officer)

v. 8. *spec. (prisoners):* blow one's copper (US: lose remission); choose up (US: select a homosexual partner); do a bit (serve time); get the Book, get the glory (become religious); give (one) the office (to initiate a newcomer); flash the range (US/Can.: scan the prison landing with a mirror); go up (the river) (to be imprisoned); have some rabbit (US: yearn to escape); lay in (US: reject exercise periods); play too close (US black: invade privacy); ride the deck, swap cans (US: have anal intercourse); cop a heel (US: attack from behind)

9. *spec. (prison officers):* bang up, dub up, chubb, miln up (UK: lock the cell door); ducket (Can.: place fellow-officer on report); get the book (US: to be reprimanded); put the block on (UK: tighten up prison regulations); ghost (move prisoners at night); case (UK: place a prisoner on report)

adj. 10. spec. chosen (US: selected as a homosexual partner); nicked (UK: put on report); scammered (homosexual)

adv. 11. *imprisoned:* away, inside, in the nick, in chokey, – stir, etc. (see n. 1.), jugged, on jankers, on the corn (Aus.), under glass, up the river; spec. carpy (UK: locked up for the night); two-ed up, three-ed up (UK: two or three men sharing a cell); stir bugs, – crazy (insane); baroning (trading in consumables)

12. *in solitary confinement:* behind one's door, buried (US), iced, OP (Can.: off privilege); spec. in the peek (under observation); on Rule 43 (UK: in voluntary solitary confinement)

13. *escaped:* away, on the lam, over the hill

phr. 14. *aimed at a complainer:* if you can't do the time, don't do the crime

495. Police

n. 1. Alice Blue Gown (gay use), Babylon (WI), bear, Big John (US black), Bill, blue meanies, bluebottles, blues, bobby, bogey, bogie, bull, button, chapper (Yid.), cop(per), cozzer, deputy do-right (US black), divine right (US black), esclop (backsl. = cop), flatfoot, flattie, fuzz, gendarmes, gestaps (US black), gum heel, harness bull, hawkshaw (WI), heat, hood (Aus.), irvine (US black), John Law, John Hop (Aus. rhy.sl. = cop), Johnny-be-good (US black), Kojak, law, little boy blue (US black), Lucy Law (gay use), mallet (US black), nab (US black), nail 'em and jail 'em (US black), Old Bill, ossifer, paddy, Peter-Jay (US black), pig, reppock (backsl. = copper), Sam and Dave (US black), scuffer, Sherlock Holmes (US black), the Man, three-bullet Joey (US black), Tilly (gay use), uncle nabs (US black), union wage (US black), walloper (Aus.), weakheart (WI), whips (US black); spec. rusty gun (veteran); active, hungry (enthusiast); saint (uncorruptible); horseman (RCMP 'mountie'); five-day wonder (UK: graduate of police college); aid (Temporary Detective Constable); dickless Tracy (woman officer); choirboys, wollies (novices); skip (sergeant); guv, guvnor (UK: any senior rank, usually as form of address) boffin (forensic expert); bobbsey twins (gay use: squad car officers); mother superior (gay use: sergeant)

2. *detectives:* ace, brains, busy, clothes, D (Aus.), eye, filth, G-man, gumshoe, jack, mod squad, Scotland Yard (US black), shoo-fly; spec. T-man (US Treasury agent); peeper (private detective)

3. *traffic police:* bald-tyre bandits, bear in the air (US: using a helicopter), brown bomber (Aus.), Freeway Freddie (US black), green hornet (Can.), grey ghost (Aus.), Kojak with a Kodak, pirates, Smokey

4. *group of police:* button mob, heavy mob, team; spec. heavy mob, Sweeney (rhy.sl. = Sweeney Todd = squad), the squad (flying squad); pussy posse, queer detail, Vera Vice (vice squad); narco (narcotics squad); bunco squad (fraud squad); Met (UK: Metropolitan Police); Home and Colonial (UK: regional crime squad); rubber heels, umbrella brigade (UK: Special Branch); rubber heels, shoo-fly (internal disciplinary officers); COs (UK: Commissioner's Office – taxi-cab authorities)

5. *police work:* the job; spec. batting average (US: arrest record); rubbish (UK: tedious duties); shout (an emergency call); SOP (standard operating procedure); advice (UK: a reprimand)

6. *police badge:* buzzer, potsy, tin

7. *Scotland Yard:* hollow tooth, Kremlin, the Yard

8. *police station:* Bridewell, factory, nick, old bill, (see also Crime: 460)

9. spec. dido (UK: internal complaint); Kilburn (rhy.sl. = Kilburn Priory = police diary)

v. 10. spec. walk the bricks (patrol); go out with (share professional attitudes); cover the sheet (fill an arrest quota); give a coating (to reprimand); cast (UK: to be discharged); put in one's papers (UK: to resign); crash (UK: drop enquiries); plot up (UK: study a given villain); blow out (UK: for a case to collapse); shape up (for a case to develop well)

adv. 11. spec. copping on the wrist, on the take (accepting bribes); over the side (UK: shirking duty for private interests); cooping (US: sleeping on duty); on dab (UK: on a disciplinary charge)

phr. 12. derog. ACAB (all coppers are bastards)

13. spec. APB (all points bulletin: general alert); ten-four (message received and understood)

phr. 14. spec. have you got a coat (UK: have you found a feasible suspect?)

CRIME: MISCELLANEOUS
496. Miscellaneous Terms, etc.
n. 1. spec. black (blackmail);
bleeding dirt, the mouse
(blackmailing homosexuals); Jewish
lightning (deliberate arson for
insurance fraud); bustle-punching
(acting as a frotteur); moprey
(exposing one's genitals to a blind
woman); copper jitters (irrational
fear of police); Follies (UK:
Quarter Sessions)
v. 2. spec. do it for oneself (UK
cabbie use: take a fare without using
the meter); torch (commit arson)

PROSTITUTION
497. Prostitution
n. 1. pussy game, the Game
2. *prostitute:* ass peddler, bangtail
(US black), bird (US black), brass,
business girl, call-girl, charlie
(Aus.), chromo (Aus.), cruiser,
Edie, flash-tail, flatbacker, grunter
(Aus.), ho (US black), hook(er),
hoowah, KP (Aus.: common
prostitute), kurve (Yid.), lady,
moonlighter, nafka (Yid.), noffka
(Yid.), open game (US black),
pavement princess, pro,
professional woman, prossie, prosso
(Aus.), puta (Sp.), short-time girl,
stepper (US black), stick (US
black), tom, working girl; spec.
square broad (non-prostitute);
industrial debutante (specialist in
conventions)
3. *part-time prostitute:* B-girl, charity
moll (Aus.), chippy, half-brass,
weekend ho (US black), – warrior,
summertime ho (US black)
4. *senior prostitute:* old timer, vet
5. *worn-out prostitute:* fleabag, over
the hill ho (US black)
6. *incompetent prostitute:* flaky ho
(US black), hold-out, mudkicker,
nag, slouch; spec. outlaw (one who
works without a pimp)
7. *experienced prostitute:* bottom

woman, main bitch, rose among the
thorns, star of the line,
thoroughbred
8. *under-age prostitute:* baby-pro
9. *male prostitute:* ass peddler,
– pro, bird taker, broad, boy, buff
boy, bunny, business boy, call boy,
career boy, cocksman, cocktail, coin
collector, come-on boy, commercial
queer, crack salesman, dick
peddler, fag boy, flesh peddler,
floater, foot soldier, gigolo, goofer,
he-whore, Hollywood hustler, party
boy, prick peddler, puto (Sp. =
whore), rent, rent-boy, sport,
sporting goods, two-way man,
trabajadao (Sp. = worked over),
trade, working girl
10. *thieving prostitute:* ginger,
rip-off artist
11. *prostitutes working for a pimp:*
flock, nest, stable; spec. choosing
money (cash given by a prostitute to
her new pimp); pimp crazy (a
prostitute who prefers sadistic
pimps)
12. spec. hand gig (gay use:
prostitute who masturbates (with)
client); vegetarian (prostitute who
will not fellate); three-way girl
(offers all bodily orifices for sex);
trapeze artist (specialist in
cunnilingus)
13. *working targets:* catch, trap;
spec. git-down time (start of
working day)
14. spec. trick baby (prostitute's
client-fathered child)
v. 15. *to work as a prostitute:* hawk
one's fork (Aus.), – one's mutton,
– one's pearly, hook, peddle pussy,
sit on one's stuff (US black), step
(US black), turn tricks; spec. break
one's luck (meet the day's first
client)
16. *work as a male prostitute:* hawk
one's brown, peddle one's arse
adv. 17. *working as a prostitute:* on
the bash, – the bat, – the battle
(Aus.), – the bottle, – the Game,

steppin', trollin'; spec. on the case (earning steadily from one client) **phr.** 18. *used by prostitute to client:* wanna do a thing?, – go out?

498. Pimps and Pimping
n. 1. mackery, the Life; spec. the Book (verbally transmitted 'book of pimping rules')
2. *pimp:* Alphonse (rhy.sl. = ponce), Charlie Ronce (rhy.sl.), fence (Aus.), hoon (Aus.), Joe Bonce, Joe Ronce (rhy.sl.), macaroni (US black), mack man (US black), ponce, sweetman; spec. bit of mess (UK: a male lover, neither client nor pimp)
3. *small-time pimp:* chili chump, – pimp, coffee and pimp, popcorn pimp, simple pimp
4. spec. boss player (superior pimp); faggotter (pimp for male prostitutes); gorilla pimp (violent pimp); promoted pimp (experienced, senior pimp); sugar pimp (kind pimp); macaroni with cheese (pimp who has other interests); Madam (male/female brothel proprietor)
5. spec. bonds (clothes given to his prostitutes); copping clothes ('best suit' used when enticing a new prostitute); kimible (noticeable 'pimp walk'); pimp's arrest (revocation of statutory bail bond for a given prostitute when she wants to leave); pimp dust (cocaine); pimp fronts (pimp-style clothes); pimp ride (expensive car); pimp shades, – tints (dark glasses)
v. 6. *to entice prostitutes:* cast the net, cop, – for, hit on, take an application
7. *to run prostitutes:* drive one's hos, put one on the block, – one on the corner, turn (one) out; cop and blow (exploit a prostitute); lock (ensure a prostitute's fidelity); ponce off (live off immoral earnings); work from a book (run call – not street – girls)
8. *to discuss pimping:* run down game, talk game
9. spec. file (to give instruction to a prostitute); rig a jig (prepare a sexual con-trick); put snow in one's game (ensnare a white person for financial gain); creep (to defraud a client); work a ginger (Aus.: to rob a client); drop a lug (US black: to confront or argue with)
adj. 10. *pertaining to pimping:* mack

499. Clients and Services
n. 1. fare, gonk, john, trick, TOS (trick off the street); spec. freak trick, special (devotee of any sexual speciality, see n. 2); phoney (mean client); champagne trick (generous client); live one (good client)
2. spec. beat (masochist); beer bottle beat (one who likes to be hit with a bottle); cream-puff freak (cake-thrower); dress-up (uses the girl's clothes/make-up); facial (the girl sits on his face); gorilla (sadist); jim, tin soldier, twank (voyeurs, 'assistants', etc.); leapfrog (one who watches two girls play leapfrog); needle freak (sadist, with needles); no freak (likes to simulate rape); phone freak (calls the girl to talk sex); sniffer (sniffs underwear); talker (only talks to the girl); underwear (underwear fetishist); word freak (listens to obscenities); toys (appliances used for bondage, S&M, etc.)
3. *sex show:* circus, dig (US black), gazoopie, gazupie; spec. T&A, tits and ass (burlesque, strip-show)
4. *services:* around the world (licking, sucking of entire body); B&D (bondage and discipline); English culture, – guidance (flagellation and bondage); fifty-fifty (gay use: alternating fellatio and sodomy); fladge (flagellation); French culture (fellatio); golden

showers (urolagnia); Greek culture (anal intercourse); party (any form of sex act); R/S (rough stuff, including sado-masochism, urolagnia, rubberwear, etc.); Roman culture (orgies); short time (basic intercourse); Swedish culture (rubber); telephone J/O (masturbation while listening to the telephone); tongue bath (see around the world); water sports (urolagnia); middle finger (prostitute's trick that speeds up orgasms); freebie, free shot (sex for free)
5. spec. ten-two (US payment for sex: $10 for girl, $2 for room)
v. 6. *to lick and suck the client's body:* go around the world, – all over town (with), round-house
7. spec. kerb-crawl (to solicit street girls from a car)
8. spec. georgy (to hire a whore and then refuse to pay)
9. spec. freak off (offer sex for free)
10. spec. sell a boy (gay use: to hire a prostitute as a 'gift' for a third party)

500. Locations
n. 1. *brothel:* barrelhouse, benny house, call house, case, cathouse, chicken ranch, hook shop, house, knocking shop, leaning house (US black); spec. punch house (US black: place where pimps and whores meet); rap parlour (euphemism for 'massage parlour'); peg house, show house (homosexual brothel)
2. *pimp uses:* office (wherever a pimp conducts business); fast track (centre of whoring in a city, US East Coast cities in general); slow track (US West Coast cities)
3. *the street:* ho stroll (US black), pitch, stroll, track
adv. 4. *on the street:* on the bricks

COMMERCIAL SEX
501. Pornography
n. 1. smut
2. *books:* eight-pager, fuck book, one-hand job, stroke book, Tijuana bible; spec. fag hots (gay-orientated material)
3. *films:* blue film, horn movie, skin-flick, stag movie
4. spec. close-ups: beaver shot (female genitals); flap shot, liver shot, meat shot, pink, wide-open beaver (inner labia, open vagina, etc.)
adj. 5. *pornographic:* adult, blue

DRUGS
502. Selling
n. 1. *seller:* candyman, connection, dealer, man, pusher, watermelon man (US black); spec. seedy (US black: seller of pills)
2. spec. buy (purchase of drugs); meet (appointment to buy drugs); green house (location, popular for buying drugs); jam house (location where cocaine is available); hop joint, shooting gallery (location where narcotics can be bought and used)
3. spec. Dr Feelgood, hungry croaker, writing doctor (doctors who write illicit prescriptions for drugs)
4. *measures of drugs:* amp (ampoule); bag (measure of narcotics); bindle, deck, paper (small fold of paper holding narcotics), birdseye (small amount of narcotics); blow, toot (one line of cocaine); brick (appx. 1 kilo of marijuana); can (1 oz of marijuana); cap (capsule); deck, dime bag ($10 worth of a drug); fifty-cent bag ($50 worth of marijuana); football (appx. 0.5 grain of a narcotic); half-lo (15 bags of heroin); jar (500/1000 pills); key (one kilo); LB (one pound weight); lid (22 gms appx. of

marijuana); line (one snort of a narcotic); match, matchbox (half-oz of marijuana); mic (one microgram, used to measure LSD); oz (1 ounce weight); paper, piece (appx. 1 oz of heroin); pinch (small amount of marijuana); spoon (2 gms heroin); taste (small amount of any drug); teaspoon (1 gm heroin); ten-cent bag ($10 worth of marijuana); weight (1 oz of heroin, 1 lb of marijuana); baggie (small plastic bag to hold marijuana)

5. *adulterated drugs:* blank ('narcotics'); catnip ('marijuana'); six and four (heavily diluted heroin)

6. spec. one-shot credit (a buyer is allowed only one default in payment)

7. spec. dog tag (a legitimate prescription for narcotics)

8. *to sell drugs:* deal, hustle, serve; spec. lay on (to offer free or sample drugs)

9. *to buy drugs:* connect, cop (for), score; spec. front (advance cash for a purchase)

10. spec. write script (for a doctor to write prescription for narcotics)

11. *to measure out drugs for sale:* bag, bag up, cap (into capsules)

12. *to sell adulterated, fake or short weight drugs:* burn, rip off

13. *to adulterate drugs:* cut, hit, step on

adv. 14. *in possession of drugs:* anywhere, carrying, holding

phr. 15. *do you want drugs?:* do you need a boy?

16. *have you any drugs?:* are you anywhere?, – carrying?, – holding?

503. Use and Addiction

n. 1. *pill-taker:* a-head, downer, freak, pillhead, pill-popper, speed freak

2. *narcotic user:* AD, hophead, globetrotter, hype, junkie, junk hawk, mainliner, schmecker, smack freak, – head, stuffer, unkjay, user

(heroin); cokey, coke freak, – head, snow bird (cocaine); needle freak, pin-jabber (one who prefers to inject); snooter (one who prefers to sniff drugs); hog (one who uses an excess of narcotics); swellhead (US black: one who has collapsed from drug use)

3. *soft drug user:* doper, druggie, freak, head, pothead, weedhead (cannabis); acidhead, acid rapper, tripper (LSD); space cadet, zonker (an excessive user); bud sesh (smoking drugs together); teahouse (place for communal smoking); bowl, chalice, chillum, cutchie (WI) (device for smoking)

4. spec. stash (drug hiding place; thus the given drug itself)

5. *addiction to narcotics:* habit, jones, monkey (on one's back); burning down habit, oil-burner habit (very heavy addiction); coffeeand habit (mild addiction); white line fever (cocaine addiction); honeymoon (early use of heroin)

6. *withdrawal from drugs:* belly habit, bogue, cold turkey, kicking (the habit), sweats, sick; spec. detox (detoxification: post-withdrawal period); chucks, chuck horrors (excessive eating that follows withdrawal)

v. 7. *to be addicted:* be strung out, have a habit, – a jones, – a monkey on one's back, hurting (for)

8. *to stop using narcotics:* go cold turkey, kick, kick the habit

9. spec. make for a stash (to steal drugs from a fellow user)

10. spec. bogart (take an excess of marijuana)

adv. 11. *using drugs:* on the needle; spec. pinned (tiny pupils, a sign of heroin use)

adj. 12. *no longer addicted:* clean, straight

504. Pills

n. 1. *general pills, capsules, etc.:*

ace, beans, blunt, candy, cap, dolls, hors d'oeuvres (US black), Jacks (and Jills) (rhy.sl. = pills), ju-ju, M&Ms, prescriptions, rainbows, roundhead, vitamins, yum-yums
2. *stimulants:* a (amphetamine); b (benzedrine); bam (bambita = amphetamine); bennies, benny, benz (benzedrine); black beauties, – bomber, – widow, blues, bomb(er), Christmas tree (deximal); crank, crystal (powdered Methdrine); dex(y) (dexedrine); leaper, meth (methdrine); olly (rhy.sl. = Oliver Reed = speed); pep-em-ups (US black), ph, pink lady, purple heart, rouser (US black), speed, uppers, ups, white cross, whites, whiz, widow
3. *depressants, tranquillisers:* barbs, blue angel (amytal barbiturate); borders, Christmas tree (Tuinal); downer, F-40s (Seconal); F-60s (Histadyl); F-66s (Tuinal); goofball, gumdrop (US black), jacket (nembutal); jiblet (US black), Lilly (Seconal); nebbie, nembie (Nembutal); reds, sleeper, slow-'em-ups (US black), sopor, tranks, Vallie (Valium); yellowjackets, yellows
4. *methaqualone:* ludes (Quaalude); mandies (Mandrax)
5. spec. silk and satin, up-and-downer (pill combining amphetamine and barbiturate); Mickey Finn (knock-out drug, poss. chloral hydrate); Monday pills (US milit: malaria pills)
6. *to take pills:* drop

DRUGS: TYPE
505. Hard
n. 1. *narcotics:* hard stuff, stuff; good stuff (better than average drugs)
2. *heroin:* beast, big H, boy, Chinese no. 3, dog food (US black), duji, gold dust, H, henry, hop, horse, junk, scag, schmeck, shit, skag, skezag, (pig Latin), stuff; spec. quill (heroin hidden in a matchbook cover)
3. *cocaine:* blort, blow, bowser, C, candy, cecil, charlie, coconuts, coke, flake, fly, freezer, girl, golden girl, gonzo, jam (US black), lady, leaf, nose, nose candy, pimp dust (US black), rock, snow, sophisticated lady (US black), toot, white shit
4. *opium:* black, brown stuff, button, canned stuff, card, green ashes, high hat, hop, mud, O, red smoker, san lo, tar, yen pok
5. *morphine:* cube, Dr White, dolly, God's own medicine, GOM, M, Miss Emma, mojo, sweet Jesus, white nurse, – stuff
6. spec. PG (paragoric); paracki (paraldehyde)
7. *drug cocktails:* 'Frisco speedball (heroin, cocaine & LSD), speedball (heroin and cocaine)
8. *drug injection:* bang (in the arm), fix, hit, Jimmy Hix (rhy.sl. = fix), jolt, shot; spec. wake-up (first injection of the day); main, mainline (the vein into which one injects); joy bang, – pop (occasional use) ab (an abcess caused by injecting); marks, tracks (scars of regular injections); hot shot (injection of poison deliberately used to murder a drug addict)
9. *hard drug paraphernalia:* gun, hypo, spike (hypodermic syringe); fit, gizmo, outfit, works (needle plus other equipment for making an injection); collar (wrapper that ensures needle and dropper fit tightly); cooker (a container in which a mixture of heroin and water can be heated); cotton (cloth through which heroin is sucked into the syringe); tie-up (a means of tying off the vein prior to injection); rope (a vein)
v. 10. *to inject drugs:* bang up, crank

(up), do a thing, – in, – up, fix, geeze, jack up, hit the mainline, mainline, pop, shoot up, take off, use; spec. chippy (to use narcotics occasionally); tie off (to isolate the vein); skinpop (inject under the skin rather than into a vein); fire up, shoot gravy, jack off (pump the mixture of blood and heroin into the arm); spill (to miss the vein); get one's wings (to start injecting drugs); brew, cook (heat a mixture of heroin and water prior to injecting oneself)
11. *to sniff or inhale drugs:* blow, get one's nose cold, horn, jam (US black), sniff, snort, toot; spec. base, freebase (to inhale cocaine mixed with ether); chase the dragon, kick the gong around (inhale heated heroin); toot (a device for inhaling cocaine)
12. *to addict to drugs:* hook
adj. 13. *narcotic:* heavy
adv. 14. spec. caught in a snowstorm (under the influence of cocaine); on the sleeve (injecting narcotics)

506. Soft
n. 1. *hashish:* charas, dope, hash, kaker (Yid.), kif, shit; spec. tincture (tincture of cannabis); THC (tetrahydrocannabinnol); temple balls, Lebanese gold, – red, Afghani, Af, black Pak, Turkish pollen (geographical 'trade' names)
2. *marijuana:* ace, baby, bale, bar, black gungeon, – moat, – Russian, bomber, boo, brand X (US black), brick, bu, bush, charge, collie, dagga, dew, djamba, dope, duby, esrar, gage, ganga, gangja, gangster (US black), gauge gear, grass, greapha, greefo, griefo, gunja, gunny, hay, hemp, herb, joy, juanita, locoweed, maharishee, mariweegee, Mary Warner, Mary, Maryanne, Maryjane, moocah, mootah, mooter, mother nature's

own tobacco, mother nature, mu, muggle, muggles, pot, reefer, root, smoke, tea, turnip greens (US black), twist, 'wana, weed, wheat, zombie (Aus.); spec. sinsemilla, Mexican green, Durban poison, Congo bush, Acapulco gold, Acapulco red (geographical 'trade' names); homegrown (home cultivated); bad shit (better-than-average drugs)
3. *marijuana or hashish cigarette:* bag of bones, bomber, bones, doobie, dubee, duby, j, joint, ju-ju, no-brand cigarette, no-name cigarette, off-brand cigarette, skoofer, skoofus, skroofus, spliff, stencil, stick, stogie, toke, toothpick (US black), tuskie (US black); burnie, roach (remains of a cigarette); crutch, roach clip (gadget to hold the hot 'roach'); papers, skins (cigarette papers); makings (content of a 'joint'); hit, toke (puff of a cigarette)
4. *hallucinogens:* acid, LSD; spec. clear light, mellow yellow, Owsley, strawberry fields, sunshine, window pane ('trade names'); angel dust, hog, steam (phencyclidine); businessman's trip (DMT); mesc (mescalin)
5. *amyl nitrate:* aroma, poppers
6. *to smoke drugs:* blast, do a number, take a hit, toke (down); spec. bogart, double-clutch (take more than one's share), shotgun (blow smoke into another's mouth); cuff (to hide a burning cigarette)

507. Experience and Effects
n. 1. *hard drug use:* rush (immediate effects of a narcotic injection); spec. OD (overdose)
2. *soft drug use:* charge, high, stone, turn-on; spec. hashover (cannabis hangover); trip (LSD experience)
3. *bad experience:* bring-down, bummer, bum trip, freak-out, horrors

v. 4. *to take a drug:* do, do up, get behind
5. *to 'get high':* blow one's mind, do one's head, fly, get Chinese, – high, – low, make one right (US black), ride the wagon (US black), – tough (US black), toot one's horn; spec. freak out (have an unpleasant drug experience; come down (to feel the effects of the drug end); go on the nod, nod, nod out (to fall asleep when using heroin)
6. *to look after a drug user:* babysit
adj. 7. *'drugged':* spacey, trippy, weird
adv. 8. *experiencing drugs:* annihilated, bent out of shape, blocked, bombed, charged up, destroyed, fried, fucked up, goofed, have the slows (US black), high, hopped up, loaded, messed up, on it, ossified, out of it, – of one's brain, – of one's gourd, – of one's mind, – of one's nut, – of one's skull, pilled up, psychedelic to the bone (US black), ripped, skulled, spaced (out), toasted, twisted, wasted; on the nod, smacked out (intoxicated with heroin)
phr. 9. DFFL (dope forever, forever loaded); someone blew out his/her pilot light

---

COMMERCE
508. Commerce
n. 1. *large sum of money:* big bucks, bundle, fat knot (US black), megabucks, packet, pile, sting, wedge
2. *small sum of money:* chickenfeed, grubstake, pin money, razoo (Aus.), walk-about money
3. *cheque:* goose's neck (rhy.sl.), total wreck (rhy.sl.); spec. bum map, frog, kite, leaper, rubber cheque, stumer (bad cheque)
4. *rent:* burton (rhy.sl. = Burton-on-Trent), Duke of Kent (rhy.sl.)
5. *corruption:* lurkola (Aus.), payola (payoffs for media exposure); gayola (payoffs that permit the running of gay clubs)
6. spec. California bankroll, Chicago bank roll, flash roll, Kansas City roll, nigger's bankroll (a roll of small bills wrapped in one large one); divvy (dividend); loose ends, mad money, money to burn (spare money); OPM (other people's money – invested in business); quick (instantly available money); rainy-day money (savings); slush fund (contingency fund); whip-round (instant collection of money); whack (a share)
7. *businessmen:* spec. breadhead (obsessed with money); damager (manager); jobber (freelance cabbie); Mr Ten Per Cent (an agent or middleman)
8. *locations:* Arthur (rhy.sl. = J. Arthur Rank), iron tank (rhy.sl.), jug, kaynab (backsl. = bank); Ma and Pa store, Mom and Pop store (corner shops); rip (off) joint (an exorbitantly expensive store); schlock shop (flashy dress shop)
9. *industrial relations:* compo (Aus.: industrial compensation); con and coal (rhy.sl. = dole); dole-bludger (Aus.: dole scrounger); greens (rhy.sl. = greengages = wages), rock of ages (rhy.sl.); time and a half (overtime); sweetheart contract, yellow-dog contract (contracts that favour the company)
10. *cost, bill:* Beecham's pill (rhy.sl.), damage, nut, tab; spec. swindle sheet (expense account)
11. spec. action (business deal); bottom line, real deal (end result, basis); cherry-picking (reviewing rival business ideas); dog (unsaleable item); Jewish piano, – typewriter (cash register); quick and dirty, quick fix (instant remedy); bob a nob (a shilling each)
v. 12. *to spend money:* push the

boat out, splurge; spec. blew in, do
one's dough (waste money); bounce
(pass a dud cheque or have the bank
refuse payment on the cheque);
catch a cold, hold the baby (lose
money on investments)

13. *to invest:* bankroll; spec. pick up
the tab (pay a bill)

14. *to earn money:* knock out (plus
sum), make change (US black), pull
down (plus sum)

15. *to become rich:* carve a slice,
coin (it), make a bomb, – a killing,
rake it in, scoop the pool, strike it
rich

16. *to sell:* flog, hype, push; spec.
whack for (to charge); go like hot
cakes (for a commodity to sell fast)

17. *to cost:* set (one) back

18. spec. headhunt (to recruit
executives)

adj. 19. *expensive:* pricey, through
the nose

20. *free:* buckshee, on the house

adv. 21. spec. hanging-up (cab use:
refusing to take unprofitable fares);
on the clock (freelance taxi-driving);
in the barrel (about to be
dismissed); staked long and deep
(US black: investing heavily)

phr. 22. *deriding a small sum of
money:* don't spend it all at once

509. Names for Money

n. 1. *money:* ace, ackers, beans,
bees and honey (rhy.sl.), billies,
boodle, brass, bread, cabbage,
cake, clams, cod's roe (rhy.sl. =
dough), coin, dibs, dinero,
do-re-mi, dough, duckies (US
black), gelt, gold, gravy, green,
greenbacks, greenies, guineas, hard
money, hoot (Aus.), Jimmy
O'Goblins, kale, kylege (WI), lean
green, lettuce, lolly, long green,
loot, mazuma, moolah, mulla, oscar
(rhy.sl. = Oscar Asche = cash),
potatoes, readies, ready, rhino, roll,
sausage and mash (rhy.sl. = cash),
scramble, scratch, shekels,
simoleons, smash, spondulicks,
sugar, tusheroon (US black),
wampum, whistle and toot (rhy.sl.
= loot), wonga, yennom (backsl.);
spec. crackle, folding stuff, soft
money (paper money); long-tailed
'un (large sterling note); paper
(money orders, etc.)

2. *pound sterling:* bar, doonups
(backsl.), funt (Yid.), oncer, nicker,
note, quid, smacker, smackeroo,
sov

3. *dollar bill:* clam, skin, slab (see
also: green, greenbacks, long green,
etc. in n. 1)

4. *small cash sums:* spec.
Abergavenny (rhy.sl. = penny),
yenep (backsl. = penny); Susy
(rhy.sl. = Susy Anna = tanner),
tanner (sixpence); tosheroon (half a
crown); caser, dollar, Oxford
scholar (rhy.sl.) (five shillings); calf
(rhy.sl.), cows (rhy.sl. = cow's calf
= half), half a bar, – a sheet (ten
shillings, 50p); pony in white (£1.25
in silver); deuce ($2.00); nickel (5
cents; dime (10); quarter (25)

5. *five pounds, five dollars:* fin,
finnif, pound note ($5.00); half a
cock (rhy.sl. = half a cock and hen
= half of ten), Jacks (rhy.sl. =
Jack's alive = five)

6. *ten pounds, ten dollars:* sawbuck,
sawski ($10.00); cock and hen,
cockle and hen (rhy.sl. = ten)

7. *twenty dollars, twenty pounds:*
double sawbuck, double sawski
($20); score (£20)

8. *twenty-five pounds:* macaroni
(rhy.sl. = pony), pony

9. *fifty dollars:* half a
yard

10. *one hundred pounds, one
hundred dollars:* big one, C, C-note,
century, hun, one bill, yard ($100);
big one, century (£100)

11. *one hundred and fifty dollars:*
buck and a half

12. *two hundred pounds:* twoer

13. *five hundred pounds:* monkey

14. *one thousand pounds, one thousand dollars:* G, grand, K

510. Loans; Debts, etc.
n. 1. *usurer:* loan shark, shark, shy, shylock; spec. Uncle (pawnbroker)
2. *credit:* drip, never-never, slate, sub, tick; spec. lay-by (Aus.: deposit paid in a shop); sharking (practising usury)
3. *interest:* juice, vig, vigorish
4. *location:* hockshop
v. 5. *to loan:* spot, sub (for); spec. nail (charge with a debt); hold paper on (stand as creditor)
6. *to pawn:* hock
7. *to purchase on credit:* drip it up, put on the slate, – on tick, etc. (see adv. 10)
8. *to pay one's debts:* ante up, brass up, pony up; spec. welch (to refuse to pay debts)
adj. 9. spec. financial (Aus.: in credit, solvent); in hock, to the bad, up the spout (in debt)
adv. 10. *owing:* into (one for)
11. *on credit:* on the cuff, – the slate, – tick; spec. on the drip, – the never-never (on hire purchase); on appro (on approval)

GAMBLING
511. Gambling and Wagering
n. 1. action; spec. Lombard Street to a China orange (the longest possible odds); cert, dead cert, million (certain winner); on the Murray cod (Aus. rhy.sl.), on the nod, payday stakes (betting on credit)
2. *gambler:* high roller, punter; spec. mug punter (foolish gambler)
3. *money:* bundle (large sum); short-end money (betting on a loss); smart money (bets made by experts)
4. *locale:* spieler (gambling club): plot (site of a three-card monte game); blower (tannoy system in a betting shop)

v. 5. *to bet:* play, punt, put one's shirt on, spiel (Yid.), splosh it on; spec. go for the doctor (Aus.), shoot for the sky, – for the moon (bet all one's money)
6. spec. make book (work as a bookmaker)
adj. 7. big (multiples of ten thousand; thus 'big nickel' = $5,000)
adv. 8. *at stake:* on the line; spec. on the short end (the unfavourable end of the odds)
phr. 9. spec. put up or shut up (bet, don't talk)

512. Winning and Losing
n. 1. *a win:* motsa (Aus.), skinner (Aus.); spec. dirty money (dishonourable gains)
2. *loss:* tap city
3. *loser:* provider, pooch
v. 4. *to lose:* dog it
5. *to beat:* clean out, take to the cleaners
6. *to pay debts:* come across; spec. welch (to refuse to pay debts)
adj. 7. *impoverished:* skinned, tapioca, tapped out
adv. 8. *winning:* hot, in the money, on a roll, – a rush
9. *losing:* in the hole

513. Persons
n. 1. *gambler:* punter; spec. hustler (professional gambler)
2. spec. hot dog (successful); hardnose (cautious); knocker (one who defaults on debts); kibitzer, railbird, sightseer (watchers, not players); shill, steerer (house player); sucker-bait (female used to lure gamblers); take-out guy (member of card-sharping team)

514. Horse-racing
n. 1. airs and graces (rhy.sl. = races)
2. *horses:* gee-gees; spec. pelter (fast horse); dead cert (a winning

horse); dead 'un (Aus.), quitter, stiff 'un, undertaker job (a losing horse); closer (horse on whom odds shorten); underlay (horse on whom odds increase)
3. *locations:* canal boat (rhy.sl. = the Tote); flapping track (small, unlicensed track); smoked haddock (rhy.sl. = the paddock)
4. *people:* chalk eater (one who bets on favourites only); horseplayer (better); hot walker (groom who walks horses after the race)
5. *the race:* boil over (Aus.: an upset); dead cert, romp (absolute certainty); the off (start)
6. *betting:* dope sheet, morning line, scratch sheet (racing form); Heinz (a combination bet); on the nose (a bet to win rather than place or show)
v. 7. spec. dope, dope out, – the ponies (to work out bets); go for the doctor (Aus.: for a horse to draw ahead); go through the card (bet on every horse); nobble (interfere with a horse); play the gee-gees (bet on races); pull (deliberately pull up a horse)

515. Cards
n. 1. bladder of lard (rhy.sl.), broads, flats, Wilkie Bard (rhy.sl.); spec. readers (marked cards); case card (last card of the four suits in each denomination to turn up); bullet (ace), deuce (two), trey (three), trips (three of a kind), whore (the queen)
2. *card games:* skin game (US black); spec. find the lady, monte, three-card monte ('the three-card trick')
3. spec. mechanic (cardsharp); tells (tics and mannerisms that betray poker bluffing)
v. 4. *to play cards:* spread the broads; spec. kibitz (watch a game)
5. *spec. poker uses:* bring it in (for the lowest card to start betting);

coffeehouse (to bluff); fold (cease betting on a hand); sandbag (bluff by checking the bet); tight-weak (weakness in play)
adj. 6. *marked deck:* spooked
excl. 7. *deal the cards:* hit me!

516. Dice; Bingo, etc.
n. 1. *dice:* African dominoes, bones, tatts; spec. flats, tops (doctored dice)
2. *dice player:* gunner, shooter
3. *playing dice:* fading game (players bet against each other and not against a bank); hard way (throwing pairs to make even points in craps); jacking off (shaking dice up and down)
4. spec. numbers, policy ('numbers' gambling); April fools (rhy.sl. = football pools)
5. *names of points in craps:* snake-eyes (pair of one 1s; 2); ace-deuce, trey (3); little Josie, little Joe (from Kokomo) (4); fever in the South, five in the South, (Little) Phoebe (5); Jimmy Hix, sixty days (6); craps (2, 7 or 12 as a loss), natural (7 as a win or 11); Ada from Decatur, eighter from Decatur (8); Nina from Carolina, Nina with her hair down (9); big Dick (from Boston) (10); box cars (12)
6. *names of numbers in bingo (many are rhy.sl.):* buttered scone, Kelly's eye (1); dirty old Jew, me and you (2); you and me (3); knock at the door (4); God's in heaven (7); garden gate, Harry Tate (8); doctor's orders (9); cock and hen, Downing Street (10); legs eleven (11); monkey's cousin (12); unlucky for some (13); rugby team (15); never been kissed (17); blind twenty (20; thus 'Blind thirty', 'Blind forty', etc.); all the twos (22; thus 'all the threes', 'all the fours', etc.); two ducks, dink-do (22); Pompey whore (24); bed and breakfast, half a crown (26); speed limit (30); all the

steps (39); half-way house (50); all the beans (57); stop work (65); clickety click (66); was she worth it? (76); two little crutches (77); two fat ladies (88); top of the house (99 or 100)

phr. 7. *toss the dice:* roll them bones!

Guide to Using the Index

1. This Index has been prepared on a computer database and as such conforms in its alphabetical order to the rules that are part of the standard ASCII (American Standard Code for Information Interchange) data transmission system. In practical terms, as experienced by the user of such an alphabetical system, ASCII listings work as follows.

Assuming that a list contains a number of examples of the same word, differentiated by capitals, punctuation marks and so on, the ASCII system will sort them thus: Fully capitalised words, initially capitalised words, lower case words, words incorporating a bracket, words incorporating a punctuation mark (!?*), words incorporating a hyphen. Thus:

AND 76.3	and 20.15	and! 94.5
And 234.1	and (and) 23.1	and-some 272.3

This order, when capitals, punctuation marks, etc. have to be considered, supercedes any non-computer-based alphabetical rules. Other than these differences, the basic alphabetical listing of individual words remains as would be expected in any dictionary.

2. For the purposes of this Thesaurus, the words listed in this Index have been designated typographically as follows.

LOVE 123–127: a comprehensive section of the book, comprising a number of subsections and identifying a wide-ranging topic which has been broken down into a number of more specific sections.

Love 123: a single sub-section of the book dealing with a single specific topic.

Love 125.1: a keyword as listed within a specific sub-section; usually one of the parts of speech defined within that sub-section.

love 125.17: the slang words included at large within the Thesaurus.

Index

a 504.2
A! 199.3
a bag 36.1
a bit swift 482.5
a bun in the oven 109.4
a Chinese 86.26
a cut above 20.5
a head 125.2
a laugh a line 276.1
a little of what you fancy 94.5
a (little) bit of all right 275.4
a mile wide 165.4
a moral 159.1
a nice how-d'you-do 252.2
a right how-d'you-do 252.2
a right two and eight 252.2
a screw loose 147.1
a-head 503.1
A1 20.2, 20.6, 27.3, 123.2, 305.8
ab 505.8
abandon 209.2, 209.5
abandonment 209
abc 438.1
abe 384.8
abergavenny 509.4
aberrant 360.23
abie 384.8
Abie Kabibble 384.8
ability 253
able person 430.2
abnormal drinks 95.11
about one's speed 253.8
about right 101.3
above one's head 167.3
absent oneself 210.6
absent-minded 150.2
abso-bloody-lutely 22.7, 159.4
abso-fucking-lutely 159.4
absolutely not! 200.3
absolutely! 199.3
abstainers 93
abstinence 100

abuse (n.) 294.3
abuse (v.t.) 294.6
Abyssinia 54.7
Abyssinia! 346.4
AC/DC 357.9
ACAB 495.12
acapulco gold 506.2
acapulco red 506.2
accelerate 49.7
acclerator 76.3
accept bribery 372.4
accept one's punishment 318.7
accepting bribes 482.6
accessories 83
accident 7.2
accidentally on purpose 206.3, 233.6
accommodation collar 489.1
accomplish 239.5
accomplishment 239
according to Hoyle 4.8
accoutrements 116.33
ACCURACY 164–165
accusation 316
accuse 316.2
ace 16.3, 18.3, 20.6, 49.4, 257.2, 273.6, 275.4, 310.6, 328.10, 430.2, 438.1, 495.2, 504.1, 506.2, 509.1
ace boom boom 438.1
ace boon coon 438.1
ace coon poon 259.1, 438.1
ace in the hole 374.1
ace it up 10.5
ace it up! 10.9
ace of spades 116.41
ace out of 310.6
ace up one's sleeve 259.1
ace(s) 27.1
ace-deuce 516.5
aces 123.3, 139.5, 164.4, 164.8, 214.2, 275.4, 305.8
aces high 494.4

aces with 328.9
achieve erection 118.11
achieve orgasm 118.12
acid 506.4
acid rapper 503.3
acidhead 503.3
ack emma 3.7
ackamaraccka 146.2, 312.1
ackers 509.1
acorn 116.34
ACQUISITION 365–371
acquit 317.3
across the pavement 478.1
across the river 112.10
act (v.) 239.2
act 311.2
act effeminately 358.4
act indifferently 271.3
act irresponsibly 208.3
act madly 208.2
act of surpassing 20.1
act on the square 305.3
act suspiciously 161.3
act the nigger 298.2
act unpleasantly 278.3
act up 276.6
act your age 146.7, 230.3
action 49.1, 276.2, 508.11, 511.1
action piece 71.1
active 495.1
ACTIVITY 236–243
Acton Hilton 195.6
actor 435.1
acts like shit wouldn't melt in her mouth 401.3
AD 503.2
ad lib 12.2
Ada from Decatur 516.5
Adam and Eve 86.27, 160.2
Adam and Eve on a raft 86.27
Adam and Eve on a raft and wreck 'em 86.27
Adam's ale 67.1
Addicks 179.1

beyond the rabbit-proof fence 38.2
bhani ghani 346.3
bi 357.9
Bible Belt 43.3
bible-banger 323.1
bible-basher 323.1
bible-puncher 323.1
bicycle 75.10
biddy 380.1, 455.1
biff 32.3, 113.4, 135.1, 359.6
biff-bang 135.3
biff-boom 135.3
big 511.7
big A 43.1
big C 125.8
big E 63.1, 224.1
big H 505.2
big O 118.5
big T 43.1
big ass 32.6
big bird 116.34
big bit 491.3
big boat 75.2
big bucks 16.4, 508.1
big cheese 18.3, 139.6, 387.1
big chief 387.1
big chill 112.1
big city 42.1
big con 480.1
big deal 18.3, 139.6, 271.7, 387.1
big deal! 292.7
big Deuce 179.3
big Dick (from Boston) 516.5
big dime 16.4
big Ditch 45.1, 67.2
big enchilada 18.3, 387.1
big fish 387.1
big foot Joe 116.34
big gun 387.1
big hearted 329.4
big hit 119.3, 491.3
big house 494.1
big how-de-do 231.2
big hunk of nothing 19.1
big idea 232.1
big John 495.1
big jobs 119.3
big Kahoona 67.2
big lake 67.2
big league 18.3
big nickel 16.4

big noise 18.3, 387.1
big note artist 401.1
big one 16.4, 509.10
big pot 387.1
big razoo 292.1
big Red 44.2
big shot 18.3, 394.2
big sleep 112.1
big Smoke 43.1
big stick 336.1
big stuff 18.3, 139.6, 387.1
big time 18.3, 27.1, 491.3
big wheel 18.3, 387.1
big wig 18.3, 387.1
big word 177.2
big-name 139.7
big-time 18.8
big-timer 413.1
biggie 18.3, 387.1
bigmouth 401.1
bike 437.3
biker 424.1
bilge 146.2
bilge artist 401.1
bill 508.10
bill 75.13, 495.1
bill of goods 310.1
bill shop 460.1
billies 509.1
billy 465.1
billyjack 142.3
bim 377.1, 380.1
bimbo 377.1, 380.1, 381.4, 381.5, 437.3
bimi 383.23
bimps 86.11
bin 82.19, 147.2
bind 252.1
bindle 366.2, 502.4
bindle stiff 417.3
bing 41.5, 73.1
bing it 362.6
binge 98.1, 276.3
bingo 494.7
bins 82.11, 116.12, 132.3
bint 381.5
bip bam thank-you-ma'am 359.2
bird 75.4, 116.34, 377.1, 380.1, 491.1, 497.2
bird dog 353.2, 456.1, 458.12
bird taker 497.9
birdbrain 431.1
birdie 180.1, 404.1

birds 115.3
birdseye 502.4
Birmingham screwdriver 69.6
birth 110
birthday suit 85.2
biscuit 116.4
biscuits and cheese 116.20
bisexual 357.9, 436.8
bit 491.1
bit of a lad 401.2
bit of all right 425.1
bit of crackling 425.1
bit of fluff 380.1, 388.1
bit of how's-yer-father 359.1
bit of mess 498.2
bit of one's mind 291.1
bit of spare 445.2
bit of stuff 425.1
bit of the other 359.1
bit on the side 441.4
bit previous 28.2
bit steep 161.5
bit tall 161.5
bit thick 161.5, 278.5
bit thin 161.5
bitch 252.4, 284.1, 289.1, 289.2, 334.2, 380.1, 396.1, 404.1, 404.5
bitch box 187.1
bitch off 284.2
bitch up 254.2
bitch's bastard 396.1, 494.5
bitched, buggered and bewildered 283.6
bitchen 27.3
bitchin 27.3
bitchin-twitchin 27.3
bite 116.40, 160.3, 284.2, 368.1
bite on that! 153.11
bite one's crank 360.12
bite one's ear 368.2
bite the bullet 265.3
bite the carpet 248.4
bite the dust 112.5, 258.2
bite the ice! 292.7
bits and bobs 19.3, 69.2
bitten 349.3
bizarre 228.3
blab 183.1, 183.7, 193.3, 193.4, 435.3, 473.3
blabbermouth 420.2, 435.3

blabs in labs 179.4
black 279.7, 496.1, 505.4
black Maria 475.3
black Pak 506.1
Black Power dance 479.1
black and white 75.4, 475.2
black beauties 504.2
black bird 384.3
black bomber 504.2
black dog 279.2
black dust 384.3
black gang 456.1
black gold 67.6
black gungeon 506.2
black justice 320.1
black moat 506.2
black on black 76.7
black Russian 506.2
black sensibility 260.2
black taxi 75.2
black 360 degrees 384.2
black widow 504.2
black wings 360.4
blackjack 217.2
blackleg 241.9, 453.5
blacks (by blacks) 384.2
blacks (by whites) 384.1
blacktop 47.1
bladder 194.3
bladder of lard 515.1
blade 69.9
blag 310.4, 479.4
blagger 458.7
blah (on) 146.6
blah 19.2, 124.4, 146.3, 185.1, 185.2, 299.2
blah! 292.8
blam 2.11, 135.1, 164.11
blame 18.10
blame 316
blame unfairly 316.3
blamed 28.2, 189.4
blamelessness 305.2
blanco 384.12
Blanco 179.8
blank 150.2, 200.1, 200.2, 224.3, 493.3, 502.5
blanket man 458.9
blanket party 494.7
blankety 18.8, 18.10, 28.2, 189.4
blap 164.11
blarney 183.2, 183.19, 184.1, 287.1, 287.2
blart 183.9

blast 113.4, 276.3, 337.7, 363.1, 506.6
blasted 101.3, 189.4
blat 183.9
blather 146.3, 184.1
blatherskite 146.2, 299.1, 401.1
blaze on 338.4
blazes 326.2
blazing (down) 66.1
blazing 18.8
bleary 101.3
bleat 188.1, 188.2, 289.2, 493.5
bleed (white) 368.3
bleed 384.2
bleed the liver 119.8
bleeder 377.1
bleeding 18.10, 189.4
bleeding dirt 496.1
bless me! 189.5
bless my heart! 189.5
bless my soul! 189.5
bless you! 285.5
bless your little cotton socks 328.10
blessed 18.8, 189.4
blessed event 110.1
blew in 508.12
blighter 377.1
blighty 45.1
blimey! 189.5
blimp 427.2
blind 18.10, 98.1, 101.3, 116.37, 311.2, 317.2
blind Freddy 414.1
blind pig 104.2
blind staggers 101.1
blind twenty 516.6
blinder 344.1
blinding 27.3
blindside 173.3
blinker 195.9, 486.2
blinking 18.8, 18.10, 22.6, 189.4
blip 164.11
blister 397.1
blithering 189.4
blitzed 101.3
blob 16.2, 95.11
block 116.4, 494.2
blockbuster 18.1, 386.4
blocked 507.8
blocker 458.15
blockhead 431.1
blockheaded 145.3

bloke 377.1, 379.1
Blondie 179.11
blood 116.28
blood 384.2, 438.1
blood claat 396.1
blood oath! 199.3
blood wagon 75.11
bloody 18.8, 18.10, 96.1, 189.4
bloody-minded 206.2
blooey 258.4
blooey! 146.11
blooie 7.4
bloomer 165.1
blooming 18.8, 22.6, 189.4
blooper 183.1
blop 41.5, 135.1, 164.11
blort 505.3
blossom 180.1
blot 116.29
blot one's copybook 165.3
blotch 69.18
bloviate 183.9
blow (it) 233.4
blow (it)! 54.6, 189.5
blow (n.) 337.2
blow (off) 184.2
blow (oneself out) 89.7
blow (out) 25.4
blow (up) 7.4
blow 7.8, 54.1, 54.3, 183.7, 211.3, 235.4, 360.12, 502.4, 505.3, 505.11
blow Black 299.2
blow a fuse 147.4, 280.3
blow a gasket 280.3
blow a raspberry 292.3
blow ass 49.4
blow away 113.4, 173.3, 337.7
blow by 361.4
blow down one's ear 183.8
blow fire 239.4
blow great guns 66.8, 289.2
blow hard 183.9, 299.2
blow heavy 299.2
blow in 52.1, 52.2, 53.1
blow in one's ear 202.4
blow it 127.1, 216.5, 280.3
blow it out (your arse)! 292.7

blow me down (with a
  feather)! 173.7
blow my nose! 173.7
blow off (at the mouth)
  183.9
blow off 251.1, 280.3
blow off steam 184.2,
  280.3
blow one away 173.3
blow one out 243.3,
  262.5, 356.2
blow one to 370.5
blow one's cookies
  118.13, 280.3, 360.12
blow one's cool 280.3
blow one's copper 494.8
blow one's cork 147.4,
  280.3
blow one's doughnuts
  118.13
blow one's gasket 280.3
blow one's glass 360.12
blow one's groceries
  118.13
blow one's head off 337.7
blow one's lid 147.4
blow one's lunch 118.13
blow one's mind 147.4,
  173.3, 262.5, 507.5
blow one's nose 472.3
blow one's own trumpet
  299.2
blow one's stack 280.3
blow one's top 147.4,
  280.3
blow one's wad 373.2
blow out 63.2, 224.3,
  495.10
blow out of 54.3
blow past 310.4
blow sky-high 291.2
blow smoke up one's arse
  312.2
blow some tunes 360.13
blow stick 116.34
blow the daylights out of
  291.2
blow the gaff 184.3,
  193.4, 473.3
blow the skin flute 360.12
blow the whistle (on)
  193.4, 193.5
blow the whistle on 473.3
blow through 472.3
blow up 7.4, 127.1, 140.3,
  243.1, 280.3

blow wise (to) 144.5
blow wise 144.4, 162.2,
  166.2
blow-job 360.2
blow-out 7.4, 89.5, 258.1,
  276.3
blow-up 258.1, 280.2,
  344.1
blowed 189.4
blowed in the glass 164.8,
  305.8
blower 195.5, 511.4
blowhard 401.1, 420.1
blown away 173.6
blown out 243.4
blowoff 10.1
blub 281.3
blubberbrained 145.3
bludge 368.2
bludger 417.1
blue 30.1, 165.1, 279.7,
  306.5, 344.1, 357.10,
  501.5
blue and white 475.2
blue angel 504.3
blue around the gills
  283.6
blue balls 125.10, 357.2
blue blazes 326.2
blue dangers 475.2
blue feature 46.3
blue film 501.3
blue funk 296.2
blue meanies 495.1
blue moon 1.2
blue papers 493.6
blue ruin 7.4
blue streak 49.3
blue vein 116.35
blue-blood 141.1, 448.1
blue-book 141.1
blue-chip 159.1, 192.10
blue-eyed boy 387.1
blue-eyed soul brother
  438.2
blue-pencil 25.4, 202.3
blue-veined piccolo
  116.34
blue-veined steak 116.34
blue-veined trumpet
  116.34
bluebottles 495.1
bluenose 419.2
blues 104.2, 279.2, 495.1,
  504.2
bluey 68.7, 428.1

bluff 404.2
blunt 504.1
blurb 285.2
BMOC 387.1
bo 125.18
Bo Peep 247.1
BO juice 120.7
boasie 297.3
boast 185.3, 299.2
boastful 299.3
boasting 299
boat 75.1, 116.5, 116.40
bob a nob 508.11
bob and weave 210.2
bob up 53.1
Bob's your uncle! 199.3
bobbish 123.3, 274.9
bobble 57.2
bobbles 83.10
bobbsey twins 495.1
bobby 495.1
bobby dazzler 27.1
bobby-soxer 381.5
bobkhes! 288.5
boche 383.8
bod 27.3, 116.1
bodge (together) 240.1
bodge (up) 240.1
bodger 28.2
bodgies 378.3
bodice-ripper 198.5
bodily fluids 116.28
bodily functions 118
BODY 116–121
body 458.1
body and soul lashing
  69.23
body lover 404.5
body odour 125.18
body queen 404.5
body-snatching 194.6
bodyguard 433.4
boff 274.2, 277.1, 337.4,
  338.5
boffin 495.1
boffins 456.12
boffo 27.3
boffola 277.1
bog 48.6, 79.1,
  107.2
bog in 238.4
bogart 503.10, 506.6
Bogey 179.8
bogey 495.1
bogeyman 325.4
bogie 495.1

bogtrotter 383.12
bogue 12.4, 503.6
boho 147.5
bohunk 390.3, 427.1
boil 88.4
boil over 280.3, 514.5
boiled 101.3
boiler 77.1, 382.3
boilerplate 4.8
boiling 18.8
boing-boing 447.2
boko 116.4, 116.9
bold 347.4
bold as brass 347.4
boldacious 231.5
bollick 291.2
bollix up 254.2
bollixed 7.13
bollock 364.2
bollock naked 117.6
bollocking 291.1
bollocko 117.6
bollocks 116.36, 146.2
bollocks up 254.2
bollocksed (up) 7.13
bollox 146.2
bologna 146.2
boloney 19.2, 146.2
bolshy 342.4
boltop 191.5
bomb 28.1, 258.2, 504.2
bomb off 258.2
bomb out 258.2
bombed 101.3, 507.8
Bomber 179.8
bomber 504.2, 506.2, 506.3
bombshell 173.1
bonaroo 27.3
bonce 116.4
bonds 498.5
bone 116.35
bone idle 245.1
bone to pick 334.2
bone up (on) 190.9
bone yard 48.6, 112.3
bone-shaker 75.3
boned 337.10
bonehead 431.1
boneheaded 145.3
boner 118.4
bones 506.3, 516.1
bong 73.1, 135.1
bonified 253.7
bonkers 145.3
bonzer 27.3

boo 165.1, 506.2
boo-boo 165.1
boob 165.1, 165.3, 390.3, 391.1, 431.1, 494.1
boob-tube 82.21, 195.1
booboisie 390.1
booby hatch 147.2
boodle 509.1
boofer box 69.25
boofhead 431.1
booful 180.1
boog 384.1
boogaloo 276.5, 364.3
boogie 276.5, 364.3, 384.1
boogie-woogie 54.3
boogieman 325.4
boogying 364.1
boohoo 281.3
boojie 451.1
book (the joint) 132.6
book 190.7
book 54.3, 194.3, 489.2
book it 190.9
book up 190.9
boola-boola 188.1
boolhipper 82.12
boom 73.1
boom-boom 119.3
boomer 18.1
boondocks 46.1
boondoggle 235.3
boong 384.1
boonie 390.2
boonie hat 82.17
boonie rat 456.1
boonies 46.1
booshwah 146.2
boost 285.2, 286.1, 286.2, 341.1, 341.2, 341.3, 479.4
booster 458.15, 479.3
boosting 479.1
boot (around) 337.4
boot (out) 24.5, 63.2
boot 32.3, 63.1, 94.8, 118.13, 224.2, 242.4, 384.2, 454.1
boot-out 63.1
booted 63.4
bootlick 287.3
bootlicker 418.1
booty 116.40, 380.1
booze 94.1, 97.3
booze artist 92.3
booze hound 92.3
booze it up 97.3

booze joint 104.1
booze-up 98.1
boozed 101.3
boozed up 101.3
boozer 78.6, 92.3, 104.1
boozing 97.1
bop 41.5, 56.1, 59.2, 73.1, 135.1, 338.3, 338.5
bopper 381.5
boppers 82.15
bopping 364.1
bopping club 378.3
bopping gang 378.3
boracic 376.5
borax 146.2
borders 504.3
bore 272.3
bore stiff 272.3
bore the pants off 272.3
bore to tears 272.3
bored 272.6
bored stiff 272.6
bored to tears 272.6
boring 272.5
born days (all one's) 1.2
born tired 245.1
born under a bad sign 215.9
born with a silver spoon in one's mouth 215.5
borrow 489.2
borrower 417
borrowing 368
Borscht Belt 43.3
bosh 28.1, 146.2, 184.1, 299.1
boss 27.3, 457.1
Boss Charlie 387.1
boss player 430.2, 498.4
boss-eye 428.4
bossman 457.1
bot 368.2
botch up 33.3
bother 252.1, 252.4
botheration 168.1
botheration! 189.5
bottle (up) 218.2
bottle 295.1
bottle and glass 116.30
bottle baby 92.3
bottle blonde 117.9
bottle out, 33.2, 296.3
bottle-a-day man 92.3
bottled 101.3
bottler 394.4, 403.1
bottom drawer 354.1

bring down the house 257.2
bring home the bacon 239.5, 257.2, 371.5
bring it in 515.5
bring one up 291.2
bring oneself off 118.14, 360.19
bring the house down 274.5
bring-down 282.1, 300.2, 507.3
briny 67.2
Bristol City 116.31
bristols 116.31
bro 438.1
broad 380.1, 437.3, 497.9
broad in the beam 37.3, 117.1
broadcast 183.9, 299.2
broadcasting 183.1
broads 515.1
broadsman 480.3
brodie 7.4, 56.1, 258.1
broke (to the wide) 376.5
broken 7.13
broker 416.1
brolly 69.21
bronco 404.5
Bronx cheer 293.1
broom 49.4, 54.3
brooming 481.1
broomstick 427.6
brothel 500.1
brothel creepers 82.15
brothel stompers 82.15
brother 273.7, 438.1
brothers 384.2
Brough 179.1
brougham 75.2
brought down 279.7
brown 360.15
brown artist 404.1
brown bomber 495.3
brown coat 456.13
brown envelope 224.2
brown family 404.1
brown hatter 404.1
brown off 284.2
brown stuff 505.4
brown wings 360.4
brown-eye 116.29, 360.5
brown-nose 287.3
brown-noser 418.1, 439.5
brown-slice 338.5
brown-tongue 439.5

brownbag 97.3
browned off 284.5
brownie 95.5, 116.29
brownie point 303.1
browning 360.5
Browning family 404.1
Browning sisters 404.1
bruiser 427.1, 433.3
brummagem 311.5
brummy 28.2, 385.1
bruno 44.2
brush 116.39, 348.1, 353.1
brush (off) 63.1
brush off 113.4, 150.1
brush one's teeth 360.13
brush-off 25.2, 348.1
Brussel sprouts 378.3
brute 252.4, 427.1
BS 146.2, 183.2, 183.19, 299.1, 299.2, 310.7, 312.1, 312.2
BSHs 116.31
BTM 116.30
bu 506.2
bub 178.3, 381.3
bubble 83.2, 193.4, 383.9, 472.1
bubble-gummer 381.5
bubbled 193.8, 473.5
bubblehead 431.1
bubbly 95.4
bubby 178.3
Buck 179.8, 179.10
buck (against) 289.2
buck (for) 205.2, 238.5
buck 72.1, 210.2, 458.1
buck and a half 509.11
buck for 238.5
buck private 410.1
buck up 128.4, 148.2, 274.6, 274.7, 295.3, 295.6
buck's night 3.3
bucket 116.29, 292.4, 494.1
bucket down 66.7
bucket gaff 480.1
bucket job 480.1
bucketing down 66.3
bucko 231.5, 433.3
buckshee 508.20
buckwheat 384.4
bud 381.5
bud sesh 503.3
buddy 178.3, 438.1
buddy up 328.2

buddy-buddy 328.7
buddyseat 76.4
budgie 473.2
buf 425.2
buff boy 497.9
buffalo 218.3, 336.2
buffer 382.2
bufu 404.1
bug 69.26, 284.2, 408.1, 494.7
bug-eyed 101.3
bug juice 494.7
bug out 54.3
bug pass 494.4
bugger! 189.5
bugger (it) up 165.3
bugger 252.4, 379.1, 396.1, 404.1, 433.1
bugger about 146.4
bugger all 23.3
bugger me! 173.7, 189.5
bugger off 54.3, 54.6
bugger off! 278.7
bugger up 7.8, 33.3, 254.2
bugger you! 189.7
bugger's grips 120.2
buggeration! 284.8
buggered 173.6, 252.12, 258.4
buggered up 7.13, 126.2
buggering 189.4
buggerlugs 328.10
buggins 180.1
buggin's turn 8.2
buggle 180.1
buggy 75.1
bughouse 146.2, 147.2, 147.5
bughutch 78.8
bugle 116.9
bugs 431.1
bugs about 270.6
buick 118.13
build-up 285.2, 287.1
building 78.1
BUILDINGS 78–81
built 35.4, 117.11, 117.12
built like a brick outhouse 32.6, 37.3, 117.12
built like a brick shithouse 32.6, 37.3, 117.12
built that way 137.3
bull (along) 310.7
Bull 179.10
bull 146.2, 146.3, 146.6,

check out 54.3, 112.5, 132.11, 156.3
check over 156.3
check-in 52.1
check-out 54.1
checked out 112.10
cheder 494.3
cheek (n.) 347.1
cheekiness 347.2
cheer one up 274.7
cheer up – the worst is yet to come! 295.6
cheerfulness 274
cheerie-bye 346.4
cheerio 346.4
cheerio! 99.1
cheers! 99.1
cheese 18.1, 116.28, 118.8, 118.12, 164.4
cheese 86.15
cheese it 211.3
cheese it! 10.9, 201.5
cheese off 284.2
cheese-eater 472.2
cheesecake 194.5, 251.5, 425.1
cheesed off 279.7, 284.5
cheesy 7.14, 311.5
chemist 456.17
cheque 508.3
cherry 116.40, 381.7
cherry hogs 78.8
cherry splitter 116.34
cherry-picking 508.11
cherrypop 359.11
chevy chase 116.5
chew (the fat) 183.7
chew face 351.3
chew on that! 153.11
chew one's balls off 291.2
chew out 291.2, 294.6
chew the cud 153.4
chew the fat 152.3, 186.6
chew the rag 184.2, 186.6
chi-ike 310.4
chic people 450
Chicago bankroll 508.6
Chicago lightning 73.2
Chicago piano 71.2, 466.1
Chicago typewriter 71.2, 466.1
chichi 116.31, 358.7
chick 180.1, 380.1, 425.1, 441.3
chickabiddy 381.2
chickadee 180.1

chicken 115.2
chicken 180.1, 296.6, 403.1, 404.5, 426.2
chicken hawk 404.5
chicken out 33.2, 209.3, 296.3
chicken queen 404.5
chicken ranch 500.1
chicken run 60.2
chicken scratchings 190.4
chicken-hearted 296.6
chickenfeed 19.6, 508.2
chickenshit 33.8, 296.6, 403.1
chicky 180.1
chico 383.15
child 381.3
child molester 436.5
chili chump 498.3
chili pimp 498.3
chill 112.1, 113.4
chill out 265.3
chiller 198.4
chilli 86.30
chillum 503.3
chimney 82.17
chin 116.23
chin-chin 346.4
chin-chin! 99.1
china 438.1
Chinaman's chance 158.2
chinch 115.4
chinee 190.2
Chinese 383.4
Chinese chance 158.2
Chinese ducket 190.2
Chinese fire drill 5.1
Chinese no. 3 505.2
chingazo 359.6
chink 383.4
chink chow 86.26
chinky 374.4, 383.4
CHINS 458.4
chinwag 152.3, 186.1
chip 478.2
chip in 183.15, 341.2, 367.2, 370.2, 370.3
chipper 123.3, 148.7, 236.7, 274.9
chippie 353.3, 437.3, 456.8
Chippy 179.8
chippy 48.6, 344.7, 497.3, 505.10
chippy chaser 395.1, 443.2

chippy on 353.3
chips 116.30
chirp up 274.6
chirpy 236.7
chisel 310.6
chisel out of 365.4
chiseler 434.1
chiv 69.9, 70.5
chive 337.6
chizz 310.6
chocolate 384.1
Chocolate City 44.1
choff 86.1
CHOICE 212–213
choice 27.3
choirboys 495.1
choke (it) down 222.2
choke a darkie 119.7
choke off 201.2
choke the chicken 360.19
choke the chook 118.14, 360.19
choked 279.7
choked down 84.3
choker 282.1
chokes and croaks 179.4
chokey 494.1, 494.2
chokka 22.2
cholo 383.15
chomp at the bit 248.4
choof 54.3
chook 115.2
choose 212.3
choose 268.2
choose off 344.5
choose up 494.8
choosing money 497.11
chop 86.1, 337.7
chop the clock 480.6
chop-chop 2.10, 49.9
chopped liver 116.40
chopper 71.1, 71.2, 71.3, 75.6, 116.34
choppers 116.8
chops 116.7
chopstick 384.11
chosen 494.10
chow 86.1
chow down 89.6
chow down! 89.9
chow-hound 423.1
chowder-head 431.1
Christ 325.2
Christ! 189.5
Christ Almighty! 189.5
Christ on a crutch! 189.5

christen 7.1
Christmas 325.2
Christmas! 189.5
Christmas hold 337.2
Christmas tree 504.2,
  504.3
Christopher (Columbus)
  325.2
Christopher Columbus!
  189.5
chrome-dome 117.10
chromo 426.2, 497.2
chubb 494.9
Chubby 179.13
chubby-chaser 441.10
chubette 427.2
Chubs 179.13
chuc 383.15
chuck (it) (up) 209.2
chuck (it) up 241.8
chuck 25.4, 41.5, 62.1,
  62.3, 63.1, 63.2, 86.1,
  118.13, 209.1, 331.2,
  353.1, 353.5, 491.2
chuck a dummy 118.13
chuck horrors 90.3, 503.6
chuck it (in) 302.2
chuck it! 136.4
chuck up the sponge
  302.2
chuck you, Farley! 189.5
chucker-out 456.5
chucklehead 431.1
chuckleheaded 145.3
Chucks 179.2
chucks 82.16, 503.6
chuff 116.40
chuffed 274.9
chug 97.3
chug-a-lug 97.3
chugalug 87.6
chum 438.1
chum up 328.2
chummy 328.7, 361.5,
  438.1, 486.4
chump 116.4, 310.4, 391.1
chump job 241.2
chump off 292.4
chump-change 28.2
chunder 118.13
chungo bunny 384.1
chunk 25.4, 71.1, 135.1
church 324.1
church key 69.8
church mouse 404.5
chutney ferret 404.1

chutzpah 347.1
cigar 106.7
cigarette 106.2
cigarette end 106.3
cigarette lighter 106.6
cigarette papers 106.5
ciggie 106.2
cinch 159.1, 192.3, 214.2,
  251.1
cinched 162.7
circle jerk 360.9
circumcised penis 116.38
circus 499.3
cities: districts 44
cities: nicknames 43
city 42
civilian clothes 82.8
civvie 377.1
civvies 82.8
civvy street 46.3
claim 489.2
clam 399.1, 509.3
clam up 201.1, 201.3,
  202.2, 209.3
clamp (down) (on) 218.2
clamp 218.1
clams 509.1
clap 125.10
clap eyes on 162.3
clap one's clit 360.20
clapped out 7.13
clapping for credit 179.4
claptrap 146.2
claret 116.28
class 35.1
classic 27.3
classy chassis 35.4, 425.1
clean (to) 22.7
clean 84.4, 305.6, 466.6,
  503.12
clean 4.4
clean broke 376.5
clean house 25.4
clean nose 305.2
clean out 7.10, 512.5
clean out of 366.6
clean sheet 305.2
clean shot 214.2
clean to the bone 84.4
clean up (on) 10.7, 257.3
clean up 113.4, 317.4,
  320.1, 320.2
clean up one's act 320.2
clean up the kitchen
  360.13

clean up the walls 196.3
cleaned out 376.5
cleaner 456.14
cleaning 4.3, 69.19
clear as mud 167.3
clear cut 82.1
clear light 506.4
clear off 54.3
clear the decks 237.2
clear to hell 22.7
clear-up 489.1
clearly 27.3
clever 12.3
clever dog 430.2
click 233.3, 257.2, 340.1
click (with) 273.3, 328.3
clickety click 516.6
cliffhanger 198.4
climb all over 291.2, 351.3
climb the rigging 280.3
climb the walls 263.2,
  280.3
climb trees to get away
  from it 359.10
climb-down 140.2, 300.2,
  302.1
climbing the walls 263.5
clincher 10.3, 163.1
clink 494.1
clinkers 119.3
clinking 18.8
clip 337.4
clip joint 78.7, 461.1
clipped 116.38
clippie 456.11
clit 116.42
clithopper 437.5
clitoris 116.42
clitty 116.42
clobber 82.1, 337.4
clobber one with 217.2
clobbered 101.3
clock 116.5, 132.6, 337.4
clock 69.17, 81.7
clock a daffy 312.2
clock in 52.2
clock off 241.8
clod 390.2, 431.1
clodpoll 431.1
close 38.6
close but no cigar 27.5
close call 211.2
close shave 38.3, 211.2
close up 202.2
closer 514.2
closet 202.5

closet case 404.5
closet queen 404.5
cloth-ears 433.1
clothes 495.2
clothes 82
clotheshorse 450.1
cloud 46.3
clout 216.1, 219.1, 479.4
clouting 318.3
clown 431.1
clown around 276.6
club 70.2, 78.7
clubs 378.3
cluck 431.1
clucky 109.4
clue (one) in 197.1
clueless 145.3
clumsy 254.6
clunk 337.4, 390.3, 431.1,
    452.2
clunker 75.3
clutch 364.2
CNR strawberries 467.1
COs 495.4
coal burner 441.9
coat 82.12
coat and badge 368.2
Coats and 'Ats 179.2
cobber 438.1
cobbler 483.2
cobblers 7.2, 146.2
cobitis 494.7
cobs 116.36
cocaine 505.3
cochealed 366.4
cock (it) up 165.3, 254.2
Cock 179.8
cock 116.34, 116.40,
    146.2, 178.3, 379.1,
    380.1, 415.2
cock a deaf 'un 210.2
cock a snoot (at) 347.3
cock a weather eye 149.4
cock and hen 16.3, 509.6,
    516.2
cock block 353.2
cock doctor 456.2
cock linnet 3.11
cock movie 195.3
cock off 258.2
cock pluck 351.3
cock sparrow 69.20
cock up 165.3
cock-and-bull story 198.2
cock-eyed 101.3
cock-hound 437.2

cock-tease 352.8
cock-teaser 352.2, 441.12,
    443.1
cock-up 7.2
cockamamie 169.4
cockeyed 5.5, 7.13, 33.5,
    40.1
cockle and hen 16.3,
    509.6
cocksman 437.2, 497.9
cocksucker 395.1, 396.1,
    404.1
cocksucking 189.4
cocktail 497.9
cocky 178.3, 297.3
coco 116.4
cocoa 87.3
coconuts 505.3
cod 310.3, 310.5, 310.7
cod's roe 509.1
codger 382.2
codology 293.2
cods 116.36, 146.2
cods up 254.2
codswallop 146.2
coffee 87.1
coffee and cocoa! 146.11
coffee grinder 75.7
coffeeand 28.2
coffeeand habit 503.5
coffeeand pimp 498.3
coffeehouse 515.5
coffin 112.4
coffin nail 106.2
cognoscenti 438.2
coin (it) 508.15
coin 509.1
coin collector 497.9
coitus interuptus 359.5
cojones 116.36, 295.1
coke 505.3
coke freak 503.2
coke head 503.2
coke stare 132.1
cokey 503.2
col 28.1
cold 31.2, 125.3
cold 27.3, 28.1, 28.2,
    38.5, 86.5, 159.3, 215.9,
    258.4
cold as a bastard 31.2
cold as a bitch 31.2
cold as a brass monkey
    31.2
cold as a well-digger's
    arse 31.2

cold as a witch's tit 31.2
cold enough to freeze the
    hind leg off a donkey
    31.2
cold feet 296.2
cold in hand 376.5
cold meat 112.2
cold shot 231.1
cold shoulder 348.1
cold snap 66.2
cold turkey 503.6
cold weather 66.2
cold-cock 337.5, 348.2
cold-deck 337.5
collapse 243.1
collar 365.2, 489.1, 489.2,
    505.9
collar and tie 404.3
collared 489.4
collect 7.11
collection 16.1
collective gossip 196.2
colleen bawn 116.34,
    116.35
college 494.1
collegiate fucking 360.8
collide 7.11
collie 506.2
Collins Street farmer
    456.16
collision 7.3,
    75.14
colly 166.2
collywobbles 125.1, 263.1
colour 30
colourful 84.5
colours 82.7
comb 120.4
combo 456.5, 465.1
comboozelated 101.3
come 116.28, 118.5,
    118.12, 359.8
come a cropper 56.2,
    165.3, 258.2
come a purler 56.2
come across (with the
    goods) 319.2
come across (with) 193.3,
    370.2
come across 164.6, 359.6,
    512.6
come and get it! 89.9
come back at 335.2
come clean 164.6, 193.3,
    319.2, 490.6
come down 11.3, 507.5

counterfeiter 483.2
counterfeiting 483
counting worms 112.10
countries: nicknames 45
country cousin 16.3
county 141.1
couple 441.5
COURAGE 295–296
court personnel 458.18
COURTESY 345–346
courtship 350
cousin 404.5
cove 379.1
cover the sheet 495.10
cover up 12.2
cover your arse 230.2
cover your ass 255.3
cover-up 202.1, 203.1
covering 69.21
cow 87.4, 426.2
cowabunga! 273.7
coward 403
cowardice 296
cowardly 296.6
cowboy 433.5, 434.1
Cowboy City 43.1
cowlick 120.1
cowpoke 456.20
cows 509.4
cowyard confetti 146.2
cozzer 495.1
crab 7.10, 7.12, 289.1,
    290.2, 405.1
crab (about) 289.2
crab (one's act) 250.1
crack (it) 239.7
crack (one) up 277.2
crack (something) up
    186.7
crack (up) 7.6, 33.2
crack (wise) 277.4
crack 23.2, 116.40, 162.2,
    183.1, 183.4, 183.10,
    238.2, 277.1, 292.2,
    302.2, 319.3, 380.1
crack a bottle 97.3
crack a cherry 359.11
crack a fat 118.11
crack a tube 97.3
crack down on 318.4
crack hand 430.2
crack it 257.2
crack on (about) 270.3
crack on 286.2, 299.2
crack one's face 274.4
crack salesman 497.9

crack the books 166.7
crack the whip 216.3
crack up 124.2, 127.1,
    147.4, 274.4, 306.2
crack wide open 319.3
crack wise (to) 162.2
crack wise 166.2, 183.13
cracked 127.2, 138.4,
    147.5, 162.7, 258.4
cracked up 263.5
cracker 27.1, 385.1
crackerbarrel 153.6
crackerjack 27.3
crackers 138.4, 147.5
crackle 509.1
cracko 147.5
crackpot 431.1
crackup 258.1
cracky! 189.5
cradle-snatcher 436.10
craftsmen 456.8
crag 405.1
cram 89.7
cramber 119.7
cramp 125.4
cramp one's style 250.1
crank (up) 236.5, 505.10
crank 76.1, 504.2
crank it out 190.8
crank one's shank 360.19
cranny 116.40
crap (all) over 5.4
crap (on) 146.6
crap 19.2, 28.1, 86.2,
    119.3, 119.7, 146.2,
    235.2, 310.1, 312.1,
    312.2
crap! 146.11
crap around 252.10
crap on 5.4, 299.2
crap out 7.6, 112.5, 215.6,
    243.1, 258.2
crapbrain 431.1
craphouse 46.2
crapout 258.1
crapped out 243.4, 247.7
crapper 48.6, 79.1
crappo 28.2
crappy 7.14, 28.2, 235.9
craps 516.5
crapshoot 214.3
crash 119.3, 247.3, 258.1,
    495.10
crash 75.15
crash (out) 247.4, 258.2
crash in 53.2

crash out 211.3
crash time 3.9
crash-pad 78.2
crasher 397.1, 417.1,
    429.1, 446.2
crawfish 209.3, 302.3,
    399.1
crawl out from under
    252.9
crawling (with) 5.6
crawling with 22.4
craze 270.2
craze-o 228.3
craziness 147
crazo 409.1
crazy 147.5
crazy 27.3, 268.4
crazy alley 494.2
crazy for 148.8, 268.4,
    270.5, 349.4
crazy house 147.2
crazy to 268.4
crazy-arse 147.5
cream 20.2, 116.28, 257.2,
    338.5, 359.8
cream one's jeans 262.3
cream-puff freak 499.2
creamie 425.1
creaming 479.1
creampuff 403.1
creamstick 116.34
crease (one) up 277.2
crease 338.5
crease up 274.4
creased 243.4
create 231.4, 280.3
create 240.1
creation 240
cred 160.1
credence 160
credit (n.) 510.2
creep 287.3, 363.2, 396.1,
    439.5, 452.2, 479.3,
    498.9
creeper 479.3
creeping Jesus 403.1,
    403.2
creeping and tilling 479.6
creeps 129.1, 263.1,
    296.2
creepsville 46.2
creepy 278.5
creepy crawly 115.4
crevice 116.40
crew 378.1, 438.2, 458.2
crewed up 339.6

crib 48.4, 78.2, 310.2, 463.3
crib-man 479.3
crikey 325.2
crikey! 189.5
CRIME 458–496
crime: accusation 473
crime: arrest 489
crime: begging 477
crime: betrayal 473
crime: booty 464
crime: coercion 485
crime: communication 469
crime: correspondence 469
crime: corruption 482
crime: devices 465
crime: establishments 461
crime: evidence 486
crime: examination of prisoners 490
crime: explosives 466
crime: food 467
crime: general 478
crime: health 459
crime: illicit goods 464
crime: illicit business 481
crime: implements 465
crime: information 472
crime: locality 460
crime: money 462
crime: observation 474
crime: persons 458
crime: pursuit 488
crime: search 488
crime: signals 471
crime: speech 470
crime: suspicion 486
crime: tobacco 468
crime: transportation methods 475
crime: vagrancy 476
crime: valuables 463
crime: violence 485
crime: weapons 466
Crimea 95.1
criminal 458.1, 478.4
criminal go-between 458.12
criminal planner 458.11
criminal sentence 491
criminal specialists 479.3
criminy 325.2
criminy! 189.5
crimp 218.1, 218.2
crimson 44.2

crinched 40.1
crinkle-top 428.7
cripes 325.2
cripes! 189.5
cripple 429.2
crispy 429.1
criss-cross 310.4
critic 419
criticise 290.2
criticism 290
critter 115.10, 377.1
crix 419.1
croak 112.5, 113.4, 258.1
croaked 112.10
croaker 456.2
crock (of shit) 28.1, 146.2, 235.1
crocked 101.3
crocko 101.3
crombie 82.12
cronky 307.4
crook 124.4, 235.8
crooked 40.1
crooked on 289.3
crookedness 40
crop 105.2
cropper 56.1, 165.1, 258.1
cross 313.3
cross man 435.1
cross one's heart (and hope to die) 164.7
cross one's palm 370.4
cross up 313.3
cross-bar hotel 494.1
cross-examination 154.2
cross-eyed 101.3
crotch 380.1
crotch cheese 116.28
crow 300.2, 426.2
crow eaters 385.1
crow McGee 28.2
crowd 378
crowd pleaser 466.1
crown 337.4
crown jewels 116.33
crucial time 2.2
crud 116.28, 395.1
cruddy 28.2
crude 67.6, 235.8, 472.1
cruise 350.4, 352.5
cruisemobile 75.2
cruiser 497.2
cruising for a bruising 252.12
cruising with one's lights on dim 147.5

crumb 28.1, 388.1, 427.4
crumb-crusher 381.2
crumb-snatcher 381.2
crumbly 382.1
crumbs! 189.5
crumbum 28.2
crumby 28.2, 278.5
crummy 7.14, 28.2, 75.4, 124.4, 278.5, 308.3
crummy with 366.5
crumpet 425.1
crunch 10.3
cruncher 458.3
crush 349.1, 441.1
crush-out 459.1
crust 347.1
crust of bread 116.4
crusty 280.5
crutch 506.3
cry (n.) 188.1
cry (v.) 188.2, 281.3
cry Hughie 118.13
cry Ralph 118.13
cry Ruth 118.13
cry Uncle! 302.2
crying 18.8
crying 281.2
crystal 504.2
crystal-gazer 430.4
CS 296.6, 403.1
cube 505.5
cuckoo 124.7, 145.3, 147.5, 165.4
cuckoo over 349.4
cuddle and kiss 380.1
cuff 506.6
cuffs 465.1
cuffs and collars 116.41
cull 451.1
cull bird 426.2
CULPABILITY 316–318
cults 378.3
culture 141
culture 143.6
culture fruit 86.14
culture-vulture 430.1
cum-freak 437.2
cunnilingus 360.3
cunning 253.2
cunt 116.40, 380.1, 395.1, 396.1
cunt-tease 352.8
cunt-teaser 352.2, 441.12
cuntlapper 395.1, 436.2
cup of tea 212.1
cupcake 116.31, 425.1

damp 101.3, 116.40
damper 218.1, 278.1, 463.3, 494.2
Dan 179.8
dance (n.) 364.2
dance (v.) 364.3
dance 479.4
dance on one's lips 337.4
dance on the mattress 359.6
dancing 364
dandy 27.3
dandy! 285.5
dang(ed) 189.4
danger 256
dangerous 256.5
dangler 116.34
dap 84.3, 164.11, 346.1
daps 82.16
darbies 465.1
Darby Kelly 116.13
dark complexioned black (by blacks) 384.3
dark meat 384.1
darkie 384.1
darkness at noon 179.4
Darky 179.8, 179.11
darling 273.6
darn! 189.5
darn right! 199.3
darnedest 238.2
darry 132.1
dash 372.1
dash! 189.5
dash in the bloomers 359.1
dash it (all)! 189.5
dashed 28.2, 189.4
date 116.29, 116.30, 354.2, 362.1
dating 350.1
daughter 380.1, 404.5
Davy Jones' locker 67.2, 112.3
day 3.1
daylight 197.1
daylights 116.12
days of the week 3.2
DE 75.4
deache 116.4
dead 112.10
dead 22.6, 243.4, 459.2
dead as a dodo 229.5, 244.3, 272.5
dead as a doornail 112.10, 244.3, 272.5

dead between the ears 145.3
dead cert 159.1, 251.1, 437.3, 511.1, 514.2, 514.5
dead duck 7.1, 28.1, 235.1, 412.12
Dead End Street 116.40
dead fetch 428.5
dead from the neck down 145.3
dead from the neck up 150.2, 272.5
dead giveaway 193.1
dead man 105.4
dead man's shame 366.1
dead marine 105.4
dead meat 112.2
dead on the vine 124.6, 272.5
dead pigeon 158.2
dead rabbit 116.35, 235.1
dead ringer 428.5
dead set (on) 349.4
dead set 27.3, 204.6
dead shot 359.1
dead soldier 105.4
dead spit 428.5
dead sure 159.3
dead time 494.6
dead to rights 159.3, 162.6, 164.10
dead to the wide 153.9, 243.4
dead to the world 150.2, 153.9
dead 'un 412.12, 514.2
dead-beat 124.6
dead-eye dick 404.1
deadbeat 412.12, 414.1
deadeye 116.29
deadhead 60.4, 431.1
deadly 278.5
deadpan 183.8, 271.5
deaf 134.5
deaf 27.3
deaf mute 125.14
deal 502.8
deal in 357.3
deal out 370.2
deal the cards 515.7
deal them from the bottom of the deck 310.4
deal with 163.5
dealer 502.1

dear John 191.6
dear heart 180.1
dearie 178.3
DEATH 112–113
death 27.3
death by shooting 113.2
death! 285.5
death on 216.6
deb 458.2
debag 85.5
debts 510
debut 358.1
debutante 404.5
decapitate 337.6
deceit 310
deceitful 310.8
deceitful person 435
deceive 219.5, 310.4
deception 310
DECEPTION 310–315
deck 41.2, 337.4, 502.4
deck ape 456.1
deck up 367.2
decko 132.1
decks-awash 101.3
declare open season on 157.1
decoke 76.9
decorate 35.5
decrease 25
deelo nam 382.2
deenach 116.15
deep 67.2
deep six 25.4
deep throat 193.4, 360.2, 360.12
def 27.3, 159.4
defeat 338.5
defecate 119.7
defecation 119
defective object 7.1
defend oneself 341.4
definitely 159.4
deflower a virgin 359.11
defraud 310.6
defug 106.9
defy union rules 241.9
degenerate 7.7
dekko 132.1
Del 179.7
delay (v.i.) 284.2
delay (v.t.) 248.3
delay (n.) 248
Delhi belly 119.5
delight 273

dip in one's business
  249.2
dip in the bush 360.13
dip it 359.6
dip one's beak 372.4
dip one's wick 359.6
dip the beak 87.6
dip the bill 97.3
dip the fly 359.6
dip the snoot 97.3
diphead 431.1
dipping in the bush 360.3
dippy 124.7, 147.5
dipshit 28.2, 396.1, 431.1
dipso 429.4
dipstick 396.1
direct a film 195.13
directed force 32.3
direction 51
directly 164.11
dirk 116.34, 196.1, 294.2
dirt chute 116.29
dirt road 116.29
dirt tamper 404.1
dirty 5.4
dirty deal 308.1
dirty dishes 486.1
dirty dowager 404.5
dirty dozens 294.1
dirty fingernails 117.7
dirty leg 437.3
dirty look 288.2
dirty money 512.1
dirty old Jew 516.6
dirty place 48.8
dirty pool 308.1, 310.2
dirty weather 66.2
dirty weekend 3.6
dirty work (at the
  crossroads) 308.1, 313.1
disadvantage 259
disagreeableness 278
disagreement 343
disappear 132.9
disappearing act 211.1
disappoint 282.2
disappointed 282.4
disappointment 282
disapproval 288
*disapproval of passing
  girl(s)* 288.6
disapprove 288.3
disapproving 288.4
disapproving look 288.2
disarrange 5.3
disbelief 161

disbelieve 161.1
discard 25.4
discharge 63.1
disclose 193.3
disclosure 193
discombobulate 169.3,
  283.4
discombobulated 169.4
disconcert 169.3
disconcertion 169
DISCOURTESY 347–348
discover 162.3
discover one's gender
  358.3
discovered 162.7
discovery 162
discs 135.5
discuss 186.6
discuss again 186.9
discuss pimping 498.8
discussion 186
diseases 125
disfavour 332
disguise (v.t.) 203.7
disguise: front 203.4
disguised 203.9
dish 7.10, 35.2, 183.10,
  183.7, 196.1, 250.1,
  282.2, 380.1, 425.1
dish (the lowdown) 192.4
dish it out 337.4
dish out 367.5, 370.2
dish out a line 287.2
dish out gravy 491.4
dish out the applesauce
  287.2
dish out the oil 287.2
dish queen 420.2
dish the bull 146.6
dish the crap 146.6
dish the dirt (about) 294.5
dish the dirt 192.4, 196.3
dish up 88.1
dishabilly 85.1
dished 282.4, 376.5
dishonest 307.3
dishonest person 434
dishonestly 307
dishwater 94.6
dishy 35.7
disillusion 193.7
DISINTEREST 271–272
dislike (v.) 332.2
dismiss 63.2, 224.5
dismissal 63.1, 224.2,
  242.2

dismissed 63.4
disorder 5
disorder 7.8
disorientated 127.3
disparage 292.3
disparagement 292
displease 278.4
displeased with 278.6
displeasure 278
DISPLEASURE 278–284
disposition 137
disreputable 140.5
disreputable person 433
disrepute 140
dissipation 309
dissolute 309.4
dissoluteness 309
distance 38
distasteful 130.2
ditch 25.4, 63.2, 67.2,
  116.40, 209.2, 209.5,
  331.2
ditso 28.2
ditty-bop 390.4
div 403.1
dive 78.1, 104.1, 203.6,
  258.1, 360.13
dive in the canyon 360.13
dive into the dark 359.6
dive into the sky 360.15
divert suspicion 486.10
divide 25.3
divil 325.3
divine 273.6
divine right 495.1
divisions of time 3
divorce (v.) 356.2
divorce 356
divvy (up) 367.2
divvy 23.1, 508.6
divvy up 25.3
Dixie 179.8
Dizzy 179.16
dizzy 101.3
Dizzie Lizzie 179.9
dj 456.5
djamba 506.2
do (it) on one's dick
  251.4
do (it) on one's head
  251.4
do (it) on one's prick
  251.4
do (it) up right 257.2
do 239.2
do 7.10, 310.6, 318.4,

a double-barrelled shotgun 145.2
doesn't know his ass from a hole in the ground 145.2
doesn't know his ass from his elbow 145.2
doesn't know his ass from third base 145.2
doesn't know his butt from a gourd 145.2
doesn't know owl-shit from putty without a map 145.2
doesn't know sheepshit from cherry-seed 145.2
doesn't know shit from Shinola 145.2
doesn't know t'other from which 145.2
doesn't know up from down 145.2
doesn't know whether to shit or go blind 435.4
doesn't know whether to suck or blow 435.4
doesn't have the foggiest 145.2
dog 35.1, 115.5, 115.10, 119.3, 296.1, 298.1, 395.1, 426.2, 472.2, 508.11
dog and bone 195.5
dog around 244.1
dog days 3.5
dog excrement 115.5
dog food 505.2
dog in the manger 206.2
dog it 50.1, 84.2, 244.1, 512.4
dog juice 95.6
dog tag 502.7
dog vomit 86.2
dog's bollocks 177.4
dog's chance 158.2
dog's cock 177.4
dog's dinner 5.1, 86.2
dog's life 278.2
dog's nose 472.2
dog-ass 28.2
dog-end 106.3
dog-knotted 359.17
dog-robbers 82.8
dogface 426.2, 456.1
dogger out 474.1
doggie 426.2, 456.1

doggie-bag 91.2
doggone 189.4
doggone! 189.5
doggy 50.4, 245.1, 399.1
doggy-do 115.5
dogs 115.1
dogs 82.15
dogsbody 453.2
doing a hundred 257.5
doing up 4.3
doings 69.2, 230.1
dojigger 69.2
dole-bludger 508.9
doley 417.1
doll 380.1, 387.2, 425.1
doll city 425.1
doll up 4.4, 35.6, 84.2
dollar 509.4
dollar bill 509.3
dolled up 84.3
dollface 425.1
dolls 504.1
dolly (bird) 380.1
Dolly 179.8
dolly 425.1, 441.3, 505.5
Dolly Varden 48.5
dollydrop 62.1
DOM 383.3
dome 116.4
domestic servant 455
Dons 179.1
don't amount to a fart in a whirlwind 235.10
don't amount to a pisspot full of crab-apples 235.10
don't ask me 145.5, 167.5, 271.7
don't ask me I only work here! 292.7
don't be absurd 146.11
don't be cheeky 347.5
don't be funny 146.11
don't be smart 347.5
don't be so conceited 297.5
don't call us, we'll call you 346.4
don't complain about prison 494.14
don't do anything I wouldn't do 256.7, 346.4
don't do anything I wouldn't do! 149.6

don't fancy yours 288.6, 359.20
don't fuck about 230.3
don't fuck about! 146.11
don't get funny 284.8
don't get smart 284.8
don't get your bowels in an uproar 265.7
don't get your knickers in a twist 265.7
don't get your shit hot 265.7
don't give me that 161.6
don't give me that! 146.11, 278.7
don't I know it 164.12
don't interfere 249.4
don't interrupt 201.6
don't just stand there, do something 216.7
don't kid yourself 161.6, 165.5
don't know from 167.2
don't know one from a bar of soap 348.3
don't know one's arse from a hole in the ground 168.4
don't know one's arse from one's elbow 168.4
don't know whether one is coming or going 168.4
don't let the bastards grind you down 295.6
don't make a federal case (of it) 265.7
don't make a production of it 295.6
don't make me laugh 161.6, 165.5
don't make me laugh! 146.11, 200.3, 214.11, 223.1
don't mind if I do 340.5
don't mind me I only live here! 284.8
don't mind me I only work here! 284.8
don't muck about 230.3
don't pick up soap in his shower 435.4
don't piss about 230.3
don't shit me 161.6
don't shoot the pianist, he's doing his best! 266.4

dreamy 35.7
dreck 28.1
dredge-head 92.3
DRESS 82–85
dress 84.1
dress down 291.2
dress one's hair 120.10
dress up 84.2
dress-up 499.2
dressed 79.10
dressed to the nines 84.3
dressed up 84.3
dressed up like a dog's
  dinner 84.3
dressed up like a pox
  doctor's clerk 84.3
dressing 84
dressing down 291.1,
  318.2
dreykop 435.1
dribble 184.1, 261.2,
  261.3
drill 337.7, 359.6
drill 69.12
drink 67.2, 372.2, 482.2,
  482.4
drink (n.) 87.6, 97.2
drink (v.) 97.3
drink at the fuzzy cup
  360.13
drink container 105
drinker 423
drinker 78.6
drinkery 104.1
drinking 97
drinking 97.4
drinking establishment
  104
drip 125.10, 403.1, 452.2,
  510.2
drip it up 510.7
dripping 296.6
dripping for it 357.11
dripsy 125.10
drive fast 60.4
drive on 337.4
drive one around the
  bend 284.2
drive one nuts 284.2
drive one through the
  roof 284.2
drive one up the wall
  284.2
drive one's hos 498.7
drive out of one's brain
  169.3

drive out of one's gourd
  169.3
drive out of one's skull
  169.3
drive the big white bus
  118.13
drive the porcelain bus
  118.13
drive up a pole 169.3
driver 475.1
drivers 116.18
driving post 116.34
drongo 431.1
droob 396.1
drool 261.2, 261.3
drop (it) 150.1
drop (of the creature)
  97.2
drop (right) in 315.2
drop 74.1, 113.4, 203.3,
  203.5, 259.1, 337.5,
  376.4, 381.3, 464.1,
  504.6
drop a beast 118.8
drop a brick 165.3
drop a bundle 369.2
drop a dime on 473.2
drop a dollar on 473.2
drop a line 191.7
drop a lug 498.9
drop a packet 369.2
drop a quarter on 473.2
drop a thumper 118.8
drop anchor 41.6
drop by 52.2, 53.1
drop dead! 278.8, 292.7
drop game 480.2
drop in 52.1, 52.2, 53.1
drop it 274.6
drop it! 201.5
drop off the twig 112.5
drop on 291.2, 316.2
drop one in it 310.4
drop one out 486.9
drop one's beads 358.3
drop one's bundle 283.2
drop one's guts 118.8
drop one's hairpins 358.3
drop one's load 359.6
drop one's roll 369.2
drop one's wad 369.2
drop sticks 479.4
drop the cue 112.5
drop the curtain 239.6
drop the duds 85.3
drop the gear 85.3

drop the hook on 489.2
drop trou 85.4
dropped 354.4
dropper 458.5
drops 462.2
drown 112.6
drug 272.6, 279.7
drug addiction 503
drug cocktails 505.7
drug effects 507
drug experience 507
drug injection 505.8
drug seller 502.1
drug selling 502
drug use 503
'*drugged*' 507.7
druggie 456.17, 503.3
DRUGS 502–507
drugstore 91.1
drugstore cowboy 446.1
drum 78.2
drum up 219.6, 311.4
drummer 456.16
drumming 480.2
drumstick case 338.2
drumsticks 116.18
drunk 101.3
drunk as a bastard 101.3
drunk as a bat 101.3
drunk as a beggar 101.3
drunk as a besom 101.3
drunk as a big owl 101.3
drunk as a boiled owl
  101.3
drunk as a brewer's fart
  101.3
drunk as a cook 101.3
drunk as a coon 101.3
drunk as a coot 101.3
drunk as a cooter 101.3
drunk as a dog 101.3
drunk as a fiddler 101.3
drunk as a fiddler's bitch
  101.3
drunk as a fish 101.3
drunk as a fly 101.3
drunk as a fowl 101.3
drunk as a Gosport
  fiddler 101.3
drunk as a hog 101.3
drunk as a king 101.3
drunk as a little red
  wagon 101.3
drunk as a log 101.3
drunk as a lord 101.3
drunk as a monkey 101.3

enough and then some 22.2
enough said! 201.5
enquiries as to health 122.3
enter 53.1
enter forcibly 53.2
enterprising person 410
entertain 239.8, 363.4
enthroned 358.10
enthuse 286.2
enthusiasm 236.3, 270
enthusiastic 236.8, 270.4
enthusiastic about 270.5
entice 220.2
enticement 220
entice prostitutes 498.6
enticing 220.4
entrance 53
entrap 315.2
entrapment 315
enuff 22.1
equality 26.1
equalizer 71.1, 466.1
equipment 116.35
equipment 69.1
er 9.2, 177.3
er? 167.4
erase 113.4
erect penis 118.4
-erino 10.4
-eroo 10.4
Errol Flynn 116.23
error 165
esaff 116.5
escape (v.) 211.3, 487.5
escape 211, 487
escape from trouble 252.9
escape punishment 318.9
escaped 494.13
escapee 487.3
esclop 495.1
-ese 176.1
eskimo 384.8
esky 69.20
esrar 506.2
essentials 164.3
ESTATE 375–376
estimate (n.) 163.3
estimate (v.) 163.4
estimated 163.6
estrangement 331
etc 135.1
ethno 385.1
-ette 10.4, 19.4
euchred 243.4

evade 210.2
EVASION 207–211
evasion 210, 487
Even Stephen 179.9
even steven 26.2, 367.1, 367.6
ever so 18.10
even the score 335.2
every Tom Dick and Harry 378.2
every man jack 378.2
every mother's son 378.2
everyone 378.2
everything 22.3
everything but the kitchen sink 22.3
everything's cool 275.7
everything's hotsy-totsy 275.7
everything's jake 275.7
everything's OK 275.7
everywhere 41.8
everywhichway 5.5, 40.1, 51.5, 151.7, 232.5
evidence 162.1
evil 306
ex 27.3, 441.7
exaggerated 312.3
exaggerator 420.5
exalted 101.3
examination 156
exceedingly 18.10
excellent 18.11
excellent 27.3
excessive 22.5
exchange stories 198.8
EXCITABILITY 262–264
excite sexually 357.4
excited 262.7
excitement 262
exciting 262.6
exciting story 198.4
excluded from a share 367.7
excuse (n.) 317.2
excuse my French 189.3
excuses to leave 317.6
execution 113.3
exercise the ferret 359.6
excercising 121.2
exert strength 32.4
exhaust 243.3
exhausted 124.6, 243.4
exhausted person 429.1
exhib 132.10
exhibitionist 436.6

exonerate 486.9
expat 383.6
expect 172.2
expectant 172.3
EXPECTATION 172–173
expectation 262.8
expensive 508.19
experience 11.1
experienced 253.7
experienced person 430
experienced person 430.3
experienced prostitute 497.7
experiencing drugs 507.8
experiment 156.4
explain 197.1
explanation 186.4
explanation 197
explosion 73
explosion of rage 280.2
EXPLOSIVES 70–74
expose 193.5
expose the genitals 357.6
exterior 76.8
extort 368.3
extract the michael 293.5
extravagance 373
eye 156.1, 495.2
eye doctor 404.1
eye-opener 97.2
eyeball 132.6
eyeful 35.2, 425.1
eyes 116.12
eyes 116.31
eyes (characteristics) 117.4
eyes like pissholes in the snow 117.4
Eyetie 383.13
eyewash 146.2, 183.2, 287.1, 310.1

F-40s 504.3
F-60s 504.3
F-66s 504.3
faastie 347.4
fab 27.3
face 116.5
face 295.1, 347.1, 377.1, 458.1
face fungus 116.10
face like a douchebag 426.1
face like a toilet seat 426.1
face the music 318.7
face the nation 360.13

give one's best shot 204.2
give one's come-uppance 371.4
give one's deserts 371.4
give orders 216.4
give over! 292.7
give some body 359.6
give some skin 346.2
give some spli 346.2
give the (old) heave-ho 25.4, 63.2
give the E 224.3
give the OK 222.2
give the air 25.4, 63.2, 353.5
give the all-clear 285.3
give the belt 63.2
give the big razoo 292.3
give the bird 293.4
give the boot 224.5
give the brown envelope 63.2, 224.5
give the brush 353.5
give the brush-off 25.4, 209.5
give the bullet 242.6
give the bump 25.4
give the business 113.4, 318.4, 350.3
give the chop 113.4, 338.5
give the come-on (to) 220.2
give the dog a bone 359.6
give the dogs a rest 56.3
give the dope on 192.4
give the double-shuffle 259.4
give the drummer some 346.2
give the duke 290.2
give the elbow 25.4, 63.2, 224.3
give the eye (to) 132.6
give the eye 156.3
give the finger 148.5, 292.3, 293.6
give the glad eye 350.4
give the go-ahead 222.2, 285.3
give the go-around 209.5
give the go-by 210.2, 210.4
give the goods on 192.4
give the green light (to) 222.2

give the hard word 224.3, 294.6
give the heave 25.4
give the high sign 182.3
give the hook 25.4
give the knife 25.4
give the leather 337.9
give the man the play 472.3
give the miss 210.4
give the needle 284.2
give the nod 288.3
give the once-over 156.3, 132.6
give the pip 284.2
give the rap 113.4
give the red light (to) 224.3
give the rough edge of one's tongue 294.6
give the runaround 210.2, 210.4
give the sack 63.2, 224.5
give the slip 25.4
give the thumbs up (to) 222.2
give the thumbs-down (to) 200.2, 224.3, 288.3
give the time of day 267.2
give the works (to) 338.3
give the works 113.4, 318.4
give the works to 338.5
give up 209.2
give up as a bad job 302.2
give up crime 478.3
give up one's face 360.11
give up rhythm 352.5
give up the ship 112.5
give up the store 209.2
give your face a rest! 201.5
giveaway 193.1
giving 370
giving up 209
gizmo 69.2, 505.9
gizzard 116.13
gizzum 116.28
glad 101.3
glad eye 132.1, 352.3
glad hand 328.1, 328.5
glad rags 82.4
glads 114.2
glamour 229.1
glamour-puss 425.1, 425.2
glance 132

glass 83.10
glass jaw 116.6
glassed 117.3
glasshouse 494.1
glaum 132.1, 132.6, 162.3, 166.2
Glaziers 179.1
gleep a cage 479.4
gleet 125.10
glim 69.22
glimmer 417.2
glims 132.3
glitterati 139.7, 448.2, 450.3
glitzy 141.1, 229.4
globetrotter 503.2
globular 101.3
glom 132.1, 132.6, 162.3, 166.2, 365.2
gloom 405.1
glooms 279.2
gloomy person 405
glop 67.7, 86.2
glory (be)! 189.5
glory hole 116.40, 360.2
glossy 194.3
gloves 83.1
glow 101.1
glowing 101.3
glue 67.8
glut 399.3
glutton 437.4
glutton for punishment 436.1
gmbu 5.5
gmfu 5.5
gnarly 28.2
gnat's pee 94.6
gnat's piss 94.6
gnaw a bone 89.6
gnaw the 'nana 360.12
go (along) with 340.2
go (and) bark at the moon! 292.7
go (and) boil your head! 292.7
go (and) jump in a lake! 292.7
go (and) take a long walk off a short pier 292.7
go (for) 266.2
go (for) the whole shot 204.2
go 1.1, 8.2, 23.2, 49.1, 156.2, 183.7, 214.1, 236.2, 238.2, 270.1

griff 194.1
grift 480.1
grifter 435.1, 480.3
grill 154.3
grilling 154.2
grin in the canyon 360.13
grind 226.1, 241.1, 241.7,
    359.6, 410.3
grind down 219.4
gringa 384.13
gringo 384.12
gripe 279.3
gripples 116.29
grisly 36.2
grit 295.1
gritch 289.2
gritchy 280.5
grizzle 279.3, 289.2
groaty 36.2,
groceries 86.1, 116.40
grockle 451.1
grody 36.2
grody to the max 36.2
grog 68.2, 94.1
grogginess 169.1
groggy 33.5, 101.3
groid 384.1, 463.1
grok 166.2
grooming 120
groove (on) 276.4
groove 260.1
groove behind 276.4
grooved 274.9
groovy 27.3
groping 351.1
gross 18.7, 22.5, 28.2,
    29.2, 36.2, 312.3
gross out 89.7, 347.3
gross-out 89.5
gross-out artist 399.3
grotty 36.2
grouch 405.2
grouchy 279.6, 280.5
ground 41.2
ground 460.2
ground rations 359.1
ground zero 9.1
group 378
group grope 360.6
group of police 495.4
group sex 360.6
grouper 439.2
groupie 437.3, 439.2
grouse 27.3
grouse gear 425.1
grow horns 280.3

grow up 146.7
groyne 463.1
grub 86.1, 368.2, 426.1,
    453.3
grub it up 89.7
grub up 89.6
grub('s) up! 89.9
grubber 48.6, 426.6
grubbies 82.5
grubble (around) 157.1
grubfest 89.5
grubstake 508.2
grudge (n.) 334.2
Grudian 179.5
grumble and grunt 116.40
grump 279.3
grumps 279.2
grumpy 279.6
grunge 5.1, 337.4, 392.1
grungy 5.5
grunt 388.1, 456.1
grunter 497.2
grunters 382.1
gub 384.12
gubbins 69.2
guck 67.7
gucky 36.2
Gucky 179.2
guess (v.) 174.3
guess (n.) 174.1
guesstimate 16.6, 163.3,
    174.1
guff 118.2, 146.2, 146.3,
    183.1, 184.1, 347.2
guggle 135.2
guinea 383.13
guinea pig 472.2
guinea stinker 106.7
guineas 509.1
guinzo 383.13
gulf 116.40
gulley 116.40
gulley hole 116.40
gullible 160.6
gullible person 391
gum 325.1
gum heel 495.1
gum things up 233.4
gum up (the works) 7.8
gum up 33.3, 250.1, 254.2
gum up the deal 254.2
gum up the play 254.2
gum up the works 233.4,
    250.1, 254.2
gumdrop 504.3
gummed up 250.2

gumption 143.1, 253.1
gums 184.2
gumshoe 8.3, 54.4, 132.7,
    456.4, 495.2
gun (it) 60.4
gun 116.34, 505.9
gun 466.1
gun for 157.1, 357.3
Gunboat 179.8
gunfire 73.2
gung-ho 270.4
Gunga Din 116.23
gunge 86.2
gunja 506.2
gunk 67.7
gunner 516.2
Gunners 179.1
gunny 456.1, 506.2
gunsel 458.4
guntz 22.3
gunzel 338.3
gush (over) 261.3
gush 184.1, 261.1, 261.2
gut 251.1
gut it 241.6
gut-wrenching 278.5
gutache 125.1, 279.3
gutless 296.6
guts 32.1, 32.3, 204.1,
    295.1, 399.2, 423.1,
    427.2
gutshoot 113.5
gutso 423.1, 427.2
gutstick 116.34
gutsy 295.5
gutted 280.6
gutter 116.40
gutty 272.5
guv 178.3, 457.1, 495.1
guvnor 178.3, 387.1,
    457.1, 495.1
Guy (Fawkes) 59.1
guy 377.1
guyver 287.1
guz 43.1
guzzle 89.7, 351.3
gynae 456.2
gyp 310.3, 310.6, 434.1
gyp joint 461.1
gyppo 384.7
gyppy tummy 119.5
gypsy 384.7
gypsy's 119.2
gyrene 456.1

H. 505.2

hold the can 216.3
hold the phone 248.2
hold the phone! 248.5
hold up! 10.9
hold water 4.5
hold your horses! 266.4
hold your noise! 201.5
hold your water! 266.4
hold-out 497.6
holding 466.5, 502.14
hole 78.1, 116.7, 116.40,
   494.2
hole and corner 202.5
hole card 202.1
hole in one 164.12, 257.1
hole up 203.6, 246.2
hole-in-the-wall 28.2
holed up 203.8
holes and poles 179.4
holier-than-thou 321.2
HOLLAND 191.5
holler 188.1, 188.2
holler copper 472.3
hollow tooth 495.7
Hollywood hustler 497.9
Hollywood swoop 60.2
hols 3.3
holy 18.8
holy Joe 323.1, 323.2
holy Moses! 189.5
holy cats! 189.5
holy cow! 18.5
holy cripes! 189.5
holy friar 435.2
holy mackerel! 189.5
holy mess 252.2
holy muddle 252.2
holy smoke! 173.7, 189.5
hombre 379.1
home 78.2
Home and Colonial 495.4
home and dry 255.6
home squeeze 438.1
homeboy 384.2, 438.1,
   452.1
homegirl 384.2, 438.1,
   452.1
homegrown 506.2
homeless 48.7
homespun philosophy
   153.6
hominy gazette 494.7
homo 404.1
homosexual (adj.) 358.7
homosexuals 404
hon 178.3

honcho 232.3, 387.1
honest (injun) 204.7
honest 305.6
honest! 305.9
honest injun! 199.3
honesty 305
honey 119.3, 178.3, 180.1,
   235.2, 425.1, 441.3
honey cart 69.19
honey wagon 69.19
honey-bunny 180.1
honey-child 180.1
honey-dipper 456.14
honey-pie 180.1
honey-suckle 180.1
honeybunch 441.1
honeyfuck 359.6
honeyfuggle 359.6
honeymoon 503.5
honeymoon cystitis 125.9
honeypot 116.40
Hong Kong dog 119.5
honk 384.12
honk for 357.3
honk on 54.3
honk out 33.2
honker 116.34, 116.9,
   409.1
Honkers 45.1
honkie 384.12
honky 390.3
honky-tonk 48.6
honyok 390.2
hoo-ha 146.2
hooch 94.1
hood 433.1, 433.4, 495.1
hoodoo 215.4, 215.7,
   327.2
hoodooed 215.9
hooey 146.2, 146.3
hoof 116.22
hoof it 49.4
hoof out 63.2
hoofer 456.5
hoofing 364.1
hook 195.5, 259.1, 310.3,
   387.1, 489.1, 497.15,
   497.2, 505.12
hook down 89.6
hook for 310.6
hook in 219.4
hook line and sinker 22.3
hook shop 500.1
hook up with 328.6, 339.2
hook-up 339.1
hooked 226.2, 489.4

hooked up 339.6
hooker 479.3, 497.2
hooking 472.1
hooknose 384.8
hooks 116.15
hookup 340.1
Hooky 179.8
hoon 498.2
hoop 360.5
hoopdie-swoop 350.3
hoopla 262.1, 274.1
hooray 448.2
hooray Henry 448.2
hooroo 346.4
hoosegow 494.1
hoosier 390.2
hoot 274.1, 274.4, 277.1,
   509.1
hootch 48.1
hooter 116.9
hoowah 497.2
hop 505.2, 505.4
hop and a step 38.3
hop in the hay 247.3
hop in the sack 247.3
hop it! 54.6
hop joint 502.2
hop on a babe 359.6
hop on it 49.7
hop the wag 54.3, 210.3
hop to (it) 241.5
hop up 236.5
hope 158.1, 214.1
hope to die 199.2, 328.7
hophead 503.2
hopped up 77.2, 236.7,
   262.7, 268.4, 507.8
hopping (mad) 280.6
horizontal exercise 247.1
horizontal jogging 359.1
horizontal rumble 359.1
Horlicks 5.1
horn 116.34, 116.35,
   116.9, 505.11
horn in 249.2
horn movie 501.3
horning in 249.1
horny 357.11
horror 426.1
horrors 296.2, 507.3
horry 359.1
hors d'oeuvres 504.1
horse 115.10
horse 125.10, 505.2
horse apples 119.3
horse around 244.1, 276.6

horse around with 277.5
horse collar 116.40
horse laugh 277.1, 293.1
horse of a different colour 26.1
horse sense 143.1
horse's arse 395.1, 431.1
horse's hangdown 431.1
horse-race 514.5
horse-race betting 514.6
horse-racing 514
horse-racing locations 514.3
horse-racing: people 514.4
horsefeathers 146.2
horseman 495.1
horseplayer 514.4
horses 60.3
horseshit 146.2
horsewoman 404.3
hose 360.15
hose down 73.3
hose one's hole 360.20
hostie 456.11
HOSTILITY 331–338
hot (for) 268.4
hot (to trot) 172.3
hot 31.1
hot 1.6, 35.7, 215.8, 276.8, 280.6, 306.5, 357.8, 357.11, 486.13, 512.8
hot air 146.3, 184.1, 185.1, 299.1
hot and bothered 168.5, 262.7, 280.6, 283.6
hot and strong 49.9
hot as a bastard 31.1
hot as a bitch 31.1
hot as buggery 31.1
hot as hell 31.1
hot chair 492.1
hot cross bun 49.9
hot damn 273.7
hot diggety 273.7
hot diggety dog 273.7
hot dish 411.1
hot dog 513.2
hot fling 359.1
hot for (it) 357.11
hot for 148.8, 204.6, 267.4, 270.5
hot honey 411.1
hot number 411.1, 425.1
hot nuts 357.2
hot off the press 1.6

hot off the presses 192.9
hot on 270.5
hot one 62.2, 153.2, 411.1
hot pants 283.6, 357.2
hot poop 192.1, 192.2, 194.1
hot potato 252.1
hot seat 154.2, 252.1, 492.1
hot shit 273.7
hot shot 505.8
hot squat 492.1
hot steer 192.2
hot stuff 35.2, 191.1, 192.2, 253.7, 273.2, 411.1, 430.2, 464.1
hot stuff! 292.7
hot time 276.2
hot tip 192.2
hot to trot 148.7, 237.5, 264.3
hot walker 514.4
hot weather 66.1
hot-cha-cha 273.7
hot-dog 413.1
hot-dogger 401.2, 413.1
hot-foot 49.1
hot-footing 49.2
hot-shit 27.3
hot-shot 387.1
hot-wire 60.6
hotcha 236.2, 270.1, 273.7
hotel 78.5
hothead 405.2
hots 267.1
hotshot 62.2, 410.1, 413.1
hotsy 273.6, 411.1
hotsy-totsy 27.3, 123.3
hottentot apron 116.43
hotter than hell 31.1
hottie 69.8
hour 3.10
house 48.2, 78.2
house 488.4, 500.1
house nigger 384.6
household equipment 69.8
how (in) the devil 232.6
how (in) the fuck 232.6
how (in) the heck 232.6
how (in) the hell 232.6
how 232.6
how about it? 232.7
how are they hanging? 122.3
how are you doing? 122.3
how are you fixed? 366.7

how are you going? 122.3
how do you like them apples? 153.12, 278.7
how does that grab you? 153.12, 278.7
how much do you have? 366.7
how the blazes 232.6
how the deuce 232.6
how the shit 232.6
how're they hanging? 346.3
how's about it? 232.7
how's by you? 122.3
how's it hanging? 346.3
how's tricks? 346.3
how's your head? 122.3
how-come? 152.4
how-do-you-do 4.1
howd'ye dos 82.15
howdy 346.1
howdydo 346.1
howl 289.2, 293.5
howler 7.2, 165.1
howling 312.3
hoy 188.3
hubba! hubba! 285.5
hubbie 444.4
huddle 186.3
huey 71.3
hug the porcelain 118.13
huge 18.7
huh! 292.8
huh? 167.4
hulluva 18.2
hully 427.2
hum and haw 207.2
humbug 489.1
humdinger 18.1, 27.1, 273.2
humiliate 300.3
humiliation 300.2
HUMILITY 300–302
hummer 62.2, 489.1
humour 277
humourist 406
hump 'em and dump 'em 359.10
hump 61.1, 279.2, 359.6
hump one's horse 360.19
humper 454.3
humungous 18.7
hun 383.8, 509.10
hunch 172.1
hung 116.34
hung for 268.4

hung for bread 376.5
hung up (on) 226.2
hung up 270.4
hung up on 270.5
hunger 90.2
hungry 236.8, 495.1
hungry 90.4
hungry croaker 50.23
hunk 390.3, 425.2, 427.1
hunkie 384.12
hunko 427.1
hunky 117.12, 390.3
hunky-dory 4.2, 27.3,
   275.4
hunkydory 123.3
hunt 157.1
hunt 224.4
hurl 118.13
hurricane lamp 417.3
hurry 49.5
hurry up! 49.12
hurry-up 475.2
hurry-up wagon 475.3
hurt (v.t.) 485.3
hurt 337.8
hurt 337.8
hurt for 268.2
hurt one's feelings
   301.3
hurt to 264.2
hurtin' for certain 36.2
hurting (for) 268.4, 503.7
hurting 264.3, 279.7,
   376.5
hurting dance 281.1
husband 404.5
husband 444.4
hush money 372.2
hush my mouth! 173.7
hush one's mouth 136.3
hush up 136.3, 202.2
hush up! 136.4
hush your mouth! 201.5
hush-hush 202.5
husky 453.3
hustle 49.1, 232.1, 232.3,
   236.1, 236.2, 236.3,
   502.8
hustler 513.1
hydraulic 434.1
hygiene 120
hype 20.3, 187.2, 286.2,
   503.2, 508.16
hyper 263.4
hypo 505.9
hysterical historical 198.5

I agree 340.5
I ain't just whistling
   (Dixie)! 199.3
I ain't just whistling Dixie
   204.7
I am jealous 333.2
I am/was embarrassed
   301.4
I approve 285.5
I ask you 161.6
I can't get that together
   167.5
I can't handle this 283.8
I could care 151.9
I could do that a favour
   286.3
I disapprove 288.5
I don't believe it! 161.6
I don't believe this 161.6
I don't buy that 161.6
I don't care 271.7
I don't give a fuck 151.9
I don't know 271.7
I don't mean maybe!
   199.3
I don't mind if I do 221.3
I don't think! 200.3
I don't understand 167.5
I dunno 271.7
I feel happy 273.7
I give in 302.5
I give up 145.5
I haven't the foggiest
   145.5
I hear you! 199.3
I mean 9.2
I mean! 199.3
I mean it 204.7
I pass 145.5
I refuse! 223.1
I should be so lucky
   158.7, 285.5
I should care 271.7
I should cocoa 146.11
I should live so long 158.7
I should say so! 199.3
I should worry 271.7
I suppose 116.9
I understand 166.5
I've won! 20.7
I want work 242.9
I want! 365.5
I wouldn't fuck her with a
   borrowed prick 359.20
I wouldn't fuck her with
   your prick 359.20

I wouldn't know 271.7
I wouldn't touch it with a
   (ten-foot) barge-pole
   288.6, 359.20
I wouldn't touch it with
   yours 288.6, 359.20
I wouldn't trust him/her
   as far as I could throw
   him/her 307.5
I'll be a Dutchman! 189.6
I'll be a (lowdown) son of
   a bitch! 189.6
I'll be a Chinaman, 189.6
I'll be a dirty word! 189.6
I'll be a monkey's uncle!
   173.7, 189.6
I'll be blowed 189.6
I'll be consarned! 189.6
I'll be damned (if I will)
   223.1
I'll be damned if! 200.3
I'll be danged (if I will)
   223.1
I'll be darned! 189.6
I'll be dashed (if I will)
   223.1
I'll be fucked 173.7
I'll be fucked if! 200.3
I'll be hanged (if I will)
   223.1
I'll be hanged 189.6
I'll be jiggered! 189.6
I'll be shot (if I will) 223.1
I'll be shot 189.6
I'll be . . .! 189.6
I'll eat my hat! 161.6,
   199.3
I'll eat my head! 199.3
I'll freeze 345.5
I'll go for that 340.5
I'll say 340.5
I'll say! 199.3
I'll say she does 164.12
I'll say you do 164.12
I'll see you in hell first!
   223.1
I'm bored 272.7
I'm on 340.5
I'm with you 340.5
ibble out 89.7
IBM 116.34
IC 379.1
ice 83.10, 113.4
ice 67.4
ice cream 86.29
ice cream machine 116.34

interrogation 154
interrupt 183.15
interrupter 458.18
intestinal fortitude 295.1
intimate 328.8
intimidate 336.2
intimidation 336
into (one for) 510.10
into 148.8, 166.4, 204.6, 267.4, 328.9
introductory word 177.3
intrude in a conversation 249.3
invalid 429.3
invest 508.13
investigate 156.3
investigation 156
invitation 191.2, 361.2
invitations to drink 99.2
involve 339.3
involved in crime 478.5
irey 27.3
iris out 54.3, 54.4
Irish 383.12
Irish confetti 68.5
Irish fortune 116.40
Irish hurricane 66.6
Irish jig 120.5
Irish root 116.34
Irish screwdriver 69.6
iron 71.1, 75.1, 404.1
Iron 179.8
iron cross 252.3
iron mikes 70.3
iron tank 508.8
irregular motion 57
irresolute 207.3
irresolute person 408
IRRESOLUTION 207–211
irrigate the tonsils 97.3
irritable person 405
irritated 284.5
Irvine 495.1
Irving 431.1
is a bear a Catholic?! 199.3
is that good or is that good! 285.5
is that . . . or is that?! 199.3
is the Pope a Catholic! 199.3, 299.4
is the bear a Catholic? 299.4
island-hop 58.2

Isle of Wight 199.3
isn't ready for people 145.2
issue 22.3
it 139., 413.1, 441.11
it fell off the back of a lorry 479.7, 481.6
if it moves salute it, if it doesn't, paint it 216.7
it looks like rain 489.7
it shouldn't happen to a dog 278.7
it takes two to tango 359.19
it will all come out in the wash 295.6
-itis 10.4, 270.2
it's (all) Greek to me 145.5
it's a great life if you don't weaken! 295.6
it's been a slice 276.9
it's been fun 276.9
it's got me 167.5
it's my story and I'm sticking with it 206.4
it's not my funeral 271.7
it's one o'clock at the water-works 85.8
it's the beer talking 97.5
it's your baby! 292.7
it's your corner 99.2
it's your little hip pocket 252.7
Italian 383.13
ITALY 191.5
itch 268.1
itchy 268.4
item 441.5
itty bitty meat 116.34
ivan 383.19
ixnay! 225.3
izzatso! 173.9
izzum 180.1

j 506.3
J. Arthur 360.9, 395.1
j/o scene 360.9
jab 238.2
jabber 184.1
jack (it) in 209.2, 241.8
jack 104.1, 125.10, 178.3, 179.8, 495.2
jack around 293.5, 352.5
jack in the box 359.1, 479.4

jack job 252.3
jack of 272.6
jack off 360.19, 505.10
jack roller 479.3
jack shit 16.2
Jack the Lad 401.2
Jack the Ripper 86.19
jack up 6.4, 338.4, 359.6, 488.3, 505.10
jack-a-dandy 95.7
jack-off 436.9
jackanape 399.2
jacked 280.6
jacked out 284.5
jacked up 283.6
jacket 494.6, 504.3
jacking off 516.3
jacks 504.1, 509.5
jacks and jills 504.1
jag 23.2, 75.4, 97.2, 281.2
jake 4.2, 164.10, 275.4
jake flake 399.2
jakes 79.1
jalopy 75.3
jam 54.3, 252.1, 351.1, 404.5, 425.1, 489.1, 489.2, 505.11, 505.3
jam duff 404.1
jam fag 404.5
jam house 505.2
jam it 60.4
jam it! 292.7
jam jar 75.1
jam one up 337.4, 338.5, 338.6
jam roll 493.2
jam tart 441.3
jam-packed 22.4
jam-rag 83.11
jamdung 45.1
jammy 273.6
jamoke 377.1
jane 380.1
jap 338.7, 384.8
Japanese 383.14
jar 173.1, 502.4
jargon 176.2
jarhead 92.3
jarred 101.3
jasper 404.2
java 87.1
jaw 183.1, 183.7, 184.2, 291.1, 347.2
jaw-jaw 183.1
jawbone 184.2
jawbreaker 177.2

jayzus 325.2
jazz 185.1, 196.1, 359.6
jazz around 352.5
jazz up 6.4, 236.5
jazzy 84.5, 298.5
jd 458.4
jealousy 333
jeez 325.2
jeff 352.7
jel 396.1
jello squad 451.1
jelly 466.3
jelly sandwich 83.11
jellyfish 403.1, 408.1
jemmy 69.5, 465.1
jerk 414.1
jerk 57.3
jerk around 284.2
jerk off 118.14, 244.1,
  360.19
jerk one's chain 284.2
jerk-off 412.12, 436.9
jerking the gherkin 360.9
jerkwater 28.2, 42.2
jerry 69.8, 143.6, 144.9,
  275.4, 383.8
Jesso 179.8
Jesus H. Christ 325.2
Jesus H. Christ! 189.5
Jesus! 189.5
jew 310.6, 399.1
Jew Canoe 75.4
Jew York 43.1
jewellery 83.10
Jewish lightning 496.1
Jewish piano 508.11
Jewish typewriter 508.11
Jews 384.8
Jewy 374.1
Jewy Louis 81.8
ji-jibe 183.1
jib 183.7
jiblet 504.3
jibone 390.3, 395.2
jickhead 92.3
jiffy 1.3, 2.10
jig 69.2, 384.1
jig-a-jig 359.1
jigaboo 384.1
Jigger 179.8
jiggered 101.3, 173.6,
  243.4
jiggery-pokery 146.2,
  310.1, 312.1
jigglers 465.1
jillion 16.5

jilting 353
jim 83.10, 178.3, 499.2
Jim Crow 384.1
Jim Crow laws 332.1
jim-dandy 27.1
jim-jams 82.14, 129.1
Jiminy Cricket! 189.5
jimjams 279.2
jimmies 263.1, 279.2
Jimmy 179.8
jimmy (riddle) 119.2
jimmy 69.5, 465.1
Jimmy Britts 263.1, 279.2
Jimmy Hix 505.8, 516.5
Jimmy Skinner 89.4
Jimmy Woodser 423.3
jimmy o'goblins 509.1
jingled 169.5
jinny 104.1
jinx 215.7
jinxed 215.9
jip (out of) 310.6
jism 32.2
jitters 263.1
jittery 263.4
jive 146.3, 169.3, 184.1,
  310.1, 310.5, 311.5,
  312.1, 312.2
jive and juke 276.5
jive hand 252.2
jive-ass 278.5
jo-jos 494.7
joanie 229.5
joanna 69.24
job 119.3
job 241.2
job 310.3, 337.4, 478.1
jobbed 486.12
jobber 508.7
jobsworth 388.1, 397.1
jock 82.20, 383.20,
  456.18, 456.5
jock major 179.4
jocker 404.1
jockey 344.2, 404.3, 453.1
jockstrap 82.20
Jodrell Bank 360.9
jody 443.2
joe 87.1, 377.1
Joe Blake 86.12
Joe Blakes 102.1
Joe Blow 377.1
Joe Bonce 498.2
Joe Gurr 494.1
Joe Public 449.1
Joe Ronce 498.2

joes 283.1
joey 494.7
jog the brains 170.3
john 48.6, 79.1, 178.3,
  379.1, 404.5, 499.1
John Bull 101.3, 383.6
John Hancock 190.3
John Henry 384.5
John Law 495.1
John Q. Public 449.1
john hop 495.1
john-john 75.1
johnny 69.27, 83.12
Johnny 179.6, 179.8
Johnny Bliss 119.2
Johnny Horner 47.3
Johnny at the rathole
  410.1
Johnny on the spot 2.14,
  148.7, 236.8, 410.1
johnny-be-good 495.1
johnny-come-lately 390.1,
  440.1
join in 339.2
join the great majority
  112.5
joint 48.2, 78.1, 494.1,
  506.3
joint possession 367
joint-joint 275.6
jointman 494.4
joke 277.1
joker 377.1, 379.1
jolly (along) 287.2, 310.7
jolly d. 27.3
jolt 32.3, 94.8, 97.2,
  173.1, 505.8
Jonah 179.8
jonah 215.4, 215.7
jones 503.5
josh 277.3, 293.5, 310.5,
  310.7
joshing 293.2
joskin 382.2
joss 215.1
journalism 194
journalistic technique
  194.6
journo 456.3
joy 506.2
joy bang 505.8
joy juice 95.1
joy pop 505.8
ju-ju 504.1, 506.3
juanita 506.2
Judas Priest! 189.5

make the legal move 355.5
make the scene 52.2, 166.2
make the sparks fly 280.3
make trouble for 252.10
make up to 287.3
make useful 234.3
make waves 360.20
make whoopee 276.5
makeout artist 411.6
makings 506.3
malarkey 146.2
male homosexual 404.1
male homosexual types 404.5
male lover 441.2
male philanderer 443.2
male prostitute 497.9
malflor 404.2
malice 334
malicious 334.6
mallet 495.1
mam 444.3
mama 404.4
mammy-jammer 395.1
mammy-jamming 189.4
mammy-rammer 395.1
mammy-ramming 189.4
mammy-tapper 395.12
mammy-tapping 189.4
mammyhugger 395.1
man 273.7, 502.1
man oh man 273.7
man with a paper ass 401.1
man with fuzzy balls 384.12
man-a-hanging 408.1
man-eater 443.1
manager 457
manana 2.1
mandies 504.4
manhandle 337.3
manhole 41.3
-mania 270.2
manky 36.2
mano-a-mano 344.6
manor 46.1, 460.2
mantee 404.3
many 18.2
maps 132.4
maps 135.4
marijuana 506.2
marijuana or hashish cigarette 506.3

mariweegee 506.2
marj 86.10
mark 391.1, 480.4
mark for death 113.6
mark one's card 197.1
mark up 337.8
marked cards 515.6
marked for death 485.6
marker 480.1
Marks 179.2
marks 505.6
marriage 355
married 355.7
marry 355.5
marrying someone younger 355.4
Mars Bars 126.1
marv 430.1
marvy 27.3
mary 506.2
mary! 189.5
Mary Ann 403.1
Mary Ellen 456.14
mary warner 506.2
maryanne 506.2
maryjane 506.2
'*masculine' lesbian* 404.3
masers 75.4
mash it on (one) 464.2, 370.2
mash note 191.6
mash the fat 359.6
masher 443.2
mashup 338.1
masses 449
massive 27.3
master-dog 457.1
masturbate (female) 360.20
masturbate (male) 360.19
masturbate 118.14
masturbation 360.9
masturbator 436.9
mat 441.3
match 502.4
match me! 107.3
matchbox 479.1, 502.4
matches 69.16
mate 178.3, 438.1
materially comfortable 375.5
MATERIALS 68–69
maulers 70.3
mauley 190.3
maven 430.1
max out 270.3

maxed (out) 101.3
maxi 82.9
maximum 491.3
Mayfair Merc(enary) 441.3
mayo 86.13
mayonnaise 86.13
mazel 215.2
mazuma 509.1
McAlpine fusilier 454.3
McCoy 27.1
MCM 451.1
me and you 516.6
me and you both 340.5
me-too 15.5
meal ticket 241.2, 391.1, 400.2
mealy-mouth 418.1
mean 27.3, 28.2, 32.6, 280.5, 306.4, 334.6
mean 28.2, 374.4
mean business 204.2
mean person 399.1
mean-hair 334.6
meanie 399.1, 405.1
meany 399.1
measure 132.1, 156.1
measure of dimension 37.4
measure of liquor 94.9
measure one's dick (for) 486.5
measure out drugs for sale 502.11
measurement 38.7
measures of drugs 502.4
meat 32.3, 379.1
meat 86.5
meat market 47.4, 362.2
meat rack 47.4
meat shot 501.4
meat wagon 475.3
meat-eater 436.2, 482.3
meathead 431.1
mechanic 515.3
medal 181.3
meddle 359.6
meddler 398
meddling 249
media 456.3
medico 456.2
mediocre 28.3
meekness 300
meet (v.) 362.3
meet 362.1, 502.2
meet with 162.4

rim queen 404.5
rim slide 494.7
rim-job 360.4
rimming 360.4
ring (in) 12.2
ring 203.7, 311.3, 360.5
ring a bell 170.6
ring in 339.3, 367.3
ring it on 310.4
ring one's bell 337.4,
    359.9
ring one's chimes 359.9
ring the changes 310.6
ring the other one (it's got
    bells on) 223.1
ring-ding 414.1
ringburner 119.5
ringer 12.1, 15.1, 75.4,
    311.1, 458.8
ringside 38.6
rinky-dink 28.2
rip (along) 49.4
rip (off) joint 508.8
rip 151.4
rip and tear 189.3
rip her guts down 359.7
rip into 241.5, 338.4
rip it up 309.2
rip off 113.4, 310.4,
    310.6, 502.12
rip-off artist 434.1, 497.10
rip-snorter 27.1
rip-snorting 18.8
ripe 101.3, 277.7
ripoff 310.2
ripped (to the tits) 101.3
ripped 507.8
ripper 27.3, 62.2, 123.3
rise and shine 247.6
rise and shine! 247.78
risk 214.5
risqué 306.5
ritzy 141.1, 229.4
roach 506.3
roach clip 506.3
roach-killers 82.15
road 47.1
road apples 119.3
road brew 95.1
road dog 438.1
roadie 456.5
roaf 16.3
roak 337.4
roaring 101.3
roast 290.2, 291.2, 293.2,
    293.4

roaster 3.1, 66.1
roasting 154.2, 290.1,
    291.1
rob 479.4
rob with violence 485.4
Robert E. 119.4
Robins 179.1
rock 505.3
rock and roll 74.4
rock of ages 508.9
rock out 243.1
rock spider 383.21
rockers 378.3
rocket 291.1
rockets 72.1
rocks 67.4, 83.10, 295.1
rocks for jocks 179.4
rod 71.1, 82.12
rod walloper 436   9
rodded 74.3, 466.5
rodge 164.1, 164.10
Rods 44.1, 179.2
rofe 491.3
roger 164.12, 275.7, 359.6
Roger the Lodger 179.9
roll 310.6, 375.2, 509.1
roll in 52.2, 366.3
roll in money 375.3
roll in the aisles 274.4
roll in the hay 359.1
roll one's own 213.2
roll out 54.3
roll over for 287.3
roll them bones! 516.7
roll up 52.2
roll with the punches
    222.2
roll your own 346.3
roll-up 106.4
roll-your-own 106.4
roller 75.4, 479.3
rollick 291.2
rolling 101.3, 365.4
rolling in 366.5
rollocks 146.2
roman candle 112.1
roman culture 499.4
romantic story 198.5
romp 514.5
romp it 60.4
roof it 359.6
rook 310.6
rooker 434.1
rookie 431.1, 454.1
rooks 295.1
room to rent 431.1

roost 41.6
rooster 437.2
rooster time 3.7
root (for) 286.2
root 359.1, 359.6, 506.2
root about 156.3
root around 156.3
root hog or die 241.6
root-faced 279.6
rooted 243.4
rooter 400.2, 438.3
rootiepoot 381.6
rope 505.9
rope in 310.4, 339.3,
    365.2
ropes 232.1
ropey 28.2
rorty 274.9
rory 79.7, 494.3
roscoe 71.1, 466.1
rose among the thorns
    497.7
rosewood 465.1
rosiner 97.2
Rosy Lea 87.2
Rosy Lee 87.2
rosy about the gills 123.3
rot 146.2, 146.6
rot your bones 189.7
rotgut 95.6
rotten 101.3
rough 142.5
rough 36.2
rough edge of the tongue
    294.3
rough end of the
    pineapple 252.3
rough it 376.3
rough stuff 337.1
rough trade 404.5
rough treatment 337
rough up 337.3
rough-and-ready 142.5
rough-house 337.1, 338.3
rough-necked 142.5
roughneck 454.3, 456.21
round file 235.2
round the houses 82.11
round-house 499.6
rounder 458.1
roundeye 384.12
roundhead 504.1
rouser 504.2
roustabout 454.3, 456.21
rout 359.6
row in 478.2, 486.5

SHAPE 39–40
shape up 230.2, 495.10
share (v.) 367.2
share 23.1
share out (v.) 367.5
share out 464.3
sharing 367
sharing 367.6
shark 434.1, 510.1
sharking 510.2
sharp 123.3, 143.6, 148.7,
    229.4, 253.7
sharp end 252.1
sharp-shooter 443.2
sharpen 170.3
sharpen up 237.2
sharpie 435.1
sharpies 378.3
shattered 263.5
shave 120.6, 120.11
shave 310.6
shaver 381.3
shazzam 236.4
she-man 404.1
shebang 69.1, 69.2, 78.1
shebeen 104.2
sheeny 384.8
sheep 403.1
sheepish 120.14
sheepskin 82.7
sheet 194.3, 494.6
sheet! 189.5
sheet music 135.4
sheila 380.1
shekels 509.1
shell out 370.2
shell-back 407.1
shell-road 352.10
shellac 318.5
shellacked 101.3
shellacking 318.2, 318.2
shemozzle 262.1
shenanigans 146.1, 231.1,
    334.1
Sherlock Holmes 495.1
shicer 434.1
shicker 91.4, 97.3
shickered 101.3
shift arse 49.5
shift the weight 316.2
shikse 384.10, 455.1
shill 513.2
shilly-shallier 408.1
shilly-shally 207.2
shim-sham 263.1
shimmy up 55.2

shin 466.2
shin battle, 338.1
shindig 98.1, 276.3, 363.1
shindy 98.1, 231.2, 276.3,
    363.1
shine 384.1
shone on 348.2
shine one's pole 360.19
shine up 170.3
Shiner 179.8
ship 75.8
shirt 82.18
shirt-lifter 404.1
shit 86.2, 119.3, 119.7,
    168.2, 395.1, 505.2,
    506.1
shit! 189.5, 278.7
shit a brick 296.4
shit a brick! 173.7
shit and derision! 189.5
shit and wish 279.3
shit bricks 296.4
shit city 252.2
shit detail 241.1
shit jacket 79.1
shit list 332.1
shit on a shingle 86.9
shit on a stick 395.1
shit on a string 168.2
shit on from a great
    height 252.6
shit oneself 296.4
shit or bust 204.2, 238.6
shit stompers 82.15
shit stopper 276.2
shit through one's teeth
    312.2
shit, eh! 173.7
shit, or get off the pot
    241.11
shit-eating grin 274.3
shit-for-brains 395.1,
    433.1
shit-hot 27.3
shit-scared 296.7
shit-stick 465.1
shit-stirrer 420.2
shit-stirring 294.2
shitbird 433.1
shitface 98.1
shitfaced 101.3
shithead 396.1, 433.1
shitheap 46.2
shitheel 396.1, 433.1
shithole 48.8
shithook 393.1

shithouse 79.1, 252.2
shitkicker 390.2, 431.1
Shitkicker, Ohio 43.2
shits 119.5
shitter 48.6, 79.1, 479.3
shitting 189.4
shitting bricks 296.7
shitting oneself 296.7
shitty 28.2, 252.11, 334.6
shitwork 241.1
shiv 69.9
shiver my timbers 173.7
shivers 129.1
shmeer 287.2
shmeggegge 414.1
shmooser 418.1
sho' 'nuff 159.4, 164.8
shock (v.t.) 262.5
shocker 198.4
shocks for jocks 179.4
shoe 450.1
shoes 82.15
Shoey 179.8
shonk 384.8
shonnicker 384.8
shoo-fly 495.2, 495.4
sho-in 159.1
shook on 270.5
shoot (off) 118.12
shoot (one's wad) 183.10
shoot 73.3, 113.5, 337.7
shoot 183.14
shoot! 189.5, 278.7
shoot a cat 118.13
shoot a line 183.7, 198.7,
    287.2, 310.7, 352.7
'shoot a line' 186.7
shoot blanks 184.2
shoot down 292.3, 348.2
shoot for the moon 511.5
shoot for the sky 511.5
shoot from the hip 205.2
shoot gravy 505.10
shoot off (at one's mouth)
    184.2
shoot off 49.4, 54.3
shoot off at the mouth
    299.2
shoot on 293.5
shoot one's best mack
    205.2
shoot one's bolt 204.2
shoot one's load 118.12
shoot one's marbles 147.4
shoot one's star 360.15
shoot one's wad 118.12

264 / INDEX